12:01

BELLA JAY

First paperback edition October 2023
ISBN 9798864771211 (Complete Experience Edition)

www.authorbellajay.com

12:01

THE COMPLETE EXPERIENCE

BELLA JAY

To everyone who deserves to get their happily ever after, even if it's a little messy. Don't let your ex stop you from finding the love of your life.

"True love is like a fine wine; it gets better with time." - Unknown

"One thing about them tables… they always turn." - Unknown

12:01

THE COMPLETE EXPERIENCE

This is the complete experience edition and includes both 12:01 and 12:01:The Aftermath.

Author's Note

First and foremost, welcome to lick back season.

In the world of 12:01, the symbolism of red and white wine runs deeper than Midnight's family being in the wine business.

Red wine represents Midnight and his character—bold, intense, and complex. Much like the finest Cabernets, Midnight exudes passion and warmth, capable of igniting desires.

On the other hand, white wine embodies Tyme, representing her true lightness and charm. Yet, like a Chardonnay, she possesses hidden depths that come to light over time.

The blending of these two personalities, like the harmonious pairing of red and white wine, forms the heart of our story. It's a reminder that sometimes, the most unexpected pairings create the most beautiful symphonies of flavor and love.

So, pour yourself a glass of your preferred wine, settle into the world of 12:01, and savor the complexities of Midnight and Tyme's journey.

Cheers and happy reading.

Content Warning

Inside this book you'll find:

- Explicit language, vivid descriptions of sex, and bdsm elements.
- Mention of the following: childhood sibling loss, miscarriage, depression, parental divorce.

If any of these things trigger you, bother you, or do not align with you, this book may not be for you. If you do continue to read, proceed with caution and enjoy the ride.

A more detailed explanation can be found on my website if you would like specifics: https://preshrodgers.com/authorbellajay/cw

CHAPTER 1

Well, *I've had worse Friday afternoons*, I thought as the door to the jail cell slammed shut behind me. I mean, there was the time I woke up to a video of my *supposed* soon-to-be cousin-in-law fucking my fiancé the night before our wedding.

Or the time I got kicked out of my own wedding for causing a scene.

Oh, wait.

Both of those things happened on the same Friday.

Twenty-six Fridays ago.

But who's counting?

Oh yeah, me... the victim whom everyone else acted like *wasn't* the victim when I crashed their stupid winter wonderland wedding this morning.

Sure did.

But suddenly, I'm the bitch? I'm the one in the wrong now because I, *quote unquote*, ruined their perfect New Year's Eve *eve* wedding.

I mean, who has morning weddings anyway? Psychopaths.

What's interesting is how much audacity two bitch-made people can have to lie about their relationship, ruin what was supposed to be *my* day, and then turn around and get married in the same fucking year.

Yet, they wanted to act surprised by what I'd done? They had to know I wasn't going to let any of that shit slide.

So, this morning, me and my bat showed up and showed out.

Their wedding at the picturesque resort was a sight to behold, overlooking the snow-covered mountains that the town was famous for. But I was determined to strip away the illusion of their perfect day, just like the frostbite nipping at the edges of my heart.

As I stormed through the venue, it was hard to ignore the cozy yet breathtaking decor, with white candles and Christmas tree lights that should have made me feel warm inside. Instead, they only fueled the fire of rage within me. This was exactly the wedding I had dreamed of, which was why I messed shit up and reminded them that it was cold outside, and the only heat they deserved was in hell.

With my sneakers squeaking loudly against the polished floors, I targeted the centerpieces, knocking a few off the tables, scattering petals with a flourish. I didn't have time to ruin all of them because security was already hot on my tail, but the chaos I left in my wake was enough to shatter the ambiance they had tried so hard to create.

And then there were the cakes, not one, but two towering confections meant to symbolize their *disgusting* love. The first cake, a masterpiece of white fondant adorned with intricate snowflake designs, stood tall and elegant, a testament to their *seemingly* flawless union. The second cake, a mirror image of the first, sat beside it, promising a sweet future filled with happiness and joy.

With one swift motion of my bat, I sent the first cake crashing to the ground, leaving a mess of frosting and shattered dreams. The delicate snowflakes smeared and broken, mirrored what I could only hope would be their relationship going forward.

The second cake trembled, on the brink of the same fate, but security intervened before I could do more damage. As the burley Robocop dragged me out of their reception hall, I smirked, reveling in the satisfaction of seeing their picture-perfect day unravel before their eyes.

The gasps of their guests, screams of my cheating ass ex, and his new heaux of a wife, and looks of horror on their faces, still played in my mind.

Overall, it was a top tier performance and with all the phones I saw pointed at me, I was excited to see if I'd go viral.

I can see the headline now: Girl Goes *Bat*shit Crazy at Ex's Wedding.

To the outside world looking in, I was the villain, but no one could tell me that what I did, wasn't well deserved.

Especially when *I* wanted a winter wonderland wedding, and Sir Cheater convinced me that a summer wedding at his parents' friend's vineyard would be better.

Little did I know, I would be very thankful for all the wine I had access to on *that* Friday because boy, oh boy, did I drown myself in it for days.

Lucky me.

So, even though I was about to catch a charge, the Friday twenty-six weeks ago still held the top spot in comparison.

To be honest, jail wasn't such a bad idea.

It seemed like the perfect place for me to sulk and disconnect from social media. Otherwise, I would spend my time using my fake profiles to stalk my ex and his now wife.

At least, that was how I'd spent many of my weeknights, weekends, *and* hours of my days these last few months.

It was a disease that I couldn't rid myself of, and I had lost friends because of it. But how was I supposed to just move on after I wasted two years of my life living a lie?

According to Sir Cheater and the bitch he fucked, I had misunderstood what they meant when they said they were cousins. They were just *like* cousins because their dads were best friends.

And then, all the bullshit fell from their lips after that.

The typical 'it wasn't supposed to happen', 'I never saw her that way', 'it was a mistake', 'I love you'.

Yet, five months later, you're standing at the altar with your mistake?

He definitely took me for a damn fool.

However, I guess I should be happy he wasn't hitting a home run with his biological uncle's daughter.

Either way, I wish them nothing but chaos.

This is exactly what I get for thinking dating a man that I met in person was going to be any better than a man I met on the internet. Turned out, the species as a whole is a lost cause.

I plopped down on the hard metal bench and finally eyed my surroundings.

The holding cell wasn't as bad as I had pictured it would be when I was in the back of the squad car. There were no smells of piss, the two other people looked nice enough, and I wasn't afraid I'd catch something from just sitting down.

Overall, I'd give it a seven out of ten if I was rating jail cells.

Not that I'd been in any before, but based on the movies, definitely a seven.

Resting my head against the wall, I thought about how I could have started my day off differently. How I could have asked God to give me the strength to let bygones be bygones and leave it in his hands. Or how I could have gone to the Amalfi Coast in Italy for the holidays, like my mom had begged me to.

According to her, she just *felt* like I needed some motherly love outside of my city. However, I didn't think being the third wheel to my mom and her boyfriend, Luke, in one of the most romantic places in the world would make me feel better about my messed up love life. Either way, maybe if I had listened, I would have never been *here*.

But I woke up and chose violence.

And the funny thing was, I'd do it again.

As time ticked away while I sat in the cold, unforgiving walls of the holding cell — and I watched my other two cellmates make bail — the adrenaline that had fueled my rage began to subside. Reality seeped in, and I scolded myself for allowing my emotions to get the best of me. Catching a charge over a man? That was never the kind of person I wanted to be.

But somehow, this was the woman my ex had turned me into. All the anger and hurt I had been holding onto had driven me to this point, and for what?

As I paced back and forth in the small cell, my mind raced with thoughts of the consequences I would face. The embarrassment of being arrested, the potential legal trouble, and the disappointed looks from my family and friends weighed heavily on me.

How had my life gotten here when six months ago, I was living in what I thought was bliss?

I was such a delusional girl, and not in the good way.

"Henley!" The guard's gruff voice had me jumping out of my skin right as I was about to doze off. "You're free to go," he said as his tired eyes landed on me.

I felt a mix of relief and apprehension.

"What?" I had been sitting in this cell for hours, waiting to be booked and processed. "I didn't even call anyone."

"That look like my problem? You coming or staying?"

After hour two, I had come to terms with the fact that I'd be spending the weekend in jail. It was the day before New Year's Eve. Who in the hell was going to come get me? My only real last standing friend was hundreds of miles away, and though I didn't doubt that she'd find a way to get on the first plane out, had she known, there was still no way she'd have made it here already.

Regardless, I leaped to my feet and made a beeline for the exit. He didn't have to tell me a third time to leave.

I retrieved my belongings and stepped out into the frigid winter weather, never once expecting to see *him* standing right in my line of vision.

"What in the hell are *you* doing here?" I asked as I moved down the steps towards Midnight Drayton. He stood against a luxury, all white vehicle dressed to perfection in a cream-colored suit that accentuated his silky, dark brown skin, showcasing his *annoyingly* impeccable taste in fashion.

I wanted to admire him, but the truth was… I couldn't stand Midnight Drayton.

He was a product of the same parents who laid down and created the devil, formerly known as my ex.

But that wasn't why he was one of the people on my shit list.

Him being a condescending asshole was reason number one.

Him being a *fine* condescending asshole was reason number two.

Reason number three, which was also tied with number one, was that it was because of him that I met his brother.

"The better damn question is why am I picking your ass up from here?" There was an obscene amount of disdain in his eyes. "Why the fuck would you pull some shit like this?" The questions were obviously rhetorical because before I could answer, he said, "Get in the car."

"Get in who car?" I gawked.

"Tyme, I'm not about to go back and forth with you when I already wasted my time having to come do this shit."

I pulled my neck back as I ignored the cold wind whipping past us. "Nobody asked you to. It honestly makes no sense that you even would. Last I checked, you don't fuck with me."

"Just get in the damn car."

"I can figure out how to get back to my hotel on my own." *Did I forget to mention that I really got on a plane yesterday to come ruin someone's wedding hundreds of miles away today? Because I did.*

"You know what. Be ignorant, that's what you're good at anyway."

"What the hell is that supposed to mean?" I raised my voice a few octaves. It was just us outside of the small precinct. It was eerily quiet, as if everyone else in this country ass town was already asleep.

He let out an amused chuckle. "Are we not standing outside of the damn police station because your *smart* ass decided to catch a disorderly conduct charge?"

"Well, it got dropped, so does it really matter?"

"Because of me. Now get in the car, I'm not asking again." He walked around the vehicle and got in while I didn't move from the curb. Instead, I opened my rideshare app, only to find that there were no cars currently available in this stupid ass town. And, of course, there were no taxis in sight either. Who has a wedding in the middle of nowhere?

Apparently, cheaters and the *cousins* they fuck.

I got into the car.

It was either that or walk the ten miles and risk getting snatched by a deer or some other animal crossing the road.

My door was barely closed before he peeled off.

"I'm staying at one of the hotels down the street from the venue," I mumbled.

He didn't say anything.

I opened my phone to retrieve the exact name of the hotel and told him. He *still* said nothing.

Reason number four: he's a rude asshole.

The short ride was painfully silent, even with the music playing. I did my best to keep my eyes staring out of the passenger side window into the darkness. It was only a little after six at night, but it felt much later. I had gotten so used to living in a big city that a small town like this just didn't feel right.

"You know that shit you pulled is all over social media, right?" The sound of his rigid voice pricked at my skin in a way that I never liked. In a way that always made me act even more like a bitch towards him.

"Now how exactly was I supposed to know that?" I turned my attention towards him. "You think they gave me the Wi-Fi code to the jail cell to pass the time?"

His jaw clenching at my words made me smile internally.

"You can't ever control that slick mouth of yours."

"I guess we *do* have something in common," I said as he pulled up to a light. He shook his head at me and then licked his bottom lip. When he ran his thumb across it, I looked away. My eyes landed on a billboard with 'Gavenfalls Inn & Resort 5 miles away' on it.

The inn where I'd been arrested.

I'd have to give it to the cheating *cousins.* Their wedding venue had been one of a kind and probably didn't deserve the havoc I'd brought to it.

Oh well.

"What did you expect to come from today? What was your goal?"

Why was Midnight Drayton talking to me?

"Why do you care? You're just gonna judge me like you've always done, so why does it even matter?"

"I don't judge you."

I cut my eyes at him as he turned onto the familiar looking road that led to my hotel.

"I don't think you know the definition of judgment."

"I try to understand you, and you take it offensively."

Bullshit!

Reason number five: He's delusional.

"Just make it make sense for me as to why you got your ass on a plane to crash your ex's wedding. I get that you're still pissed about what they did to you, but what you did ain't change nothing."

"Well, it made me feel better to fuck up their day."

"Did it?" he asked incredulously, with a hint of 'you're a dummy'.

I stood my ground. "That's what I said." My leg started bouncing, and I could feel a rush of anxiety coursing through me at his questions. At his words. At his *judgment.*

Even though I expected to get this same line of questioning, potentially from family and friends, I couldn't stand that it was coming from someone I hated.

Why the fuck did I get in this car with *him?*

"You'd rather ruin your life over that nigga? Come the fuck on, Tyme. I know we don't see eye to eye on a lot, but Mal ain't never been it."

I don't know why his words felt like a knife stabbing an open wound, but they did, and I hated that silent tears started rolling down my face. *Fuck.* I quickly wiped them away and opened the bag that held my belongings to search for my room key.

I didn't swipe the tears away fast enough because good ol' Midnight Drayton had to remind me that he never missed anything as he pulled into a parking spot.

"I know you not over there crying over a nigga that's probably knee deep in the bitch he cheated on you with." Gut punch to the heart. "Woman up because—"

"Fuck you, Midnight," I seethed, throwing the seatbelt off of me so hard that I jumped when it clacked against the window. The nighttime air didn't even bother me as I rushed out of the car, making sure to slam the door as hard as I could.

The tears started falling harder and by the time I made it to my room, I could barely keep it together. I dropped the key card three times, and on the third time, someone else picked it up.

Midnight Drayton was back in my space.

Haven't I gone through enough?

I ignored him as he pressed the card against the reader, unlocking the door.

He said something as he followed me inside, but I continued to pretend like he wasn't there. I didn't have the energy to fight with him about what I had decided to do. He didn't understand. He wasn't the one who had been embarrassed, hurt, and tossed to the side.

I headed straight for the bathroom and locked myself inside.

Maybe he'd go away.

Maybe I was dreaming.

Maybe I hadn't been as stupid as he made me sound.

Sike.

As I looked at my tear-stained face in the mirror, I realized Midnight was wrong.

I wasn't crying over my ex. I was crying because of what he'd turned me into, and Midnight's words ate me up inside. I had just spent my day in a jail cell, thanks to a fuckboy who never deserved me in the first place. I was indeed ruining my life over someone who had still picked another woman over me.

How pathetic.

CHAPTER 2

Midnight Drayton

Why was I still even here? My thoughts overwhelmed me as I paced the quaint room, trying to decide if I wanted to leave or stay.

I *shouldn't* be here.

I wanted to leave.

I *needed* to stay.

This was the type of back-and-forth bullshit that made me always keep my distance from *her*. She was—

The creak of the bathroom door jolted me out of my thoughts, and I turned to see the bane of my existence—Tyme Henley.

Like clockwork, my body betrayed me with a stupid reaction that sent my heart racing. Despite her puffy red eyes, messy ponytail, and frown, she was still way too fucking beautiful. But I knew from experience that external beauty didn't always mean much.

We'd played this 'I hate your entire being' game so long that I truly could not stand her. Yet, I also couldn't bear to see her like this—especially over my fuck ass brother.

"Why are you here, Mid?"

I didn't have a good answer for that because I had no real clue why I'd decided to do anything I'd done today.

That was bullshit.

I had a clue; I just didn't want to own the fuck up to it.

The moment I saw Tyme taking that bat towards everything it, or her hands, could get ahold to, I wanted to play captain save-a-crazy-ex.

I also wanted to laugh.

What she'd done had been messed up, but I'd be lying if I said it wasn't well deserved. However, I also meant what I'd said to her. What she did hadn't changed a got damn thing.

I had to fight tooth and nail with my bitch ass brother, his conniving wife, and our parents about not pressing charges. Suddenly, I was her lawyer, she was on death row, and I was determined to save her because based on history, her actions were justified.

It didn't mean they were smart.

There were better ways for her to get back at my brother that didn't involve almost catching a charge.

After everyone saw things my way, or at least agreed to disagree, I called the precinct to drop the charges. They told me I'd have to come in to complete some paperwork, and that led to me watching Tyme walk out of the police station six hours after she'd wreaked havoc.

I hadn't intended on waiting for them to release her.

But I did.

I hadn't intended on giving her a ride back to her hotel.

But I did.

Despite the nigga she thinks I am, what I'm not is one who would leave a woman stranded. Even with all the shit I was talking in front of the station, I had no intention of abandoning her without knowing she'd gotten back here safely.

I also never intended on making her cry.

But, once again, I did.

She always had tough skin when it came to dealing with me, which was why I never felt the need to handle her with care. Not to mention, her attitude wasn't one that deserved much grace. I stayed on go mode when it came to her ass.

"I didn't have to come at you the way I did," I said, not really answering her question as I leaned against the nearest wall.

She crossed her arms over her titties. They were hiding beneath her oversized sweatshirt, but they were still sitting pretty.

"Is that an apology?" Her brows inched up her forehead.

My right ankle crossed over my left as I bit back what would have been a typical rude response in alignment with our usual interactions. Instead, I held my composure and reminded her, "I apologized when I walked in."

"I didn't hear that, but you should ha—"

"Can we not do *this* for five fucking minutes?" I motioned between us and our constant need to argue. "Again. I'm sorry for what I said. You clearly are still not over my brother, and it ain't up to me to tell you when and how you should move on. And it damn sure ain't up to me to tell you how to release whatever emotions you're feeling. Today was a fucked up day for you."

She narrowed her pretty, mahogany brown eyes at me as wrinkles formed between them.

"What? You want me to apologize again?" *'Cause I'm not.*

"No," she held up a hand and I spotted a very minuscule smile hanging off the side of her lips, "I just—I'm shocked you were able to say all of that without judgment." I wanted to cut my eyes at her, but I refrained. "And all it took was for me to cry. You might have a heart and not be a complete tin man."

"Whatever. At the end of the day, Malachi ain't never gonna be worth your tears, but get them out if that's what you need to do."

She walked away from me and against my will, my eyes followed her body as it continued to the bed. The curves of her thick frame couldn't be hidden, no matter how big her sweatpants were.

"It's not Mal that I'm crying over," she revealed, sitting down on the bed. "It's the idea of the life I had planned with him. I wanted it so bad, and I know you're gonna judge me for it but I—"

"Stop thinking I'm gonna do something I'm not."

"Well, I know you and—"

"Damnit, Tyme." She was so fucking hardheaded. "I'm waving the white flag because you look like you need someone. Stop—"

"I don't *need* anyone." The words damn near flew out her mouth. "Especially someone with the last name Drayton, or better yet, someone who looks way too much like the person who fucked me over in the first place."

Her guard was back up to the ceiling. Maybe even heaven.

"Look, you asked me why I was here. I don't really fucking know, but despite how it seems, I do have places to be, yet, I'm still here, trying to give you the space to get out whatever you need to get out."

"Do you want me to say thank you? Because I won't."

This damn girl.

"I want you to stop acting like you don't need anyone or anything when you clearly do."

"I don't."

"Tyme." I hated how her eyes met mine as soon as I said her name. Or how that one loose strand of hair fell over her face, causing her to push it behind her ear. It all irked me because it was a reminder of how effortlessly charming she could be. The way she looked at me with those deep, soulful eyes only added fuel to the fire of my annoyance. It was like she knew exactly how to get under my skin, and I hated that I noticed it. "We might not always be on the same page about a lot of things, but I promise you, I know exactly what you need. You can lie to yourself all you want to, but that ain't my problem."

"And what exactly is it that I need?"

Besides to be fucked by a nigga who ain't fucking his supposed cousin?

"Why would I tell you when all you're gonna do is debate me?"

She gave me an annoyed look that brought a sense of justice to my soul. "Humor me."

I shook my head at this woman.

"I can't tell you, I can only show you."

She blinked rapidly, and I could see the confusion forming on her face as she jumped to a conclusion. "If you think—"

"Is that all you brought with you?" I cut her off, pointing at the open duffle bag on the bed. It was mostly packed, but there were a few items around the room.

"Why?"

I let out a deep breath. "Why can't you just answer a question sometime?"

She shrugged, a hint of relief crossing her features as she tugged down her bun, letting her hair fall free. The strands were naturally black, complementing her brown skin, and flowed past her shoulders. As much as I tried, I never could deny that she had a certain captivating quality about her. "It's a valid question," she repeated, as if daring me to challenge her further.

And I would.

I pushed myself off the wall I'd been leaning against. "Get your stuff together and come with me."

She looked at me like I had three heads. "Excuse me?"

"Either you want to know the answer to your question, or you don't. If you do, have your ass in my car within thirty minutes." With that, I walked out of the room.

I was done playing her game. If she wanted to know what she needed, then I was in charge.

CHAPTER 3

There were twenty-eight hours left in the year, so I might as well say to hell with logic. I had already made multiple bad decisions all year; what was one more before the year came to a close? At least that's what I kept telling myself with each step that I took towards Midnight's car. And because I wouldn't be me if I hadn't, I waited until I had two minutes to spare before I left my hotel room.

It took me less than ten minutes to repack the items I had out, and then I took a fifteen minute shower to rinse off the stench of jail.

Taking my sweet time was also my way of letting the universe decide on what really was going to happen next. If he was gone when I got to the parking lot, then it wasn't meant for me to make another stupid decision.

However, he was still there.

God must've been watching my life for his entertainment this year.

I threw my duffle into the backseat before climbing into the front. I expected him to say something, but no words left his mouth as he pulled out of the hotel parking lot.

"Where are we going?"

"The airport."

"Oh."

I don't know why I was expecting him to say we were going to his hotel because I was almost sure that when he said he knew what I needed, he was alluding to sex.

Was I really willing to fuck my ex's brother?

Well, you did hop your ass up in this car so...maybe?

Did I need sex?

No comment.

"My cousin is having a New Year's Eve party tomorrow night. So, we heading there."

"Oh."

"Since when don't you have more than five words to say out that mouth of yours?"

"I just— I don't know what to say. You think I *need* to party?"

The right side of his mouth turned up a little. "I already said I'm going to show you what you need. Stop tryna figure it out."

"Okay," I conceded, even though my brain wanted to ask a hundred more questions. "Is this one of those kissing cousins or...?"

Mid let out a snort followed by a genuine laugh, and I hated that it sent a tingle of delight through my center. I'd heard him laugh before, but this was different. This was with me.

"Nah," he said, still chuckling. "For one, pussy is my drug of choice and that nigga ain't got one. Second, we blood cousins. Same last name and all."

I heard the rest of his sentence but the way he said *pussy* made mine jump, and I wasn't sure how I felt about that. I didn't like it. This was Midnight Drayton. *We* hated him. *We* definitely didn't get turned on by him.

"Well, that's good."

"It's Neo. I'm sure you've heard of him, but y'all never got to meet. He's been hosting these parties for a few years now."

He was right. The name did ring a bell, but I couldn't match it to a face. Just as Neo was a question mark, so were these parties—which was interesting because my ex and I had spent two years of us watching the clock strike midnight side by side, and it was intriguing that he'd never thought to mention these bashes Neo threw as an option for us to attend.

Classic move from Sir Cheater, I guess.

Silence took over us because what the hell did we have to talk about? I didn't need him bringing back up the dumb shit I'd done today, and I was racking my brain trying to figure out why I was in this car with him and going to the airport. How in the hell was I trusting my life with Midnight Drayton after despising him for these last two and a half years? I was really out to make this year the worst year of my life.

To combat the stress of all the scenarios going around in my head, I closed my eyes and allowed myself to doze off. When I woke up an hour later, it was due to him lightly shaking me awake.

"Come on," he said once I laid eyes on him standing in front of me. The car door was open, and he had my duffle on his shoulder with his hand wrapped around the handle of his suitcase.

It took another second for my body to register what was happening. Blinking a few times, I undid my seatbelt and stepped out of the car, realizing that we were right next to a plane.

A private jet? Was I dreaming?

I watched as Midnight greeted a few people, handed the rental car keys to someone, pointed at me, and then continued his conversation. I was too in shock to pay attention to what was happening, until I felt his hand against my arm.

My eyes met his, and I found myself entranced by the depth and beauty of his gaze. His eyes were bold and big, yet so dark and mysterious, as if they held secrets only he knew. Midnight once told me that his mother gave him that name because when he was born, his eyes reminded her of the soothing darkness that envelops the world at night. She wanted to get lost in them forever. And so, he became Midnight. Of course, it also helped that he was born right after the clock struck twelve on the first day of December, but to him, it was his mother's love and admiration that made the name truly special.

I had always thought it was a beautiful story. It reminded me of the story my mom had told me for why she'd named me Tyme. It was different, but similar in thought in that when she saw me, she wanted to stop time and stare at me forever.

Our names were how we'd once connected, before things between us went to the deepest parts of hell.

I hated to admit it, but sometimes I wondered, what if. What if we hadn't gotten off to the wrong foot? What if he hadn't been such a fucking asshole?

Would things have been different?

Would he have been the twin I picked?

Or, would I have still picked a fuckboy either way?

"Come on," he pulled at my elbow, "we're already behind because of us."

I pushed the ill thoughts back down to where they'd come from and followed his lead. I had never been on a plane this small. There were only enough seats for seven people in the main cabin. The seats were those comfy oversized ones that I'd seen in movies when rich people flew private.

But I wasn't rich, and though I knew Midnight and Sir Cheater's family had money, *money,* I didn't know it was *private jet* money.

Though it made a lot of sense with how flashy my ex could be at times.

The Drayton family had been in the wine business for over twenty years. Their dad started M.D. Winery and in the last seven years, they had expanded to five lounges across the country, each with its unique personality. The Drays, as their wine bars and lounges were called, were hidden gems known for their extensive selection of wines, carefully curated to please even the most discerning palates. Walking into The Drays was like stepping into a luxurious speakeasy, where the ambiance was as intoxicating as the wine.

According to my ex, business was good, but I had no idea it was *this* good.

Maybe it was because *we* never flew private, but then again, we'd only traveled outside of our state once during our entire relationship. Dating a businessman, who was determined to be the son who was passed down the title of CEO, meant that he was always working.

At least, that's what he told me.

For all I knew, he was sexing his faux cousin.

It could also be because I never inquired about his finances. I didn't know what his bank account looked like. I minded my business because I didn't want to be *that* girl — the one who seemed too eager to know how well off he was.

He'd said on more than one occasion when we first started dating that the women he'd dated in the past had been gold diggers. I didn't want to come off as one of them. I wanted to *be* his wife. Or maybe just *a* wife. *Somebody's* wife. That made me ask fewer questions so that I wouldn't become a walking red flag.

Because I'd been called that before.

I tended to come on too strong about what I wanted in a relationship, what I was looking for, *who* I was looking for, and how I wanted my life to go within the next two to five years. Apparently for some men, if you tell them that too soon— they're turned off and have a lot of rude and choice words about how they deem as you being desperate as hell.

So, I toned things down *just a smidge* when I met my bitch ass ex. I let him lead and went off of his energy. Somewhere along the lines, I let *Mr. Wrong* tell me all the right things I wanted to hear.

The icing on the cake was that he *wanted* a wife. His exact words were that he was tired of having girlfriends— he was ready for the woman who would have his last name.

I stupidly thought he meant me.

Maybe if he had, I would have seen the more luxurious life of being the future Mrs. M. Drayton.

Because I knew there was no way he wouldn't fly private if his brother did. *Mr. Kissing Cousins* always did the most. He liked people to know he wasn't average and that his family had money.

And what he didn't like was for his twin to outdo him.

Midnight, on the other hand, exuded money naturally, but with an air of humbleness that surrounded him. Anyone could tell from the clothes he wore, the way he carried himself, and his luxury cars, that he wasn't broke, but he never let it go to his head.

He was just a man who had money, whereas my ex was a man who needed people to *know* who he was *and* that his bank account wasn't hurting.

But yet and still, I didn't know his bank account had private jet money.

Or better yet, I didn't get to experience it. I felt a little bamboozled.

I bet that fake cousin did.

"Where are we going?" I finally asked after we got settled into our seats. I noticed the guy he'd been talking with earlier was the pilot.

"Chasington County."

I had heard of the area. It was along the coast, a few hours away from Southgate, our city in Clampton County. However, I'd never ventured out that way since moving to the city.

"Oh," I responded as if the location of where we were going really mattered. What mattered was that a bitch was flying private and living life on the edge after being arrested less than twenty-four hours ago.

This Friday had turned out better than I'd thought.

I WOKE UP AND PINCHED MYSELF, HARDLY BELIEVING THE SIGHT BEFORE ME. The lavish, blue-green ocean waves crashing against the shore felt so surreal that it seemed like a dream, but I knew it wasn't. I was in a luxurious hotel right off the coast, and my room had the perfect view of the ocean.

We'd arrived in Chasington County a little after eleven at night and drove for another hour to reach Chasington Beach. I slept the entire way, and by the time we got to the hotel, the only sounds I could hear were the distant crashing of ocean waves. Check-in was a breeze, and as soon as we entered the one-bedroom suite, we headed straight to bed.

I was fully prepared for Midnight to tell me that I would have to take the pull-out couch. However, he offered me the room instead, which was shocking, considering he'd never been so gracious towards me before. Of course, I didn't argue with him about it, and I took it. As a result, I slept much better than I had in a long time.

The cozy, grey fleece robe hanging in the closet beckoned to me as I slipped out of bed. My voluptuous body didn't need to be on display for my arch nemesis, even if he'd been treating me like he had more sense than I'd ever thought he'd had.

Tiptoeing out of my room, I hurried across the hallway to the bathroom to freshen up. Despite his unexpected courteousness, I wouldn't let Midnight Drayton catch me slipping with morning breath.

Afterwards, I headed into the living room area and was disappointed in myself for feeling a way when I saw that *Mr. I Know What You Need* was nowhere to be found. The couch he'd slept on had been put back together, and his covers were folded and placed off to the side.

Why wasn't I surprised that he was a neat freak?

I retreated back to my room to grab my phone before going into the kitchen to see if there was coffee. I didn't expect to find a message or anything from Midnight because we had never exchanged numbers. Instead, I was ready to face the backlash from the consequences of my actions.

Last night I had already seen a few via the missed calls and messages from my mom, best friend, and even my God brother— who barely called me unless my mom told him to.

After texting them to let them know that I was okay and not behind bars, I turned my phone off to protect my mental energy. As much as I wanted to see if Midnight's claim about my actions being all over social media was true, I chose rest over rumors and slept soundly.

But this morning was different.

With a steaming cup of coffee in hand, I settled into a plush lounge chair with a breathtaking view of the ocean. It didn't take long before curiosity got the best of me, and I couldn't resist checking my social media. My mouth dropped open as I was inundated with over a hundred notifications, confirming that my recent shenanigans had indeed made waves online.

The videos *(yes there were more than one from different angles)* of me going ham at Sir Cheater's wedding were viral on multiple accounts, and people who knew me had tagged me in them, which caused strangers to also feel the need to mention my username when they had shit to say about what I'd done.

I went down a rabbit hole of reading the comments on the post that With Shade On Top (WSOT) had posted. WSOT was the top source for trending celeb news, exclusive interviews, videos, and more. How had *I* made it there?

"The dick better had been that good for sis to do this..."

"I heard that he cheated on her with that girl he married... seems justified to me."

"Baby... get you some therapy 'cause why would you do this?"

"I would have beat her ass and been in jail with her if this was my wedding! TF! @thatgirladalyn @thetessahwarwick"

"This is hilarious af. I wish I was there."

"Did she used to play baseball or sumthin? Sis needs to be on a team expeditiously."

"Um... anyone know who the security guard was who effortlessly grabbed sis? Asking for my kewchie."

"At least they had two cakes because damnnnnnn!! Babe, come see this @deucethealmighty"

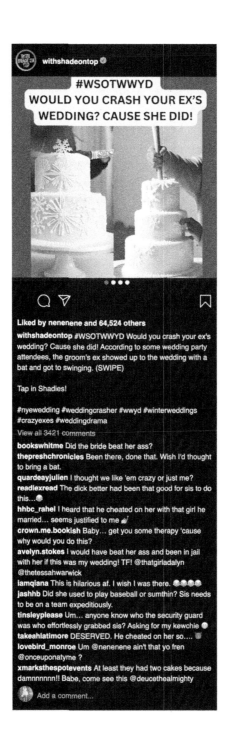

withshadeontop ✓

#WSOTWWYD
WOULD YOU CRASH YOUR EX'S
WEDDING? CAUSE SHE DID!

Liked by nenenene and 64,524 others

withshadeontop #WSOTWWYD Would you crash your ex's wedding? Cause she did! According to some wedding party attendees, the groom's ex showed up to the wedding with a bat and got to swinging. (SWIPE)

Tap in Shadies!

#nyewedding #weddingcrasher #wwyd #winterweddings #crazyexes #weddingdrama

View all 3421 comments

bookswhitme Did the bride beat her ass?

thepreshchronicles Been there, done that. Wish I'd thought to bring a bat.

quardeayjulien I thought we like 'em crazy or just me?

readlexread The dick better had been that good for sis to do this... 🍆

hhbc_rahel I heard that he cheated on her with that girl he married... seems justified to me 💅

crown.me.bookish Baby... get you some therapy 'cause why would you do this?

avelyn.stokes I would have beat her ass and been in jail with her if this was my wedding! TF! @thatgirladalyn @thetessahwarwick

iamqiana This is hilarious af. I wish I was there. 😂😂😂😂

jashhb Did she used to play baseball or sumthin? Sis needs to be on a team expeditiously.

tinsleyplease Um... anyone know who the security guard was who effortlessly grabbed sis? Asking for my kewchie 😏

takeahlatimore DESERVED. He cheated on her so.... 🍵

lovebird_monroe Um @nenenene ain't that yo fren @onceuponatyme ?

xmarksthespotevents At least they had two cakes because damnnnnnn!! Babe, come see this @deucethealmighty

Add a comment...

People had even tagged *the kissing cousins* and the next thing I knew, I was on one of my burner accounts looking at their wedding pictures. Even with all the damage I'd done... things really still continued.

They *were still* husband and wife.

They *still* had a reception where people celebrated *their* love.

They *were still* on their honeymoon.

And most importantly, they *still* didn't give a fuck about how they'd ruined my life.

My chaos hadn't done anything but put a little hiccup in their love story. Meanwhile, I was who people saw as the "batshit" crazy one. Even though I had wanted to go viral, I hadn't considered the backlash I'd receive from people who didn't know the facts.

As my thoughts were spiraling down a dark path, a sudden beeping noise jolted me back to reality. I turned to see Midnight walking in, dressed in casual athleisure wear with headphones draped around his neck.

My eyes swept over him, taking in his relaxed appearance. I had gotten so used to seeing him in that suit that had been tailored to perfection for his body, I almost forgot that he unfortunately could make a potato sack look good against his physique.

Hate that for me.

"I went out for a quick run along the beach and then picked up breakfast." He held up a bag with 'Nani's' on it.

Watching Midnight Drayton walk into a hotel room where I was, returning with food as if he was my man, had me confused as fuck.

Maybe not confused. More-so a word that I refused to let slip from my tongue or thoughts.

"Oh. Um. Thank you." He placed the large bag of food down onto the counter that separated the living room from the kitchenette. As he started pulling out what was inside, I made my way over to see bagels, cream cheese, oatmeal, and fruit. Everything looked good.

"The poppyseed one is yours."

"Thanks," I dragged out, trying to figure out how he'd known to get me that one. It was my favorite.

"We need to go up to the city in a couple hours, so we can get you the stuff you'll need for tonight."

"What do I need?"

"You'll see. Eat first," he replied, his tone demanding as usual. Despite his bossy demeanor, I found myself strangely compelled to obey him as we both sat down at the compact dining table. What was wrong with me? *Did he drug me?*

We ate in silence, each engrossed in our own phone screens. I could feel his eyes on me every now and then, but I refused to look up. The air between us was oddly comfortable, and it made me uneasy. It was strange to be alone with him in a hotel room without spewing our usual slick comments at each other. As much as I wanted to hate him, there was something different about him this morning.

Out of nowhere, he asked, "How'd you sleep?"

Midnight Drayton was asking me normal questions.

I looked up to see him staring at me with those intense, ebony eyes. For a moment, I forgot how to breathe. "Great, actually," I managed to say, trying to sound casual.

"Cool," he nodded, and went back to scrolling through his phone as I finished off my bagel.

I couldn't help but steal a few more glances at him, wondering what was going through his mind. Why was he being so normal?

After a few more minutes of comfortable silence, I couldn't take it anymore. I put my phone down and looked at him.

"Are you dying or something?" I blurted out. "Why are you being so nice to me?"

He burst out laughing, a deep guttural sound that echoed through the room. I couldn't find anything funny about this situation.

"I don't like it," I grumbled.

He continued to laugh, and my frustration mounted.

"What's so funny?" I demanded. "Asking me how I slept was what was comical because we both know you couldn't care less."

He was still laughing, and I couldn't take it anymore.

"Midnight!" I exclaimed, trying to get his attention.

"What?" he asked through his obnoxious laughs.

"I'm serious!"

"I know, that's what makes this shit so funny."

I kissed my teeth and crossed my arms over my chest.

"Do you really want to be stuck with me for the next thirty-six hours and all we do is go back and forth? 'Cause that ain't how I wanna bring in my new year. I can not fuck with you and still speak to you like I got some sense."

"I just never knew you had sense. Maybe that's what I can't wrap my head around."

"Fuck you."

That made me chuckle.

Holy cow, I was sharing a laugh with Midnight Drayton.

"I guess you're right." I stood to my feet. "Besides, I got enough shit to be stressed about— being a whole celebrity and all." I waved my phone before heading into the kitchen to dispose of my trash.

"Exactly," he said, watching me from across the counter. "So how about a truce until we get back home?" He leaned back in his chair, revealing his impeccably trimmed goatee and small gold hoop glinting from his left nostril. I found myself fixating on the details of his sharp jawline but also felt uncomfortable under his intense gaze, even though there was a whole countertop and table between us. It felt as if he was trying to memorize every detail of my face, making my skin prickle with discomfort.

"A truce?" I repeated.

"I think we can handle that."

"So, like no slick comments? At all?" I asked, skeptical.

"You can't do it, can you?"

The little smirk on his face didn't go unnoticed. He was challenging me. "I can do it. I don't live my days thinking of ways to keep you in your place."

He stood up and walked into the kitchenette, coming face to face with me. Well, face to neck. I was five-six (and three quarters), and he had me by a good four inches.

"Is that what you think you do?" Each word of his question seemed to tickle the hairs that were standing on my skin. I was thankful I was leaning against the counter because I *needed* something to hold me up. He didn't let me answer as he continued to move closer into my space.

"Wha— what are you doing?"

He licked his lips. They were a warm shade of brown with just the right amount of thickness. His eyes went from mine and then lowered to the parts of me that were my new enemies.

"You're standing in front of the trashcan. Excuse me."

Motherfucker!

"Oh." I damn near tripped over myself getting out of his way. "Sorry."

I heard the soft chortle as he put his trash into the bin.

"You gonna answer the question?" he said, turning back around towards me.

What quest—oh, right. "I'll let you think what you want." What a dumb response.

"Right." He walked past me. "I'm gonna go shower. We can head out around eleven. Cool?"

"Yeah," I responded because I was still mentally in a bad place. A place that had me thinking thoughts I'd never imagined I'd ever think about Midnight Drayton.

But yet, here we were. *Fuck my life.*

CHAPTER 4

Midnight

Watching her sweat from me being so close in her space, had been even more entertaining than my normal routine of getting her so riled up, she wanted to murder me with her bare hands.

This truce might actually be fun.

Or if nothing else, it'll allow me to not have to be on go mode every time she opened that pretty little mouth of hers. Not that I should be thinking about how her mouth looked. It was perfect with a natural, dark lining around the outer parts of her lips. And when she wore those dark colored lipsticks she liked with a gloss on top… *shit.*

The thoughts had me wrapping my hand around my dick and rubbing a nice one out while I was in the shower.

Yeah, I hated myself for that, *but* my penis didn't seem to care that the juicy ass lips, sweet ass eyes, and thick ass body *he* was thinking about was attached to Tyme fucking Henley.

After I let out a well needed nut, *we* had a long ass talk.

When I got out of the shower, I found Tyme back on the lounge chair and once again, on her phone.

"Don't you get tired of scrolling social media?"

"Nope. You know people really do have a lot to say about things they know nothing about. Some of these comments about why I did what I did are a little wild. It's pretty fascinating."

"If you say so." I wasn't a big social media person. I used it but most of the time when I was on my phone, it was because I was watching YouTube videos.

"Is that judgment?"

"Absolutely not, your highness."

She looked back at me, like I'd been hoping she'd do since I came into the space, and I enjoyed the way her eyes widened at me being in only a towel. She tried to hide it, but I caught it. Just like I caught her earlier, eye fucking me. And whether I could stand her annoying ass or not, I was a man who enjoyed being admired.

"Could you not stand there like that?"

"I had to come get my clothes. Some of us don't have a whole room."

"Touché," she said, turning her head back around.

I grabbed what I needed and retreated to the bathroom.

After that, I didn't see her until it was time for us to leave.

The drive to Chasington Bay was a quiet one. I had been laughing at her comments about this setup between us being weird, but she was right. I didn't know how to be *me* around her because I'd gotten so used to making sure my inner jackass was turned on at all times when she was around.

But now, for more reasons than one, it didn't need to be, and figuring out how to navigate this new normal, even if temporary, wasn't easy—especially since my penis seemed to lose all common sense when our guard wasn't up.

"We're gonna check out a couple of these boutiques. We need to get you a dress or something," I said as I drove into the parking garage.

"Or something?" she questioned, looking over at me. By dress, I meant one of those lingerie night dresses, but I wasn't going to say that.

"The theme is Playboy Mansion meets *House Party*. So, something to go with the theme," I said as I pulled the rental into a parking space.

Her chin lowered. "That's an interesting theme."

"Last year was Golf Pros and Tiger's Hoes. This is much more classy. Luxury pajamas and shit is what my cousin said to think about."

"It's kind of giving pimps and hoes in silk."

I let out a chortle. "Maybe, but it'll be fun."

"What are you getting me into?" she asked as she removed her seatbelt, and I did the same.

"Exactly what you need, remember?"

"Correction, what *you* think I need. I'm starting to question it for real at this point."

"Well, we already have a truce in place; it's too late to go back on anything now."

"I don't think that's how truces work."

"In my world, they do. I'm not being nice to you for nothing."

She rolled her eyes and I wondered how she'd look— *don't.*

"Come on." I cut the engine and exited the car, shaking the thoughts out of my head. At the end of the day, fuckboy or not, she *was* Malachi's girl, and I was doing my damnedest to respect that.

"What are you wearing?" Tyme asked me as we stepped into our third boutique.

"Why? You wanna match with me?"

"As fucking if."

"We can take one of those couple pics and post it, and then I'll have proof that there was a point in time where you didn't hate me."

"I would never allow such things," she said, walking away from me and to whatever had caught her eye. "How about this?" She held up a standard pajama set. It would do, but it wouldn't do *her* justice.

"It's straight."

"You've said that for the last seven things I've picked out. I don't have a clue of the look I'm supposed to be going for, Mid. I'm just tryna find something cute enough for whatever it is you're getting me wrapped up in."

I knew she was trying to subtly dig for clues about tonight, but I'd given her the key details about what she needed to know.

"You mind if I pick out a few things for you to try on?"

She gave me a questionable look but then conceded. I took ten minutes gathering five different options for her to choose from that ranged from lingerie to what I'd consider sexy lounge wear.

"Absolutely not," she said from behind the changing room curtain. "This barely covers anything."

Well, respectfully, you got a lot to cover. The words almost slipped out my mouth, but I caught them. Tyme wasn't a small woman. She was curvy with thick thighs that most men would be happy to be suffocated by. Her figure was voluptuous and inviting, with hips that swayed as she walked and thighs that begged for attention. Her ample chest only added to her allure.

I didn't want to, but I couldn't stop myself from imagining the way her body would feel pressed against mine, the softness of her curves enveloping me. I appreciated her body for what it was — a stunning work of art.

After a moment of silence, Tyme spoke up, her voice slightly muffled by the curtain. "Excuse me?"

I replayed the last thirty seconds in my head. Did I say that shit out loud? "Huh?"

"What did you just say?"

Shit. "I said, let me see."

She peeked her head out through the curtain, looking at me incredulously. "You did not say that."

"Yes, I did," I lied, hoping that the smile I was holding back wasn't slipping through.

"So, this truce has made you a liar?" She disappeared behind the curtain.

"I thought I said that shit in my head," I admitted, feeling my cheeks flush.

"Mmhmm," she sang.

"You do gotta lot of hips, thighs, and ass. Respectfully."

"So, you be checking for me?"

"You not gon' let me see how the set looks?" I bypassed her question, but I forgot who I was dealing with.

"I know you heard my question." She opened the curtain, and the air slowly drained from my lungs. *Yeah, absolutely not.*

She wore a sea green lace and mesh lingerie set that I was cursing myself out for picking up. The sheer robe barely covered her ass cheeks when she did a quick three-sixty.

She looked insatiable.

Calm the fuck down, I reprimanded my dick.

Yeah…*absolutely the fuck not.* Otherwise, I'd forget my morals.

"This is too much; I'm trying on the next one."

The next two weren't as seductive, but they were decent. However, the fourth one was it. It was a three-piece silk ensemble, in a rich bronze color that was perfect against her medium brown skin. The pants had a delicate lace trim that flowed down the sides, and the matching robe featured the same lace detail along the hem and sleeves. The top was what caught my attention. It was sheer with a lace overlay and a plunging neckline that left little to the imagination. It was the perfect mix of sexy and sophisticated, and she felt comfortable in it. I couldn't take my eyes off of her because the way it fit her body was chef's kiss.

With this one, I could also keep my hormones in check since I had to see her in it for hours.

"You didn't have to pay for it," Tyme stated as we walked out of the boutique. She had tried to stop me from tapping my phone against the machine when she was checking out, but I told her to chill out.

"Why wouldn't I pay?" I questioned, with squinted eyes as I looked over at her— back on her phone, of course.

She glanced up at me as she shrugged. "Because you don't have to. I'm not with you or anything. You don't have to do things for me because of the truce either."

When I first met Tyme, she was a live-in Nanny. I had no clue how much that paid, or if that was still her profession, but it really didn't matter because I had money, which meant hers was null and void.

"Even if the truce wasn't in place, you're technically my guest and therefore my responsibility."

"I'm not your responsibility. I'm not five."

"I don't mean it like that," I countered. "I just mean, I got you as long as you're here with me. Calm down."

"You know telling women to calm down is how men get their asses handed to them?"

"You just can't stand not arguing with me, huh?"

"Because you always have to be right."

"I'm not tryna be right, I'm just letting you know what it is when you're with me. I don't know what kind of men you've been around in the past, but I take care of those I associate with. It's just money... I'll get it back."

"Rich people's problems." Her slick ass just can't help herself.

"Something like that," I shot back as we started walking down the sidewalk. She was a few steps in front of me, which meant my eyes were disrespectfully watching the back of her.

"Thank you," she finally stated. "I guess it's the least you could have done after admitting you be checking me out."

"I never admitted to shit."

She peeked over her shoulder, and I wouldn't be surprised if she caught me staring, since it took me almost running into her before I noticed she was looking back at me. Her eyes gave me a once over as she smirked and said, "Be fucking for real. Now can we eat? I'm starving after all that shopping you made me do to get one lil' thing."

CHAPTER 5

"What are you doing?" Midnight asked me as we waited for our food. We'd picked a ramen spot since we both loved noodles.

Look at us, having things in common. How cute.

"Nothing." *Well, if nothing meant doing what I shouldn't have been doing.*

"Checking his profile is not going to change anything."

"I'm not checking his profile." Before the word 'profile' was even fully out of my mouth, Midnight had snatched my phone from my hand. On instinct, I reached back for it, but he moved it out of my range.

I hated the little ugly smirk that popped up on his sexy ass face.

Not that I thought he was sexy.

"Checking the wedding hashtag is just as bad as checking his profile."

He placed my phone back down on the table. I grabbed it with a hard roll of my eyes before locking it and putting it away.

We were quiet again, and I busied myself with people watching. I wondered what everyone was thinking about as we all wrapped up the last day of this year. Had their year been as *eventful* as mine? Or had it been full of abundance, prosperity, true love, and happiness?

The things I had once thought this year was going to be about for me.

There were couples who were laughing with one another, friends who were enjoying each other's company, people who were solo but devouring their meals, and families too.

Then there was us: two people who damn near hated each other twenty-four hours ago. *And* I use the term 'damn near' lightly because I was sure I hated Midnight.

And now... now I was eighty-two percent sure of something else.

But I was trying to hold onto reality, and the harsh truth was Midnight was a certifiable douchebag who had rightfully earned one of the top spots on my personal list of 'men I hated because they were true assholes'.

As much as I didn't want to admit it, letting my guard down around Midnight brought back memories of a time when we didn't despise each other. It was a time when we were strangers, and I was foolish enough to think that he could be "the one."

We had matched on a dating app twelve days before I met his twin brother, and for forty-eight blissful hours, it felt like we were truly connecting. We talked about our unique names, our mutual love for Japanese cuisine (especially ramen), and his appreciation for wine, planes, and food videos, as well as my desire to have a family and be a loving wife.

But just as quickly as it had started, everything fell apart. The shit hit the fan, and I was left with the bitter taste of disappointment and resentment—something that I unfortunately wasn't new to when it came to men.

According to Midnight, I came on too strong. He called me desperate for marriage and told me that I was a walking red flag. And I told him to go fuck himself before un-matching— and *maybe* reporting his profile.

I can be petty at times.

Almost two weeks after my disastrous encounter with Midnight, I decided to take his suggestion and check out the wine bar he had recommended. It wasn't because I wanted to run into him and give him a piece of my mind in person, though. I just wanted to try meeting someone in real life, and The Drays seemed like the perfect spot.

Plus, as a newcomer to the city, I figured it couldn't hurt to explore the places Midnight had suggested. Little did I know, this hidden gem he had touted as a great spot to check out, was actually owned by his family.

It was there that I met Sir Cheater. My first impression of him was that he was handsome, charismatic, and knew how to say all the right things to make a girl feel like she was the only thing that mattered in the room. He put his hooks in me, and I fell for his charm effortlessly.

Like a dummy, I thought the universe was on my side and had used Midnight as a catalyst to bring my actual true love into my life. Unlike Midnight and me, fuckboy and I were on the same page about what we wanted in life. He brought up kids, marriage, and settling down right away, and I was happy to follow his lead.

Especially since the men I had dated in my twenties didn't ever seem to want anything as serious as I did. I either found myself in situationships that didn't meet my needs, or with someone who just wanted to go with the flow. My ex was the first man who seemed in complete alignment with me, so when things between us moved fast, I didn't complain.

Okay so looking back on it, maybe I was a little desperate.

In my defense, I was twenty-eight and had this warped idea that I had to find my husband — *and preferably be married* — before I was thirty. Thirty-one at the latest on the marriage tip, so the clock was ticking. I wanted love and a family— something I once had as a child that was snatched away from me as a pre-teen due to a tragedy that was outside of my parents' control. What was so wrong with that?

Nothing, except I focused so much on what I wanted that I missed *(the correct term for some of them might be ignored)* all the yellow, orange, and big red flags.

And now I was thirty and looking goofy as hell.

Two weeks into dating, Sir Cheater asked me to be his girlfriend and then introduced me to his family. Some might consider that a red flag in itself, but my silly behind was just excited that someone was taking me serious enough to introduce me to their loved ones.

That's when I met his twin brother and I was left *gagged*. His features had always seemed oddly familiar but I could never put my finger on the reason. They were fraternal twins, yet looked eerily similar when they were next to one another.

Or sitting in front of you.

While their facial features, skin tone, and bone structure were almost identical, making it difficult to tell them apart at first glance, they did have their differences.

Midnight's hair was kept in a tapered curly fade, which contrasted with Sir Cheater's mid-fade with waves. Midnight's eyes were a dark, intense ebony, whereas Sir Cheater's were a softer hazel. Midnight's upper body was covered in tattoos, while Sir Cheater had none. And one stark difference was that the proven fuckboy was a couple of inches taller.

But at times, it was unnerving how much they looked alike. It was like looking at two versions of the same person, one with a darker edge and one with a more polished façade.

I had a weakness for men over six feet, which was probably why I was so easily drawn to my ex. But when I started talking to Midnight, I found myself making an exception. Despite falling an inch*ish* short of my usual type, I was willing to give him a chance because our conversations were just that good. However, he showed his true colors and I had to block his mean ass out of my mental space.

That was, until I was being introduced to him by my *boyfriend*, and he was giving me a menacing stare. From that moment on, our mutual hatred for each other bloomed into top-tier animosity.

It was quite fun having an archenemy — if I do say so myself.

The smell of ramen tickling my nose brought my attention back to the moment. We ate in semi-comfortable silence before he ruined it by bringing up the past.

"You never did tell me, what was the point of fucking up their wedding?"

What did he mean what was the point? Wasn't that obvious?

"I thought the point was clear, and I told you I did it to make me feel better."

"I don't believe that. When I brought it up yesterday, it made you cry, and I apologize for that again, but I really want to understand why you did what you did. And before you say it, I'm not about to judge you."

"Right."

"I'm serious, Tyme." I was starting to realize, I didn't really like him saying my name. I started doing Kegels every time he did. That couldn't be good, right? "Truce is in play. That makes this a judgment free zone."

I contemplated my next words as the noodles I'd just placed into my mouth danced on my tastebuds, distracting me from what was happening between my legs.

Did it matter if he knew why I had chosen violence?

"I want him to regret what he did to me." The words came out slow as if I had to make sure I pronounced each one to the fullest.

Midnight nodded. "So, you want him to want you back?"

"No, I—"

"I ain't the one you gotta lie to. If you want—"

"I don't want him back!" I stated matter-of-factly. "Why would I want someone who did me like that back?" He shrugged, which was better than him having something judgmental to say. "But fine… I do want him *to want me* back. What's wrong with that?"

"Nothing, except you're going about it all wrong. You doing all this crazy shit ain't gonna do anything but make Mal think he made the right decision. He was ready, right with Tia, to press charges against you and thought that shit was funny. You ain't doing nothing but making yourself look like you're not over him, and if I know anything about my brother… that shit makes *him* feel like he won."

He was right.

I hated that he was right.

The more time I spent worrying about what *the kissing cousins* were doing, the more it made it seem like I was still hung up on the relationship we once had.

That was false.

I didn't want him back, but I did want him to suffer. I wanted him to understand the pain he'd inflicted on me and feel genuine remorse. I wanted him to regret losing the best thing that could have happened to him, because desperate for love and marriage or not, I was still that fucking girl.

The issue was that my pride and ego wouldn't allow me to let go. My heart had moved on, but my ego wasn't ready.

"Well, since you know your brother so well, what do you suggest I do instead?"

Midnight stopped eating and leaned back in his seat.

"Show him that you've moved on."

Not him giving me the obvious answer. And here I was, starting to think he was the smart twin. "Clearly, that would be the easy thing to do, but the idea of dating right now makes me sick to my stomach."

"Then don't date. You just gotta make it look like you've moved on." He picked up his phone and aimed it at me.

"What are you doing?" I questioned, allowing my chopsticks to rest in my bowl.

There was that ugly *sexy* smirk again.

"Are you recording me?"

He ignored my question and stated, "Mal always wants what he can't have…"

"Midnight." I reached my hand out to block his phone, but he moved it and kept doing what he was doing.

"… and it's even worse when I have it."

He stopped aiming his phone directly at me.

"Were you recording me?" I asked again before his last sentence registered fully in my mind. "And what do you mean by 'it's even worse when I have it'?"

"Mal can't stand if his "younger brother" is doing better than him. He's way too competitive for his own good. So, if he sees that you're with me, that's gonna fuck with him."

I couldn't deny what he'd said. During our relationship, Sir Cheater always went out of his way to outdo Midnight. At first, I didn't pick up on it but as time went on, I noticed he'd brag about having the bigger house, more expensive materialistic things, and being the one who was going to be the next CEO of their family business. He took those twenty-two minutes he was born before Midnight to heart.

Another red flag I ignored.

Midnight started doing something on his phone. "What are you doing?"

"Posting this video of my date for the evening to my close friends."

I was sure my eyes got as wide as saucers. "What?!" I leaned over and snatched his phone, but it was too late. The video was already posting. "Midnight!"

"Trust me, Tyme. Don't delete it." That was exactly what I was waiting to do. "As soon as Mal sees that video, it's gonna fuck with him."

The video finished uploading, allowing me to see it. It was literally of me asking him if he was recording me and trying to take the phone back. He'd replaced the original sound with the chorus of "Essence" by Wizkid featuring Tems. But what really made me wanna scream was the added text: *she always wanna be difficult but in reality, she knows she excited to be my NYE date*.

"Not you with this bold-faced lie."

"Is it, though?" he asked with a smirk.

"Yes." I scoffed. "Anyway," I paused with my finger hovering over the three dots that would take me into the settings. "None of this makes any sense. He knows that we don't get along. Why would he even care?" I sat his phone down momentarily to tend to my food. He had until I finished my next bite to change my mind.

But nothing could have prepared me for the words that came out of his mouth. "He does know we don't get along, but he also knows that I wanted you before he did."

CHAPTER 6

Midnight

And *apparently still do.* I left that part of the sentence out.

"Excuse me?" The noodles she was about to put into her mouth fell back into her bowl of ramen, but her hand position with the chopsticks didn't change as she stared at me in disbelief.

It was cute.

Everything about her was starting to be fucking cute, which was why I didn't know why I'd made that bold ass suggestion. Except for the fact that I was tired of seeing her in such a funk over a nigga who never deserved her.

I wasn't a saint, but I was damn sure a better man than my brother — and I always knew that—but when they got together, that wasn't my business. Besides, they seemed like two peas in a pod— both ready for love, family, and marriage— everything that I was so far removed from at the time.

Which was why I kept telling myself that I didn't want her.

She was too much for me.

She was a walking red flag— okay, maybe I was the red flag and wanted to protect her from me. I knew back then that all I wanted was someone to play with, and she was looking for Mr. Forever.

I wasn't him.

But Malachi… Malachi was supposed to be him.

Despite all of my brother's flaws, I'd hoped Tyme would be the one to turn him into a better man. It would have been a bitter pill to swallow, but I thought he would end up making me regret those texts I'd sent her when we first met, calling her desperate and accusing her of asking for too much too soon.

The Midnight Tyme had matched with was an immature man who'd lied to himself about not needing love. But the truth was, during that time, I was still hurting from a past relationship where I wasted four years on someone who rejected my proposal and told me I wasn't marriage material — just the type of dude you fuck and enjoy until someone better comes along.

So, who was I to go against what was apparently my winning qualities?

I knew from our very first conversation that Tyme was someone special. She wasn't someone to play around with, and that's why I let her off— harshly.

Because I'm a dick.

I never expected to talk to her again, let alone have her show up in our group chat. Malachi was boasting about some hot girl he'd met at our wine bar, and when he sent her picture, I was stunned to see Tyme.

I debated whether to confess I'd matched with her on a dating app weeks earlier. I knew I'd messed up my chance with her and didn't think my twin had much of a chance either. It wasn't until a few days later when he mentioned he was planning on bringing her to an upcoming family function that I knew I had to speak up.

Of course, Malachi brushed it off as no big deal, because in his mind, he was the one she wanted now. His ego loved it.

The day I was introduced to her, I recognized her immediately— even from across the room. Her pictures never did her justice, even though she was photogenic. However, they couldn't capture her timeless beauty or good-natured energy that she exuded the moment she entered a room.

It took my breath away each time— and, of course, I despised it.

"What do you mean he knows that you wanted me before he did? He doesn't even know that we knew each other beforehand. I mean, if you want to even call it that…" She started rambling. Her hand was still holding up the chopstick as if it was a frozen prop. "Wait, wait, wait," the utensil finally dropped back into her bowl of noodles, "what do you mean you wanted me?"

"Which question would you like me to answer first?"

"Midnight, please." There were multiple emotions covering her face, but the one of her being tired of my bullshit stood out the most. It was one of my favorites.

"I don't know how much clearer I can be. I wanted you from the moment we connected, thought that was obvious."

"I mean, I guess," she stumbled over her words, "but—"

"There's no but."

"Yes, it is because then you told me how much you didn't want me after you judged me because…" she swirled her hands around as she pointed at me, "*you're you*. Then, you proceeded to taunt me my whole relationship with your lookalike."

From the moment Mal told me he would continue dating Tyme because he could see her becoming *his* Mrs. Drayton, I made an executive decision. Not only did I have to dislike her, but I also had to make her detest me even more. It was the only way I could stomach being in the same room as her without my dick getting hard.

"We taunted each other. You're never really good with the facts."

"Whatever," she waved me off. "The question now is, why would you ever tell him about us? *We* agreed that *we* wouldn't say anything."

Tyme didn't seem to recognize me right away when we first met. It wasn't until Malachi said my name that the pieces fell into place for her. I remember watching her face subtly change as she connected the dots. My dating profile was filled with side profiles and half-face shots intentionally. I only had one full-face, forward-facing photo, but apparently, it wasn't memorable enough. Or maybe she was just too caught up in Malachi's bullshit to notice the resemblance between us.

Even as fraternal twins, our family genes were strong, which meant that sometimes, we could look like we shared an egg. Our main physical difference — one that Mal loved to brag about — was our height. He had me beat by three and a half inches.

Those inches I was missing went to my dick. *Yeah, mine was bigger,* but I didn't rub that in his face. He already did enough extra shit to make up for his barely average dick syndrome.

"I lied," I admitted. "By the time we had that conversation, Mal already knew about us. I didn't want you to feel uncomfortable about it, so I lied. I knew he'd never bring it up."

"How could you have been so sure?"

"I might not fuck with my brother like that... but I know him and how he moves."

I watched as she processed what I had said before asking her next question. "How did you find out about me and him?"

"Malachi likes to brag about his conquests; you were in the group chat."

Her mouth dropped open.

"After I saw it was you, I hit him up and told him that we had matched on the app."

"*And* that you wanted me."

I tried to hide my smile, but I guess I didn't do it well because of the way her eyes narrowed at me.

"Mal knew I frequented dating apps for a good time. All he cared to know was if I'd smashed. I told him you weren't on that type of time, so you weren't my type." She tilted her head, but I didn't bother explaining that I didn't mean physically, or that I had been lying to myself either way. "He then confirmed that I did want to bless you with the pipe at one point, and I told him I did."

I could practically feel Tyme's eyes on me as she processed my words. "He was okay with pursuing me after that?" she asked incredulously.

Internally, I shook my head. Her line of questioning showed me that she didn't know the man she'd almost married. She had no clue who Malachi was behind the façade he must have put on for her.

"For Mal," I explained, "the fact that he now had something I once wanted made you even more valuable to him."

"So, I was just something for him to check off a list?" Tyme asked, hurt radiating through her words.

"No," I quickly rebutted, not wanting her to feel that way. "But you know how he is, always needing his ego stroked and feeling like he's won something. It's not about you, it's about him," I added, hoping to reassure her. She continued to twirl her chopsticks in her ramen, lost in thought. "Look at me, Tyme," I said softly, hoping to bring her attention back to me.

Well, that was fucking stupid.

As soon as her eyes met mine, I regretted it because an image of her tied up, with a blindfold on, and headphones in her ear flashed into my head, and my dick immediately bricked up.

Her not breaking eye contact with me and waiting for me to say what I had to say didn't help.

"You'll never be something that someone just wants to check off a list. Don't ever fucking disrespect yourself by thinking some bullshit like that, you hear me?"

"I do but—"

"No buts. That's what the fuck it is and that's it."

"Even with the truce, you still work my nerves."

"Is that your way of saying 'Thank you, Midnight, for reminding me that I'm that girl'?"

"Sure."

"I'll take that because I know you can't say thank you."

She rolled her eyes. "Long as you know." We went back to eating our food, and I was sure hers had gotten just as lukewarm as mine. "So now how does all of this tie back into you posting me on your social media?" She picked up my phone. "Because I'm still ready to del—" A small gasp escaped her mouth as it lit up. "Fuckboy just messaged you."

She tossed the device back at me like it was lava.

"Oh my god, what did he say?" she squeaked.

"Why didn't you read it?" I shook my head as I clicked on the notification to open the app.

One message.

Two messages.

Five messages, back-to-back, came into my direct messages.

@THEEMALACHIDRAYTON

???????

yo what the fuck you doing out there with Tyme?

I know you ain't takin' her with you

to 12:01

that's flaw if so

I handed the phone back to Tyme and watched as she scrolled through the messages, her eyebrows knitting together, causing wrinkles to form in between them.

"What is 12:01?" she asked, looking up at me for an explanation as I finished off my last bit of noodles.

"That's what my cousin calls his party every year," I replied.

Tyme eyed me skeptically. "Why would it be flaw for me to go?" she asked.

"I thought I told you not to ask any more questions about tonight," I said, trying to keep my tone firm.

"I *meannnn,*" she twirled her pointer fingers around one another as she dragged the word 'mean' out. "He's making it sound like it's something sketchy."

"It's not sketchy," I reassured her. "You'll be safe, and anything you don't wanna do, you don't have to do."

Her brows furrowed even deeper. "Um, you definitely made it sound even sketchier. I'ma need a little bit more. Is this some kind of cult party I'm walking into or some shit? Am I gonna have to sacrifice my firstborn?"

I chuckled at her exaggeration as our waitress approached to see if we were done with our food. We were.

"I'm not at liberty to give you much more than that. Host's orders. Just trust me, for once. Can you do that?"

She pulled her bottom lip into her mouth, and I sucked in the deepest breath I could muster.

"I can."

CHAPTER 7

Tyme

T he sound of my phone vibrating against the bathroom counter made me roll my eyes and almost mess up the lashes I was already failing at applying. I should have taken Midnight up on his offer to pay for me to get my makeup done, but I already felt like he was doing too much.

Was he doing too much? Or was I afraid of letting him do too much? 'Tis the real question.

Either way, I enjoyed getting all dolled up on my own — with the exception of lashes. I had a love-hate relationship with putting them on and aligning them perfectly.

Besides, had I gotten my makeup done while we were out, I wouldn't have been able to get in the nice nap I took when we got back. And naps were a priority when I had no clue what was going to happen tonight.

I glanced down and saw a number that wasn't saved calling me. A number that had called me three times in the last three hours and sent four text messages.

It was Sir Cheater — calling from a different number than the one I had him saved under —and boy, oh boy, was he showing his ass. I had to admit, it was quite comical, which was why I hadn't blocked him.

When Midnight put this plan into action, I thought it was stupid, a little childish, hella petty, and most importantly, it wouldn't work. Mr. Fuckboy would not be bothered by a little video of me on his brother's social media account when he should have been — as Midnight put it — knee deep in his new wife's vagina.

He was on his honeymoon for goodness' sake... why on earth would he care? He'd gotten the girl he really wanted, right?

Well, right or wrong, his actions were showing that he still gave a damn about me—enough to waste his time and energy blowing my phone up. Even if it was out of pure jealousy, it sent a ping of satisfaction through me.

I pressed ignore and as I got my lash situated to my liking, a text came flowing in.

> 333-987-6543
>
> So y'all both ignoring me?

And another one.

> If u on some get back shit, this just shows me u weren't loyal anyway.

I couldn't let that slide.

> Fuck off, please.

> What the hell u doing with Mid?

> Why do you care? How's the honeymoon?

> I doubt your wife would be happy about you texting me.

> Don't worry about my wife. She got me, unlike u.

> Yet you're the one on my line. That's concerning.

> Because why u with my brother?

Why you in my business?

U know he's just tryna fuck right? If he hasn't already. Don't be surprised when u end up being just some pussy to him.

Before I could respond to his ignorance, knocks sounded against the bathroom door. "You ready?" Midnight's voice came flowing in.

"Almost," I called back, swinging the door open and then having to immediately catch my damn breath.

He was shirtless— again.

Seeing him this way this morning was already enough for my vagina. We were at capacity.

The tattoos that covered every inch of his chest, upper arms, back, and torso were like little demons begging me to lose my religion. But no, this *was still* Midnight Drayton at the end of the day.

Even if those silk pajama pants told me something I already peeped over a year ago— my arch nemesis had a premium size dick. That was probably why my bitch ass ex was blowing me up... he didn't want his brother to blow my back out the right way.

Sex with my ex had been good (even if his penis wasn't that big), occasionally even great, but the way my core was contracting as my eyes tried to act like we weren't looking at *what we were looking at* told me that there was no occasionally with Midnight.

"You're not even dressed." His voice pulled my attention up to his face.

"Well, that's why I said almost, duh." I moved past him and back across the hallway to my room. "Besides, you said we were leaving at six-fifteen. It's only six-oh-five." As if I'd be ready in ten minutes.

"For somebody named Tyme..."

"Don't finish that sentence," I threatened, and he laughed. I hated that I was starting to like that laugh. "I got distracted by your brother calling and texting me again."

"I hope you ignored his ass like I've been doing."

I grimaced, forming a deep frown.

"Tyme." He sighed.

"You never said I shouldn't respond. He was saying some foul shit and as you told me not to forget, I had to remind him that I'm that bitch."

"What the fuck he say?"

It was the way the words came out of his mouth that made my stomach tighten. It was a very much 'do I need to fuck him up?' tone, and it was at that moment, it clicked as to why one of my estranged friends loved her men to be a little rough around the edges. They did not play about their women.

But I wasn't Midnight's woman. Yet, the tone said he'd protect me.

Or at least, that's how it made me feel. Protected. Safe.

And that was something I hadn't felt in a long time from a man.

I hadn't even realized it until *now*.

I always felt wanted by my ex and knowing what I know now— maybe it was because he saw me as a trophy he had "won". But I never felt the way that Midnight had made me feel with five little words.

"You can see for yourself." I handed him my phone. My teeth sank deep into my bottom lip as his eyes scanned the thread.

The muscles in his jaw flinched a few times before he finally said, "This nigga such a fucking bitch. I swear I wanna lay his ass out sometimes."

Why was the thought of that sexy?

His eyes met mine. "You do know he's just running his mouth, right? He needs a response to feel better."

"I know." I nodded. "Did his heffa of a wife see your post?"

"No, I purposely made a close friends list with only him." *Smart.* "Just to see, as I expected, if we would bait him."

"And you did. I can only imagine what will happen if *ol' girl* find out he's blowing us up like this."

"He won't let that happen." I, more than anyone, knew that was probably true. My ex clearly knew how to be a sneaky ass person.

"By the way," Midnight said as he scrolled through the texts once more, "I'm definitely not tryna fuck." There was an air of playfulness in his voice, plus that ugly *sexy* smirk of his.

I sucked my teeth. "As if I would give you the time of day."

"Aye, you wanted to once, let's not forget."

I snatched my phone from his hand and pushed him towards the door. "Please get out with your bullshit so I can change."

"I know you just wanted to touch my chest. You might be the one —" Before he could finish, I slammed the door in his face.

I couldn't see it, but I felt it in the burn of my cheeks: there was a huge grin on my face. I hated that for me.

I wasn't ready for another twenty-five minutes.

I thought the silk pajama set was cute at the boutique, but I looked damn good. The wine color against my skin was heavenly. Not to mention the black lipstick I'd picked up earlier today gave me an edgy look that I always loved. I loved a good dark lipstick; they always suited me well.

I gave myself a final once over as I took a moment to adjust my hair, coaxing the curls to fall just the way I desired.

"She cute!" I complimented the beauty in the mirror.

I had always been a chubbier girl, but the weight never really bothered me. Of course, I had my days where I felt fat as heck due to mother nature— *mother naturing*, but overall, I loved my curves.

I had a good amount of ass and titties with a few rolls to match. My bottom-heavy frame was definitely something I inherited from my mother's side and sometimes, I did ask my thighs and hips to chill out, because they be doing just a little too much.

Unfortunately, they never listened, and I'd learned to embrace my grown woman, size sixteen on a good day, body to the fullest.

Besides, a little fat never hurt anybody or prevented me from riding somebody's son's face.

"I knew you weren't almost ready," Midnight's voice sounded before I even walked out the room.

"Yes, I was." I stepped into the living area to see he was standing next to the balcony doors. It was almost seven, so that meant it was pitch black outside, but that didn't seem to stop him from staring out into nowhere.

His back was to me, and it was in that moment that I noticed we were wearing the same color. My brain must have been too busy focusing on the wrong thing earlier to take note of the color of his pajama's bottoms.

"I'm starting to think we're taking this couple thing a little too far."

He turned around, and I wanted to fight myself for the way my heart skipped a beat. Why would God make my arch nemesis this damn fine? Had I not been through enough turmoil this year?

Sir Cheater was handsome — they obviously looked alike — but Midnight... Midnight was— *fuck*. He was the epitome of the type of man who *actually* should be on the cover of those 'Sexiest Man Alive' magazine editions.

But it wasn't just the way he looked.

It was the way he carried himself.

The way his sex appeal spoke for itself.

The way his confidence entered a room thirty minutes before he did.

He exuded a dangerous amount of fine, flirty, and fuckable.

Add in his faux bad boy vibe, and he'd have most women ready to risk it all for one night with him.

I didn't want to be most women.

Did I?

"Oh, so we're a couple now?"

"I-I—" I stumbled because I was about to lie and say 'I didn't say that' but the words had literally come out my mouth five seconds ago. "I didn't mean it like that, but you are matching me." I motioned between us.

He moved closer to where I was standing, the glint of his nose ring catching my eye. "I'm pretty sure I had my 'fit first. You tryna be like me, Sweets?" Midnight said, tugging at the hem of his shirt.

"Don't pet name me," I snapped, crossing my arms over my chest.

"You said we were a couple," he reminded me, his eyes sparkling with amusement.

"But I—"

"No buts."

"Midnight!" I hissed. He was impossible to deal with. "You are really annoying," I finally said, gritting my teeth.

"I like being annoying to you. There's a difference," he replied, a mischievous glint in his eye.

"No there's not," I retorted, my eyes locked onto his. "Plus, being purposely annoying is going against the truce."

"Is it?" he challenged, raising an eyebrow.

Why was he staring at me like that?

I felt my cheeks flush with heat.

Focus, girl.

"You're poking the bear and if I curse you out, you're gonna say I'm the mean one," I warned him, trying to steer the conversation back on track.

"You are the mean one," he shot back, his gaze roaming over my body for a brief moment before returning to my eyes. It was all of three seconds, but it felt like a never-ending plank hold. "You look stunning, by the way."

I think I forgot how to breathe.

"And this wasn't the color you tried on at the store." I didn't think he'd even notice I'd swapped the bronze for the wine color. The boutique clerk had already bagged it up before he got to the register to pay. "But I'm glad you switched it out. It'll play better into our game-plan. Plus, you look good in it."

"Stop with the compliments," I said, my heart still racing from the first one.

"See, you don't want me to be nice, you want me to be an annoying asshole."

My head fell back. Midnight Drayton was going to ruin me and not in a good way. "Can we go?"

CHAPTER 8

I was damn glad I'd chosen to wear boxer briefs instead of free-balling it. After seeing the way Tyme's eyes dropped to my print earlier, I knew I needed to contain the beast. But I couldn't resist flirting, even though I knew it would only make things more difficult.

I had a natural inclination to flirt, but with Tyme, I had learned to channel my flirtatious tendencies into being an extra asshole. However, since we had agreed to a truce, I was playing with fire by indulging in my old habits.

As we entered the gates of the private villa, Tyme's awestruck expression caught my attention. "Whoa," she breathed, taking in the exquisite sight before us. My cousin had been renting out this particular spot for his annual event for the past few years, and it never failed to impress. The villa was straight out of a magazine with fifteen suites, over ten full bathrooms, a spa, a multi-level saltwater pool, and an array of other shit.

"Oh, your cousin has money, *money*. Must run in the family," she said, smirking.

"He's doing alright with his business, but the villa belongs to his best friend's family. They're real estate tycoons all over Chasington County."

Tyme nodded thoughtfully. "It's all about who you know, right?"

"Most of the time, it is. So don't be afraid to mingle with the people you meet tonight. You never know who could help you with whatever's next for you."

"You mean after we break up tomorrow?" she joked.

I chortled. "Exactly." As we waited for the valet, I asked, "So, what have you been up to? Still nannying?"

"Sort of," she replied, her expression contorting briefly as if she had tasted something sour. "To be honest, I've dropped the ball a lot over the last five months. The breakup didn't put me in the best headspace, and I know it sounds stupid, but I let it mess up my bag."

I was about to say something when she added, "But don't worry, I'm not struggling. Your brother paid for everything, so I was able to save a lot of money from my job. I had a nice cushion to fall back on. But, I'll need to start working again by Spring if I don't want to drain my savings. I'm just not sure if I want to go back to nannying or try something else in my field."

"What is that?" I asked, taking a moment to admire her. Her hair was down, with soft, voluminous curls cascading around her face, framing her features perfectly. And the way she had applied her makeup was impeccable. I appreciated the dark lipstick she wore, with a hint of gloss on top, which gave her a bold and edgy look that I found irresistible.

"Interior design. I've been dabbling in it a little bit again and realize I miss it."

"I didn't know you had an eye for things like that. That's pretty dope," I said, twirling a strand of my goatee around my finger.

"Thanks," she said as we approached the valet. One of them opened her door and helped her out while another opened mine and gave me the ticket I'd need for when we left.

Tyme waited for me at the bottom of the steps that led up to the entrance, looking up at the grand villa with anticipation shining in her eyes. "I'm kind of excited," she said as I approached her.

"Good. It's gonna be a great night. My cousin throws one hell of a New Year's Eve party," I replied with a grin.

She glanced down at her phone, and I wondered if Mal was still bothering her. After he'd sent me the direct messages, he had called and texted me a few times as well, but I left him on read. I hadn't heard from him in two hours, but I was sure he was still in his head about what was going on between me and Tyme. He knew what type of vibe our cousin's party would have, which is why my plan to get under his skin was working even faster. As the twin who easily let shit roll off my back, it was quite satisfying to see him struggle.

"By the way," I said, absentmindedly stroking my goatee and placing a finger under her chin so that she'd look at me. "Breakups are hard, and they sometimes cause shit to fall out of place. That doesn't make you stupid." She gave me a confused look. "In regards to you calling yourself stupid in the car. Stop belittling yourself, especially around me. I won't have that shit."

She sucked her teeth, playfully knocking my hand from her chin. "Do the women who *are* your type like how demanding you are?"

"I don't know. *Do you?*" I loved watching her get caught up in how to respond to me. "Come on, let's get to the fun."

At the top of the stairs were the door staff dressed in sleek black attire, accessorized with the iconic Playboy bunny ears and bow ties. Knowing my cousin, I was sure no detail was overlooked when it came to staying true to the theme of the night.

As we approached, one of the bunnies greeted us with a flirtatious smile and welcomed us to the party. Tyme couldn't resist a chuckle as we made our way past them and into the house, taking in the lavish decorations and the lively atmosphere.

Before we could join in on the fun, we had to go through the necessary precautions to gain entry. My cousin's annual event was an exclusive gathering, with only thirty to sixty vetted guests allowed in. If you weren't familiar with Nehemiah Drayton, then you had to be a VIP guest of someone he trusted.

"I am starving. Please tell me there's food," Tyme said, placing her hand around my bicep. My dick twitched at her touch.

"Plenty," a familiar voice caught us both off guard, and I turned around to spot the host himself. "Middie Mid!"

"Cuzzo!" I greeted back, as we slapped hands and pulled each other into a hug. My cousin was dressed like a modern version of

Hugh Hefner, complete with a red smoking jacket and black silk pajamas, giving him the air of sophistication and playfulness. His hair was slicked back, and he had an un-lit cigar in his hand, which he waved in the air as he talked. "You look like *Neo Hefner*. How you feeling about tonight?"

"Oh, you know me," he said with a smirk, taking a fake puff of his cigar. "Always ready for a good time. I'm less stressed than I was a few hours ago, but everything is good now. I already had a couple shots, and I'm ready for some good ol' fun."

"Same," I concurred, turning my attention to my *date*. "This is Tyme. Tyme, this is my *blood* cousin I've been telling you about, Neo."

Tyme gave me her signature side eye, and I winked.

"Nice to meet you, Tyme. Welcome to 12:01. I hope it's going to be an experience like none other."

To avoid any potential awkwardness, I messaged my cousin earlier to let him know that I was bringing Malachi's ex. Neo hadn't gotten the chance to officially meet her during what was supposed to be her and Mal's wedding weekend, but he was in both the extended family group chats — one for everyone, and one exclusively for us cousins — so he was well aware of who she was and how shit crumbled between them. Yesterday, both chats were lit with talk of Tyme and her now legendary bat.

Funny enough, the jokes about the situation got so intense that both Mal and Tia ended up removing themselves from both chats. It happened after Tia sent a message *telling* everyone we needed to be on their side and to stop making jokes. One of my cousins, who has absolutely no chill, responded: 'Karma said BATTER UP'. That had me laughing for a good five minutes.

But amidst the laughter, there was a tinge of disappointment. Tia had been part of both chats from the time they were created because *some of us* genuinely considered her family. I wouldn't deny that she was in love with my brother; however, I still wished they'd both owned up to their feelings long before they got Tyme wrapped up in their bullshit.

"So, I'm guessing you're the one who can tell me more about what Midnight here has gotten me into?"

Neo grinned at us. "Tonight's theme is 'Playboy Mansion meets *House Party*.' I wanted to mix luxury and fun, and your matching PJs fit the bill perfectly. I've set up games all around to awaken that inner child and remind us of the good ol' slumber parties and house parties we used to have. It's like a nod to 'Kid 'n Play,' but we're all consenting adults here, so we might take it up a notch."

"Oh, well that seems innocent enough."

Neo and I gave each other a look before he said, "For now, but it's not called 12:01 for nothing. So until then, you two enjoy yourself. There's a shit ton of food and drinks in the kitchen. Mid knows where it is. I'll see you both around. Have fun."

"Remember how I said I was excited?" Tyme asked after Neo walked away. "I'm back to being nervous."

"Remember to trust me. Now let's get you some food." *You might need the fuel for later.*

CHAPTER 9

Someone spiked the mango pineapple punch.

Okay, no one spiked it. It was clearly marked that the 'Play's Punch' was a cannabis infused drink and now, my ass was high as a kite as we played musical chairs. I loved that all the specialty drinks that were being served had been named after the characters from the *House Party* franchise.

I had never had an infused drink and it hit quicker than I expected. Midnight had warned me, but it was *him*, so of course it was only right for me to be a rebel and do the opposite.

Big mistake, huge!

The music started playing again, and the seven of us that were left started moving around in a circle. I was determined to win because all the other games had been kicking my ass. But musical chairs used to be my shit. It was my time to shine. Besides, if I didn't, I had to take a shot and I needed to reframe from getting too tipsy.

Too much alcohol made me horny and for that reason, I needed to stay far from it.

Of course, I could just turn down the shot — but I was no punk bitch. I surely was not finna be one in front of Midnight Drayton.

The music stopped and I snagged me a chair right in the nick of time.

Then there was six.

Then five.

Four.

Three.

And now two: me and my arch nemesis.

"You know I'm not gonna let you win, right?" he taunted me.

"You won't have to let me; I'm just going to. I hope you don't mind getting beat by a girl."

The banter between us, as we both circled the final chair, had those looking on laughing at our expense.

"Besides, I got a lot of ass, remember? It's gonna knock you out the way."

He sniggered at my shade, and I hated how my low vibrational vagina simmered at the look on his face.

Please have some fucking decorum. This is not someone we purr for.

See. No more liq.

"I might not—" his sentence was cut short due to the music coming to a halt. I grabbed the seat, almost breaking a nail, and dropped into it at the same time as he did.

"Move!" I grumbled, trying to push him off but the portion of his body that was on the chair didn't budge.

This had everyone watching in a cackling uproar at our antics. Two grown ass people refusing to lose. It was a solid minute of struggle before the host of the game suggested a tie breaker: rock, paper, scissors.

Oh, he was going down.

"Best two out of three," the host stated before we did the first round.

"Rock, paper, scissors, *shoot!*" we said in unison. I kissed my teeth when his paper beat my rock. Must have been bad boy luck.

The second round was all me. I stood beside rock, and he switched it up with throwing scissors. *Loser!*

"Looks like I'm about to secure my win," I declared smugly as we prepped for the final round.

"Ain't nothing more cuter than your competitive side showing right now," Midnight commented, successfully throwing me off my game with his compliment and winning the final round. "Now what was all that mess you were talking?"

"Shut up." I stuck out my tongue before I reluctantly took my loser's shot of liquor.

Next stop, water.

We continued around the mansion, playing a few more games such as Mario Kart on the Nintendo system and Red Light, Green Light— which took me *way* back. I had to take my shoes off for that.

This was definitely turning into my kind of party.

The games had been nostalgic, and I felt like a kid but was enjoying every minute of it. It was true what people said about letting your inner child out to play. It was the distraction my brain needed from all the bullshit of this year.

"Want to see what's happening outside? It's a little chilly, but there's heaters out there."

Chasington County weather was warmer than what I was used to. The average low at the end and beginning of the year was somewhere between the high forties and low fifties. Tonight, it was fifty-three and it felt a lot nicer than the low teens I'd experienced back in Gavenfalls. *Or* the mid-thirties back home in Southgate.

Nevertheless, I was glad there were heaters since this thin pajama set would have my nipples on full display out in that cold.

"Sure, but I'll meet you out there, I need to go to the restroom." We parted ways and I made my way to one of the guest bathrooms on the main floor.

This villa was a complete dream. It had everything you could imagine being inside of a home this size—a game room, indoor sports court, theater (where they were currently playing the *House Party* movies), board room, gym, and even its own spa.

My favorite area so far had been the piano bar. It was beautiful, and the view into the dining area with retractable glass walls was breathtaking.

When I first stepped into that space, I just stood there for a moment and took it all in, basking in the view of the lush greenery leading out to the back area of the estate.

There was so much to see.

They'd blocked off the upstairs area, but Midnight told me that was where the suites were.

After freshening up, I walked out into the outdoor space where the multi-level pool and hot tub were. Glancing towards the bar on the terrace, I spotted Midnight with his back to me, having a conversation with a woman I'd seen earlier. She had been on the opposing team when I'd played Jenga. I couldn't forget her face because she was just plain ol' gorgeous. Like the classic kind of gorgeous that can't be missed, especially with her height, long limbs, and golden skin. I had wondered if she was a model with the way she oozed elegance.

Love a Black woman from infinity to infin.ni.ty!

And if it wasn't for that, it was also because this party was quite intimate, so after seeing a face two times max, it was hard to forget. If I had to guess, there were no more than fifty people in attendance.

I lowkey loved it.

It made interacting a lot easier and fun when everyone was getting drunk or high. Plus, I noticed most people seemed to be familiar with one another, but even as an outsider, everyone was very welcoming. The vibe had been nice, and everybody was serving a look with their take on luxury *jammies*.

However, for a house of this caliber, I expected more people, but that was none of my business.

My business was being a bad bitch who was living her best life, bringing in the new year— something I would have never thought would be happening when I was sitting in that jail cell. But here we were, and these last twenty-four hours had been some of the best hours I'd had all year.

To think it had been with a man I swore I hated.

And we still did... let's be fucking for real, Tyme. You're high and liquored up... you're not thinking straight. This truce is not forever. He's still enemy number two.

Upon reaching the bar, I caught the tail end of their conversation.

"... to see you, Mid. I was hoping you'd be here. I'm a little sad about this, though… Clareese and I were looking forward to an encore presentation."

Midnight let out a soft laugh. "There's always next…" He cut his sentence short as he peeked over his shoulder to see me. "I thought you got lost," he said, and the head-to-toe look he gave me didn't go unnoticed.

Those fucking eyes are soul suckers.

"And yet you didn't come search for me?" I batted my eyelashes.

He flashed a smile, and I wanted to hide some place where life made sense again, because why did my body tingle at that pretty pearly white smile of his? *WHY?*

"I was catching up with a friend." He turned his attention back to the woman as I came up beside him.

"I see," I smiled. It was a genuine smile too, but Midnight had to play around.

"You jealous?" he teased.

I pursed my lips. "Not in the least."

"Not even a little bit?"

His tongue swiped over his bottom lip, then the top, and I was in a millisecond trance before I finally said, "Nope." I made sure to make a popping sound with my lips.

"Come on Sweets, don't embarrass me in front of Mercedes."

"Too late for that," Mercedes said, grinning and getting us to stop acting like a bickering married couple. *Disgusting.* "You two are cute together. Now I see why we went with the black," she said to him, and I had no clue what she was referring to. I also wanted to vomit at the 'you two are cute together'.

Please girl, I thought we could be friends and now you say things like that?

"Mercedes." She outstretched her hand to me. "We were playing Jenga together, right? I didn't know you were with Mid. Nice to meet you, first timer."

"I was, and I'm Tyme." I shook her hand. "Nice to meet you, too." *Evil person who clearly wants me to throw my ass back in a circle on my ex's twin brother.* "How'd you know it was my first time?"

"Your wristband, darling." Her eyes bounced down to my wrist. I forgot I was wearing one. I noticed hers was yellow. It wasn't until that moment that my mind started to register the different colored wristbands.

Mine was white. Midnight's was black. Some people even had on more than one. *Interesting.* "Anyway, I need to go find my wife. Hopefully, I'll see you both around later." She gave a wink and floated away in only a way someone that dazzling could do.

"She is very pretty," I commented, turning my attention towards him.

"You into...?" he cocked his head to the side and raised a brow. "'Cause I can put in a good word for you if—"

"Oh my god, no!" I quipped and he laughed.

"Nothing wrong with it. I'm definitely not gonna judge you about that." He gave me an exaggerated wink. God, why was he being this cute? *Howww* was he being this cute?

"I bet you wouldn't, and I can appreciate a beautiful woman without being sexually attracted to her. Considering you're *almost* forty," I said to be shady, "I hope you know that."

"I do, but I was curious about your preferences."

"Well, nosey, to each their own, but I only prefer gummy worms and not Swedish fish, if you get my drift."

He balled up his face. "You still high, aren't you?"

I laughed because I was. "Speaking of liking coochie," I caught the words about to come out. "Actually, never mind."

"Hell no, I like coochie. Speaking of what?"

"You know, you actually might be funny sometimes," I commented, unable to pause the giggles still flowing out my mouth.

"I know that. Now back to what you were saying."

Reason number six of why I hate Midnight: He's cocky, and it's annoying because he's sexy with it.

I let out a theatrical sigh. "Your brother asked me to be in a relationship with him and *girl*."

The look Midnight gave me had the chuckles coming back. "You lyin'?"

I shook my head. "Nope."

"When? Today?"

"Oh God, no." I laughed harder, but at the same time, I could have imagined him doing that with the way he had blown me up. "After I found out about him and her getting engaged." *A mere five weeks after our break-up.* "I was furious and sent him this long ass dissertation that he probably laughed at." The amount of shit I'd allowed myself to do post break-up over Sir Cheater was so out of character, but heartbreak apparently made me stupid as hell. And conversations like this were starting to make me much more aware.

"Don't call yourself stupid!" Midnight's words about me belittling myself rang in my head.

Wow. Now he was living in my core memories. *Had I died and gone to hell? Was that it?*

"He replied, telling me that he still loved me as much as he loved her and if I was open to it, he could get her to agree to a poly relationship."

"He's always had an unhealthy amount of audacity in his blood. I swear, sometimes, I wonder how we share the same DNA."

I'm starting to feel that way, too.

"Assholes, jerks, and fuckboys are one in the same, so don't jump too far left."

Midnight moved his head left to right. "Breaking the truce and breaking my heart, all within ten minutes."

I pulled my neck back, squishing my eyebrows together. "Breaking your heart? How?"

"You tried to embarrass me in front of your girl crush. I ain't forget."

I slapped his arm while kissing my teeth. "She is not my girl crush! And nobody embarrassed you. You lucky I ain't tell you not to call me Sweets like I wanted to."

"I like calling you that, though. I think it comes with the faux bae vibes."

"Faux bae?"

"You the one who called us a couple. Don't get in your head. It's all for appearances, remember?" *I'm trying to.* "And since we're on the subject, we need to take a picture. That nigga has been watching my stories like a hawk all night. I know he's waiting to see if I post you again and if you're actually here with me."

"You *really* think you need to post me again? He's already in his feelings."

"If we're gonna do this, we gotta go all in."

Exactly what is all in? That's what I should have said, but instead I asked, "For how long?"

"Just tonight and maybe tomorrow for good measure. Calm down."

"What did I tell you about that calm down?" My arms crossed over my chest.

"Nothing that I listened to." That ugly sexy smirk was back on his *ugly sexy* face.

"You're very aggravating."

"Only for you, *Sweets*."

"Whatever, *Tin Man*." I rolled my eyes at his amusing behavior as he pulled out his phone. I wanted to disown my body for the way goosebumps ran up and down my arms when he positioned me against his chest. We took a few selfies and each one gave, *Spending New Year's Eve with bae.*

"What is your family gonna say when they see your story?" The one from earlier had been on his close friends. This one, this one was a free for all. His mom used social media just as much as me. She was surely going to see it and put it in their family group chat.

"You still don't know me well enough if you think I give a damn about what they have to say. Besides, if they do, all the backlash will fall back on me, not you. I promise."

Every part of me believed his promise.

I don't even need Whoopi Goldberg to tell me I'm in danger.

I cleared my throat, noticing we were still embracing one another as if we hadn't stopped taking photos. I broke away and suggested we go find a place to sit before getting back to the party festivities. The night was still young, and we had almost two hours before it was time to ring in the new year.

"Would you like a *Zora*?" one of the servers asked, approaching us. This was a sweet and spicy cocktail named after Queen Latifah's character.

I grabbed the alcoholic beverage because I wasn't the smartest cookie in the jar.

Midnight passed on the Zora and asked for a Bilal—a bold drink made with blueberries, lemon juice, honey and bourbon.

It wasn't until we both had our drinks in hand that I worked up the courage to ask, "Did you know?"

Midnight eyed me and did that thing where he quickly gave me a once over. "Did I know what?"

"About Malachi and Tia?" It still felt like I was subjecting myself to fire any time I let their names roll off my tongue. I had trained myself over the past five months to call them everything but what their parents had named them, but it was time I stopped letting them have such control over me. That didn't mean that saying their names hadn't felt like I had burnt the roof of my mouth and bit my tongue at the same time. "Did you know that he was cheating on me?"

"I didn't know until the wedding." He meant when I put everything on blast as soon as I got to the altar. I wanted to wait until it was my turn to say my vows, but the moment I saw both of their faces when I walked down that aisle, I lost it. I still didn't know how I'd managed to hold it together for almost six hours after I got their low-level sex tape *anonymously.*

To this day, I was sure anonymous's name was Tia.

"There's no way I would have let you walk down that aisle had I known. Everything I learned about him and Tia was during the aftermath. I didn't know they had some kind of situationship for years prior to you. We've all been cool our whole lives. They were closer, but them messing around never crossed my mind. Whatever shit they were doing, they hid well."

"Yeah, it's easy to hide behind the 'she's my cousin' façade. I never even thought to question it. I thought she was really family."

"To me, she is. I've always seen her that way, but according to Mal, they realized they had feelings for one another in high school but didn't pursue anything because of how close our families are. But a drunken night had them crossing the line over and over *and over* again. Per Mal, he was against them being more yet couldn't stop fucking her."

"And that was very clear from the video."

"We don't have to talk about this, Sweets."

Stomach flutters. *Embarrassing* stomach flutters.

"You really aren't gonna stop calling me that?"

"I like the way it makes you aggravated with me. I kinda miss that attitude you gave me on sight."

"I mean, if you want it back that bad... we can drop the truce."

"Nah, I like the truce. But messing with you, with the truce in place, is top tier."

"You are a pest, and I suggest you get your head examined next year because it's giving sick and twisted."

"I think you kind of like it."

"Please," I stressed, pushing one of my curls behind my ear before doubling back to what he'd said. "Anyway, talking about the bull crap wasn't as sucky as I thought it'd be... maybe because I'm inebriated." I raised my already half empty cocktail.

"Or maybe it's because I got your ass out here having fun."

"I guess *this* is what you thought I needed." I tapped my chin.

"It's part of it."

Raised brow. "What's the other part?"

With a grin on his handsome deep brown face, he said, "Me beating your ass in Twister. Let's go play."

He stood and extended his hand for me to take.

I did, without hesitation.

A warm sensation settled around me as he squeezed my hand and led me back into the villa, making me grab a water bottle along the way.

There were some hard truths I had to face from this moment on: I still didn't like Midnight Drayton, especially because we had just unlocked a new reason to hate him.

Reason number seven: I wanted to fuck Midnight Drayton.

CHAPTER 10

Midnight

This wasn't a regular game of Twister.

Of course not.

But I knew that before we started playing.

So I shouldn't have been surprised when 'right foot green' landed me in hell for two reasons.

The closest one to me not only had a shot of liquor on it, which I had to take in order to keep playing, but it also put me in the position of my dick being pressed up against Tyme's succulent ass.

These last few hours, thanks to God's favor, I had been able to control my body's reaction to how good she looked in this pajama set. The bronze color had been nice, but upon further inspection, the wine color was true perfection against her highly melanated skin that seemed to shimmer from whatever magical lotion she was wearing.

And speaking of magical — the way she fucking smelled.

"You're tryna put all your weight on me so I'll fall, stop cheating!" she whined, wiggling her body and I wished — prayed — she stopped before she got me hard.

The liquor and weed flowing through my system had me ready to give Tyme what I really thought she needed.

Fun was definitely part of it but so was pleasure. However, I had never planned on doing the pleasing.

Unfortunately for us both, having her pressed up against me like this had the nastiest thoughts floating through my mind.

Flashes of my dick being swallowed whole by that pretty mouth of hers. Or my face submerged deep between her ass cheeks while my tongue ravished all of her holes like we were digging for buried gems.

My favorite, though, had been the way I imagined her screaming out my name as I made her cum until she couldn't take anymore. Until she forcibly pushed me away from her as she convulsed over, and over, *and over* again.

I had been so caught up in my wild thoughts, that I missed the host calling out the next move and was only brought to the realization when my arm started crumbling beneath me. The soft, warm, thick body I had been pressed up against moved, and I fell.

I came out of my trance to see Tyme sticking out her tongue at me, and I almost couldn't believe how much I wanted to suck on it and see if it tasted like all those drinks she had been sipping on tonight.

Almost.

The moment I put the truce into play, I knew the risks of me letting my guard down with her. It was why from the time I got her out of that winery on her wedding day, I knew I needed to keep my distance from her.

It was essential for her to be out of my life now that she wasn't with my brother anymore. *Or else.*

The 'or else' was currently eating away at me. But I loved being the one to help her fuck with Malachi. He deserved it for what he did to her.

My brother and I had a complicated relationship. It was why our younger sister, Mickie, called us frenemy twins. Our dynamic was complex, sometimes even volatile. From a young age, we competed in everything, from school grades to sports. While Malachi was always driven to win, I took a more laid-back approach, content with my own pace. Yet, no matter how nonchalant I seemed, he couldn't help but feel the need to measure up to me. It's like he was constantly trying to prove something, not just to me, but to himself.

Despite our rivalry, there were also moments of genuine friendship between us. We had shared secrets, inside jokes, and supported each other when it mattered most.

There was no doubt that I loved him despite his flaws, and if he needed me to go fuck somebody up with him, I was there. However, because of those same flaws, we rarely saw eye to eye on things. He always seemed to be in competition with me, even when it wasn't necessary. In reality, he was competing with himself because most of the things he wanted, I didn't want. I had always been cool in my lane.

The exception: Tyme Henley.

As I grew as a man, it became clear that she was the one that got away. I was still willing to let her go, though. I just had to make it through the night. By this time tomorrow, we'd be home and back to living our lives without each other in it.

"The way you're looking at her is probably why Mal called me." My cousin's voice jolted me out of my trance as I stood off to the side, waiting for Tyme to finish playing.

I turned my head to face him, quirking an eyebrow. "What are you talking about?"

Neo nodded towards Tyme, who was switching from right hand green to right hand blue. "You've been staring at her for the past five minutes, man. And Mal saw the picture you posted on social media."

I rolled my eyes, trying to hide my smile. "It was just a couple of selfies. No big deal."

"Clearly, it was a big enough deal for him to call me and ask what's going on between you two."

I chuckled because I had turned my phone on do not disturb so he couldn't bother me. "Let him wonder."

Neo shook his head, a smirk playing on his lips. "You got that fool pressed, bro. I told him I didn't know anything."

"Good. Let him sweat it out a bit," I said with a shrug.

"His pride won't but hey, he got the one he wanted, right?"

"Exactly, so why is he worried about what his ex is up to?" I asked, feeling a grin spread across my face as I adjusted my nose ring.

Neo shot me a knowing look, and we both burst out laughing. He had always been more like a brother than a cousin to me, and we had each other's backs, no matter what. We were two sides of the same coin, both wearing masks that hid our true selves, even if those masks were also true to who we were, just on a more tamed level.

I glanced back at Tyme, feeling a rush of warmth and affection for her. Maybe I *had* been staring a little too long. She had a way of capturing my attention and holding it hostage, even when I didn't want her to.

"With the way you're staring at her, no wonder he's about to ruin his honeymoon, worried about what you two are doing here. Are you tryna take it *there*?" Neo's playful smirk was gone now, replaced by a serious expression.

I turned to face him fully, feeling defensive. "No." And I wasn't *trying* to.

Neo's head cocked to the side, but he didn't push the subject. "Alright, but that leads me to my next question. Have you told her about what happens after midnight?" He looked at me expectantly, his arms crossed.

I stuffed my hands into my pockets, feeling guilty. "I haven't."

"Cuz," Neo grumbled, "now you know how I feel about wildcards. She's new to this. You need to prepare her."

"I know. I am, after this."

"Yeah, you better. From that video in the group chat, she's good at swinging a bat, so you might not want to test her gangsta." Neo laughed at his own joke, and I waved him off.

I turned back to the game, just as Tyme lost her balance and fell to the ground.

"I'll see you later," I faintly heard Neo say as Tyme looked up at me with a pout, but it quickly turned into a grin.

"At least I beat you," she said triumphantly, as she approached me. I felt a small weight on my shoulders. I wondered how she'd take the info I needed to tell her. Neo was right. This wasn't something I could just let her walk into.

"I guess," I replied to her teasing, trying to put on a façade of nonchalance. But I couldn't keep it up for long. "Let's go somewhere and talk. I need to tell you something."

I appreciated her not fighting me and instead just placing her soft hand into mine so that I could lead us down the hallway to the one room no one on the main floor was probably occupying—the boardroom.

As we walked, I noticed how seamlessly her hand fit into mine. But I shook my head, trying to focus on the task at hand. We reached the door to the boardroom, and I took a deep breath before opening it and leading her inside.

"What's up? Is it your brother?" Tyme asked.

"Nah. It's about to be midnight," I replied.

"I see you know how to tell time. I'm very proud," she joked.

"Shut up. Anyway, typically, Neo prefers us to wait to reveal part two of the night. However, we're also supposed to vet any new people we bring to gauge how they'd react to the reveal."

"React to the reveal?" She repeated my words as if she needed to hear herself say them. Her lips poked out before she said, "It is a cult, isn't it?"

She giggled, but it was short-lived after I let the cat out of the bag. "It's a play party."

"A play party?" Her eyes moved side to side. "Like how we're playing games?"

I wanted to laugh, but I didn't because I wasn't sure if she was feigning innocence or truly didn't know what a play party was. "A pleasure party," I clarified.

Her head tilted to the left. "Like sex toys?"

"Kind of… but on steroids. At 12:01 this," I motioned around for emphasis, "turns into a sex party."

Her eyes widened. "Excuse me?"

"The theme of 12:01 is all about bringing in the new year with passion, fun, releasing inhibitions, and cleansing your energy with pleasure. The motto is: We end the year with fun, we start it with pleasure."

Her eyes were still enlarged. She blinked a few times before she whisper-yelled, "You brought me to a sex party? And you didn't think to tell me beforehand? No wonder everyone's been so nice… they're all just waiting to fuck."

"It's not like that."

She huffed. "Then what is it like? Oh my goodness." She placed her hands along the sides of her face. "That's why you said you could arrange for something with me and Mercedes. *And* is that why she said..." she started rambling about the part of the conversation she'd walked up on between Cedes and me. "This is some bullshit. Even for you, Midnight."

Damn, she's a little more upset than I thought she'd be.

Okay, I really didn't know how upset she'd be, but I had hoped less than this. I knew it was going to be a gamble. I had never brought a plus one before, and the reason was that Neo had an entire list of questions to ask in order to vet potential attendees beforehand. He preferred that they didn't have a complete understanding of the experience, but he also wanted to ensure they were open to the idea of attending a play party. If it hadn't been me, I wasn't sure if he would have trusted anyone else to bring someone like Tyme, who was a complete wildcard.

She turned to leave, and I grabbed her by the elbow. "Wait, Sweets."

"Don't call me that, and don't touch me!"

I released her, holding up my hands in surrender. "My bad, okay? We can leave if you're not comfortable. That's not a problem."

"Why on earth would you think bringing me to a sex party and not telling me would make sense? So, at midnight, everyone is just gonna strip and start fucking and I'm supposed to join in?"

Again, I wanted to laugh, but I knew better than to try her life in this moment.

"It's nothing like that, I promise."

"You promise?" She pinched the bridge of her nose. "You promised I could trust you and instead, you got me in the middle of some freaky deaky party. Why the hell wouldn't you tell me?"

"I didn't think it through," I answered honestly. "It was a last minute decision. I felt you needed something that would get you out of the funk you've been in over my brother. Tapping into a side of you that is outside of your comfort zone is what I think you need."

"Well, you're wrong."

"You once told me you liked to be spontaneous."

"Yeah, like 'show up to my ex's wedding with a bat' spontaneous, not *this*." She pointed at the ground.

"You're funny when you're mad."

"Go to fucking hell." She headed towards the door, and I walked behind her. "*Don't* follow me."

"We can leave."

She stopped in her tracks and spun around.

We were close.

As close as we were when we were taking those pictures together earlier, and I had to suffer through smelling whatever intoxicating perfume she was wearing.

"I'm s—" I started but she cut across me.

"I want to be away from you— please." Every word was distinctive and intentional. I took a few steps back from her before she turned on her heels and stormed out of the room.

Shit.

CHAPTER 11

Tyme

I was hiding in the gym *and* sipping on another glass of Play's Punch.

One of these two things were a bad idea.

Or maybe both.

Because why was I still here? Why hadn't I hightailed it the heck up out of here as soon as I sprinted out of that room?

He told me we could leave.

Why didn't I respond, "let's go"?

The truth: Because I didn't know what the hell I wanted to do.

Because I'm curious.

Thinking back on it, the signs had always been there, but I wasn't looking for them. Malachi's message about 12:01 made a hell of a lot more sense now. Not to mention Neo's comment about 'consenting adults', and the fact that it was an intimate party at a big ass mansion.

There were signs.

I finished off my glass of punch and then pulled out my phone. I needed to call the one person I hoped would help me get some clarity about what the hell had transpired in my life since yesterday evening.

"Hey, my little jailbird," my best friend, Nene, sang into the phone. "How does it feel to be a free woman?"

"Please stop," I said with a titter. "I have real problems. Are you busy?"

"Nah. Mo and I are just watching TV, waiting for the countdown. What's up? What's wrong?" I could hear her shuffling around, which meant she might've been going somewhere private.

I let out a sigh. "I should probably start with the fact that I'm with Midnight."

"Midnight who?"

"How many Midnights do you think I know?"

"I'm hoping more than one because last I checked, *weeee* hate the one I know of."

Nene and I met randomly at an art museum shortly after I moved to Southgate. We were both by ourselves and kept running into each other and offering to take pictures for one another. After the fourth time, Nene suggested we explored together. We clicked instantly and had been cool ever since.

She had been around for the entirety of my and Sir Cheater's tragic love story. What I loved most about her was that she didn't abandon me when I spiraled like a few other friends had. There were times where she had been against some of the things I did or wanted to do, but she still loved me as a friend, and I appreciated her for that.

For most *crazy ex* things I wanted to do, Nene was down for. And I left her out of the things that I didn't think she would be.

Showing up to the wedding would have been a no for her, which was why it wasn't until she saw the viral video on social media did she know what I'd done. And even still, she didn't judge me for it.

Nene had always been someone who accepted me for who I was, flaws and all. I valued that about her because it reminded me of how much I hated when people assumed things about me.

Ever since I was young, I'd never appreciated someone jumping to a conclusion about me when they didn't even truly know me. As far as I knew, it didn't stem from anything and was just an innate feeling that made me immediately go on defensive mode.

And once I felt judged by someone, it became hard for me not to expect that from them, which was why, prior to these last twenty-four hours, I always assumed any commentary from Midnight came from a negative, judgmental place due to the way things initially went between us.

But unlike Midnight, Nene wholeheartedly embraced my sometimes over-the-top, childish, or extra behavior from the beginning, and it meant the world to me. She understood that we all had our quirks, and that was perfectly fine. Her acceptance was a comforting reminder that I could be myself without fear of judgment or misunderstanding.

Maybe she enabled my toxicity at times, but that's what some friends are for, right?

Which meant, prior to yesterday, *we* both hated Midnight and his lookalike.

"Yeah, so..." I started and then gave her a quick rundown of my last twenty-nine-ish hours. Everything from him getting the charges dropped to initiating a truce. "... and now we're at this party his cousin throws for new year's, and he just dropped a freaking bomb on me."

"I don't think I have enough popcorn for another bomb."

"It's a sex party, Nene!" The line went quiet. "Did you hear me?"

"Girl, my mouth is wide open. Is he tryna smash?" She whispered the last part as if she couldn't talk regularly. Sometimes she was dramatic for no reason.

"I don't know. I don't think so. I do—" I took another deep breath so I could stop repeating the same words. "Earlier today, *the ex* told me Midnight only sees me as some coochie and—"

"Wait, I feel like you didn't give me the full story. Fuckboy knows you're with his brother? This tea is first class!"

"*Shit,* I forgot to mention he suggested we make Mal jealous." I explained to her what we'd been doing to make my ex think I'd moved on.

"Not you saying *Voldemort's* name like it's cool."

She made me sick. "I'm trying to release the power he and Tia have had on me. Honestly, it has a lot to do with Midnight. Wild, right?"

"Yes," she agreed, and I could imagine her nodding vehemently. "All of this is *crayyy-zee.*" I couldn't agree more. "But Tyme!" she squealed. "Talk about getting your lick back, bitch! You *should* fuck him. I approve."

"Chenethia!" I screamed and then covered my mouth as if I wasn't in this gym all by myself.

"Ain't nobody bringing somebody to a sex party if they ain't tryna slide up in them guts. Mal already about to have an aneurysm thinking y'all did... you might as well let the rumors be true."

"She right, though!" I heard Nene's significant other.

"Oh my god! Do you have me on speaker?"

"No! But you know Mo nosey. She all up in my mouth. However, I am right. Focus on that."

"How about we focus on the fact that I'm at a sex party!"

"Well based on what you told me, it's not a sex party *yet*. You could always leave... yet, you haven't. Why is that, ma'am? Is it because you wanna see which twin is better? I know we hate Midnight, but I hear men who be humble be sexing the hell out of their women."

"PLEASE, NENE!"

"You deserve to get them Sonic Rings knocked out of you BY YOUR EX'S TWIN!!"

"Why are you yelling?"

"Because if I could end or start my year by riding my ex's twin's face, I would." I shook my head. "Baby, I mean if I didn't love you, duh. Besides, you don't even have siblings, you good." A soft laugh slipped out of my mouth as I listened to Nene and Mo bicker for a second. "Anyway, what's the worst that can happen?"

"You mean besides people saying I'm not shit. They already think I'm the crazy, psychotic ex who can't let go."

"Listen, if Mal and you had ended on different circumstances, then I wouldn't be encouraging this. However, he did you dirty, so you should ride his brother into the new year. It's only right."

"The year of the lick back!" Mo's voice came through clearly.

"But I'm not even supposed to like Midnight."

"You don't have to like someone to get your body knocked out of alignment."

What if I'm starting to like him? Then what?

That was the question I wanted to ask, but I couldn't bring myself to say it.

I couldn't even bring myself to tell her that prior to Midnight dropping this bomb on me, I was already struggling to accept the fact that I *did* want the Sonic Rings, Mario Coins, and whatever else, knocked out of me by my arch nemesis.

That was probably the real reason I hadn't run out of this house.

I wanted to be fucked by Midnight Drayton... the question was, did he want me just the same?

"What are you going to do? It's twenty minutes until the ball drops. You gonna have balls dropping in you or what?"

"On that note, I'm hanging up. Good night and Happy New Year."

With lots of giggles, she wished me a happy new year, and we ended the call.

"What in the hell am I gonna do?" I mumbled to myself. Nene had given me more to think about and though the answer was clear as day, I still couldn't come to terms with it.

My phone vibrated in my hand, and I jumped. The punch was working its magic on me again after Midnight's revelation had sobered me up. I glanced down and thought that God really had to be playing in my face or trying to get me a first-class ticket to hell.

BLOCK LATER

attached picture

If u tryna make me jealous it ain't gonna work.
Y'all not fooling me.

A screenshot of one of the selfies Midnight had posted made me chuckle. For someone not jealous, he was truly not acting that way.

K.

Tia always told me u probably weren't the good girl u pretended to be.

You mean the same girl who was bussing it wide open for you as the side chick while pretending to be your cousin? Of course she did. Hoe behavior.

Watch ur mouth.

> How about you go be with your WIFE?

Yeah the wife u wanted to be. That's why u showed up to my wedding! But since u couldn't get me back u out here spreading ya legs for my brother "suddenly"

Unless y'all were always smashing.

> I thought we weren't fooling you? *hmm emoji*

> Now get off my line before I send your COUSIN these messages.

I had seriously thought about it because Midnight was probably right. Tia more than likely had no idea that her HUSBAND was embarrassing her like this. And I could really be *that* girl and show her all she'd won was a defective prize. However, I wasn't coming to her woman to woman about nothing.

BLOCK LATER

Fuck you, Tyme.

> You won't but someone else surely will *shrugging emoji*

If u wanna be the bitch Mid fuck for his yearly one night stand, go ahead. Have fun.

> And did. *blowing a kiss emoji*

God if this was your way of trying to talk me out of being the girl who did both brothers... this wasn't it. Because now, it was to hell with Malachi Drayton!

> BTW, you should take some tips from your "little brother" so you can please your wife better. Don't want karma coming back to bite you in the ass *winking emoji*

As soon as I saw the message had been read, I blocked him. Sir

Cheater — Malachi — didn't deserve me consulting my moral compass about what was or wasn't the right thing to do.

I was going to do whatever the hell me and my coochie wanted to do and if he felt away about it, he could go cry into the pussy of the bitch he cheated on me with.

"I've been looking every damn where for you." Midnight's voice almost had me going to the upper room. He hadn't come into the gym via the way I had; he'd entered through the entrance that was within the house.

After pulling myself together, and with my back still to him, I said, "Well, I guess I picked a good hiding spot. Besides, I don't know why you were looking for me. I told you to leave me alone."

Why must you do him like this?

Because it's Midnight Drayton, duh.

"Tyme."

"What?" I snapped, doing the dumbest thing by turning to look at him. How did he look finer?

"You're acting childish."

I scoffed. "I'm acting childish? Please don't act as if I don't have a reason to be upset." Was I even still upset? *I wasn't.* However, being back in his space sent so much fire through me that I couldn't help but to come off snippy. I *had* to give him attitude.

Attitude that I wanted him to sex out of me, might I add.

But I couldn't tell him that.

Better yet, I didn't know how to tell him that or how to cross that line. I had never been one of those girls who were comfortable shooting their shot. It's not like I ever had to.

"You right. I fucked up. I'm sorry. However, when you're with me, I need to know that you're safe. At all times."

I rolled my eyes, crossing my arms over my nipples that didn't seem to know that we didn't care about how his need to protect us made us want to come undone in every way possible.

"Afraid someone is gonna drag me into an orgy? What, the freaks come out after midnight?"

"I don't mean it like that. No one is going to bother you with that wristband on, for one. For two, the people here are not like that. This ain't some wild free-for-all. There are boundaries, there are rules... for most people here, it ain't their first time at one of Neo's play parties. You don't have to worry about no bullshit. I would have never brought you into a situation where you wouldn't feel safe or respected."

"Whatever. If that's the case, why were you worried about where I was?"

"I thought you left, and I doubt you know how to get back to the hotel so..." He didn't finish the sentence.

I *wanted* him to finish the sentence.

Had Midnight Drayton been worried about me? How cute.

Pussy juices are flowing.

"So, you were worried?"

"The last person you were seen with was me. I wasn't tryna be the number one suspect if you'd disappeared."

Look at him trying to save himself. Also cute.

"Yeah, whatever. Just admit you were worried and *maybe* we can be truce friends again."

"How about you give me your number if you're gonna be disappearing. That way, I don't have to deal with this kind of back-and-forth bullshit. Or at least unblock me on social media."

Shit, I forgot he was blocked.

"Is it bullshit or are you upset because I know you were worried? Either way, I like you not having my number or quick access to me. I like you worrying."

His jaw twitched. I was seconds away from cumming from his facial muscles... that couldn't be good.

Hopefully, flirting could work as shooting my shot because that's as far as my *moral-less* inner bad girl seemed to be willing to take it for now.

"Whatever you say, Sweets." Oh, so he's taunting me. "I'll have the valet bring the car around right after the countdown."

He turned and headed back towards the way he came in. I waited until he got to the door before I blurted out, "What happens if I want to stay?"

His head swiveled to the left, giving me a nice view of that tantalizing profile of his. "Is that what you want to do?"

"Maybe… if you answer my question."

He did a full one-eighty. "Nothing you don't want to happen. I already told you—"

The DJ coming in through the intercom, asking everyone to head to the grand room for the countdown, interrupted whatever Midnight was going to say.

"Let's head upstairs. I'll answer any questions you have, afterwards."

CHAPTER 12
Midnight

After her outburst, I didn't expect the words 'what if I want to stay' to come out of her mouth. But leave it to Tyme to keep me on my toes.

We made it upstairs with a minute to spare. The countdown ensued, and the awkwardness followed as we both seemed to be uncomfortable as everyone around us shared a new year's kiss.

"Happy New Year, Tyme," I spoke first, pushing my glass of champagne towards hers.

"Happy New Year, Midnight." Her glass clinked mine, and her eyes immediately reverted back to everything happening around her.

"Are you sure you want to stay? You look uncomfortable."

"I'm not uncomfortable," she shot back.

"Are you sure?"

"Oh my god," she huffed. "I'm anxious. Happy?"

I grabbed her elbow, gingerly turning her to me. Everyone around us seemed to be moving quickly, but in this moment, it was just us. "If, at any time, you want to leave, promise me you'll let me know."

"Okay," she said genuinely. "I will."

At exactly one minute after midnight, Neo's voice rang through the microphone.

"Happy New Year, everyone, and welcome to part two of 12:01!" Sounds of people saying 'Happy New Year' echoed around the room before he continued. "If you're new here, you're in for an experience. If you're not new... then you already know how we do. For the newbies though, let me make things very clear: 12:01 is meant to be a pleasurable way to bring in your new year. We ain't about the bullshit, disrespect, overstepping boundaries, or fuckery of any kind. We're about having fun, enjoying pleasure in the way that you wish, and most importantly, being safe.

"I call this experience 12:01 because, for me, that is the start of a new day and in this case, a new day as well as a new year. With either one of those is another day to start fresh, to start anew, and what better way to do it than to say fuck whatever happened yesterday — or last year — and focus on the present in the most freeing way. Pleasure — when done right — lets us lose ourselves, even if for only a few moments. It's one of the best times where we can let go of all our inhibitions and step out of our comfort zones. That's what I wish for you and why I created this experience.

"If you have a white wristband, the person you came with should be able to answer any more specific questions you have, but your first step is to get another wristband and familiarize yourself with the house rules if you choose to stay.

"If you wish to end your 12:01 experience now, I advise you to head out within the next thirty minutes because after that, it might get a little wild. Veterans who have rooms, they have been assigned to you, and you should have received the details. They have been set up as requested. The play store is located on the second floor in the sports lounge, and you're welcome to grab any additional things you need. Now without further ado, let's get to the pleasure. Have fun, everyone!"

Everyone cheered as the DJ started the music back up.

"You told me this wristband was because I was your guest. The truce does make you lie," she said, garnering my attention— though, I had been watching her out the side of my eye the whole time Neo had been speaking to gauge her reaction to his speech.

"I didn't lie. It means you're new and you're a guest of someone. You'll need to head over there," I pointed towards a table, "before one." The table had been set up specifically for handing out the wristbands and making sure those who were new to the experience were well equipped.

"What do they even mean?"

"Neo uses them to help everyone immediately get an idea of each person's 'level of play' as he calls it."

"Interesting."

"How about we grab something to drink and explore a little while I break things down more for you and answer any questions."

"Okay," she agreed, and we headed towards the kitchen. We both grabbed bottles of water and snacks before I led the way to some of the key spots.

"Alright so," I started, "blue means you're here alone. Orange means you enjoy being watched. I'll tell you now… you're gonna see people fucking— prepare yourself."

"Well, I kind of expected that. Seems like it comes with the whole sex party territory." Her eyes moved around the area we were passing through to get to the stairs. "Things actually are calmer than I thought."

"For now. Everyone is settling in. They don't just jump to the fucking."

That got a laugh out of her. "Good to know."

"Plus, this area is a safe space." I explained that there were a few areas throughout the villa that were sex-free zones. "Anyway," I continued as we headed upstairs, "usually, those with blue or orange will have more than one wristband on to indicate their level of play. Black," I held up my wrist, "means you're not here for sex, but here for the experience. It's also for those who enjoy watching people engage in sexual activities."

Her brows inched up her forehead before she leaned closer to me. Her perfume once again made me want to twist her into a pretzel. "You like watching people?"

"Sometimes." The truth was, I got black because I was here with her. Blue and yellow were usually my go to. "Yellow means you're open to discuss sexual actions with others. Green means you're down for whatever."

She rubbed her temples. "It's like a fucking rainbow. How do you remember?"

I chuckled. "I'm used to it, I guess. Plus, there's an app."

"An app?" she gawked.

"Yeah, they'll tell you about it when you get your wristband. It basically has the rules and shit, villa floor plans, where you can find certain things, and all of that."

We reached the sports lounge that had been converted to a mini sex store. Neo was the owner of Books and Ecstasy, a local bookstore that doubled as a sex shop in Chasington Bay.

"You can grab whatever you want or need from here—condoms, toys, lingerie, lube, throat spray, etcetera."

"Throat spray? You tryna be funny?"

Immediately, my brain went to her *throat baby* abilities, and my dick jerked. I didn't need to think about her deep throating shit. "I was pointing out the things you can get. Simmer down."

"We've gone from calm to simmer. You're learning."

I chuckled. "Don't start your shit."

"How much is everything?" she asked, picking up a blindfold. I imagined it covering those pretty eyes of hers as she begged me to make her— *fuck.*

"It's included with your ticket."

She turned to me. "Oh... I didn't know...You paid for me to attend this?"

"I did."

The sides of her mouth turned up. "I'm starting to think you like me, Mr. Drayton. It's quite disgusting."

"Or, I'm a kind person who's trying to give you an experience that will start your year off right, so you can move past my brother."

She scoffed. "Let's not mention him."

Didn't have to tell me but once. "Done."

"Good." Her fingers brushed over her hair, her gaze fixed on me. "How much were the tickets?"

My eyes swept over her. "That's not a concern of yours. Come on."

The tour continued, and I showed her more safe spaces, including a cuddle area (she was surprised to see that everything wasn't about sex) and an Aromatherapy Room in the spa area, where we decided to take a break and enjoy the calming scents.

"We need to head back upstairs in twenty minutes," I reminded her.

"*The pressure is getting worser*," she whined. "I really do have to pick one, huh?"

"It's preferred. Makes it easier for everyone to know where you stand. But also, you need to sign a confidentiality agreement and agree to uphold the rules." Her eyes widened. I had come to realize I loved when they got big like that. "What happens at 12:01, stays at 12:01," I clarified, and she let off a soft laugh.

"Y'all serious about y'all lil' orgy, huh?"

"Gotta keep shit under wraps. The agreement covers what is and isn't allowed, the rules, and expectations, such as being open and honest about your sexual history. It also breaks down what can and cannot be disclosed about the event."

"Wow."

"These are exclusive play parties with some big names in different industries. Neo wants to make sure everyone feels safe." This was also why it was important for us to vet any plus ones before bringing them because if they ran their mouths, it'd fall back on the person who brought the guest. "As far as sexual history, it's also for safety. Most of us veterans get up to date testing prior to this, and transparency is expected."

"Makes sense."

"However, Neo encourages the use of condoms and other safe sex tools, unless it's one hundred percent with someone you trust and don't mind living on edge with."

"That also makes sense." Things got quiet again before she said, "Wait, you never told me what red means. I've seen a few people with that color."

"Red means you're not interested in engaging in sexual activities with anyone other than the person you came with."

"Oh." She pulled her bottom lip into her mouth.

We were quiet again.

"You ever played seven minutes of heaven growing up?" I gave her a look. "You know, the game where people spin a bottle and then the person it lands on and the spinner have to go into a closet for seven minutes, usually to kiss or cop a feel. *First base stuff.*"

"Yeah, yeah, yeah." I nodded as the game came back to me. "I played that in middle school. Pretty sure that's how I felt my first boob." Her eyes rolled. "Now look who's being the judgy one when you brought the game up."

"How about we play?"

I pulled in my brows. "Why?"

She sucked her teeth. "Just agree to playing because you want to pretend to be my fake man who wants to do whatever to make me happy."

I smirked. "So, I'm your man when it's convenient?"

The way her eyes fluttered made my dick tingle. "We playing or what?"

"If it'll make you happy, *Your Highness.*"

"It will." She cheesed and I suppressed my smile. I couldn't let her catch me finding her mannerisms cute as fuck. "Okay," she said, doing something on her phone." Seven minutes on the clock starting...now."

"Okay." I didn't know what the purpose of us playing this game was, but I was *that* dude. The dude who would do just about whatever if it meant it'd make his girl smile. Not that Tyme was actually my girl, but for truce purposes. "Is this the part where I get to cop a lil' feel?" I joked.

"No, this is the part where you get to kiss me."

"Huh?" I *should* have seen that coming, but I didn't.

She straddled me, and I had to immediately start reminding myself who she was. "We're in seven minutes of heaven. Kiss me."

"I don't remember the girls in middle school being this demanding."

"Shut up and just do it." She pushed her hair out of her face.

I ran my tongue over my lips as a I took in the captivating beauty in front of me. "Come here," I said, causing her to lean towards me. As her mouth got closer to mine, the amount of blood begging to have free rein to rush down into my dick was a harsh reminder that I couldn't have her lips on mine.

Meeting her halfway, I planted a soft kiss on the side of her mouth instead before leaning back onto the seat.

Her eyes flew open, squinting. "We're at a sex party and you peck me on my cheek?"

I sniggered. "It was actually on the side of your mouth."

"You might as well have kissed me on my forehead."

"You didn't say where I had to do it."

She gave me a death stare. "You know where I wanted you to do it. Be for real, Midnight."

"It ain't that deep, Sweets. Don't trip."

She tried to hide it, but I saw the flash of hurt in her eyes as she positioned herself back next to me. I missed the warmth of her weight on me, and I also hated to see that turning her down bothered her. But I couldn't put my lips on *hers.*

With her eyes closed, she leaned her head back against the wall.

"You okay?" I asked as I internally fought myself over the *right* thing to do and say.

Her voice was soft and low, almost a whisper, but there was an edge to it that betrayed her vulnerability. "Why don't you want to kiss me?" she asked, her eyes still closed.

Because I will completely lose the minuscule amount of control I have left.

"Kissing is intimate," I said, hoping that would be enough. But who was I kidding? This was Tyme.

She let out a huff as she sucked her teeth. "No shit, Sherlock. I shouldn't be surprised that you're one of those men who won't kiss unless it's someone you love. Your tin man is showing."

I let out a soft chuckle at the tin man comment. Her using it as a nickname for me hadn't gone unnoticed, but now her reason was starting to click. "I didn't say that. All I said was that it's intimate."

"Honestly, you suck as a fake boyfriend. I guess I should go find someone who's willing to kiss me. I *am* at a party full of men willing to please me," she said, her eyes closed.

I bit back the retort that came to mind, knowing I had no right to be jealous or aggravated by her words—though I was. Instead, I stood up and suggested, "I'm starting to think you might need some more water."

"I don't need no damn water! I'm tipsy, not drunk," she shot back, opening her eyes. "You," she pointed with a playful air in her tone, "just don't wanna kiss me."

I could feel the heat rising to my cheeks, but I tried to hide it by running my hands down my face. "We need to go get your wristband."

"See! You *really* don't wanna put your raggedy lips on mine. Is it my breath?" She blew into the palm of her hand and sniffed it.

"Now you're being dramatic," I replied with a chuckle.

"Do I need to show you my most up to date test results in order for you to give me a little tongue? 'Cause I can tell you now, I haven't had sex with anyone since your brother, and of course I got tested after all that was said and done."

Perfect time to bring up the reason why we shouldn't be tonguing one another down.

"You know what's funny," she pulled my undivided attention back to her as she stood up, "the kissing cousins be kissing," *this damn girl,* "but I can't get one lil'—"

She shut the hell up when I snatched her ass to me and buried my head into her neck. I swirled my tongue around the top of her ear and down the back of it before I planted kisses down the side of her neck. Her soft gasps for air tickled my eardrums and made my dick twitch in delight.

I wanted to fuck the shit out of Tyme Henley.

Guiding her back down onto the couch, I continued to lick and suck the parts of her body that were exposed—the top of her shoulder, her collarbones, the tops of her breasts, her stomach — and then back up, even though I wanted to go further south.

But I didn't. We shouldn't. *I* shouldn't.

Thankfully, the alarm on her phone went off.

"Game over," I said, stopping abruptly and standing up. After she snapped back into reality, her eyes were ready to murder me. If she had that bat of hers with her, I'd be a dead man. "We need to head upstairs for your wristband."

"You know what," she let out an annoyed chuckle, "whatever." She stood, moving around me and my eyes followed her. "I can go by myself." She fixed her pants before glancing over her shoulder at me — definitely catching me being mesmerized by that ass of hers. "And you still didn't kiss me, *punk*."

CHAPTER 13

Midnight Drayton was gunning for the number one spot on my people I hate the most list. I didn't think he could outdo Malachi, but leaving me horny as all hell — at a sex party — and making me feel desperate was almost as bad as cheating on me with your *cousin*.

Okay, it wasn't even on the same playing field, but it bothered the hell out of me. It took an obscene amount of vulnerability for me to ask for that kiss, just to be turned down and left looking like a *desperate* fool. It was like a slap in the face and a big fat reminder that this wasn't the first time he'd rejected me. And I think that was what had me spiraling the most.

Maybe the chemistry I felt brewing between us now that this truce was in place was all in my head. *Maybe* nothing had changed, and he still saw me the way he did on that dating app.

Bullshit!

It was definitely bullshit because the way he wouldn't kiss me yet played in my face by teasing my body with his mouth, told me that I was indeed *not* imagining things.

Either way, I hated that he made my entire being feel like it would die of sex deprivation if we didn't have him fill us up without mercy.

I could still feel his breath on my skin.

The way it made my soul tingle, my pussy thump, and my mouth water.

And his lips… they were so soft.

I wanted them on *both* of mine, and I wholeheartedly hated myself for it.

What had he turned me into?

How did this man take me from wanting to punch him in his throat ninety-six percent of the time, to wanting to sixty-nine with him?

I definitely had to have been drugged while in jail.

In just fifteen minutes, I selected my wristband, signed the confidentiality agreement, and reviewed the twelve rules. They were all about one thing: making sure everyone felt safe, respected, and comfortable. The guidelines hammered home the importance of consent, clear communication, hygiene, and confidentiality.

I headed towards the stairs and tried not to make eye contact with *Mr. I'm Too Cool To Kiss You*, who was watching my every move. Why did he do that? And why did, as each hour passed, he look finer, as if he was aging like fine wine right before my eyes? Like, his demeanor just screamed *fuck me*. Yet, he didn't seem to want to fuck me.

"Black," he commented, staring down at my wrist as I got closer to him. "You wanna be me so bad huh, Sweets?" *A-he-he, no. I want you to be in me so bad. There's a difference.*

Ignoring him, I continued towards the elevator.

"What do you want to do now?" he asked, coming up beside me. I guess he didn't get the memo that I wasn't interested in being tormented by him — and shut down like I didn't look damned good tonight.

Like I didn't look like the meal he needed on his tongue.

"Mind my business."

You got it bad, sis. My inner voice scolded my immaturity. I was acting as if my *real-life man* told me no to some dick that belonged to me. Pouting like a certified brat who hadn't gotten her way over a damn kiss. Am I thirteen or thirty? *This is sad.*

Midnight was introducing me to a side of myself I had never met.

The kiss was one thing, but that was just supposed to be a gateway drug to the dick, and I had never been this thirsty for penis.

Penis I had never even had at that.

Penis that was attached to Satan's second born.

Penis that belonged to my ex's twin brother.

I am disgusted.

Except about that last one because it's fuck Mal. But still, I was appalled that he'd really had the audacity to curve me at a sex party of all places. Make that make sense. *It didn't.*

And to think during the whole 'tour', I had been trying to work up the courage to ask him for what I truly wanted: premium dick attached to a beautiful dark-skinned Black man who would ruin my life.

And who I didn't even like.

So, we're still running with that lie?

But I didn't have the ovaries to do it.

Now I'm glad I didn't, since I couldn't even get a dang kiss.

Let it go, boo.

"Aww Sweets, you mad at me?" As the elevator reached the first floor, I continued to act like he wasn't talking to me because *gots to see it through, my boy.* "Damn, you wanted a lil' smooch that bad, huh?"

Oh, he thinks he's a comedian, now?

"Fuck o—Oh — um." The elevator doors opened, and I fumbled over my words as my eyes landed on a couple getting it *in*. Like they were hunching—*hunching*. The woman's back was against the wall, legs wrapped around the guy's waist, and he was drilling the hell out of her.

Elevators weren't sex-free zones. *Noted.*

"I'll take the stairs," I spitted out.

The couple barely blinked at us before the elevator doors closed back.

Though the words had left my mouth, I hadn't moved a muscle. I looked over at Midnight, who of course, wasn't nearly as caught off guard as me, and the laugh that escaped my throat had him chuckling as well.

Yup, I was definitely at a pleasure party, and people had surely started getting pleased. Must be nice.

On my way to get my wristband, I'd seen a couple getting hot and heavy in the hallway, another couple getting friendly on the dining room table, and potentially an orgy on the horizon in the great room.

However, as I walked from the Aromatherapy Room to the main area, I was on high alert for people doing grown up things. But this one, this one, I wasn't ready for, and it had me in a fit of giggles.

"Yo," Midnight said as we climbed the stairs, "why were they fucking in silence?"

"Oh my god," I laughed harder, grabbing his bicep — *damn*, "that's what got me rolling. Like, they were just slapping skin in silence!" The skin slapping was so loud that I was a little shocked we hadn't heard it before the doors opened. But that was it, no moans, no grunts, just *slap slap slap.*

This had us both laughing as we made our way to the second floor, stopping in front of the sports lounge that had been converted to a sex shop.

"What do you want your experience to be?" he asked after we both pulled ourselves together.

I shrugged. This time, not purposely ignoring him since the elevator debacle had me letting go of my childish grudge, even though my vagina was still asking to be Midnight's dirty little secret. I guess that was the experience I wanted, but I wasn't about to put myself out there again—even if I knew, that he knew, that WE knew he wanted to give me the D I needed. "I thought you were gonna be my sex party tour guide. Shouldn't you be curating my experience?"

"I am, but I need to know your level of comfort."

"Such the gentleman," I commented, batting my eyelashes. "Watching people in the act or getting into the act is more intriguing than I thought it'd be," I confessed.

"Cool. We can float around or stay here to get an overhead view of what's on the rise down there." He leaned over the glass railing that overlooked the great room. The *potential* orgy I'd seen earlier was definitely about to be a full-on group project. I counted six people, and two more were walking up. "We can also get a more private show. It's up to you."

My head turned towards him, brows raised in question. "A private show?"

Of course, I was hoping he meant us, but I knew better.

"Yeah." He grabbed my hand. "I'll show you."

I sucked in air at the way my body reacted to his touch. My mind zoomed right in on the memory of his mouth and tongue exploring the side of my neck.

We walked down the hall towards the bedrooms.

"If the rooms have an orange ribbon on the door," he explained, "they welcome spectators." We walked around the floor. There were ten bedroom suites. Three of them had an orange ribbon on the door.

"So, I just walk inside and be a Peeping Tom?"

Midnight chuckled. "You can bring popcorn too, if you want," he joked. Or at least, I *think* it was a joke.

"What if they ask me to join?"

"Wristband."

"Right." I nodded. "I'm curious," I admitted, lightly placing my ear against the door we were in front of. Between the music in the hallway coming through the house speakers and the music on the other side of the door, I couldn't hear much of anything.

"Just go inside. That's a good one."

"How you know?"

"You wanna go in or what?"

"Now I see why you don't like me answering a question with a question. But sure, I guess — let's do it. You first, though," I chuckled.

He led the way.

No knocking, no asking if they're decent or having sex, no nothing, except for a twist of the knob and walking right inside as if he belonged there. I followed suit and allowed my ears to adjust to the music that was playing in the room.

It was classic R&B flowing around mixed with light moans.

I had stepped straight into a real life porno.

But what was different about this— these weren't *strangers*. We didn't *know know* one another, but I *knew* them. I only recalled one of their names, the one my eyes landed on first: Mercedes.

She was sitting on a couch while two men and a woman were on the bed, getting in an intense round of foreplay. The mystery woman was making out with one man, while the other was leaving kisses up and down her leg — lucky girl.

I had spent all night interacting with these people, had conversations with them, and now they were doing the nasty right before my eyes.

How had this become my life?

Mercedes motioned us over to the couch, and she moved to the armchair closer to the bed. She was dressed in a strappy leather lingerie set with a chain garter that screamed 'I'm the bitch in charge'.

After we sat down, Midnight filled me in on the *cast* as we watched the show. The woman was Clareese, Mercedes's wife who was bisexual. The two men were Zion and Kobe. The men both had on blue and yellow wristbands. Clareese's own was the same color as her significant other's—yellow. According to Midnight, Mercedes got off on watching her wife get pleased.

"You good?" Midnight's voice tickled my ear five minutes into the super spicy live action movie. He was close. I turned my head towards him.

Fuck. He was *way* too close.

I looked down at his soft brown lips before he moved his head back an inch.

He was *still* too close, especially with everything that was going on around me.

Without a doubt, I *had* to be in hell.

Did I actually die in Gavensfall and now I was living out a nightmare that was turning into a fantasy?

"I'm good but…" I hesitated, not knowing if I wanted to admit to Midnight Drayton what my body was experiencing. But, *fuck it*. It's not like he was going to do anything about it. No point in being shy now. I might as well live my best life, which was also a conclusion I'd come to when I'd gotten my wristband and signed over my life.

"I'm oddly turned on," I confided to him. "Is this normal? I mean," I rushed out, "I know it's normal to be turned on by porn, I'm not a prude; but like, is *this* normal? To be in a room watching someone and wanting to get off on it?"

I felt the urge to slap the little smirk peeking out on his face. I knew I wasn't explaining myself very well, and his *judgmental* ass found it amusing.

"Yeah," he answered simply. "Remember, this is all about pleasure, releasing your inhibitions, and leaning into things out of your comfort zone." I nodded as I crossed my legs, hoping to simmer down the feeling between them. However, I should have known it would only make matters worse.

I looked away from him and back at what was happening six feet in front of me.

I was *real life* in a 5D porno.

I was *real life* watching a woman get pleased by two men while her wife sat off to the side, watching it all go down with a sex toy planted firmly on her vagina.

And I was so horny from all of it that I, too, wish I had a vibrator at my disposal. But would that be rude? To start pleasing myself while in their space?

"Get out of your head." *Why was he so close again?* I turned towards him once more, feeling the heat of his body next to mine.

His demeanor was so calm, so relaxed, while mine was rigid and on the verge of exploding at the same time.

"What are you feeling like you want to do?" I watched his mouth as it formed each word.

God, let me have this man. I deserve to get my lick back.

"You can tell me, Sweets." He ran his forefinger across my chin. *Now why would he do that?* "If you're turned on, then you probably want to get that release out."

"I do," I breathed out without hesitation as Clareese's pleasurable moans floated through my eardrums. At this point, there was no point in being sheepish about what my body was in need of.

If that's the case, why not just tell him you want to have sex? We don't have to kiss. Kissing is overrated.

Wow, you are desperate, I scolded my vagina, *there's no way we're having sex with someone without getting kissed.*

I focused back on the threesome to see what had her screaming out in delight. Zion was filling her up with his penis as Kobe sucked on her breasts.

"Then touch yourself. No one's stopping you."

Eyes back on Satan's second born. "Would that be inappropriate? I don't want to break any rules."

"No, they enjoy when people get off to them. That's why they have their room open. Step out of your comfort zone, Tyme."

His last phrase played over and over in my head as I zoned in on the pleasure everyone else in the room was experiencing. I let my imagination take me away as I pictured myself as Clareese. Instead of Zion pulling out and then burying his head deep between my thighs, it was Midnight, and he was devouring me into a grave oblivion.

I started off simple by toying with my nipples, but it didn't take long before my hand was making its way to the band of my pants and finding the folds of my vagina. I was dripping and that turned me on even more, but I almost disintegrated when I caught Midnight watching me out of the side of my eye.

"Don't watch me." I paused what I was doing, but that didn't stop what was brewing in the pit of my stomach.

"Why not?" He wet his lips and I wanted to choke him for taunting me in only the way he could. He had to be getting off on playing with my emotions.

"Because you won't even kiss me." *Because you won't fuck me.*

He smirked, fiddling with his goatee. "We still on that?"

"We are. I really know how to hold a grudge."

"Oh, I see."

I bit down on my lip as my fingers said, 'forget about Midnight and let's get back to what really matters' and started moving in circles around my clit. "Stop looking at me."

"Why? Am I making you uncomfortable?"

No, you're making me want to cum, and that's the problem.

"Because I said so." I could feel my orgasm getting to its sweet spot quicker just from having his gaze on me. I redirected my eyes.

"You wanna call the shots, Sweets?"

"Don't talk dirty to me."

He smiled and it didn't make matters better at all. "Is it making you wet? Or," he leaned in to whisper directly into my ear, "should I say wetter?"

He was definitely playing in my face.

"Shut up, you're distracting me." *Lies.*

"You're the one talking to me. I was minding my business."

"No, you were minding *my* business."

I looked back at him just as his mouth formed the words that only someone who had been born in the depths of hell would say. "I wanna watch you nut. Is that such a bad thing?"

"Yes, because I don't want you staring at me like that."

"And how is that?"

"Like you want me when you don't." I squeezed my eyes shut and turned my head away from him again.

"If you truly want me to stop, I will. Tell me you seriously want me to stop watching you please yourself."

I said nothing because we both knew the truth.

"I'll take your silence as I can continue to enjoy the show." I imagined that ugly sexy smirk on his face, and it only made my core contract harder.

I hate it here.

A couple of moments passed before he continued to prove to me that there was no way I was imagining what was happening between us.

"Open your eyes, Sweets. That's how you get the full experience. And," I sensed him coming closer and then felt his breath on my ear, "that's how you'll have one of the best orgasms you've ever had just from touching yourself."

"I can't focus on them and making myself cum at the same time. Besides, just hearing them is enough to get me there." Moans were always a turn on for me when I watched porn snippets. The right kind of moans anyway, not those extra dramatic ones that really sounded like they were doing too much. But the kind where you knew the woman was getting some of the best dick ever.

"Can I help you?" My eyes flew open at that. *Could he help me what?* He must have read the confusion on my face because he clarified. "May I touch you, Sweets? Can I help you cum?"

He wouldn't *be intimate* with me in the way I'd asked, but he'd do this? Part of me thought about cursing him out but the other part of me stared at him in disbelief for a solid ten seconds before finally nodding my answer.

Because let's be real, why on earth would I tell this man no? I don't even think I knew how to say no anymore once the option was put on the table.

Me and my low vibrational vagina wanted nothing more than his hands — and other body parts — on us.

"Tell me I can." He ran his fingers down my collar bone as his soul-sucking eyes never left mine.

I was at his full disposal. "You can," I breathed out. *I am so fucked.*

"Keep your eyes on them," he instructed as his hand found its way between my legs. He placed his pointer and middle finger on top of mine and helped me to keep playing in my pussy. My fingers, with the pressure of his, immediately had me dangling off a cliff of pure oblivion.

And if that wasn't enough, his soft lips found the parts of my neck that were weak in the *veins* for his sweet kisses. *Shit, shit, shit!* I screamed internally as the orgasmic feeling coursing through me heightened.

"Aht, eyes open, Tyme," he breathed into my ear. I was so engrossed with pushing out my nut that it didn't even click that I wasn't watching the show anymore. My eyes opened to see something I would have never thought I'd ever see in person—Clareese getting *double* dicked down in a whole new position. Kobe was lying on his back at the edge of the bed, Clareese was riding him, and Zion was hitting it from the back — literally.

And then there was Mercedes, who was convulsing on her seat as she squirted.

Oh, my fucking goodness.

It all made me start tremoring with pure delight.

"There you go," Midnight's voice was euphoric to my body. "Get that nut, Sweets."

On demand, waves of pleasure rushed through me ruthlessly. I could no longer hold back what my body needed to set free. Not taking my eyes off the sex scene in front of me, I gave into what was happening as Midnight's fingers took over completely without missing a beat. As my body filled up with heat and the best kind of tingles, I screamed out as a release of pure unadulterated glee ran through me.

"Fuck," I sputtered as my vaginal muscles continued to contract and release several times post nut. A few more curse words tumbled out of my mouth as I struggled to catch my breath. He had been right. That was by far one of the best orgasms I'd had from masturbating— even if I'd gotten a little help.

I removed my limp hand, but Midnight's continued to gingerly massage my pussy folds.

I closed my eyes in an attempt to find a normal breathing pattern. This time, he let me and allowed me to come down from my orgasmic high, and as I did, reality begin to trickle back in in the form of embarrassment.

The scream I had *scrumpt* was loud as hell and because I felt my juices trickling down my ass crack, I was almost positive I'd left a mess on the couch. There had been towels placed beside it, but I didn't grab one because cumming all on it— or in *this* room at all — wasn't on the agenda.

Joke's on me.

And let's not forget that I *knew* Midnight's fingers were covered in my special sauce, and that had my nerves on high alert.

He really sat here and played in my coochie and talked me through a nut. But he wouldn't— don't say it.

"You good?" I loathed that my body had graduated to loving him whispering in my ear *and* checking on me.

It was the protection for me.

I nodded.

"You sure?"

I reluctantly opened my eyes to look at him. "I am."

My orgasm had completely caused me to be tuned out of the *porno* for a moment as I gathered myself, but gradually, the sounds of moans and grunts filled my ears again. They were still hunching, as if they were the Energizer Bunnies, but in reality, it probably hadn't been *that* long.

Mercedes was taking a break from pleasing herself and was rolling a blunt. Oh, to be the Queen Bee.

"Great." Midnight pulled my attention back to him as I felt his hand removing itself from between my legs.

I expected him to grab one of the towels from the side table, but consider me turned the hell on *again* when he licked my cream off his fingers as if tasting me was a typical part of his day-to-day routine.

My mouth slipped open, and I swiftly closed it back before he caught me. His eyes met mine.

"Now I know why I call you Sweets." *Oh, I hate you so much.*

He smirked, grabbed a hand towel from the towel steamer, and told me to stand to my feet. I did and he positioned me in front of him.

I stared down at him and though I *heard* the other people in the room, it felt like it was just us.

"Can I clean you up?"

Never have I ever been asked that before.

"Um, yes," I hummed, because once again, why would I ever say no to being serviced? He was speaking to my number one love language.

He grasped the sides of my pants, pushed them down and around my ass until they were hugging my knees, and then proceeded to clean me up as best as he could.

Not him staring right at my pussy and not eating it. Am I a joke?

After taking care of me, he grabbed a disinfectant wipe and rubbed down the couch area, even though I hadn't left any of my secretions on it like I'd thought, but it was nice to see that cleanliness was a priority.

"Can we go?" I blurted out after he tossed the wipe into the trash can next to the side table. His brows knitted together. I had had enough of this torture and his bullshit ass mixed signals.

He can't play in my pussy *and* play in my face, so that only meant one thing: I was going to fuck this man all night, and he was going to let me.

CHAPTER 14

Midnight

Why was her pussy so fucking thick and pretty? The moment my eyes laid on it, it was like it winked at me and called out my name because it was supposed to be mine.

And I fucking wanted it.

I loved how it wasn't completely bald, because I didn't mind a little hair. But the slit, and the way her inner lips peaked out like a flower in bloom, had my dick losing its mind.

From the smell emitting from it *alone*, I knew it would ruin me. But when I licked her juices off my fingers, I damn near wanted to *move* into Tyme's vagina to see what that be like.

I was a fucking goner for Tyme Henley.

With her hand in mine, the way I liked it to be, I led us out of Mercedes and Clareese's room.

"How you feeling?" I asked, as we stepped into the hallway. I didn't know if she was getting tired of me checking in on her, but I couldn't control my need to protect her and make sure she was still comfortable— even if she was outside of her comfort zone.

"I'm good, but what was that about?" Her head nodded towards the suite's door.

"What?" I asked as we positioned ourselves against a free wall.

"The look you and Mercedes gave each other when we were leaving."

"An acknowledgement. Nothing for you to be jealous about," I teased, even though I was being honest. We'd given each other a nod as we headed out, out of respect.

"Why would I be jealous? At this point, I'm sure you two have had sex before."

There was sarcasm in her voice, and it was cute.

She *was* jealous. "Like I said, there's nothing to be jealous about."

"And like *I* said, I'm not."

Technically, she ain't say that, but because the truce was still in play, I'd let her be great. "Okay, Sweets."

She squinted her eyes at me. "So y'all *have* had sex before?"

My mouth curved into a smile. "I thought you didn't care."

The piercing glare she gave me didn't go unnoticed. "I don't, it's small talk."

Right. "Me, her, and Reese had a little fun last year."

"Interesting." She turned away from me, resting her back on the wall. As I leaned up against it, I ran my hand absentmindedly across my nose and loved that her scent still lingered on my fingers.

The amount of control I'd managed to have since I laid eyes on Tyme in front of the police station until now, should have gotten me some kind of award. *Especially* after she straddled me, and definitely after what happened less than fifteen minutes ago. Add in the fact that she *still* smelled so damn good, per my calculations, I deserved a Nobel Peace Prize.

"I had sex with Reese, not Cedes," I clarified. "I told you she gets off on watching her wife get pleased. We did some other things, but Mercedes doesn't do dick at all."

She dropped her head to the side before glancing over at me. Her hand wrapped around my arm, and she pulled me in front of her. The heels she'd worn had been ditched during our tour and replaced with slippers Neo made available to the guests, so that allowed me to hover over her.

"Tell me more," she murmured, her interest surprised me, but I was learning that there was so many layers to Tyme, and I enjoyed the ones that kept me on my toes.

Continuing to stare down at her, I dived into the details of my 12:01 experience from last year with the couple in question.

"Did you reciprocate?" she asked as I gave her a high-level play-by-play of the festivities — one of which was them giving me head at the same time.

"I mean, I'm not a selfish man, and I need to eat." I winked. I didn't mean to bait her, but my flirting ways didn't get the memo.

She let out a visible breath. It was soft but the sexiest shit I'd seen all night with the way her top lip trembled. When she rotated her head away from me, and drew her bottom lip into her mouth, I wished it was *me* she was sucking on.

Fuck me. Literally.

Her head slowly snapped back towards me, and the way her lust-filled eyes took me in, I couldn't fathom how I was ever going to make it through the rest of the night without hearing her moans again. The way she'd screamed through her orgasm, I could only imagine how loud she'd get when she was getting deep stroked in the way she deserved.

"Why are you looking at me like that?" I asked. "You mad at what I said?" Her energy told me she wasn't, but I was trying to keep the conversation flowing and my hormones in control. I needed to break the trance she was putting me in.

I was almost sure there was nothing Tyme couldn't get. Her eyes were like mind control, and though I had been holding out— I was faltering.

"I'm not mad." She paused, and before I could say something else to get us on a subject that didn't have my dick ready to risk it all, she said, "You talking about what you all did has me flustered."

There goes keeping my hormones in check.

"I think this party is turning you into a voyager. You want to—"

"Or maybe it's you," she cut me off as I was about to suggest what we could do next to avoid me fucking her in the hallway. "Knowing what you did to them turns me on. I'm so wet just thinking about it."

Houston, we have a problem.

I should have stopped her, but I didn't— *couldn't.*

I let her take my hand and guide it back inside of her pants and down to the warmth between her plentiful thighs. My fingers had a mind of their own and started massaging the soft folds of her pussy until she pushed my hand to where she desired it. A gasp escaped her throat as I entered my pointer and middle finger inside of her. The heat and wetness on my fingers alone had me yearning to nut.

Got damn!

I pressed my forehead against hers as she whimpered in pleasure while I fingered her.

"I want you, Midnight, and I *despise* myself for wanting you." I didn't have words for that because I knew the exact feeling. We were both at war with ourselves, consumed by the emotions coursing through us.

We didn't fuck with one another.

She was the bane of my existence.

I spent two plus years convincing myself of every negative thought I had about her, just so I could accept the reality of her becoming my sister-in-law.

Now that that wasn't happening, I wanted to please her in every way I could.

And with the way I'd give her what she was asking for, she'd never think about my brother again.

Yet, when she leaned in to kiss me, I couldn't bring myself to accept what I really wanted— *once again.* Instead, I buried my head in her neck like a fool. It was no surprise when she quickly shoved me away.

Horny Tyme had me damn near flying into the wall across from us.

"Are you freaking kidding me?" she snapped, "You're confusing the hell out of me, and I can't do this anymore with you!"

An apology for my actions would have been useless because I sensed she was about to metaphorically beat my ass with a bat.

And I deserved her wrath.

I was confusing my damn self with all my contradicting actions. Did I want to have her? Yes, *but* according to the bro code — *literally* — I shouldn't have her.

But I kept tiptoeing on the line all night, and she was fed up with my shit. I was too.

"You'd play in my pussy, tease me, suck my juices off your fingers…"

She pointed at me as if I were Exhibit A in a court of law, calling out my recent action. In my defense, what else was I supposed to do? Let her juices fall on the floor? *I think the hell not.*

"… but not kiss me? What kind of game are you playing? Because it's not one I'm interested in. Let's get to the real… do you want to fuck me or not?"

Nothing turned me on more than a woman being direct as hell *and* putting me in my place at the same time. Which was why Tyme always had a piece of me wrapped in her entire existence. From the moment she told me off for calling her desperate, until this very one of her telling me to stop playing with her, I should have known she would be my downfall.

I was positive, *this* Tyme wasn't the one my brother had gotten. She'd altered herself for him, and I felt partially to blame for it.

I owed her the truth.

I walked back into her space, caging her in.

"Midnight, I can't—"

"I want you, Tyme," I cut her off, "I have never *not* wanted you. Instead, I forced myself to think the worst of you because you were with Mal, and now—"

"And now, you can have me. So have me. Kiss me, please."

The strength to not devour her in that moment had to have come from God himself. "Don't beg me, Sweets. I'm weak enough, and I'm trying to be the voice of reason for us both. If I kiss you, I'm going to want you in every way you'd let me have you. And if we sleep together… there's no going back. We've been teetering on the line, but we will completely cross it, and I don't want you to regret it. Despite how it may seem, being the one to bring you pleasure tonight was never my plan."

She rolled her eyes. "With the way you've been playing in my face all night, trust me, I know."

"There go that slick mouth I like."

"Well, this slick mouth is tired of your bullshit. You think I *want* to want you? I am utterly disgusted with my vagina's choices. I think this truce was rigged."

That got a laugh out of me.

"There's nothing funny, and what makes you think I would regret it?" she asked. "I'm not expecting anything but the night you promised me. If I'm going to step out of my comfort zone," she paused to reach into her pocket, "then I get to pick who I want to please me and get me to let go of my inhibitions." My eyes saw the color red before the wristband was all the way out of her pocket. She'd gotten more than one color. "I want *you* and I'm not gonna say it again," she held it in front of my face, "*and* per the wristband, only you, so I trust you to give me what I *need*."

Checkmate.

"What about Mal?" It was one thing to make him *think* we'd done something based on him seeing us together. It was another if he actually found out we did have sex. I could deal with the backlash that would come from it, but she was already stressed about my family seeing us together. I needed to make sure she was ready to face the consequences of our actions.

She screwed up her face. "What about him? He never stopped to think about me, and even if he did, he still married the person he cheated on me with. I'm tired of giving him power over me." Her head cocked to the side as she then revealed, "Besides, I already told him we had sex." Didn't see that coming. I knew my eyes went wide. "Might as well make an honest woman out of me."

"Wait… when?" I let off a chuckle.

She dragged me closer to her by the rim of my pajama bottoms. "No time for small talk when the important question still remains, 'are you going to give me the goods or not?'"

I gave her a lopsided smile. "So, we skipping over the kiss?"

"Well," she kept her eyes on mine, luring me in, "you said if you kiss me, then you're going to have me in every way I'd let you. Therefore, the kiss is already implied."

I ran my tongue over my lips. Either we were going to regret this, or it was going to be one of the best nights of our lives.

I was willing to take the risk since she was all in.

"Well, it seems like I don't have much of a choice now do I, Sweets?" I lowered my head, zoning in on her luscious lips.

"You don't," she whispered right against my mouth, "but it was cute that you ever thought you did."

And then it was no turning back.

The kiss alone was as good as sex.

The way she melted into my arms, the way it electrified my entire being, and the way our tongues moved around each other's seamlessly as if we'd been doing this for decades, led me to believe we were in for a night of pleasure, passion, and intoxicating sex.

I was ready to lose myself in Tyme.

CHAPTER 15

As of this year, Midnight Drayton might tell me a joke, but he'd never tell me a lie.

There was no going back after that kiss.

We had stepped into our villain era, and we had to own it.

He kissed me in the most intimate way, and I almost felt like I'd never been kissed right. It was as if we were two people melding together and oblivious to everything else in the world.

I never wanted it to end.

But it did.

"Come on, let's go to my room."

"Your room?" I clarified as my hand settled into his, and we headed towards the stairs. I hadn't thought far enough into the future about what would happen after we kissed. I knew what I wanted to happen, but the whereabouts hadn't really been a thing. I guess deep down, I figured we'd find some secluded place in this big ass house to do the do, since I did recall his cousin saying the rooms had been reserved.

Clearly, I was willing to get sexed wherever the D was being given.

"Yeah, it's on the third floor. I always get a room."

"Why am I not surprised?"

He glanced over at me and little mini pricks of ecstasy poked me all over my body. I was *almost* ashamed by the way every part of me was reacting to him just having those beautiful eyes of his on me.

Even if this was only for tonight, I was going to bask in every second of it, because when else would I get the chance to have my ex's brother eating and stroking my coochie at a pleasure party?

I was thinking never. Might as well live in the moment, which was why I said—

"Wait," I stopped him from ascending the stairs, "I want to see what's going on with the orgy." I could hear the moans, and after what I'd just experienced with Cedes and crew, I wanted to get a peek.

"Look at my little Peeping Tom."

I flipped him off with my free hand as we walked to where we could look down into the great room with ease. Before, the *group project* was about to get started; now they were deep in it. Booty, boobs, and peen were everywhere.

We watched in silence.

With the right person, I'd always had the mindset that I'd be open to a threesome— but an orgy? I don't know if I'd ever be open to that. There was so much happening but from my point of view, everyone was enjoying themselves, and it had me and my vagina ready to test our limits.

"You ever played Never Have I Ever?" I peeked over at Midnight to see that he was watching me.

Multiple coochie flips.

"Yeah…"

"Why did you say it so dry like that?" I giggled.

"Because you and these random 'you ever played' questions. The last one had you about to fight me."

I rolled my eyes. "Because you had me out here looking thirsty. Look at me," I gave him a twirl, "I don't ever need to be thirsty for no man." Now I could talk big shit, but we both knew I had been acting dehydrated as hell.

But let's not focus on the past.

"So, I guess I'm the exception?" he grinned.

"You think you're funny?"

"And cute."

So damn cute.

"Hmm," I leaned up against the glass railing, "the only reason you're the exception is so I can get my lick back," I joked.

He grabbed his heart, feigning hurt. "And here I was, thinking I was using *you* so I could have one up on my brother, but you're the one *using me*? Damn."

It took everything in me not to smile. That's the one thing I always enjoyed about the connection Midnight and I shared — even when we 'hated' one another, our bickering and bantering was top notch.

"You didn't think I'd go from hating you to wanting you just because you've been all sweet to me, did you?" I asked.

"I haven't been sweet to you."

I detested the way he licked his lips.

"Or because you were worried about me?"

Since he was licking lips, I was nibbling on mine. Two can play this seducing game. He came closer into my space, sending my heart rate into overdrive.

"Definitely haven't been worried about you."

I turned my body to face him head on and could feel the wetness pooling in the seat of my panties.

"Or because you keep making sure I'm okay, safe, and comfortable?"

He placed his arms along the sides of me, locking me into place. "I really don't give a fuck about you, Tyme."

I wouldn't falter first so I went in for the kill, "And because truce or no truce," I stood on my tippie toes and leaned in to whisper, "you've always wanted me… remember?"

His lips were on mine in half a second.

This kiss was full of need and desire as we groped and grabbed at one another. He spun me around and pushed me up against the railing, wedging his dick up into the crack of my ass. I had had the pleasure of feeling it on me as we played Twister, but now he was nice and erect. Mentally, I confirmed that he was definitely the twin with the big dick.

My robe fell down and around my back, leaving the upper parts of my body exposed. He planted wet kisses along the tops of my shoulders, up my neck and around my ear before whispering, "Let's go before I have you leaning over this railing while I eat your pretty ass pussy from behind."

Ding, ding, ding... sir, you fell right into my trap!

I turned and stopped him in his tracks. "You be trying to throw me off my game... but remember I asked, if you've played Never Have I Ever."

With a smile, he draped his arms around my waist and then let his hands glide down my ass. "I said I did."

"Well, I want to play another variation of it right here." He gave me an incredulous look. "I'm calling it Never Have You Ever."

"Is that right?" His hands gripped my ass cheeks in unison. My coochie was enjoying having him this close a little too much, *but* when at a sex party, you do as the freaks do.

"Mmhmm. Wanna play?"

"As your faux bae, I don't think I have a choice."

"You're learning." I cheesed.

He planted a peck on my lips. "It better be worth us not already being upstairs, though."

I kindly removed his arms from around me and put space in between us.

Here goes nothing.

"I think so." I paused to remove my robe and tossed it a few feet away from us.

Bitch, are we really about to do this?

"Never have YOU ever..."

His eyes never left my body as I pushed my silk pajama bottoms down to the ground and stepped out of them, kicking them towards where my robe now laid.

The people downstairs can see your ass cheeks.

"... leaned me over this railing and ate my *pretty* pussy from the back."

The moment I stood in front of him in just a thong and the laced top, lust filled Midnight's eyes... but when I finished my statement—

they were filled with another level of sexual hunger that had me crumbling into a billion pieces.

I had no doubt this man was going to demolish my pussy.

"You either have to drink," I found the courage to continue my game, "or do it." He swiped his tongue over his lips and smiled. "And *oops*," I held up my hands as I shrugged and looked around dramatically, "there's no drinks up here except from what's dripping from between my legs."

With care, he placed a hand around my throat as he gripped my left ass cheek, "You sure you want everyone around to hear you beg me to make you cum, Sweets?" He was whispering into my ear and with each word, I was losing my ability to remember how to stand on my feet. "'Cause once I start eating this pussy, I'm not gonna be nice about it, and you're only gonna get the orgasms I let you have."

Did he say let? Bih, this is no longer Satan's son; we're messing with the Devil himself. Run.

"I want an audience," I confirmed, breathlessly.

I probably would regret that, but I didn't see myself getting a moment in life like this a second time. With God's willing, I'd never see these people again. Might as well give them a show.

"You can keep these on." He tugged at the thin string of my underwear. "I like having to maneuver to get to the prize."

He planted a kiss on my lips and then spun me around. It wasn't long before he was commanding me to spread my legs wide as he started kissing and nibbling on my back. The wetness of his sweet kisses mixed with the fabric of my lace top made my body tingle in a way I didn't expect.

I let out a soft moan as my eyes landed on the people down below. There were seven of them on the couch and all but one was wrapped up in the fuck fest they were having. The one who wasn't involved had his eyes on us, and I peeped the black wristband he was sporting.

I closed my eyes and shook the nerves of being watched by a stranger out of my head, and instead leaned into how sexy it felt to be watched by said stranger.

"I'm going to eat the hell out of this pussy," Midnight said as he sent a hard slap to my exposed cheeks. I yelped and gripped the railing tighter, wondering how much longer I had before my juices would start rolling down my inner thighs.

He continued his torture of kissing, licking, and nibbling before he stuck a finger inside of me and groaned into my ear. "If you cum before I say you can, I'm not going to be happy, Sweets. You do understand that, right baby?"

I nodded vehemently because a bitch had lost all words with that *baby*.

"I know you're going to make me proud." He yanked my head back and my mouth couldn't get to his quick enough, and then play time was over. He positioned me back the way he wanted me, dropped into a squat, and had me regretting the whole audience thing because I was about to embarrass the hell out of myself. They hadn't been paying attention before, but I was about to give them something to watch.

His tongue had barely *poked* my pussy, and three things immediately became true: I was *not* going to make him proud. I was *not* going to be any semblance of a good girl. I was going to cum, and I was going to cum as many times as I could, whether he liked it or not.

His hands palmed my cheeks as he spread them open and ate my pussy *and* teased my ass as if he'd been waiting for this meal all his life.

All his life he had to fight — so he could eat my pussy.

"I knew you wouldn't listen." I managed to make out his words, even though he still had a mouth full of me in him. I could do nothing but continue to let my body shake against his face as my first orgasm rocked through my soul.

I moaned disrespectfully loud as he gripped my wide hips and sucked on my clit harder. I couldn't see him, but I felt his whole *face* in my coochie.

"Look at this pussy cumming again," he mumbled. "You might as well give that shit to me." Another forceful slap to my ass and I let it out.

I prayed this glass railing was put together with the best of strength with the way I was leaning all my weight against it. If not, I'd be going to glory with a smile on my face and my coochie licked so clean, God might think I was a virgin. *Hallelujah.*

MY BRAIN WAS STILL FULL OF ORGASMIC BLISS BY THE TIME WE WALKED into his suite. He'd *let* me cum four times before we decided that the people who were privy to him eating me out, had had enough of my *opera* performance.

And my coochie needed a break.

He'd ate me clean.

Yet, *I* was ready to be butt booty ass naked for this man the moment we walked inside. Because honestly, the way I would let this man bleepity, bleep, bleep, bleep, bleep me— was insane.

And I wasn't even ashamed about it anymore. Maybe once I woke up and we got back to "reality", things would be different. But right now, all I cared to do was what my best friend had suggested: Get the Sonic Rings knocked out of me.

However, he had other plans for us.

"You know we not sleeping tonight."

"Sounds like you're trying to ruin me." I wiggled my brows.

He gave me a lopsided grin as he stood — per usual — too close for comfort. "In order for me to give you the treatment you want," my eyes zoned in on his lips, "so that you can continue this year knowing exactly how you deserve to be treated, loved on," he leaned in closer, "and fucked... I'm going to need the rest of this night."

There was a huge lump in my throat from the way he said *fucked* but I swallowed it and said, "Sleep is for the weak, anyway."

"Exactly, so I want us to relax first, talk about some things and then we can get back to the fun." He winked.

"Talk about what?"

"Getting your pussy ate don't stop you from asking questions, I see."

"Fuck you," I snorted, and he joined in on the laugh as he started removing the jewelry he wore. My brain was slowly acclimating to the room around me, and the first thing my eyes took hold of was the plethora of sex toys laid out on the work desk. "Um," I pulled my top lip into my mouth, nibbling on it as I pointed at the items. "What's all that?"

Midnight looked up from what he was doing by the nightstand and followed the path of my finger. He smiled.

A devilish one.

He placed his luxury watch that was in his hand down before coming over to me. "Why we need to talk." He planted a kiss on my lips. "I'm gonna run us a bath."

I nodded and he left me where I stood. I waited until he disappeared into the bathroom before going over to the desk. There were condoms, lube, blindfolds, vibrators, dildos, anal toys, nipple clamps, handcuffs, different types of restraints, and a few things I didn't even recognize.

What kind of wild shit was Midnight Drayton into?

And how was I now wrapped up in it?

Girl, we went from being in jail to about to be tied up in chains... Happy New Year?

"Come on." Midnight's voice pulled me out of my thoughts, and I headed to the bathroom. As soon as I walked in, the first thing I saw was the free-standing garden tub. It was perfection.

The water was still slowly pouring into it, but the subtle romantic gestures didn't go unnoticed. Rose petals were sprinkled on the floor, and a few candles had been lit around the tub.

Was Midnight Drayton the type to wine and dine a woman?

"Does the tin man have a romantic side?" I gushed.

"I won't answer that."

I smirked as I continued to take in the spacious bathroom. Beautiful marble floors, face to face vanities, and a separate walk-in shower that could fit three people comfortably.

Midnight came over to me, removing his shirt in the process. I hadn't forgotten how sexy he looked without it, but *by fucking golly* — he'd definitely gotten finer by the hour. No one could convince me otherwise.

My heart rate started to increase at the thought of him taking off his pants. It was one thing to feel his manhood against me, but to see it— I needed to prepare myself.

"Am I undressing you?" he asked.

'It's the manners for me!' my coochie yelled.

"You can," I answered. He circled me, stopping behind me and placing his hands on my waist.

My body shivered at his touch as I watched him through the mirror.

He pushed my pants down, and once they got over my ass, they fell to the floor with grace. I stepped out of them just before I felt his teeth on my right ass cheek.

I hated how effortlessly he had me moaning.

"I couldn't help myself," he said, standing back up.

"I bet," I commented, and he popped me on the booty.

Next, he removed my lace top, allowing my boobs to finally be free.

Lastly, my thong that had been drowning in my juices all night.

His hands caressed my body before one of them made its way up to my neck. He massaged my throat and then pulled it back against him. "You're really just so fucking beautiful, Tyme," he whispered into my ear, and I could have melted into the floor.

Even though I was comfortable in my skin, and loved my plus sized body, I still had to remind myself not to use my hands to cover up the parts of me that felt exposed. Truthfully, I didn't know many women, size be damned, who didn't get nervous the first time someone saw them completely raw.

But leave it up to Midnight to make all my nerves disappear with just seven words.

The silk piece of clothing he had clad on his body brushed against my bare skin as it dropped to the floor.

I almost made myself go blind as I looked out the corner of my right eye and watched him remove his boxer briefs next. The way his dick popped out to say hello, I wanted to scream *"heyyyyy, best friend"*, but I had a little sense left.

Midnight turned me around and planted a sweet kiss on my cheek. With everything in me, I kept my eyes on his upper body as he told me to get into the shower, so we could cleanse off the residue from the evening before soaking in the tub.

It made me smile internally every time I saw small things that we had in common shining through. I was the type of person who always showered before taking a bath because who wanted to soak in dirty water? *I didn't.* For me, baths were for relaxing, not cleansing.

My nasty mind expected Midnight to have me pressed up against the tiled wall within ten seconds of entering the shower, but to my delight, he took a washcloth and begin to bathe me.

It was the way he was so gentle with every part of me that had me in a daze of lust, admiration, and complete fervor for this man.

Midnight Drayton knew exactly how to handle a woman like me, and I was at a complete loss of words. Part of me wondered if I stepped into an alternative universe and that's why I was experiencing a version of him I had convinced myself didn't exist. How was *this man* the same man who'd called me desperate; yet, now, he was treating me like someone he'd move the world for?

I guess some things didn't need to make sense. At least not tonight.

After he cleansed me, I returned the favor. I started with his chest and left his dick for last. When I got to it, I studied it and committed it to memory. It was the prettiest shade of brown to me. The thickness of it had my coochie walls thumping with anticipation, while the length had my stomach doing flips.

"I think I'm clean now," he joked after I'd soapily stroked his penis.

"Oh," I smirked, "I was making sure I didn't miss any spots." Seduction dripped from my lips like a heathen in heat — *which I was.* How did *he* have more self-control than me? I was appalled.

He ran his tongue over his lips, staring down at me with a look that sent shivers across my bare body. "You're nothing but trouble, Tyme Henley."

I finally released his member. "Don't act so surprised. I think you like trouble."

He kissed me on my cheek and then whispered into my ear, "And I do, you'll see how much later." Another kiss before he turned off the water, and we transitioned from the shower to the tub.

It had been at least ten minutes since the tub had stopped filling with water, but the temperature was still perfect when we got into it.

Midnight laid between my legs and lovingly massaged the parts of my lower body that held him in place. We silently enjoyed each other's company as the sounds of his playlist played throughout the bathroom.

Though I had told Midnight that sleep was for the weak, I was pretty sure I was running off orgasmic fumes, mixed with a fear of falling asleep.

I was afraid of waking up from this nightmare turned beautiful dream and I didn't want to miss a moment of it. I didn't want to take the chance that this wasn't real and any minute now, I'd wake up in a cold jail cell, pissed at myself that I'd been dreaming about getting my coochie popped like a champagne bottle by my ex's brother.

"You not falling asleep, are you?" Midnight tilted his head back to get a better look at me.

I smiled. "Actually, I was thinking about how I'm not sleepy at all. It's like I'm on a high from everything and eventually I'll crash, but until then, I'm gonna vibe."

"That's what these play parties will do to you. I still remember my first one. It was a lot."

"Oh, you mean this ain't your first one?" I teased, feigning shock and he laughed. "How many have you been to?"

"Three."

"I was expecting you to be like about eight of them— at least."

"I'm starting to think my *supposed* judging nature has rubbed off on you."

"That's what happens when I'd been forced in such close quarters with you for over twenty-four hours."

"Whatever," he shot back, playfully splashing some water my way and causing me to giggle.

Midnight Drayton made me giggle… *how annoying.*

"I was only counting play parties, and this is only Neo's fourth year doing 12:01. I've been to a couple sex clubs as well, but those are different. Not as intimate. I like how cuz has set these up to be not only about the pleasure aspect, but fun too."

"I do like that. It gives people the opportunity to get to know someone a little before they *get to know them.*"

He laughed. "Exactly. Breaks the ice."

"Now, Mr. Freaky Tin Man, how did you get into all of this?"

"Whoa," he gasped, "whoa. Wait a minute. *You* calling *me* freaky? Which one of us asked to be bent over a railing and ate out while watching an orgy?"

My face flushed because why he had to bring that up?

"Sir, please," I begged, chuckling while I fingered his goatee. "I don't know who that girl was."

"Yeah, but I bet I bring her back out."

Not him having my coochie blowing bubbles in anticipation.

"Anyway," I pushed at the back of his head, "answer the question."

He gave my thighs a squeeze as he answered, "A bad breakup and curiosity. I figured it'd be fun. I had never been to anything like it prior to Neo deciding to do one."

I blinked at the back of his head. "A bad breakup?" I repeated.

"And curiosity."

"Sounds to me like you don't wanna talk about the bad breakup part."

He shrugged. "I don't care to bring that type of energy back into my space."

I waited ten seconds, thinking he was going to give me *more* than that but when he didn't, I said, "Okay."

"We need to discuss what you like and don't like when it comes to sex," he said, changing the subject.

A simple statement that made me wonder if I even knew what I liked and didn't like. "I guess the *normal* stuff. I probably sound so vanilla."

"You don't got any kinks? I know a lot of y'all women are into praise kinks these days."

The sides of my mouth turned up. "If you think I wanna be a good girl for you — of all people — you must not know me as well as I was starting to think you did."

"See, I'm tryna be a gentleman right now, but it seems like you're just tryna get fucked in this tub saying shit like that."

I meannnnnn.

"I'm just saying being a good girl hasn't gotten me far."

"It's gotten you farther than you think, Sweets." It was the way the words rolled off his tongue with such lust and admiration that I wanted to see if he could breathe while eating my coochie under water. However, I practiced self-control.

"Anyway, if you wanna praise me, I won't mind it. Now what else do you want to know?"

"How about I ask you a few things? You yes or no them and we'll go from there, finding your comfort level. Cool?"

"Mmhmm."

"Choking?"

"Yes, but don't try to kill me. I already think this was a set up as is."

"Fuck you," he chortled. "Anal play?"

"Oh, we skipped far ahead," I nervously laughed. "Anal play, yes. Anal sex, hard pass. If you wanna eat my booty like *Jhene Aiko* said, I won't stop you. As far as toys, I'm open to trying the smaller ones."

"Sensory deprivation?"

"Like being blindfolded?"

"Yes, but other things too that can deprive one or more of your senses. Are you open to that?"

"I'm open to it, yes."

We continued this for a little longer, with me also finding out things he liked, didn't like, and was open to. Everything from sex positions to boundaries were discussed. He'd also made me aware of safe words we could use. Red for stop completely, yellow for don't stop but dial back the intensity, and green for keep going.

No nigga had ever given me safe words. *Bitch,* I internally yelled at my vagina, *are we safe?*

It didn't matter because *we* were about to live dangerously tonight, and that was apparent with that lust that danced in both of our eyes as we exited the tub, dried off, and made our way back into the bedroom.

On the outside, I was calm — *I think* — but inside, my nerves had just taken a line of the white stuff that have crackheads bouncing off of the walls.

I was about to do *the do* with Midnight Drayton.

My *ex's twin brother* was about to stroke me into a coma.

From this day forward, I would be one of those girls who smashed both brothers.

And I was giddy as hell about it. Nerves be damned.

"You okay?" Midnight's voice drew me back into what was happening around me. He'd placed a few of the candles from the bathroom, around the room. The light from the moon mixed with the candles gave the perfect amount of illumination.

"You're always asking if I'm okay, but I haven't asked you if you're good. Are you?" I questioned, sitting down on the bed.

"Question with a question," he joked.

I shook my head. "I'm great. Are you?"

He lit one final candle before coming towards me as he replied, "I'm good as long as you're good, Sweets."

"Okay," I hummed as my eyes made their way up and down his body, twice. He smirked, but at this point, there was no need to hide my ogling over one of God's best creations he'd made thirty-seven years ago.

"You know," I said when he stopped two feet away from me, "you've been pleasing me all night. It's high time I return the favor."

I reached for his towel, ready to suck the devil out of him, but he stopped me.

"Not that I don't appreciate the gesture," he caressed my hand, "however right now, the focus is still on you. Lay back."

Gulp!

As hard as it was, I ignored his request. "You do know this isn't a one-sided thing. I want to make sure you're satisfied as well."

He smiled slyly. My towel was still tautly hugging my body, but his dark eyes were gazing down at me as if he could see every ounce of my flesh. "Trust me, I've been nothing short of satisfied from the moment you came all over my fingers."

Another gulp.

"It is not the same as me giving you head, I'm sure."

One of those ugly smirks graced his sexy face. "Head is *damn* great, but it's definitely in competition with the way you were moaning my name while you trembled all over my face as an orgasm rocked through you."

What the hell do I say to that?

"And I want that again."

Or that.

"What you're failing to understand here, baby, is that I'm a pleaser."

"A pleaser?" I questioned, almost wanting to laugh at myself because why was I always so damn inquisitive with *this* man without shame?

"That means you have no idea how much pleasure I get from pleasing you. I want to make you cum as many times as possible. I want to watch you completely lose yourself and forget how to breathe because of what I'm doing to you. It's so rewarding to know that you're leaking all because of me."

I had no words.

None.

Zilch.

However, one thing was for sure. I was leaking and ready to let him drown in the deep end.

"So lay your ass back."

CHAPTER 16

Midnight

S ome men loved a woman with a t-shirt and no panties on, but I was a sucker for a woman in a towel and nothing else. Knowing that all it took was one lil' tug and I had the luxury to see her in all her glory did something to me every time.

Every single fucking time.

That was partially the reason I didn't have the patience for that shit Tyme was spewing.

Did I want some head? Yeah, but my moment would come eventually. Right now, my soul needed to drink her holy water because I hadn't quenched my thirst yet.

I didn't know if I ever would.

"So lay your ass back," I instructed, after explaining to her what I meant when I said I was a pleaser. When I was younger, sex was all about getting my nut. If the woman got hers, cool, but she had better made damn sure of it because back then, that was none of my business.

But then I grew up.

I started *actually* dating women long term and one of them humbled me. I was twenty-six, and though I was selfish when I fucked, I still thought I was delivering top notch penis because no woman had ever complained.

Nicci Collins did.

Thankfully, she was nice about it, even though my cocky ass wasn't trying to hear it at first. However, I really liked her ass — literally and figuratively — so I put my pride aside and listened.

And that shit changed the game for me.

The way my mind, body, and soul reacted to a woman, especially one I was into, being pleased by me had me seeing sex and all forms of intimacy in a new light.

By the end of this night, Tyme's soul might be yelling out *'praise Nicci'* because I was determined to take her to a place her body had never been.

I watched as the beauty before me listened this time and laid down. Hovering over her, I tugged on the towel, causing it to open and reveal the gorgeousness hiding behind it.

Damn, I was going to enjoy kissing, licking, loving, and indulging in every inch of her stacked ass body.

To start, I pressed a kiss against her forehead, then her nose and mouth. I paused to suck on each one of her nipples, and even under her breasts— taking note of the hidden tattoo beneath her left boob. I showed it some love, wondering what the date meant, before proceeding to tease other key parts of her body until the toes of her left foot were in my mouth, as my right fingers slid in and out of her gushy center.

She moaned, groaned, whimpered, and squirmed while I relished in every millisecond of it.

"You want me to make this pussy cum, don't you Sweets?" I goaded as I lowered myself to the ground, letting her foot fall beside me as my face aligned with my new favorite toy.

I shifted my eyes up to see her nodding wildly at my question.

I sniffed the air. Her pussy smelled liked every wet dream I'd ever had. *Fuck me.*

"I don't know, she don't seem wet enough for me." I twirled my thumb over her clit. "You think you can make her wetter for me, baby?"

"Yes," she said through a pleasurable moan that had me massaging my dick through my towel.

"You sure?" I replaced my thumb with my mouth and gently sucked on her sweet spot.

"Yes," she cried out again and I smiled.

"Play with her for me." I sat back on my knees, licking my lips.

She stared at me for a moment, clearly catching her breath. Her arm moved from its position but then stopped and a devilish smirk danced on her face as she said, "No."

I cocked my head to the side. "No?"

Her smirk widened. "That's what I said. What are you going to do about it?"

"Oh," I said, nodding, knowing exactly what she was doing.

"You might as well get to eating." She tapped her pussy. "This is what *you* wanted to do. We both know she's already soaking wet; what I look like doing *any* of the heavy lifting? I'm a passenger princess — orgasm edition."

That had me chortling in the key of 'you about to get fucked up'.

From our conversation on likes and dislikes, she was aware I got off on that bratty shit. She would pay for it though, and she knew that, too.

"Bet." I tucked my hands under her legs and jerked her closer to the edge of the bed, bringing her pussy opening a mere inch or two away from the tip of my tongue.

Because I couldn't help myself, I sucked in her natural smell *again*, allowing it to tickle my nose, and then blew air out of my mouth that caused her to tremble.

"If you want me to eat her, you better start playing with her," I threatened before my tongue circled her entrance and she gasped. Dragging my tongue up and through her lips, I waited until she moaned to pull my head back. "I guess you would rather me not feast."

"Stop teasing me," she begged.

"I will when you do what I say." I planted kisses between her thighs, up and down her legs, and even along the crevices of her pussy.

"Midnight, please…" she moaned every time my tongue got close to where she wanted it most. I hated how I could only resist her sweet cream on my tongue for only so long. It barely took three 'Midnight, pleases' before my face was searching for gold between her thighs.

Two orgasms later and I was ready to fully take it to the place of no return. While Tyme recovered, I ditched my towel and grabbed protection. When I returned to the bed, she had her legs spread as she played with that juicy pussy of hers.

Now she listens.

"Mmm," I hummed, enjoying the show as I wrapped up. Her manicured fingers moving round and round on her clit, mixed with her bottom lip pulled into her mouth as she eye fucked me, was a mental image I wanted to become a core memory. "Yeah, just like that, Sweets," I encouraged her, stroking myself, "get her dripping for me again."

"As if she hasn't stayed dripping for you." She winked and all I could think was, *say that shit a-fucking-gain. 'Cause I know that's fucking right.* "How do you want me?" she cut into my thoughts. Her voice was so seductive in that moment that I could've nutted just from her words.

"Right where you are," I responded as she stuck two fingers inside of her, pulled them out, and pointed them towards me.

I crawled onto the bed, allowing her to put her soaked fingers into my mouth as I positioned myself at her opening. The way she moaned from me slurping her juices off her hand, had me wondering how nasty Tyme could really get when she was in a space where she felt safe.

I wanted to give her that space and more.

Her fingers retreated out my mouth and repositioned themselves behind my neck. Gripping it, she drew me into her. Our lips caressed one another as we shared a kiss that said a lot more than I was willing to accept in that moment.

Don't ruin me, Tyme Henley.

Pushing my way inside of her, I hissed at how the walls of her vagina sucked me in like it was my own personal vortex.

"Shit," I groaned, immediately needing to slow down my pace, because it was Tyme, and she was meant to be savored.

Finding our rhythm, we began to lose ourselves in one another. I found myself loving the way she held onto my neck as I thrusted in and out of her as if she was afraid to let me go. I also loved the way she arched her back and lifted her hips so that I could stroke her as deep as possible.

It was taking every trick I had in the book to not cum too early, but Tyme's pussy wasn't out to play fair. However, I wouldn't be caught slipping— except for in and out of her good ass coochie, of course.

Flipping her over, I gave my dick a second to chill while I spanked her ass for that 'no' she'd told me earlier.

Spanking was a yes for her without question and the way the hole to her vortex contracted at each slap, I saw why.

"You gon' listen next time I tell you to do something?" I asked, sending a nice smack her way.

"Maybe," she said, looking back over her shoulder at me devilishly. The smirk only lasted for so long because when I gripped her hips and thrusted my way back into her warmth, she yelped in pleasurable pain.

"Yeah, we gon' see about that maybe. Now throw that ass back for me, baby." *Fuck*, I yelled like a little bitch in my head. If she felt this good with a condom on, I could only imagine what her walls felt like in true form.

I would have nutted on impact.

She cried out my name as she met each of my strokes right on cue, as if we were putting together the perfect puzzle pieces.

"Fuck, baby," I seethed as she collapsed onto the bed, causing me to drill into her in one of my favorite ways that had her talking to me in a falsetto. Every ooh, oh, and whimper had me entranced in her goodness.

"Ooh, shit, baby," she whined, raising her ass up and moving it in a circular motion. "Fuck, Midnight!"

I moved my mouth next to her ear. "This what you wanted, ain't it?"

"Mmm, yes," she cried out.

I buried my head into her neck, sucking on it as I continued to let her pussy suction me into her, as if I was being punished in the best way. I wouldn't mind being sentenced to life *inside* of Tyme.

"Damn, baby," I whispered into her ear, slobbing all over it and basking in the way her body responded to it. "I feel that nut, you might as well give it to me." She gripped the sheets, making the sweetest of moans as I continued to give her body what it was begging for. "You gon' give it here?"

Her head moved up and down as she said through gritted teeth, "I'ma give it to you, baby!"

"I want it now." I held her tighter, moving in and out her at the perfect pace that had her creaming all over me within the minute. Without giving her much time to recover, I flipped her over onto her back and re-entered what I wanted so much to call mine.

Staring down at her beauty, I continuously fused my body with hers, which sent an overwhelming amount of emotions through me. It was the way her eyes never left mine, the way her hand held onto mine, and the way her breathing was perfectly in sync with mine.

How the fuck wasn't she *mine?*

We didn't need to speak to know how good this felt for the both of us.

But it didn't hurt when she moaned, "You fucking me so good, baby, I don't know if I deserve it."

"You deserve it and more, and don't you forget that shit."

I kissed her, pushing her legs back at the same time to go deeper. I was close, but I *needed* her to cum with me.

"Fuck," I growled against her mouth.

Her pussy squeezed my dick and from the gasp that escaped her throat, she didn't even have to tell me, "I'm cumming again, baby."

"I know," I hummed as she began to come apart and soon thereafter, we released together.

"Shit," I said, fighting to hold my weight up, but not wanting to remove myself from the monster that was still contracting between her legs.

She let out a deep sigh and soft giggle. "That was..."

"Yeah," I responded because we both knew what it was without her needing to finish the sentence.

"Kiss." She poked out her lips and I obliged before slowly pulling out.

It took another second before I was up and heading to the bathroom to dispose of the condom. On the way back, I grabbed two washcloths from the towel steamer.

I cleaned off myself before tending to my kryptonite.

"You good?" I asked as I returned to the bed after tossing the washcloths off to the side with the other used towels.

"I'm still trying to remember how to use my legs and breathe at the same time, but other than that— yeah. Fantastic."

I basked in her response as I slapped her on the thigh, taking joy in the jiggle and her yelp.

"You're an asshole." She pouted, rubbing the spot I'd hit.

"You want me to kiss it?"

I leaned down. "Aht!" She pushed me away. "Because you're not finna get no more sex from me for at least another fifteen minutes."

Shit, I needed at least another twenty minutes my damn self. Thirty if I'm being honest. Forty wouldn't hurt. But I mean my tongue was free. Little did Tyme know, if she kept fucking with me, I was gonna eat her ass out of coochie.

I pulled my neck back. "Damn, I can't even be intimate? What a little kiss gon' do?" I grinned.

"That Cheshire cat ass grin on your face is why I don't trust your kisses right now." She sat up, pressing her back against the headboard.

"Meanwhile, a few hours ago, you were begging for 'em. My, my, my how quick things change once someone gets the dick."

"Boy, fuck you." She stuck up her left middle finger and I knocked it away. "By the way, sorry for being a brat about that kiss."

"It was cute and entertaining. Besides, I like brats," I winked and she bit down on her lip, the sides of her mouth curling up.

"Don't I know," she teased. "Now on to more pressing matters… I got the munchies."

"Shit, me too," I rubbed my stomach.

"You think I can make it to the kitchen or are people still being nasty all over this house? I think I've seen enough hunching for the night." I laughed at that. "It sounds quiet out there." She outstretched her neck, as if she could hear what was happening two floors down.

"Well, them folks definitely gonna be going at it all night. Lucky for you," I opened the top drawer, "Neo already thought that through." The drawer was full of a variety of snacks including chips, candy— regular and *adult* kind—cookies, and energy and protein bars. There was also a mini fridge with drinks. "What you want?" I asked, giving her a rundown of her choices. We both made our selections and settled back on the bed, dressed in the provided robes.

"These are the best Oreos I've ever had," she said, devouring her last one in the six pack. We'd been talking about the most random things: if we believe Aliens existed (she thought they were already amongst us; I didn't disagree), our favorite Black sitcoms growing up (mine was *The Fresh Prince of Bel-Air*, hers was *A Different World*), and if we'd try to survive a zombie apocalypse (we both said fuck all that *The Walking Dead* bullshit — we out).

"Oreos are lit, but these Grandma's cookies?" I twirled the sand-wich cookie between my fingers before placing it into my mouth, "Bussin' harder than you."

Tyme damn near choked on the cookie still going down her throat. "Now why would you say that?" she asked, patting her chest and grabbing a water.

"That shit was funny and true." I winked, eating another cookie.

"Nasty."

"You haven't seen anything yet. It's only," I glanced at the digital clock, "Four. I'm not done."

"Wouldn't expect you to be."

We finished our snacks and transitioned to cuddling. I liked — *loved* — having her fat ass pressed up against my center. The fact that a bigger part of me wanted to *just* lay with her and not quickly transition back to being inside of her said a lot.

With majority of the women I'd dealt with after my ex, 'after care' was an afterthought. But I wanted that and more with Tyme—so much so that I was inclined to open up about shit I didn't usually care to talk about.

"Veronica."

Tyme moved her neck to look back at me with her right brow lifted. "Well, I *know* you *know* my name, so you can't be calling me another woman's name without reason."

"I still have vivid images of you with a bat in your hand. Trust me, I wouldn't dare." I immediately wanted to take that sentence back for fear it'd have her thinking about Malachi, but her energy didn't shift.

Instead, she said, "Exactly, so play with someone safe. Now who is this woman?"

I kissed the side of her temple. "The other party to the bad breakup."

"Oh." Her head repositioned itself onto the pillow. "I thought you didn't want to talk about that."

"Yeah, but you being nice to me has me doing dumb things. We gotta dead this shit soon," I joked.

"Who you telling? Truce got me popping it open for Satan Junior."

I slapped her ass for that comment before diving into the story of Ronnie and me.

"We were together for four years. I loved her, but she only saw me as a nigga to pass the time with while the person she really loved was in prison. Apparently, she only continued to entertain me as long as she did because she didn't see me as anything more than a good time and good dick."

"What?"

"Yeah," I dragged out. "I missed all the signs that she was never as into me as I was to her."

"Wow," Tyme mumbled. "How did the breakup happen?"

That shit. "I proposed on Thanksgiving, in front of her family — after asking her dad and all that bullshit — and she turned me down. It was the way she did it that set me off. She thought the shit was funny because she'd been planning on breaking up with me; yet, here I was, down on one knee.

"I had never been so embarrassed in my whole life. The hurt was also on another level, and the anger soon came after that when she revealed to me that I had been a placeholder she was just supposed to have fun with. According to her, I should have known she didn't want to marry me because she had never brought up marriage. She saw me as consistent dick, money, and fun on demand, while I saw her as wife material.

"It was a rude awakening of how blind you can be when you love someone; you force yourself to only see the things you want to see. Looking back on our four years together, there were glaring signs that we weren't as compatible or as serious as I told myself we were."

"So, she's why you're a tin man?"

"I'm not a tin man."

"You were when we met."

"I have a heart, Sweets, but when we met, I had suppressed any desire to use it. I allowed myself to *be* the type of man she'd told me I was. One that was only out to have fun and fuck, anything more— I didn't have it to give."

"I'm sorry."

"What are you sorry for?" My brows crinkled.

She flipped over to face me. Her left hand pressed against my cheek as she moved her thumb up and down it. All I did was stare at her. I didn't think I'd ever get tired of taking note of how stunning she was.

"That you allowed her to cause you to lose yourself because I know what that's like. You might be judgmental," she winked, "but the reason I'm lying beside you right now is because you're the type of man who protects those he cares about. You've made me feel nothing but safe, appreciated, beautiful, cared for, worthy, deserving, desired, seen, and so much more. All the things that women want to feel when they're with someone. If you treated her even half of the way you've treated me in this short time, the reason she refused to appreciate it was because of her own messed up reasons. It had nothing to do with you, I hope you know that now."

"I do." And I did. You can't force someone to love you when they're too caught up in someone else. "Veronica was never open to me, she never allowed herself to be because I wasn't who she wanted. It hurt at the time, though, but I've since gotten over it. I just don't care to talk about it. I like to let the past be the past and don't care to bring that shit back into my energy once I'm really done."

"Good." She planted a kiss on my lips. "And understandable, but thank you for sharing that with me anyway."

"You're welcome, and I'm the one who owes *you* an apology." She blinked a few times. "You met me during the aftermath of that relationship. That app was a means to an end. Good fucks and that's it.

When we matched, the way the conversation started off, I knew something with you would be different. And you proved me right.

"At the time, I was so far removed from wanting the things you were upfront about because of Ronnie. Typically, I would have still tried to smash," I smirked at the way her face scrunched up, "*but* with you, something told me to be an ass upfront instead. I figured you'd block me. You ain't have to cuss me out, though."

She kissed her teeth. "Nah, you deserved that more than the block."

"I won't deny that. I will apologize, and I been should have said sorry for the things I said, Sweets."

"I guess I can forgive you."

"You guess?"

She flipped back over and pressed her ass back against me. "Only because *Veronicaaa* was wrong for what she said *when* she said it, but the girl didn't lie. You do got good dick."

CHAPTER 17

I n less than forty-eight hours, I had let Midnight Drayton get me to be nice to him, take me out of my comfort zone, forget my morals, and become dickmatized by him.

If flabbergasted was a person, it would be me.

All it took was that very first thrust inside of me, and there were no doubts in my mind that I'd fucked up.

But in a way that I knew I'd never regret because you couldn't ever be remorseful about getting sexed by someone who would suck your soul out of your body and then stroke you so well you feel like you're in a different dimension.

Midnight had the type of dick that would make a girl do foolish shit. I don't condone people using someone, but no wonder his ex wasted his time. She was getting superior sex on demand.

I was honestly a tad bit jealous and wanted to beat her ass because had it not been for her bullshit, maybe I would have never ended up with the wrong twin.

"Is that right? You think I got good dick, Sweets?" Midnight's voice in my ear had my pussy juices immediately simmering. I didn't even have to respond because of the way his tone had dropped a few octaves and his dick inflated against my ass cheeks, I already knew he was about to test the theory.

"I asked you a question," he said, sticking a hand in my hair and yanking my neck back so I would look at him. Those fucking deep, dark, alluring eyes of his on me never ceased to send me into a downward spiral.

In seconds, our lips had crashed into one another. Sloppy kisses ensued, and I fell back into my Midnight haze.

He played in my hair and fondled my breasts as my hand found his erect penis beneath his robe.

It didn't take long before I heard the crinkle of the gold wrapper. My heart swelled as cool air hit my backside when he pushed my robe out of his way and slid into my home base. I let out an audible gasp of pure relief.

When Midnight was inside of me, my entire being exploded with a sense of reassurance and relaxation. Every piece of distress I'd felt over the last few months faded away and was replaced with happiness, joy, contentment, and bliss.

It was as if he was my own personal psychedelic.

Psychedelic Drayton needs to be his new name from hence forth.

He lifted up my right leg and moved in and out of me as if he owned my pussy. And at that moment, he did. It was his.

From this day forward, till death do my coochie and Midnight part.

My hands gripped the sheets as he pressed my shoulder down into the bed and had me feeling like I was doing one of those twisted yoga poses to stretch out my spine— or break it.

But I wasn't.

No, I was getting fucked.

I was getting sexed in the way I wanted to get sexed for the rest of my life. The man damn near had me ready to sing 'A dick worth fighting for' to the tune of *Mulan's* "A Girl Worth Fighting For". And I would've sung my heart out.

ONE DAY AFTER 12:01

We weren't supposed to fall asleep. I was supposed to get dicked down, tied up, blindfolded, and ate like soft serve ice cream all night. But that last session took us both out. One second, we were cuddling, and the next, I was opening my eyes to see the sun rising.

Midnight's arms were still wrapped tautly around me, and a small portion of my brain was still struggling to catch up with the reality of how I'd brought in my new year.

I wanted to pinch myself, *but I didn't.*

Even though I knew I wasn't dreaming, I didn't want to chance waking up from this sweet dream or beautiful nightmare. It was all too good to be true.

Succumbing to sleep again, the next time I woke up, Midnight's spot in the bed had been replaced with a tray of breakfast food— pancakes, waffles, sausage, eggs, and fruit. Plus, a note.

I would have text you, but someone's still withholding their number. I went for a run. Eat up, Sweets. ~ TM

TM?

The moment it clicked, I burst out into a fit of giggles: Tin Man.

Well played, Midnight Drayton.

I took my breakfast platter, along with the glass of orange juice he'd sat on the nightstand, out onto the balcony. The view into the back of the villa was peaceful. No one was outside, and I wondered how many people were still here. Did they have sex all night and day? Or, did they wake up this morning and continue about their new year as if they hadn't been at a play party the night before?

One thing was for sure, 12:01 had done its job for me. I felt this renewed sense of life dancing through my veins. I was ready to tackle this year and *finally* let go of the bullshit my ex had put me through.

I didn't know if it was because I had allowed myself to have fun again, or if it was because I'd been sexed so well by my *former* arch nemesis.

Because let's be real, there was no way Midnight could go back to being a top tier enemy of mine when he broke the record for giving me the most orgasms I'd had in one night.

I came twelve times within five hours. At this point, I wasn't sure if I had any cum left to give.

It could also be because I'd had sex with my ex fiancé's brother. The same ex who KNEW there was a high probability that I'd *actually* had sex with the person he'd shared a womb with and was now (hopefully) on his honeymoon in pure turmoil over me getting my lick back.

At least, that's what I envisioned as I sipped on my orange juice: Malachi curled up in the fetus position bitching and moaning about me fucking his family out of spite.

Maybe my imagination was over exaggerating the truth because I was sure he was putting on the perfect husband façade for his wife, but I was going to stick beside it because it made me feel so good to know I'd said to hell with Malachi Drayton.

Come to think of it, it was all three.

My phone vibrated on my lap, interrupting the music that was playing through the room's Bluetooth speaker, and I looked down to see it was my mother calling me.

"Hey lady, Happy New Year," I greeted, happy to see my mother's smiling face. She was glowing, and I loved that for her. I didn't need to know about her sex life, but I knew my mama was having too much fun traveling the world with her *lil'* boyfriend who was eleven years her junior.

"Happy New Year, my baby. How are you?" Her question was a loaded one. I'd assured her via text and voice notes that I was fine after the whole wedding debacle, but she wouldn't be Apryl Henley if she didn't quadruple check. Surprisingly, she hadn't been too hard on me about the arrest— case in point that Luke definitely helped regulate her blood pressure in a way that I didn't need to know.

"I'm really good, mommy."

"You sure?"

"Yes," I stressed with a smile. *I was damn good.*

"I believe you; you're glowing." Her eyes narrowed. "Where are you? That background does not look familiar."

"Okay nosey," I joked. "I'm in Chasington Beach. I took a mini getaway to bring in the new year. After Friday, I thought I needed it."

"A solo vacation is always a good way to clear your mind and recenter yourself. No wonder you look refreshed; I'm glad you did it."

Solo. Right.

"How's Italy?" I redirected the conversation. My mom and I had a pretty decent relationship because after she and my dad got divorced, it was just us and we endured a lot together. However, I wasn't about to tell her that she'd raised a city girl who was out here going from brother to brother and sleeping with the enemy. She'd obviously met Midnight before, and she was very well aware of the fact that I could not stand him.

At least when she met him, I couldn't.

Besides what about 12:01 was an appropriate mother-daughter convo? Nothing. Therefore, there was nothing to tell.

"It's stunning here. We extended our trip another week. Then, we're going to take a train around Europe for a month or so. There's always an open invite for you to join. Luke will even cover your ticket." Though my mom was older than Luke, she wasn't his sugar mama. He was a freelance IT consultant who did well for himself and spoiled my mother.

"I know and I appreciate it. Maybe next month. I really want to spend this month focusing on getting back to me."

My mom's whole face smiled. "I'm so happy to hear that, Tyme. I really am. You deserve to move on past all that mess with that Drayton family. Someone better will come along, and you'll know why God took you through this lesson."

Whew, if only she knew.

My mom spent another ten minutes telling me about her and Luke's time in the Amalfi Coast before she had to let me go because they had dinner reservations.

I went back to listening to music, and it wasn't long before I sensed his presence. I didn't hear him come into the room, but my skin tingled when he was close. *How disgusting.*

But not as disgusting as him walking out on the balcony, giving me a kiss, and looking scrumptious as hell in all his sweaty glory.

"Good morning," I sang.

"Afternoon."

"Shit," I hissed, checking my phone and seeing that it was indeed touching on one. It made sense, considering I woke up at eleven-thirty. I'd been sufficiently in a fog of new year, new me (*or was it new year, lick back me?*) that time hadn't been a focus. "It is. How was your run?"

"Great. There's this path I like to do out here."

"Cool. I hope you got in enough running for the both of us because I ain't doing that."

"And you don't have to. That ass don't need to be going nowhere." He squeezed my hip before sitting down in the chair beside me. I didn't even care that he kind of stank.

I am in deeeeeepppp. Send a fucking intervention.

"Did you enjoy your breakfast?"

"I did. I left you some because I didn't know if you'd ate."

He smiled. "A lil' bit. I ate the bacon."

"So, you just said forget me and my tastebuds. What if I wanted some bacon?"

He cut his eyes at me. "You don't like bacon."

I tilted my head to the side, struggling to hide my shock. This was like the poppyseed bagel all over again. "How do you know that?"

The sides of his mouth turned up. "The same way I know all the things I know about you. I pay attention."

"Why?"

"Why what?"

"Why would you have been paying attention to me? You had no reason to."

He shrugged. "And yet, I couldn't help myself."

Those six words shut me the hell up. My throat went dry. My coochie did the exact opposite.

"By the way," he said, breaking the silence, "I grabbed you a hoodie set to put on when we leave."

"A hoodie set?" I glanced over my shoulder to see the deep green colored outfit.

"Yeah. Neo keeps them in the shop as party favors. They have 12:01

branded into them. I figured you wouldn't want to put back on your pajama set."

Yeah, that set had my pussy juices marinating in it.

"Cool. Thank you."

"No problem. If the size not right, just let me know," he said, looking over at me and standing to his feet. "Come shower with me."

"That sounds like you're trying to get some more of my goodies." I pressed my pointer finger against my chin as I got up from the lounge chair.

"We don't have time for the way I'd want to be deep in you. We gotta be outta here in thirty minutes. The cleaning people are coming to put everything back how it's supposed to be."

I nodded at his back as I followed him into the bathroom.

"Question," I said as he turned on the shower.

"Are you gonna ask me if I played 'Hands Down Vanilla Five' before?" I flipped him off and he laughed. "What's up, though?"

"How did your cousin get into hosting play parties?" When he mentioned this was only Neo's fourth one, I was shocked. Not that I had any prior play party experience, but I was sure this one set the bar high.

"An older woman he used to date introduced him to the kinkier side of the world when he was younger and got him wrapped up in it."

"Oh, wow."

"Yeah," he removed his shirt, and I tried my damnedest not to stare. "Y'all women be the ones who be the freaks and then wanna act like it's us. I peep game."

I giggled, putting my hair up into a messy bun. "Boy, hush."

He reached his hand inside the shower stall to test the water. My eyes landed on his workout pants, in search of his print. I had no self-control.

"How come you had workout clothes?" I asked as he pushed his pants down and gave me the peep show I wanted.

"I might have packed me a bag and threw it in the trunk while you were getting ready… just in case." He headed towards me — dick just a bouncing.

I was clearly in my lucky girl era.

I pushed out my lips. "You just knew we'd stay, huh?"

"I didn't, but ain't nothing wrong with being prepared."

"Mhmm." I rolled my eyes as he removed my robe and let it slither down to the ground. "We both know you tricked me into being here."

He chortled. "I left out a key fact, but, I also gave you multiple outs. *We* both know *you* wanted to see how wild you could get."

"And speaking of wild... actually, never mind." I walked into the shower. The water against my skin was pure perfection. The shower head must've released water from a magical source.

He smacked my ass. "Nah, say it."

I nibbled on my lip before letting the words slip out, "I'm a little bummed out that we didn't get to any of the sensory play." During our likes and dislikes talk, he told me how he loved incorporating sensory deprivation into things— hence, some of the sex toys I'd seen.

Initially, the idea of being restrained and having multiple senses taken away was nerve-racking, but the way I wanted to please this man and make him happy was something that needed to be studied.

Because who the hell had I become? *How* did he turn me into this girl who barely could think straight when he was so close?

I was still low-key convinced I'd been poisoned.

"I ain't wanna look like a simp for the pussy, but," he started lathering his body, "on my run, I did consider asking if you wanna spend one more night here. I can extend my hotel room... if you want me to. 'Cause there's nothing more I'd rather do than have you tied up, blind folded, and cumming for me."

I had no words, just actions.

Gripping his freshly washed penis, I dropped into a squat and had it tickling my tonsils in record time. I had been wanting to suck his dick for so long that nothing but pure satisfaction rushed over me as he let out a gutty groan.

Midnight Drayton was definitely every bit of a pleaser, but it was high time I returned the favor. My mouth went to work: licking, teasing, kissing, and sucking him so well that he used the Lord's name in vain as he struggled to contain his balance.

"I'm guessing that's a yes," he said, as my tongue teased the head, giving him a small break from my pleasurable torture.

Looking up at him, I smirked and then swallowed him whole again as my response.

CHAPTER 18

Midnight

I was staring at Tyme like I ain't have no home training. It was a
shame that this girl already had me wrapped around her finger,
and there was no getting away from it.

Not that I even wanted to.

I had a very much love-hate relationship with the way she had me
feeling right now. It was embarrassing the way my stomach twisted as
I watched her mouth spread into a smile before she laughed at whatever was on her phone screen.

"Order number twenty-one!"

I snapped out of my trance and grabbed the food I'd ordered up
from the food truck's pick-up window. After checking to make sure it
was correct, I trudged back down the beach to where we'd set up shop
for the bonfire.

After we left the villa, we headed back to the hotel and slept away
most of the afternoon. When we woke up, I had a text from my cousin
about a New Year's Day bonfire that was happening on the beach
across from us, so we decided to check it out before I got back to
digging for gold between her thighs.

It had only been six hours since I was last inside of her, and the fact that I was already having withdrawals had me wondering how I was going to go back to "normalcy" once we got home tomorrow.

But I wasn't going to worry about that right now.

Right now, all I cared about was making the vivid image, in my head, of Tyme tied up and at my disposal, come to fruition. It had been living rent free in my mental space long enough.

"What got you cracking up?" I asked, outstretching my arm with her food order towards her.

She took it out of my hand with a smile. "Nene was sending me screenshots from some of the comments from the viral posts. People on the *innanet* be hilarious with trying to find out the whole story."

"Oh, you still social media famous?" I asked, getting comfortable beside her. Some part of me had to be touching her. It was my knee at this moment.

"Apparently, but I refuse to log into the app. The notifications are becoming overwhelming."

"My little celebrity." I bumped her shoulder as I dug into my food.

"Oh," she smirked, "now I'm yours?"

I chuckled, finding her reaction endearing. I took my time finishing the mouthful of seafood gumbo, savoring the moment, before finally responding. I wanted to see how she'd react, knowing she already knew the answer.

"The truce got extended, per your request, so yes. Is that a problem, Sweets?"

For a moment, her eyes darted away, and a hint of warmth glowed on her cheeks. It was in those tiny nuances that I found her irresistible —how she bit her lip when flustered, how her playful demeanor gave way to moments of vulnerability. I loved the way she allowed me to tease her as well as the way she let her guard down and displayed her true emotions.

She regained her composure and retorted, "Not at all, Tin Man."

I smiled. The fucking nickname had already grown on me.

"And don't start your lies on the first day of a new year. You're the one who made the request."

"Because you said you wanted the full *Midnight* treatment. It's okay that you want more time with me, Sweets." I winked and then laughed at the way she scrunched up her face at me.

"You seriously need help."

"Is that right?"

"Mmhmm," she hummed, eating a spoonful of her conch salad.

I placed my food down beside me before leaning into her space. My hand settled on the side of her waist furthest from me, and I took pleasure in squeezing on her love handle. Her skin was so smooth and supple that I could have spent hours running my hands up and down it for no reason at all, except for the fact that it felt good against my fingertips.

She cut her eyes at me as I lowered my mouth to her ear to whisper, "Is it my fault this sweet pussy of yours makes a nigga crazy?" My hand slithered down from her waist to between her legs, and I shamelessly scooped her fat pussy into my hand. I squeezed and rubbed her mound through her leggings, not caring one bit if someone saw me. There were only adults out here anyway. "Huh, baby?" This time, I was whispering against her parted lips, "Is that my fault?"

"No," she breathed, yanking me to her and causing a passionate make-out session. Someone passing by whistled, and we reluctantly went back to keeping things PG.

By the time we finally broke apart, my dick was saying to hell with the s'mores we'd been excited about making. He was ready to head on back across the street. But I told him to act like he had some type of sense instead of a horny little eighteen-year-old who didn't know how to control his hormones.

"You okay?" I asked after I returned from throwing away our food boxes and grabbing our free s'mores making kits.

"Yeah," she answered me. "I'm just thinking."

"About?"

"Everything," she said. "I know this isn't some kind of never-ending dream, but everything still feels so surreal, like I'm not quite awake. Does that make any sense?"

"I think you're processing all that's happened. You've had an eventful couple of days."

"Who you telling?" She pushed a piece of hair out of her face. "I've *crashed* a wedding, been to *jail*, gone to a *sex* party, become social media *famous*, had the *best* conch salad I've ever had outside of the Bahamas, and *slept* with the enemy. Life is *lifing*."

I cackled at the 'slept with the enemy' part. "Not to rub it in but you forgot: been *semi* nice to said enemy and took incriminating pictures with him too."

She got you talking about yourself in third person — bruh, you're pussy whipped.

"Those selfies we took were not incriminating." She giggled.

"Tell that to the family group chat." Her eyes bulged and I laughed.

"Oh my god." Her head dropped into her hands.

"Chill, chill, chill. It's not that deep, I promise."

"Yeah right." She puffed out her cheeks and blew out the air. "Consequences of my actions."

"Nah, consequences of *his* actions, but come on, let's make these s'mores and get your mind off shit that don't matter."

"Fine," she dragged out but smiled. All I wanted to do was keep that smile on her face.

"Wanna know a secret?" I said as the fire crackled in front of us as we each opened up our kit, which came with enough ingredients to make four s'mores.

"You're a secret agent who's been hired to ruin my life, but you messed around and fell for me instead." She wiggled her brows at me.

"You wish." *At least about the 'ruin my life' part*, I thought to myself. "I've never had s'mores before. At least not *like this*. I've had s'more-flavored things and all the ingredients that make it up, but never an authentic s'more." Her eyes widened. "You're judging me."

"I'm not you, so never would I ever." She grinned. "But I've never met someone at *your* big age who's never experienced such perfection."

"My *big* age?"

"I said what I said." She raised her shoulders in a nonchalant gesture. "Anyway, I'm appalled because s'mores are one of my favorite snacks. I make them in the oven at home at least once a month, and I'm always experimenting with different kinds of chocolate and extras."

"Oh damn. So I'm with a s'more connoisseur."

She giggled. "Something of the sort. So, follow my lead." She winked and I watched as she grabbed the graham crackers from the kit and placed the remaining things back on the beach chair that was between us. "First, we take two graham crackers and break them in half to form four squares," she explained as she demonstrated.

"Bet." I copied what she'd done.

"Then, place your chocolate on the graham cracker. Now, it's time to toast the marshmallow. You only need to make sure it's golden brown, but I like mine a little burnt."

"'Cause you're a rebel," I said as I placed my marshmallow onto the skewer.

"Sure am." As many others around us roasted their marshmallows, I savored the sweet scent that filled the air as I thought back on the tattoo that I'd seen under Tyme's left breast. I had explored every inch of her body and found no other ink, so I knew this had to have significance.

"I got a question."

"Not you trying to be me."

I cut my eyes at her. "What's significant about January eleventh?"

She took her focus away from me and onto her marshmallow. "My little sister's birthday."

"I didn—"

"She died when I was ten. She was six." *Fuck.* "Drunk driver who jumped the curb while she and my dad were walking home from the park."

"Damn. I'm sorry, Tyme." I wrapped an arm around her shoulder and kissed the side of her temple.

"Thank you. Okay, you can place your marshmallow on top of the chocolate on your graham cracker squares but don't take the skewer out just yet." I did as she instructed. "So, this is where you can fuck this up."

"Really?"

"Who's the expert here?"

I held up my hand in surrender. "You right. What now, *Your Highness*?"

"Take the other graham cracker square, place it on top, and then press down *gently* and take your time pulling out the skewer."

"You do it first. I ain't tryna have you talking shit if I mess up."

She snickered. "Watch me work, baby."

My eyes focused in on what she did. "Oh, you pulling that skewer out as if it's a dude making sure the condom don't slip off after he nutted."

Her head dropped to the side, and she shook it back and forth. "Did you really just say that?" She burst into a fit of giggles while I slowly removed the skewer from mine.

"I did, and damn this shit look good." I twirled the s'more around in my hand.

"A delicacy."

We *cheered* our handiwork before taking a bite at the same time. Tyme's eyes rolled to the back of her head, and I definitely understood why. This was delicious.

"Now I gotta have one every day to make up for lost time."

"As you should." We stayed quiet for a moment, enjoying our goodness and the warmth of the fire.

"I'm really sorry to hear about what happened to your sister. What was her name?"

"Serenity."

"Tyme and Serenity. I like it."

"My mom did too. But yeah, her death made for a very hard pre-teen to early teen years as you can probably expect."

"I can," I empathized.

She took another bite of her dessert before saying, "My dad blamed himself for not being able to save her, even though it was a hundred percent the fault of the woman who had been drinking and going forty miles per hour in a residential neighborhood. His grieving process led him to drinking, while my mom tried to hold it together as best as she could for me, though she ended up falling into a deep depression.

"I honestly didn't know what to do as that was my first big experience with death, but thankfully, my God mom and uncle stepped up a lot. They were Godsent until my mom was able to parent again."

"I'm glad you had some kind of support," I said as we roasted another set of marshmallows.

"Me too because it was tough. It wasn't until I was fourteen that things started getting better. My parents got a divorce, and then my mom and I started going to therapy. That helped a lot and allowed me not to be too fucked up by the time I became an adult." She smiled at the end of that. "At least not more than normal."

"Yeah 'cause we both know you're a lil' special."

"And is." She bumped my shoulder and almost caused me to drop my newly prized s'more. "At least that's what my mom says."

"Parents be lying."

"Shut up," she snorted. "Anyway, on my sixteenth birthday, my mom and I decided to get matching tattoos in honor of Serenity."

"I love that."

"Me too."

"Mickie been hounding me about getting matching sibling tattoos."

"That sounds like something she'd want." McKinley Drayton was my one and only little sister and typically, a pain in my ass. "With all the tats you have, you can spare a space for her. Don't be an ass."

"You would be on her side," I snickered.

"Girl power."

"Yeah, yeah, yeah."

Most things I'd learned about Tyme were either through observation or via my brother volunteering information. I'd intentionally made it a point throughout their relationship to not ask him about her. But listening to her now, I realized that Malachi had never really touched on the topic of her relationship with her father or even the fact that she had a sister. After hearing what had happened to Serenity, I wanted to understand more about this part of her past.

"You and your mom seem close. What about you and your dad?" I asked, trying to keep my tone gentle and non-intrusive.

She took a bite of the s'more in her hand, taking a moment before she replied, "I don't really talk to him. After what happened with Serenity, his life went downhill, and I don't think he ever recovered. My mom tried to get him help for his grief, but it seemed like he found solace in a liquor bottle instead."

The pain dancing in her eyes was evident, and it tore at my heart. Tyme continued, sharing her attempt to rekindle a relationship with her father after graduating college. However, it didn't go as she had hoped. "It felt one-sided," she admitted, her voice tinged with sadness.

I low-key wished I hadn't started this conversation because now all I wanted to do was take away her pain. But I let her continue, listening intently as she shared her story. Her father's guilt over the tragedy had caused him to push her and her mother away, asking them to move on without him. "We haven't talked since then," she said, her voice heavy with emotion.

"Baby, I'm sorry," I murmured, wishing there was something I could do to ease her pain.

"It sucks, but I've accepted it," she said, her resilience shining through. "It's been almost eight years. My mom found out a few years ago that he unfortunately didn't stay sober."

"So she still keeps tabs on him," I remarked, realizing the complexity of her family situation.

"She did, but she has since stopped, which is why I'm so happy she has allowed herself to find love again," Tyme shared, seeming to find solace in her mother's newfound happiness.

"I'm glad to hear that too. You both deserve that," I replied, pulling her into a comforting hug. "Thank you for sharing that with me, though."

"Thanks for asking," she said softly.

We shared a tender kiss before deciding to make one more round of s'mores for a late-night snack or two. Eventually, we migrated back to our original spot, still close enough to feel the warmth from the fire but also allowing us the privacy to savor each other's company.

"Questionnn," Tyme sang, after we'd sat in silence for a few minutes and enjoyed the sounds of the ocean and fire crackling.

I could tell from her tone that she was back into her normal energy.

"Here you go," I held back my smile. "Yes, the sky is blue; it's just nighttime right now."

She chuckled. "Shut up, asshole."

"What's on your mind?"

I looked over at her to see she was nibbling on her lip. My hand found its way onto her knee, rubbing it as a way to encourage her to say what she had to say.

"Have you heard from Mal today?" The words came out robotically, but they felt like poison to my soul, nevertheless. I didn't know if it was because it felt so left field after the conversation we'd just had, but I immediately became defensive.

I removed my hand from her and leaned back onto the blanket. "Damn, I guess the 12:01 experience didn't work since you still worried about him, huh?" I focused on everything but her.

"Is this jealousy?"

There was a hint of amusement in the question but instead of me playing into our normal banter, I said, "Is this you avoiding the question?"

My eyes reverted towards her, and I witnessed her facial expression transform from amused to confused, and finally settling into a look of pure anger. "Um," she dragged out the word, the attitude already dripping from it. "Are you serious right now?"

"As serious as you are."

Her face contorted in response—her eyes squinted, and her nose scrunched up. "Correct me if I'm wrong, but you were the one who wanted to do all this stuff to ruffle his feathers, so what's wrong with me asking how the plan that *you* came up with is working? I'm confused as to why you have an attitude."

"I don't have an attitude." *Bruh, you are definitely acting like a little pussy.* "But I don't know why you asking me when you can just unblock him if you care that much."

I couldn't stop the word vomit that was happening.

Because you're jealous.

No, I'm not.

Yes, yes you are.

I don't really give a fuck.

You sure?

She let off a stoic chuckle, snapping me out of the battle between my inner thoughts. "I see you and your brother do have something in common, *besides me*, but I'm not about to deal with the childish bullshit, so I'm going to head back to the hotel."

Shit. "It's not even that deep. You trippin'."

She frowned. "And yet, you couldn't answer a simple question. Now who's the one letting Mal get under their skin?"

I clenched my jaw. There was way too much truth in that one statement.

I woke up this morning with no intentions of going for a run. I would have rather stayed in bed, snuggled up in Tyme's softness, but I fucked around and checked my texts when I went to the bathroom.

Malachi was off his rocker in my text thread. The nigga had me ready to hop on a flight to the Caribbean so he could catch these hands with all the bullshit he was spewing.

But I also understood it.

I knew what we were doing would mess with him, which was the goal. I also knew the potential backlash that would come from us *pretending* to be spending time together— but Tyme telling him that we actually *did* fuck sent him off the rails. He was losing his shit, trying to figure out if we were just messing with him or not.

The way he was acting, I almost thought I had slept with his wife and not the woman he cheated on throughout their entire relationship.

He was a nigga scorned, and it showed.

Which meant the disrespectful shit he texted me was at an all-time high.

> That bitch ain't deserve me any fucking way, you can have the hoe.

> Tia always used to tell me the way y'all acted around each other was fake so I wouldn't be surprised if y'all BEEN fucking. You think you that nigga 'cause you got some mediocre pussy?

> If you wanted to slut her out, we could have done it together... you ain't have to be a sneaky ass bitch about it.

> Of course you'd want my sloppy seconds, you've always been second best anyway little brother

You really fucking my ex bitch after she was just making a whole ass fool of herself at my wedding? She ain't over me but I guess you don't care because pussy is pussy huh? You gon' fuck that girl up more than I did.

She gon' play you just like Ronnie did your ass, karma is a bitch.

Those last two texts were definitely the ones that got his ass blocked and had me going on a run to clear my head.

Even though I believed Tyme when she said she was over him, and didn't want him back, there was an insecure part of me that still wondered *what if* she still had feelings for him? *And* why did that even matter if what we were doing was only temporary anyway?

I had kept my feelings under lock and key because I never wanted to have to wonder about some fuckery like this. But here I was, completely intoxicated by a woman who had once belonged to a sorry excuse of a man. A *little ass boy* who was so bitchmade that he had to continue to drag her through the mud to make himself feel better, as if he was the real victim.

And I hated that for her.

So, for her to even be wondering about his dumb ass took me to a dark place. Especially since his actions were a reminder that had I not been a messed up individual when Tyme and I met, none of this would be happening.

She would have already been mine and I wouldn't be falling for someone I couldn't have.

Correction— shouldn't have.

"Cat got your tongue on that one?" Tyme asked, snapping her fingers in my face as she stood to her feet. I blinked a few times to adjust to the woman who might as well have had hot air blowing out of her nose and ears. I used to like making her mad, but not like this.

She folded her hands across her chest, rolled her neck and then dropped her shoulders, causing her head to bob. I let my eyes trail down her body and away from the intense look she was giving me before I said, "I blocked Mal this morning, so no, I haven't heard from him. You happy?"

Bruh, nooooo! Why the hell you say that at the end? My dick scolded me because we both knew with every idiotic word that continued to come out my mouth, we were moving further and further away from having the night all *four* (me, Tyme, her coochie, and my dick) of us wanted.

She huffed and I didn't have to make eye contact with her to know she was ready to strangle me. "Do I look happy?" Sand came flying all over me and the s'mores we were saving for later.

"Yo," I erupted, knocking the sand off of me. "That wasn't necessary."

"Neither is your attitude, yet here we are." She turned to walk away, and I grabbed her leg, holding her in place.

"I'm sorry, okay?" I glanced up at her.

She glared down at me. "No. Now let me go."

"Sit down, Tyme."

She broke away from my hold. "Go to hell, Midnight," she quipped, storming off.

I kissed my teeth. "I'm not finna come after you," I said before she got too far.

Stopping in her tracks, she glanced over her shoulder with annoyance still written all over her face. "And I don't *need* you to." She flipped me off and continued on her way, making me watch her ass from afar until I knew she made it safely to the hotel.

Yet and still the bane of my fucking existence.

CHAPTER 19

"**N**ot to be on the devil's side, but why *were* you asking about fuckboy?" Nene asked me.

After I left Midnight and his childish games on the sand, I came back, showered, and then closed myself in the room. I replayed our conversation over three times before I called Nene to see if I was overreacting or if Midnight was being a judgmental jackass.

"I don't know, Ne, I guess habit? One minute I was opening up about my dad and then the next, Mal was on my mind. It's like talking about my dad triggered the anxiety in me about what's going to happen when we get back and..." I dragged off, trying to find my words and make it make sense. "I did tell him we slept together, and Mal can be irrational at times... I'm afraid this is all going to blow up in my face. Mid already mentioned something about their group chat being in shambles."

"The group chat is to be expected because who doesn't love other people's drama?"

"I know," I dragged out. "I just didn't expect to feel this much anxiety around what we're doing *or* for shit to get this complicated with Midnight." As soon as I finished that statement, I heard the sound of the front door opening. "Shit, he's back," I whisper-yelled. "I can't believe I've let *him*, of all people, have me stressing out over whether or not I was in the wrong about something. This is abs—"

"Ty, chill out!" Nene cut off what was about to be an intense rant about me being so stupid enough to catch enough feelings for Midnight Drayton that it had my stomach in knots, because I didn't want to fight with him. All I wanted was for him to make me feel safe and protected again. For him to call me Sweets and get me together with just one look. But how could this be? How could he have this grasp on me like this? "Breathe," Nene's voice pulled me back down to earth again, and I took in a large amount of air. "Now let it out." I did. "How you feel?"

"The fucking same."

"Bitch," she quipped, and I let out a much-needed laugh. "I hate you for making me say this, but you're literally getting your back blown out by your ex's twin brother. Who might I add happens to unfortunately — yet now fortunately for you — be fine as hell. Who *also* gave your coochie a record amount of orgasms in one night, and you're worried about your weak behind ex? You won, boo. You have won," she reiterated. "His feelings, emotions, and whatever else do not matter. Hell yeah he's gonna be in his feelings because look at the material!!" I cheesed at my best friend gassing me up while reminding me that Malachi deserved whatever he was feeling. "At least for now, focus on enjoying the rest of your time smothering our enemy to death with your thighs."

"Oh my god," I snorted as I stopped pacing and went back to sitting on the bed. "You're an idiot."

"But a funny one."

"Hush, and I am trying to be in the moment. These last two days with Midnight have been obscenely amazing. I'm embracing the whole idea of 12:01 but—"

"No buts," she cut in.

"Chenethia!" I could have kicked her for saying that because it only made matters worse. It was like a sign from the universe or something. How dare she?

"What?" We weren't on video, but I vividly pictured her scrunching up her face in pure confusion at me full naming her.

"Why would you say one of his *catch phrases?* He stay saying that."

"Ewww," she cried.

"Exactly, and here I was, thinking you were my best friend."

Nene sighed dramatically. "Ugh, I'm really becoming team Midnight; I'm so grossed out with myself right now. This is all your fault 'cause nobody told you to take your fast tail to the boonies, get arrested, and then end up sleeping with *our* enemy! Now you got me looking like I'm not loyal."

I couldn't hold in the laughs. "Ma'am, please hush." I was mid chuckle when the room door opened. No knock, he just waltzed his half naked ass inside, as if he'd paid for the room.

Yeah, I know he did but still.

I shouldn't have been shocked because when we returned to the hotel today, his stuff had been moved from the living room to the bedroom — for obvious reasons. Therefore, his bag was in the room. However, I was going to assume he only barged his ass into here to get a reaction out of me. I hadn't decided if he would or wouldn't.

"I didn't know *the bakery had chocolate cake.*"

"Girl, huh?" Nene questioned, not picking up on the code.

"You heard me."

"…the bakery had chocolate cake?" She repeated it four times before it hit. "Oh shit, he's in the room, huh?"

"Yep, the one right off of Garrett Avenue." I tried not to look at him, but I almost went blind following his every move with my peripheral vision. Every time I saw him fresh out of the shower, shirtless, I wanted to *be* one of his tattoos. To be that close to his body. *In* his skin.

Was that healthy?

I'd never wanted to *be* in a man's skin. Honestly, I'd love to be the skin on his palm because then I'd get to play with his veiny ass dick all the time.

Yeah, no, this can't be healthy.

"What is he doing? Text it! He must be half naked because you breathing like you in heat."

"Go to hell, Nene," I snapped out of my trance as I sent her a text.

He's definitely taunting me. He's been digging through his bag and not even pulling shit out.

"Well shit, taunt him back. Just get naked, you can't go wrong with that," she responded verbally to my text.

"You have no home training. How does Mo deal with you?"

"I get naked a lot."

"Bitch," I snickered long enough to take my eyes off of Midnight and when I looked back his way, he was staring at me.

I matched his energy and for a good ten seconds we had a who will blink first contest. I lost because my best friend was in my ear, asking me what was happening.

"What?" I asked with a sharp tone. "I'm on the phone."

"Get off the phone."

"Oh shit," Nene squeaked.

"No." I moved my head back and forth because who did he think he was dealing with?

He let out a small sigh of exasperation. "Get off the phone, *please*." I narrowed my eyes at him in defiance. "Tyme."

My self-control evaporated with the way he said my name.

"Girlll, bye. That man is not about to play with you," Nene said, giggling. "And I'm not about to be in the middle of this and be responsible for him snapping your spine into quarters. Talk to him and then get you some premium dick."

"Ne—" I started, trying to regain my composure.

"See you tomorrow, byeee."

The call ended and I attempted to make a beeline for the bathroom.

"Sit down, Tyme," he demanded in a tone that made my weak behind want to say *'yes daddy'*, but I didn't because I knew how to stand my ground, even when I was falling apart at the seams.

"Damn, I can't go pee?" I snapped, pausing near the door frame.

"Not when I think you're running from me."

"I'm not," I said, refusing to look at him as I rushed across the hall. Damn right I was running, but I also did have to make sure I hadn't peed my pants from the way he'd said my name.

After removing my damp panty liner, I threw water on my face and then reapplied my moisturizer to waste time. By the time I put my big girl panties back on, a good seven minutes had passed before I walked back into the room with my head held high like I wasn't crumbling.

"Come here, Sweets," Midnight said before both of my feet were even past the doorway. I opened my mouth to say something slick, but he deaded that. "Please, Tyme. I don't want to spend any more of our time in this energy. Let me apologize." He held up a blindfold, and it was at that point I noticed what he'd done while I was in the bathroom.

The sex toys were back.

My feet floated over to him because clearly, they were controlled by my vagina that had started contracting like a whore in heat. I stood in front of him and forced my eyes to stay on his and not venture down.

"When I like someone," he started, "I get a little territorial. So, you bringing up Mal, did have me jealous. It's stupid because we both knew what this was before we crossed that line, however, hearing you ask about him after I've had the pleasure to have you, had me feeling a way. I apologize for being immature."

I pursed out my lips as I dropped my head to the right. It took everything in me not to cheese at his words. Instead I said, "So you like me?"

Midnight kissed his teeth and pushed me away from him, causing me to giggle. "Don't say that shit out loud."

I grinned as I started dancing to my own beat. *"You think I'm gorgeousss, you want to kissss me…"* I sang, imitating a line from one of my favorite movies.

He scoffed. "You think you're Miss Congeniality now?"

Him knowing the reference surprised me, but I didn't show it.

"I might be."

"What you might be is Miss Screaming-My-Name-And-Begging-For-Me-To-Let-You-Cum. How about that?" He snatched me to him, and I was ready to fold like a flip phone. "Can I show you how sorry I am by making you cum until you beg me to stop?"

Hello, 911? There's a homicide on the rise.

I gave him a verbal response — which was yes because not even a nun would say no — and then he turned me around and blindfolded me.

"Yes, I like you," he whispered in my ear. "I like the way you say my name when you're mad at me. I like the way you grab my neck when we kiss. I like the way you suck my dick like you own it. I like the way your body convulses against my face when you're cumming on my tongue and I get to bask in your *sweetness*. I like the way you snort when something's very funny to you. I like the way you pretended to hate me."

Now wait a minute. "I was not pretending."

I yelped from the sting of him slapping my ass. "This is my story and I said what I said. You're already about to be in enough trouble for leaving me on the beach."

"How much trouble?" I breathed out. I wanted all the smoke he was willing to give me.

"Always a bad girl, huh?" he asked as he led me through the room.

"Good girls ain't no fun. Besides, you like when I'm bad."

"I love that shit," he confirmed. "I'm going to undress you." I nodded in understanding. "While I do that, tell me the safe words."

I spewed out the words green, yellow, and red, along with their respective meanings.

"What about when I do this?" He tapped his fingers along the inner side of my wrist. "Or this?" He tapped along the outer side.

"I let you know if I'm okay." The words came out calm, but my heart was pounding through my chest in anticipation as cool air tickled my naked skin. Just from my sight gone, everything already felt heightened.

He planted a kiss on my collarbone that made me shiver, and then my pussy started to stir as he whispered into my ear. "You're always safe with me, Sweets, so cum as much as you like." His tongue twirled around my ear as he gripped my throat with his free hand.

Was I supposed to cum right now? Because I was about to.

With his lips fervently on mine, he guided me onto the bed. My need to see him, feel him inside of me, was already building and we had only just begun. When his mouth left my lips, they landed on my neck, then breasts, and my stomach where he gave it extra attention. He didn't have to tell me how much he appreciated every part of my body; he showed me in every way he touched and loved on me.

He gingerly turned me over onto my stomach and then propped me up into a position where I was sitting back on my knees.

"Don't move," he instructed me, "I'll be right back." I nodded my head in understanding. It didn't take long before shivers trickled down my spine as he used a kiss on the back of my neck to signal his return.

He grabbed my arms and placed them behind me. "This is where the fun begins, Sweets." His breath against my ears had my coochie thumping. "I'm going to say this one last time. If you're ever uncomfortable, you better tell me. Do you understand?"

He asked this question while placing two fingers into my honeypot, causing me to moan out my 'yes' in response.

My left wrist was tugged as he attached it to my left ankle with what I assumed was the handcuffs. He repeated the process on the right side. It wasn't long before my face was pressed into the pillow and my knees were spread wide. The restraints had me completely at his mercy. I could do nothing but lay there with my ass tooted up in the air, waiting for what would happen next.

I thought my nerves would be shot, but Midnight didn't give much room for that. He continued to explain every single thing he was doing to deprive me of my key senses. It kept me calm and very much turned on. I was starting to see that my vagina went to another level of wetness when *we* felt safe and protected by him.

However, a bitch would be lying if I said my anxiety didn't heighten when he placed the headphones over my ears; all I could hear was the sound of heavy rain.

I couldn't move, I couldn't see, and now I couldn't hear what was happening around me either?

Yeah, Midnight Drayton had city girls down by a thousand because how could I explain letting my arch nemesis have me at his mercy like this?

I was gonna have a long talk with myself once this beautiful nightmare was over.

My bottom lip slipped into my mouth as his fingertips glided over my skin. He caressed every inch of my body, gently kneading out any knots he came across.

With my sense of smell elevated, I couldn't help but inhale the intoxicating cocoa scent as he massaged my shoulders.

Leaning deeper onto me, he planted soft kisses down the center of my back. My core contracted at his hard dick being pressed up against the slit of my ass.

"Mmmmm, fuck," I cursed, not sure if I'd said that out loud or in my head. Either way, it didn't stop a full-on visual of him sliding his pretty chocolate- coated penis, in and out of me, from appearing in my mind.

As his warmth retreated, my heart rate continued to rise.

What was he about to do next? Suck the pussy juices slipping out of me? Or maybe take me out my misery and rearrange my insides, like he was trying to knock the senses he'd taken away from me, back into me?

The anticipation was killing me; yet, I was oddly in pure ecstasy not knowing when or how he would touch me again. Every part of my being was in a state of hypersensitivity, and the lack of control had my coochie dripping.

The rain sounds faded out and then "Wetter" by Twista started playing. *How fitting.* As Erika Shevon started singing the 'rain down on me part', something warm ran down the crack of my ass, followed by something freezing cold. *And then* a stinging sensation.

I gasped and lightly bucked as he repeated the process. The stinging from whatever he was using sent me closer to the edge each time. I wasn't a hundred percent sure, but it felt like a leather tasseled flogger with the way it slapped against my skin and then trickled away.

When he switched to using his mouth to run the ice down my back and then let it once again slide between my cheeks, I was ready to explode. My skin was prickling all over. I needed to release.

"Please, Midnight, make this pussy cum for you," I begged, and the way he slapped my ass, I knew he'd heard me. I imagined him growling as he watched my ass jiggle for him and saw my swollen pussy lips because of what he was doing to me.

His teeth sank into my right ass cheek and I barely could contain myself anymore. Pleasure shot through my veins the moment I felt his tongue twirl around the rim of my ass.

"Yes, baby," I hummed against the pillow.

Another slap of my ass and then Midnight started devouring my pussy like it was an ice cream cone, and he refused to let it melt anywhere but in his mouth.

I let out the deepest of moans as I lost control of my body as Erika Shevon got to the 'I'm calling you daddy' breakdown. In that moment, I was more than willing to call Midnight *daddy* with the way he was eating my pussy off the gristle and playing with my ass at the same time.

Just as I thought I was done cumming for the fourth time, he stuck his tongue deep into my asshole and had me screaming his name all over again.

I could barely hear myself through the music massaging my ear drums, but I knew that I was being over the top. I wouldn't be surprised if someone ended up calling hotel security on us because they thought I was in trouble.

In my defense, he was indeed murdering both of my sacred holes with a deadly weapon—his tongue.

This wasn't the first time I got my ass played with, but it *was* the first time that the orgasms from it left me in a full state of delirium.

As my breathing fought to regulate itself, I laid there, not knowing what to do with my life.

Not like I could do anything. The devil had turned me into his tied-up play toy.

Midnight tapped my wrist, and I somehow let him know I was okay.

But shit, was I?

Hell, I wasn't even sure if I'd even stopped cumming yet with the way the contractions were still happening between my legs.

My damn goodness, if this is what punishment felt like, I never wanted to be good.

CHAPTER 20

TWO DAYS AFTER 12:01

"I t feels like I've been gone for weeks," Tyme said as we got situated in the car that had been waiting for us after we got off the plane. "And it's only been days."

We were back on Clampton County soil and back to reality.

"That's what happens when you get dicked down right. You forget your days," I teased, and she slapped me on the arm as she told me to shut up.

Today hadn't been any different than the last day or two.

We woke up, sexed each other down, ordered in breakfast, sexed each other down again, checked out, and then headed to the airport. I thought about doing a road trip back to our city since it was less than five hours away, and that would prolong our time together, but I put back on my real nigga draws and stopped being a simp.

"Two stops, correct?" The driver confirmed as he got into the SUV.

"Yes," I said. "Unless the pretty lady beside me wants to spend one more night with me."

I loved the way Tyme's brown cheeks flushed. Even through her melanin, I could see how flattered she was by the offer but in true Tyme fashion, she held it together. "Nope."

"Ouch," I placed a hand over my heart, and she rolled her eyes as our driver started on the journey to her house.

"Stop being dramatic," she directed my way. "You know that wouldn't be a good idea, especially when we should probably nip things in the bud before they get too far gone. The weekend and 12:01 was fun, but," I wanted to cut off her *but*, but I let her finish, "that's not our reality."

"Right," I said, biting my tongue because I knew she was correct in her thinking.

I had been ignoring the questions in the group chats and calls from my immediate family, but I knew that I couldn't avoid them now that I was back. The only good thing was that Mal's ass was still on his honeymoon, and I didn't have to worry about him just yet.

Either way, I couldn't care less about what anyone thought, as long as they kept the animosity towards me. If they brought it Tyme's way, I already knew I wouldn't handle it well. Yeah, we had both crossed a line, but at the end of the day, I was the only one who owed Mal any kind of loyalty.

Though his ass wasn't deserving of shit.

"I have a question I've been meaning to ask," she said halfway through the drive.

"And you held it? Shocker."

"Shh," she said, her laughter tinkling like wind chimes. "Do you always fly private? Mal never mentioned you having your own plane, and we both know that's not something his competitive ass would have let slide."

I chuckled at her statement until she finished it off with, "Granted, he and I never flew together, so I don't know how he was flying..."

I felt a pang of sadness at the thought of my brother's lackluster relationship with her. Couldn't be me, I refused to let my future partner miss out on the luxuries I could provide.

"Depends on my plans," I replied. "I had to get from the wedding to Chasington County, and commercial flights would've meant layovers, and I'm good on those."

"Ahh okay," she said, giving me a nod of approval. I wasn't one to brag about my wealth like my brother did, but I never hesitated to spend money if it made things more convenient.

"Just to be clear," I added, "I don't actually own the plane."

"Oh, I figured because it was the same crew…" she explained.

"A friend of mine owns it. She lets me rent it from time to time when she's not using it. The pilot and flight attendant are her crew, but I'm cool with the pilot too. He's been teaching me how to fly," I said, watching her eyes widen with surprise. "I thought it'd be a cool hobby. Might impress the ladies." I added a wink for effect.

She kissed her teeth. "Just when I was gonna be nice, you ruined it."

"Gotta keep you on your toes, Sweets," I said with a grin.

Her head shook back and forth. "Of course, you do," she paused before saying, "I do recall you mentioning your love for planes when we first met." A small thrill of pleasure shot through me at her remembering this detail. "But all of this is cool. Thanks for letting me be nosey."

The rest of the ride was quiet, with our hands finding each other's and intertwining as she rested her head on my shoulder. My stomach contracted when we pulled into the driveway of the townhome, and I saw a gray truck parked there. I assumed it belonged to Chenethia, who she had moved in with after her break up.

"I got her bag," I told the driver as he opened the door for her, and I stepped out of the car on my side.

I slung the duffle bag over my shoulder and followed her up the walkway to the front door.

"You're not coming inside," she said as she searched her crossbody bag for her key. "Nene is in there."

"Is that the real reason?" I asked, amused by her evasive statement as she twirled the key around her finger.

"Midnight," she said with an exasperated tone that made me smile because I knew I was getting under her skin. "Stop asking questions you already know the answer to."

"Then I'm right to assume that you won't let me in because you think I'll end up tapping your cervix."

The sheepish look on her face had my dick tingling.

"Okay, goodbye. Have a nice life." She grabbed her bag from me and turned towards the door.

I let out a laugh, stopping her from inserting the key. "I'ma miss fucking with you, Sweets."

"I bet," she said with a roll of her eyes, turning back towards me, and placing the duffle on the ground. My eyes couldn't help but to watch her every movement. How had God made someone as lovely as her?

"*And* fucking you," I continued being a menace.

"Oh my god!" She pushed at my chest.

I licked my lips as flashbacks of our session last night invaded my thoughts. After I had my face buried lovingly between her juicy ass cheeks, it transitioned to me being deep within the depths of her soul. It ended with her sucking mine out of me. By then all of her senses had been returned to her. I thoroughly enjoyed her staring up at me as drool ran down her mouth and my seeds coated the back of her throat.

Afterwards, we cuddled as I checked in with her about her first sensory play experience. I was glad to know she enjoyed it because nothing had been sexier than the way she entrusted me to guide her through that experience. It was a memory I wanted to cherish forever. I definitely saw myself jerking off to the thought of it for years to come.

Yes, years.

"I'm speaking the truth here," I teased.

"Please go back to speaking judgmental bullshit then. I think our truce was over once we landed."

The truce was over the moment you came all over my fingers.

"We both know we can't go back to hating each other," I said.

"We can try," she responded with sass.

"Is that what you really want?" I asked, a rebuttal that also expressed genuine curiosity about her desires. Just because she had said one thing earlier didn't mean it was truly what she wanted.

"Does it matter? We're not going to run into each other or anything," she said dismissively.

"You never know," I countered.

"Whatever you say, Mid," she said, shutting down the conversation. The truth was, our paths didn't often cross. Our circles of friends were separate, and even if they did overlap, she would go out of her way to avoid being in the same place as Mal and Tia. The only place we might run into each other was at my family's wine bar, and I doubted she had plans to visit anytime soon. "Anyway, thanks again for a great weekend and for making sure I didn't catch a charge."

"Trust me, you've thanked me for that well enough," I said, smirking at Tyme. She frowned, her annoyance with me clear on her face. I couldn't help but enjoy it.

"I am so sick of you," she retorted.

I took a step closer to her and placed a finger under her chin, lifting it up slightly. "You're welcome, Tyme," I said, my voice low. I ran my thumb across her cheek as we stared at each other, both of us silent.

"This is getting romantic comedy awkward so…" Tyme said, trying to break the tension between us.

I grinned. "Give me your phone." I held out my hand.

"Why?" she asked, raising an eyebrow.

"For once, be nice to me," I joked.

Tyme smiled and handed over her phone. I quickly added my contact information and sent myself a text before handing it back to her.

"Since you won't give me your number, here's mine," I said, "In case you ever need me to be your fake boyfriend again."

Tyme's face balled up into a playful scowl. "I don't know, it kind of feels like your plan backfired," she said, "I *mean*, look at all this drama you've already caused."

I licked my lips. "*You* wanted him to want you back. Drama was gonna happen."

"True," she agreed, "but how he was acting, Mal gonna come banging on my door once he gets back."

There was an air of playfulness in her tone, but I wished Malachi would pull some stuff like that. "Keep his ass blocked," I told her.

"I will, father."

"Mal will be alright, though," I reassured her, "He'll be in his feelings for a little bit because we made him feel out of control, but that's about it."

"You better be right because I didn't sign up for a stalker," Tyme replied, half-joking.

"If I'm not, promise me you'll let me know," I said, serious now.

"You're the violent twin, aren't you?" she teased.

I frowned. "I'm serious, Tyme."

She softened. "I promise to let you know if he does something wild. But I'm not worried, I know you got me." A small smile played at the corners of her mouth.

"I always do. Now give me a hug so I can go get some rest. Someone's daughter been keeping me up."

She rolled her eyes before walking into my arms. I held her tightly, my senses taking in the familiar scent of her hair, her skin. I knew I had to commit this moment to memory, savoring every second of it. When we eventually pulled away, I placed a gentle kiss on her forehead.

"Thank you for trusting me, Tyme," I said, gazing into her eyes.

"Thank you for being there," she replied, her voice barely above a whisper.

We shared one last kiss before I watched her walk into the house and out of my life. It wasn't easy, but it was the right thing to do. I had to let her go and trust that the future held something better for us both.

CHAPTER 21

I wanted to cry.

I hated that I wanted to cry.

But as soon as the front door closed behind me, my chest tightened, and I felt like I'd lost the love of my life.

However, that didn't make sense.

Midnight *wasn't* the love of my life. He was the person that had come in and reminded me that life could go on after heartache.

That *my* life *should* go on after the bullshit his brother put me through. He showed me how I deserved to be cared for, protected, and sexed.

That's why I thought he was the love of my life.

But he wasn't.

He *couldn't* be.

"Can you really see anything out of the peephole?" My soul left my body as my head whipped around to see my best friend standing a few feet away from me.

I'd come in, dropped my duffle to the side, and was so caught up in my thoughts and feelings that I didn't even realize that Nene and Mo were in the living room. Granted, I'd have to take about three steps from the entryway to see the common areas, and I hadn't left the door.

I was pressed up against it, watching Midnight like a hawk go back to the SUV.

Waiting for it to drive away.

Waiting to be able to breathe again.

"Bitch," I spat, hand still on my chest.

"Not you name calling your bestie who you haven't seen *all* year."

"Please," I sang, walking into her open arms. She engulfed me with one of her comforting hugs that I always loved. They really had come in handy when I was going through it with Malachi.

"You look good, friend," she commented as we broke apart.

"By good she means freshly fu—"

"Simone!" Nene cut across her girlfriend.

"What?" Mo asked, snickering from the couch.

Nene kissed her teeth. "Now you know that was supposed to be my line!"

My mouth dropped open. "I'm going to move out," I lied, plopping my bag back onto my shoulder and heading towards the stairs.

"But you do, though. I like this look on you. Even if the enemy gave it to you."

"Are you done?" I said over my shoulder, not even bothering to look back because I already knew she wasn't too far behind.

"I missed you, friend!" She gave me another hug as we made it upstairs to my room.

Chenethia had truly been Godsent. I sometimes couldn't thank God enough for allowing our paths to cross because I didn't know where I'd be without her. *Probably* back home living with my mom and potentially messing up her newfound happiness with Luke. I definitely didn't want to do that, so I was grateful Nene was so quick to open up her home to me after everything went down. My other friends at the time were also helpful and there for me, in their own way, but Nene was my rider.

I loved her down bad.

"Missed you, too, boo."

I rummaged through my bag and yanked out my charger so I could give my phone some much needed juice. As I stripped out of my clothes and threw on some lounge wear, Nene caught me up on what she and Mo had been up to today before she went back to being my nosey ass bestie.

"So," she sang as I relaxed on my bed, "what happens now that you're back home?"

"Now I figure out how to get my life back on track. Damn near six months of mourning over a relationship that probably wouldn't have lasted is enough."

"That's fucking right. I'm excited for you, Ty. *But,*" she pulled her mouth to the side, "I was actually referring to you and Midnight." She wiggled her brows.

Of course, she was.

"We go back to being Tyme and Midnight— independent of each other. It was fun ruffling feathers, but that's not our reality."

"Hmm," she hummed.

"What?" I eyed her as she rested her head on her fist.

Ever the beauty, Chenethia had a radiant light brown complexion that perfectly complemented her stunning features. Her button nose and big, rosy cheeks added an adorable charm to her face. But it was her vibrant personality that made her a force to be reckoned with, despite her short stature.

"Oh, nothing." It was definitely not nothing. "However," *see.* "I figured since you let the devil's son know where you lay your head, there might be more there. I mean, you did say he dismantled your insides… we don't just give that up."

Completely demolished them.

"We do when it's attached to my ex, drama, and potential bullshit. Besides, good sex isn't hard to find." Well, *good* sex wasn't, however, what I'd had with Midnight definitely was, but she didn't need to know that.

She pursed her lips. "Ion know, sis, the girls on social media be complaining that these men ain't out here slinging it like they used to."

"Please shut up."

We shared a laugh.

"But cool, as long as you're happy, Tyme, and the lick back was worth it, then I'm happy for you." She gave me another hug before leaving me to settle in.

It didn't take long before Midnight was back on my mind. I instinctively reached for my phone. As much as it pained me, I had to let him go. Our reality was harsh and inescapable: he was my ex's brother, we despised each other *(yes, I was back to that)*, and we simply couldn't allow ourselves to fall for one another.

I opened up my text messages and chuckled at what he'd saved his number as: Tin Man.

I clicked on his thread and took a deep breath before typing out one final message:

ME

> I know I've said it before, but one more time won't hurt your ego: Thank you. I truly appreciate everything you've done for me, even if I didn't know I needed it. You're a special person, and I wish you all the best, Tin Man. Have a great year.

I hit send and closed the thread, feeling a sense of closure wash over me. It was time to move on and let go, but I knew I would always cherish the memories of our time together.

SEVEN DAYS AFTER 12:01

"What do you think about a cozy Bohemian vibe?" Nene posed a question, her hand resting on an exquisite wick chair. The piece of furniture was truly striking.

"I see the vision," I said as I sank into the chair. Surprisingly, it was even more comfortable than it looked.

Chenethia had made a career in real estate. She and Mo met in a program teaching them how to buy, rent, and sell mobile homes three years prior. They not only fell in love but also became business partners. Today, we were browsing for decorations for the fourth mobile home they had bought and were renovating.

After Nene found out about my interior design degree, I had hesitantly assisted with the decorating of their third one. It was supposed to help me move on from my *'I'm-supposed-to-be-married-but-got-cheated-on-instead-and-now-he's-marrying-her'* funk back in October, but it didn't. Nonetheless, the experience reminded me of how skilled I was at turning a room into something extraordinary.

As a result, I had become their unofficial mobile home interior decorator or, at the very least, their advisor.

"We could do those airy yellow curtains we saw at Target and then…" I started spewing off things that were coming to mind.

"Gah!" Nene wrapped her arms around me, "You're so good at this, Ty. Mo and I would never be able to pull it together the way you do."

"Aww thanks, Ne." I grinned, feeling like a kid in a candy store as we continued to browse through the overstock warehouse, now that we had a clear theme in mind. I spent the next couple of hours scouring through various items, trying to find the perfect pieces that would bring their vision to life.

After two hours of hunting for treasures, we were ready for a break. We headed to our favorite local café, Lattes & Bagels, and luckily, we arrived early enough to avoid the mid-afternoon rush. I breathed a sigh of relief, knowing I could still snag a poppyseed bagel before they ran out. We settled into a booth, ready to indulge in afternoon snacks and drinks as we basked in the satisfaction of a successful shopping trip.

"Look at you not getting coffee," Nene commented when the barista graciously brought over our drinks. I wasn't a die-hard coffee drinker, but I had my moments. I could go days without it, then suddenly crave four cups in one day. It was weird.

"This tea was calling my name." I savored a sip of the warm beverage, letting out a contented sigh before biting into my poppyseed bagel.

Nene chimed in, "Yeah, that apple cinnamon ginger tea always smells like bliss. Besides, tea is probably better for your throat." A small, mischievous smile played on her lips, and I narrowed my eyes suspiciously.

"Why'd you say that?" I asked, taking another bite of my bagel.

"Because of the way you were screaming Midnight's name in the middle of the night." My mouth dropped open at her sentence. I didn't even care that I hadn't finished chewing the food inside. "I'm honestly surprised your vocal cords are still intact." She chuckled, biting into her slice of banana bread.

"Oh my god, you heard me?" I was sure the blood was draining from my face. "Why weren't you sleep?"

"Can I not get thirsty in the middle of the night?"

"I was not *that* loud," I said through gritted teeth.

Nene looked at me out of the corner of her eyes as she sipped her coffee. "Chile, I had to check outside for a stranger's car because I almost thought he was in there literally dicking you down. But apparently, it was just you and *Kofi*."

I would like to disappear now, God.

Kofi was the name of my dildo. Aptly named after Kofi Siriboe—no explanation needed.

"Were you trying to manifest the nigga?" she continued.

"Please, Chenethia!"

She burst out laughing. "It's a valid question. You said his name so many times, I thought you were trying to conjure him up out of thin air."

Take me out of my misery, God.

I leaned onto the table and whispered, "I don't wanna talk about this *in public*."

"Girl, bye. Ain't nobody paying us no mind."

Palming my forehead, I said, "I need a new best friend."

She grinned, "I'm not abandoning my role, so good luck with that."

I rolled my eyes as I savored my drink. She made me so sick.

It was not even the fact that she had heard me pleasing myself. It was that she'd heard me *saying* his name like he was the Candyman. Because no matter how much I'd tried in the last five days, I couldn't stop thinking about Midnight Drayton.

Thoughts of him, and his premium dick, consumed me, and for the past three (of the five) days, I found myself needing to masturbate in order to get some kind of relief. Each orgasm gave me a two to four hour mental break from wondering about him and how he was doing post 12:01.

Correction— post our time together.

Despite receiving a response to the text I sent when we got back, I refused to initiate any further contact. Instead, I simply liked his response and left it at that.

I had to detox him.

Nene reached across the table and placed her hand over mine, interrupting my thoughts. "Real talk," she said, "you've been different since you got back, Tyme." I pulled back slightly, not sure where this was going. "In a good way," she quickly added. "Like, the happy version of you. It's good to see. But," she hesitated, "you've also had this air of sadness around you."

I tried to deny it, insisting that I was fine and felt better than I had in months. And it was true — thanks to 12:01 and Midnight, I felt a shift in my mental state over the last few days. I woke up feeling excited about my days, started working out *(okay I only worked out once)*, and had only felt the urge to log into my fake social media accounts to spy on Malachi and Tia a few times.

But even with those urges, I hadn't given in.

That alone felt like a victory, especially considering that just a week ago, I was checking their accounts (and their friends' accounts) at least once a day. It was a disease that had consumed me.

Now, though, after getting what I *needed* thanks to Midnight— I felt like a weight had been lifted off of me, and I was ready to figure out how to get my life back on track.

"But I feel amazing," I protested. "I'm smiling, energized, and I haven't even thought about sending you screenshots of those two idiots."

Nene nodded, acknowledging the positive changes she had seen in me. "I didn't know what to expect when you said you were ready to get your life back on track, but whatever Midnight did, it's working. I don't think it's just the sex, though. I think you miss him, and that's where the sadness comes from."

"I don't miss him," I said quickly, hoping to convince myself more than Nene.

"You don't have to lie to me, Ty. You know I'm always team you. It's okay if y'all's truce *revealed* the truth."

"You thought you ate with that sentence, huh?"

She playfully shrugged as she finished off her snack. "And did, but don't try and change the subject."

"I'm not. We spent seventy-two hours together, Ne. I miss the idea of him because I got used to him being around, aggravating me." Despite my words, I couldn't shake off the feeling that Nene might be right.

"Or you miss him because the feelings you both had suppressed, since y'all had to, came crashing back with a vengeance."

I rolled my eyes. "Or you're reaching."

"Am I, though?" Nene tapped her chin. "You liked him from the beginning. Remember how you said the chemistry between y'all was insane from the moment y'all matched on that dating app? But then he messed it up. Once you started dating fuckboy, *I* think y'all only started hating each other because it pushed you further away from one another and forced any lingering feelings away. But last weekend, there was nothing but space and opportunity, and we know how that went."

"Yeah, we had lots of sex. End of story," I shrugged, trying to dismiss Nene's analysis. But the truth was, her words had struck a chord. I hated to admit, there was an immense part of me that missed Midnight.

"*Sure, Jan,*" she said, quoting one of her favorite memes from *The Brady Bunch*.

I rubbed my temples, trying to ignore the gnawing feeling in my gut. "Chenethia, you know why Midnight and I won't work. He's my ex-fiancé's brother, for goodness' sake. We can't just ignore that."

Nene gave me a knowing look. "I know, I know. But you can't deny there's something there. You wouldn't be this defensive if there wasn't."

I thought because she hadn't brought up my former arch nemesis since the day I got back, she'd wholeheartedly believed what I'd said before and I was scot-free from any more interrogation. I see she was just waiting for me to slip up.

"It would be a constant uphill battle for us. Any feelings I *might* have for him, will run their course soon enough."

Her face lit up at me giving into the truth. At least kind of. I wouldn't admit aloud that I was indeed enamored with Midnight Drayton.

"Well, you might wanna stop calling out his name during solo sexy time if you want that to happen."

I tossed a balled-up napkin at her. "You are a menace."

"Yet, you and Mo both still keep me around." She shrugged and I shook my head, finishing off the last of my food and drink. "And Tyme," she said, after she downed the rest of her coffee, "some battles are worth the war if the result means the best and happiest version of you."

CHAPTER 22

"We've got the Foster wedding and the Painted Lady event this Saturday. Mal's covering the wedding, and you're handling the makeup event at the wine bar."

As my dad went over things I already knew, I nodded along, letting him do his thing. Marcus Drayton was a hands-on CEO, and at sixty-one years old, he wasn't ready to give up the reins just yet. Malachi had been ass-kissing him for years, hoping to take over the business, but I didn't think that was going to happen anytime soon. My dad loved what he'd created, and he was determined to make sure it didn't go awry.

He still handled a lot of the major events, even though Mal or I could have done it. The business was his baby, and he never wanted to lose that family aspect that made it so special.

It wasn't until this past year that he'd finally stepped back a little. That was mostly because my mom complained about wanting to enjoy the fruits of their labor while they were still healthy and didn't have any grandchildren to run around after.

That was definitely shade being thrown at my siblings and me since we were all in our thirties, still kid-free, and living our best lives. My sister had already broken my mom's heart on multiple occasions about not wanting kids, so now she had to depend on me and Mal to give them to her.

Now that his whack ass had a whole wife, I knew it wouldn't be long before they finally got their first grandchild.

"I spoke with Shon from the Painted Lady, and they want the Double-Barreled Cab to be served first, followed by Pinot..."

The mention of Tyme's favorite wine immediately took my mind out of business mode and into a sunken place of thoughts about her. It was both amusing and disheartening to realize that I knew her preferences even when she had never explicitly shared them with me. My subconscious had paid closer attention to her than I had ever consciously realized, and now those little details resurfaced at the most inconvenient moments, like this one.

We hadn't spoken since the day I dropped her off at home, and that was exactly a week ago. Every day since, I had to talk myself out of sending 'just checking on you' texts.

Everything about her was on my mind constantly, from her laughter that filled the room, to her quick wit and the way her eyebrows furrowed when she was annoyed with me. I couldn't shake the memory of her scent, the way it lingered on my clothes long after she was gone. Even her endless curiosity and the way she answered my questions with more questions was missed. But most of all, it was the way being near her made everything feel right, like we were meant to be together. The comfort of her presence and the effortless companionship we shared made me realize just how deeply I cared for her. It was like there was a hole in my chest that I couldn't fill, no matter how much work I threw myself into.

I'd be lying if I said I didn't know there was a chance of everything going left from the moment I invited her to leave Gavensfall with me. But I thought I'd have a better handle on my feelings for her. I thought I could fight them. Instead, I found myself drowning in everything I felt for her. It was as if I was being held underwater — and even though I had a life jacket on — I still couldn't stay afloat.

When she and Mal were together, I did my best to suppress the feelings that had been brewing inside me and convinced myself that I was just infatuated with the version of her that I had created in my mind. I had built this idea of her based on our initial interactions and what I saw through the lens of my brother.

However, I had miscalculated just how timeless she truly was. After experiencing her fully, I couldn't imagine a life without her. In such a short time, I had never wanted to know someone as deeply as I wanted to know her.

All I wanted to do was get my Doctorate in Tyme Henley.

I needed her to stay in my life. I needed to make her happy, to see the real her — not the version that Malachi had molded her into. How could I let her go when all I wanted was to be near her, to protect her, and to give her what she deserved?

My mind kept flitting between us fussing outside of the precinct to us fucking anywhere we could. It was almost unbelievable how quickly we had let our guards down with each other, revealing more than I'm sure either one of us ever intended.

I tried to convince myself that it was purely physical, but I knew deep down that my attraction to her was about much more than just sex. Her confidence, her beauty, and her soul had all drawn me in, and the more time we spent together, the more I found myself opening up to her in ways I never had before.

She listened to me without judgment and offered comfort and support without even realizing I needed it. Even though I was over my ex, hearing Tyme tell me that I was worthy of love and more than a guy who was just good for delivering elite dick made me want to give her everything I could.

With Tyme, it was easy to be vulnerable because I knew my secrets were safe with her. It wasn't just women who craved security; men needed it too, at least I did.

Now without her presence, I felt lost.

Unbalanced.

Trapped under water.

I hated it.

I thought what I'd felt after my breakup with Veronica sucked — and it did — but it was true what the old heads and those Shakespearean dudes said: 'It's better to have loved and lost than to never loved at all'.

Tyme and I had only just begun, and it was the "what ifs" of what we could be that hurt the most.

Suddenly, the sound of tapping snapped me back to the present.

"Aye, you heard me?" I blinked a few times and my eyes landed on my dad knocking his water bottle on the desk to get my attention.

The word 'huh?' tumbled out of my mouth before I quickly said, "Yeah."

"What you over there thinking about?" He eyed me with genuine concern.

"The event," I lied, and I knew *he knew* I was lying. "I heard everything you said. Everything will be ready and good to go for Saturday."

"Yeah, it better be." He paused as if he was contemplating his next words. "I know you and your brother got whatever mess happening between you two, but I ain't ya mama... I'm not about to get in the middle of it as long as it don't interfere with the business."

Today was the first time I'd seen anyone in my immediate family because I had still been avoiding them as if I owed them money. Not because I was scared to face them, but because I needed to mentally prepare myself for what was to come. Especially my mom, who had been sending me daily Bible verses ever since she saw the photos of Tyme and me in the family group chat.

The photos I'd posted of us on my social media stories were suggestive, but besides the chemistry that bounced between us in the pictures, nobody could say for sure if we'd actually crossed a line.

My mom assumed the worst because that was in her nature, and not answering any questions about the accusations probably didn't help.

"It won't," I assured him. This was personal; we knew better than to let it interfere with the money.

"Good. But just so I can tell Kinley I did my due diligence, what the hell were you thinking, son? You were only supposed to get that girl out of jail, not screw her."

Deep sigh, here we go.

"Just because we were together don't mean we had sex."

"You take me for a fool?" He leaned back in his chair.

"I thought you were staying out of it."

"I am."

"I don't know why everybody tryna act like Mal some fuckin' saint and didn't just marry someone he cheated on Tyme with the night before *their* wedding."

"Your brother messed up, and I already told him karma would come back around for what he did. I don't think he thought it'd come back in the form of *you*, though." Before I could interrupt, he continued, "I know you slept with her. The way you're defending her now and the way you came to her defense after the wedding shenanigans tells me everything I need to know."

"If you think we were messing aroun—"

He raised his palms in a placating gesture. "I'm not implying that. What I'm saying is that whatever feelings you have for her ain't just pop up overnight."

I slumped in my seat, letting out a defeated sigh. "It wasn't supposed to go down like this, pops." There was no point in hiding the truth.

"You don't think I know that? The problem is, it did, and now yo' mama acting like she so stressed. Now I gotta take her spoiled ass to Zanzibar next month because y'all keep "embarrassing the family"." I couldn't contain my smirk at him mocking my mom.

Kinley Drayton was big on appearances, and I had no doubt that she was already the talk of her wealthy wives' circle of friends *once again*, thanks to the wedding fiasco. My mother had already endured the scandal of her son cheating on his fiancée and getting married to his *home wrecker* in the span of a year. But if news got out that I was entertaining Malachi's ex-fiancée — the same one who had tried to ruin the wedding — I could only imagine the kind of gossip that would spread. And that was on top of the occasional criticisms they already had about my sister for simply being "too much of a free spirit", according to them.

The funny thing was, my mom would also tell those ladies to go fuck themselves if they did too much, but she preferred to keep the peace and not show the side of her who grew up adjacent to the hood.

"You know I don't like them long ass flights," my dad continued, "and y'all drama coming into my relationship and wreaking havoc got me having to give in to Kinley."

"Mom was gonna get that Zanzibar trip out of you for Valentine's Day anyway. Don't try to blame me."

He sucked his teeth, "I'm blaming somebody."

I let out a laugh and so did he.

"Anyway," he went back to getting me together, "you and Mal have always had your differences, but I know you wouldn't intentionally do some backstabbing shit like this. You've always been more logical like me. We think things through and weigh out the consequences of our actions, so it goes without question that Tyme is worth whatever flack is coming your way. However, blood is blood and I expect you to fix this ASAP, so yo' mama don't drive me crazy."

"Fix it how? I'm not apologizing."

"That's that stubborn shit you get from Kinley. The bro code wasn't invented by your generation. It ain't ever been cool to sleep with a friend or family member's ex behind their back—especially if y'all plan to be together."

"That's the thing, pops, we don't."

He folded his arms across his chest. "So, you caused all this ruckus not to even be together? Y'all young folk are something else. Raising my wife's blood pressure just for some *trim*."

"It's not like that." I refrained from snapping on my dad because I didn't want him, or anyone else, to think all I wanted was to smash Tyme.

"Well if it's not, it sure do seem like it, but like I said, I'm not getting in the middle of it."

"Right," I said with a half-smile, calling out his bullshit. I stood to my feet. "I'ma head out. I'll see you later, pops."

"Don't forget Sunday dinner."

Shit, I thought, scratching at the side of my face. My mom always hosted family dinners or brunch every third Sunday of the month. Since the first Sunday of the year was on New Year's Day, it threw off my internal calendar, and I thought I had one more Sunday before I had to face that lady.

I rubbed my throat. "I think I'm coming down with something."

"Yeah, an ass whooping if you don't show up, but that's between you and the woman who brought you into this world."

"Just gon' leave me hanging like that?"

"You damn skippy." He came around his desk to give me a hug. "I love you, son. Think about how you can fix this shit."

"I'll try. Love you, too."

As I stepped out of my dad's office, his words echoed in my mind. Fixing things was easier said than done.

Fifteen minutes later, I was still sitting in the parking lot, lost in thought about my situation when my phone sent me a notification. Pole_N_Pour was live. I clicked on it, and my social media app opened to reveal my sister's live video.

Mickie had three loves in life—wine, pole dancing, and gossiping. To her surprise, she found a niche that catered to all three when she gained over a million followers on a popular short-form video platform. As a lifestyle influencer, her content revolved around her pole dancing, sipping wine while telling stories, and promoting sponsored products.

A lot of the wine companies that she had brand deals with were also companies who ended up being wines we sold in our bars.

Her pole dancing and love for strip clubs was why my mom's friends tended to think she was too much of a free spirit.

"… y'all they really started fighting in the middle of the stage. Do y'all know how hard it is to fight with stripper heels on?!"

I shook my head as I sent a comment.

usermindmybusiness:
i'm on my way over.

Before she even noticed the comment, a few others had to say something.

blaxkrosexx:
Oop who inviting himself into your space.

toytalkstoyou:
Look at @usermindmybusiness trying to get on.

sip_then_read:
Mickie you got a man and ain't giving us the tea?

"Y'all chill, that's my brother. If you coming, bring me some food. I'm starving."

confidentleeme:
Which brother? The one who wedding got fucked up by his crazy ex? Or the one with the tats?

authorbriyannamichelle:
The whole family so fine. Adopt me.

settieb77:
The one with the tats can break my spine for free.

usermindmybusiness:
text me what you want fathead

moniecedejon:
Can we get a story time about the wedding? I want firsthand tea!!

"No y'all can't get no story time. I already said that last time I was on. I'm not talking about things I don't have permission to talk about. *And* don't be in my comments calling my brother's ex crazy, you don't know that girl."

sip_then_read:
Okay but which brother sis?

maggiesuniversee:
@sip_then_read Aren't they twins? I would take both.

shontheauthor:
it's probably the short one -_-

confidentleeme:
Not you tryna defend the crazies.

"And you're blocked," Mickie said, and I knew she meant that. "Bro, I'll text you in one sec." She sent me what she wanted and went back to her story time, and I closed out of the app.

By the time I made it to her spot, she was still on live. I placed her food within her reach and headed to the couch to dig into the wings I'd gotten.

"Now y'all know he's not finna get on live, so that should tell you which brother…"

I tuned her out and started watching a random episode of *The Fresh Prince of Bel Air* to pass the time. I was halfway through another episode when Mickie said, "Not you tryna steal 'problem child' away from me."

I hadn't realized she'd wrapped up her live until she plopped down next to me. Partially because, though I had been watching TV, my mind was doing that thing it did where it kept replaying scenes from my weekend together with Tyme.

I couldn't shake her. *Everything* somehow reminded me of her. Watching *Fresh Prince* took me back to our post sex conversation where we talked about the most random things and binged snacks.

Seeing Mickie reminded me of us sitting on the beach and her sharing with me what her tattoo meant.

Everything.

"Don't start," I said, getting up to toss my trash.

"You knew I would before you even decided to come to my house, so don't even start acting brand new just because you haven't seen me since the wedding *and* since you started all this drama."

I clearly was in the mood to be tortured because I *did* know she'd start her bullshit and apparently, the conversation with my dad wasn't enough for the day.

"In my defense," she said as I came back to the couch, "I didn't even text you trying to get the tea. I deserve a thanks for that."

"A thanks you won't get."

"Asshole."

"Yo' mama."

"I'ma tell her you said that too." She stuck her tongue out at me. "She already mad at you for starting all this drama within the family; you might get told to go pick a switch." Mickie laughed at her own statement.

"I ain't start shit."

My sister contorted her face at me, her expression showcasing the high cheekbones inherited from our mother. Mickie was a shade lighter than me and Malachi, matching our dad's skin tone, but her skin was still a beautiful rich brown color. Her deep dimples accentuated her contagious smile, and her eyes, much like Mal's, were a softer hazel color that they'd both inherited from our maternal grandmother.

"I didn't. All I did was *help* give your brother a taste of his own medicine."

"Mhmm," she sang, "anyway, cut the crap. Did y'all or didn't y'all?" She dropped her chin into her neck, raising her brow. "I've been waiting all week to hear this in person."

"I'm actually about to head out." I pretended to get up.

"Diamond is right under this couch. Play with yo' mama, don't play with me."

"You think that weak aim of yours scare me?" I joked. Diamond was her Glock 43X and despite what I'd said, her aim was anything but weak. She had dated a sharpshooter for two years, and he'd taught her a lot about guns and how to use them.

"I bet you don't get up though."

"Shut up," I said with a chuckle.

"Now spill, you know I live for twin drama."

I moved my head from side to side. "We did but—"

"NOPE! *No buts,*" she jumped up and down on the couch, "no wonder Mal is losing his shit! I can't believe y'all really did!" She continued to bounce as she gripped my bicep like a giggly schoolgirl.

I explained to her the same thing I'd told my dad, that this wasn't supposed to happen. But unlike my dad, my sister wanted every little detail.

"So, like who came on to who?" she pressed, her hands fluttering in the air, urging me to continue.

"Calm down, fathead," I chuckled.

She huffed dramatically, giving me an impatient look. "If I had some weed, I'd be a lot more patient, but I don't. So, hurry up and give me all the deets."

Giving into her request, I told her how everything went down from the precinct to the truce and how shit hit the fan after some flirting at a New Year's Eve event.

Mickie knew that I tended to spend New Year's Eve with Neo, but even though she was a grown ass woman, she didn't know anything about 12:01, and as far as Neo, Mal, and I were concerned, she never would.

"Have you always had feelings for her…?" Her eyes glistened in anticipation, locked in on me.

"I gotta tell you something." I slowly rubbed my hands together.

"Oh, my goodness, there's more?" She pressed her pointer and middle fingers against her temple. "I *definitely* need weed for this." She re-adjusted her position on the couch, waiting for me to drop the bomb, which was how Tyme and I actually met and where my feelings stemmed from. Outside of Mal and Tyme, no one else had been let in on that information, and up until six months ago, I thought no one else ever would.

"So technically, Mal took Tyme from you and then had the audacity to cheat on her. *Thennn* you and Tyme decided to be on some petty get back shit TOGETHER — literally. Ohhh, this is MESSY and I'm living for it."

"Mal didn't take her from me, I let him have her beca—"

"Because you were an idiot."

Facts. "I'ma let you have that."

"Because I'm right. Either way, I'm living for it because in my eyes, Tyme pulled one of the ultimate lick backs. She slept with her ex's twin brother. Y'all shared a fucking womb! That's a bad bitch right there."

She wagged her pointer finger. "I knew I always liked her. My internet besties would love this."

My eyes narrowed. "You better not."

She kissed her teeth. "Now you know I won't, I'm just saying they'd eat this story up! Anyway, you know I don't play favorites. I love you and Mal, so I'm always gonna keep it a hundred with you both. You're kinda foul for what you did because that's your blood, *yet* I can't be mad at you about it because Mal was fucked up for cheating on her with Tia."

I nodded in agreement before she continued.

"I already know if a dude would have did that to me, y'all would have beat his ass and I would have shot him. And don't let it have been a girl who had been *keke-ing* in my face for the entirety of my relationship— oh, they both would have been sharing a casket while I was sitting pretty in prison being someone's bitch."

I shook my head. "Your violent ass."

"That's what happens when you grow up with brothers and boy cousins." She shrugged.

"Touché." Mickie got roughed up a lot growing up. It was all in love, though.

"This was already elite drama; however, this gets juicier knowing you *been* had feelings for her. What you gon' do about that?"

"Nothing."

"What do you mean nothing? Are you really cool with just letting things go?"

"That's what she wants and for obvious reasons, it's probably for the best. Us being together will cause too many problems."

"Shit, the problems already here, might as well see it through. Don't punk out now—especially since it's giving S-N-E."

"S-N-E?" I reiterated.

"Sad nigga energy."

"Fuck off, McKinley."

She cackled. "It is, though! Them big ass eyes of yours are snitching on you, big bro."

"Chill out," I spoke with a tinge of frustration in my voice.

"You already let her get away once, you really gonna do that again?"

"What do you suggest then Mickie? She's still Mal's ex."

"Yes, the ex *whom* he cheated on, with a person who was supposed to be his family! *And*, let's not forget Tia was pregnant at the wedding, and yet, he still would have married Tyme knowing he had a baby on the way with his side piece. Your brother ain't shit."

A hard truth that I hated to know made my blood simmer, and I silently prayed that Tyme would never find out.

Malachi and Tia's engagement, only five weeks after he and Tyme broke up, was something Mickie and I couldn't wrap our heads around.

We decided to have a sibling intervention.

Despite me and Mal's differences, it didn't sit right with me that he'd moved on so quickly with Tia. He had already admitted to us that they had been messing around for years, but he conveniently left out the pregnancy part.

During the intervention, Malachi confessed he found out that Tia was six weeks pregnant the night before his wedding. She had threatened to abort the baby if he went ahead with marrying Tyme.

To Tia's delight, the wedding didn't happen, and she kept the baby.

Unfortunately, she lost it a month later.

After her miscarriage, Tia went into a depressive state and was afraid that Mal was going to leave her and get back with Tyme. To appease her and ensure her that he was where he wanted to be, he asked her to marry him.

It all came off as very manipulative behavior, but that was none of my business.

I had always treated Tia like family and genuinely loved her. However, as we entered our thirties, her conniving, sneaky, and manipulative behavior began to show more often. Initially, I didn't pay much attention to it since it didn't impact me directly. But when she and Mal fucked Tyme over, my perspective changed. I couldn't overlook her actions anymore and decided to keep my distance. Although we remained cordial, the bond we once shared was no longer the same.

"Love him to death," Mickie continued, "but I know a trash ass man when I see one. I truly hope he's better to Tia than he was to Tyme."

"With the way he's been so worried about me and Sweets, I doubt it."

Not that Tia was innocent in this; they both better watch out for karma.

"Which she clearly has no clue about," Mickie sighed. "She called me the other day gushing about all the things they'd been doing on their honeymoon, but I think she really wanted to see what info I had on you and Tyme. She asked me if I had seen your post."

I absentmindedly twirled my thumb around the edge of my nose ring, thinking about how I hadn't even thought to check if she'd seen it.

"I told her yeah," Mickie said, crossing her arms and smirking, "and before she could even ask, I told her I didn't have a clue what was going on. Then I flipped it back on her and asked her if Mal knew anything."

"Of course your petty ass did," I chuckled, shaking my head.

"She said Mal was unbothered by it," Mickie continued, rolling her eyes, "and that Tyme clearly is just looking for attention once again since she couldn't ruin their day."

"Wow," I hummed, letting my voice trail off slightly, my eyebrows lifting in mock surprise.

"They both delusional," my sister said through giggles. "I guess that's why they belong together."

"We gon' see," I said, clapping my hands together and rubbing them eagerly.

"We are, but don't think just because we got on the subject of Tia that I missed the fact that you gave Tyme a pet name!"

I ran my hands down my face as I sucked my teeth. Of course, she didn't miss that with her aggravating ass. *Who created sisters?* "This why I can't tell you shit."

"You didn't tell me, you let it slip because you done caught feelings for your brother's *exxxxxx*!" she sang, having too much fun at the expense of all the mayhem in my life.

"Are you done?"

"I will be once you tell me you're gonna do something about it because I'm a firm believer that love is not something we can control. How y'all got into the situation was messy, but at this point, you might as well go the distance."

"Hol' up, love is a stretch." I cocked an eyebrow, and she squinted her eyes at me.

"You don't have to be *in* love with her to love her. You care for her; you want to keep her safe and protected… that's a big deal. We also both know you couldn't care less about what kind of chaos this could cause, but you're putting your feelings aside out of consideration for her. Which I," she placed her hand on her chest, "love. Nevertheless, if you think she's your person, you gotta convince her that it's worthwhile and fuck what everybody else has to say about it."

"You must like stressing out moms," I replied, a wry tone in my voice. Because there was no way in hell my mother would be okay with me dating her *almost* daughter-in-law. I don't think she ever cared for Tyme. She tolerated her, sure, and was kind to her, but I could tell she never really warmed up to her, not in the way you'd hope your mother would for your future wife. I think it had a lot to do with the fact that she secretly always wanted Mal and Tia to end up together.

"Absolutely not. She blames me enough for her high blood pressure. I'm looking at it from the perspective of Mal got the girl that he wanted, so he can't be mad about you getting the one he lost out on. And Kinley will just have to deal with that. It's the circle of *brotherly* love or something like that."

I shook my head at her antics. There was a lot of truth in what she'd said. Ninety-eight percent of me didn't give a fuck, and if it was up to me, I'd be somewhere loving on Tyme at this very second, basking in the magical way she smelled, stealing kisses from her, cracking jokes that would have her side eyeing me or playfully threatening my life, and just being in her presence.

And of course, munching on her essence.

But then there was the remaining two percent that *did* care about how this made my brother feel, even though he wasn't deserving of that grace. However, we were still blood, and if Tyme and I did move forward, we would eventually need to clear the air.

On top of that, I kept wondering if I was being selfish for wanting more with Tyme, knowing how this could affect her.

All the thoughts put me in a state of stagnation. Yet, the conversations with my dad and Mickie had me realizing one thing: I was scared.

This wasn't just anybody. This was me getting a second chance with the woman I thought was the one I let get away. And if I was going to go for it, I couldn't fuck it up. However, what if I still wasn't the man for her?

That thought played in the back of my mind more often than I liked to admit.

What if we risk it all and everything blows up in our faces? Or worse, she sees why my ex said what she said?

I was afraid I might not live up to the man Tyme deserved.

"Ready for the million-dollar question?" my sister sang, resting her head on my shoulder before tugging on my goatee.

"Shoot."

"How are you finna get your girl?"

CHAPTER 23

ELEVEN DAYS AFTER 12:01

"**M**o's here early," I said to Chenethia when the doorbell rang.

Nene's face balled up. "Since when do you know Mo to ever ring the doorbell or be up before nine? That's not her. Are *you* expecting someone?"

"No," I mumbled as we both shuffled towards the front door. The small screen above the house alarm showed someone standing with flowers in hand. I smiled, knowing Mo was spoiling my friend again. "Aww," I sang as Nene opened the door and greeted the person.

"I have a delivery for Tyme Henley."

My body stalled. Nene's head turned towards me as if it was on a swivel, and then her chin dipped as her mouth formed into a Cheshire grin.

I raised my hand like I was a meek little girl. The delivery guy handed me the stunning bouquet of yellow Tulips and an accompanying card while Nene scribbled a signature on his pad.

"Please tell me those are from *our* new bestie," Nene squealed as we returned to the kitchen.

"Not you calling that man our *bestie*."

"Enemy just doesn't fit anymore, and you know why. Now open the card." She moved her hand swiftly in a circle, motioning for me to hurry up.

I wanted to rip open the card, but I didn't want to seem so damn pressed. It had been nine days since we last spoke (not that I was counting), and I still hadn't detoxed him. If this was a twelve-step program, I was still at step zero.

I don't know how this day usually goes for you, but I thought it'd be nice for you to get some serenity in your life to honor your sister on her birthday. I booked a spa day for you and Ne at the Ritz at ten-thirty. If y'all can't go, let me know and I'll reschedule it. I hope this brings you some peace today, Sweets. ~TM

"Oh my god, what did it say?" Nene asked, coming closer and wrapping her arms around me. It wasn't until that moment that I realized I was crying.

Bawling.

We stayed like that for a moment before we finally broke apart, and I handed her the card to read. I couldn't read it again.

Grief fucking sucks.

It was my sister's birthday, and he remembered. He had no clue how this day tended to affect me; yet, he cared enough to make sure I had a good day regardless. Why in the hell was he so good to me?

Why would God make him like this knowing he was off limits?

Knowing that we *needed* to stay away from each other.

Knowing that my coochie and heart were already struggling as is and then he popped back up like this?

On days like this, I never knew how grief would hit me. It had been twenty years since my sister passed away, but some days were still tough.

This morning when I talked to my mom, we chatted about how we each imagined how twenty-six-year-old Serenity would be. Even though I was young when she died, I remembered so much about her, and I couldn't help but wonder what life would be like if she was still here with me.

In my alternate universe where my sister was alive and well, I pictured her as a fashion icon or designer because she had always loved playing in my mom's clothes and dressing up her Barbie dolls. She also loved to draw, even though she wasn't that good at it yet.

I had always thought we would grow up together, and now I felt like a part of me was always missing.

"Wow. This is," Nene wagged the card back and forth, "...this is thoughtful. Damnit," she huffed, "I like him."

A light snort escaped my lips. "Very thoughtful." I sucked in a deep breath of air and then let it out. "How do I thank him?"

"I mean, I'm thinking spectacular head, sitting on his face, riding his dick... stop me when you disagree."

I was staring at her in disbelief.

"I recently heard about this *Fruit Roll-Up around the D* thing and—"

"Chenethia!!!"

She kissed her teeth. "I guess a text or call could work too. If you wanna go the safe route."

I shook my head at her and instead of pulling out my phone to text him, I finished off my breakfast before it got too cold.

Some people might call that stalling.

"We *are* going, right?" Nene asked, grabbing my plate to wash.

"Oh, absolutely."

I pulled my mouth to the side as I put on my big girl panties and sent the text.

ME

> Thank you for the flowers. They're beautiful. And the spa day... we're going to go. Nene said thank you as well.

He responded almost immediately.

TIN MAN

You're welcome. How are you mentally doing today?

> Your note made me cry :(but overall I'm good. The spa day will definitely help.

Good. I'm happy to hear that.

> How are you?

I wanted to ask him how things were between him, Mal, and his family, but I knew he'd sugarcoat it regardless.

I'm straight.

> Just straight?

I set myself up asking that question.

I miss you, Sweets.

Breathing slowed.

I want to see you.

Breathing non-existent.

Let me take you out tomorrow night.

Flatlined.

And I stayed dead because like a punk ass heaux, I left him on read.

When Nene and I arrived at the Ritz's spa resort almost two hours later, I was still pondering over what to reply. But I pushed that aside, knowing that Midnight had gone out of his way to ensure our relaxation and enjoyment. And he didn't disappoint.

With the custom spa package he'd booked for us, we were free to choose up to three services each. He had even arranged for a credit for food and drinks.

I started my spa day with a detoxifying sea water bath, followed by an eighty-minute bamboo massage, recommended by the receptionist. She assured me it was a healing treatment designed to relieve deep tension throughout the body, and she was right.

Leaving the massage room, I felt a sense of complete wellness, calmness, and positivity. I was still on a high when Nene found me later, lounging poolside in a cabana.

"How was your massage?" I asked her as she approached.

"Girl," she squealed, "I think I'm going to dump Mo for my masseuse. The problem is, he don't even like coochie, but we can figure it out. I'm sure his hands know how to give out happy endings."

I erupted in laughter. "Ma'am!"

"Listen," she sang, "that man hands were out of this world. I feel as loose as I'm acting." She wiggled her body for emphasis before sitting down next to me. "Did you already order?"

"I was waiting for you," I said, handing her the menu for the onsite café.

The Ritz-Carlton spa in Clampton County was among the best in the country. It was located in Willow Grove, an inner ring suburb of Southgate. The spa was massive and almost felt like a separate destination. In only three hours, I felt like I was on a wellness retreat, worlds away from the outside world. The spa offered incredible treatment areas, as well as other amenities like a salon, barbershop, café, garden, and lap pool.

She cheesed. "You love me."

"And do."

After we ordered our food, we chatted about the spa treatments we'd gotten so far and what we were doing after we relaxed for a little and ate.

"Not to be nit-picky," she said, dipping a chip into the side of guacamole. "But I don't recall Sir Cheater ever doing anything like this for *us*."

"He paid for our Disney World girls trip last year for my birthday," I reminded her as I mixed together the ingredients of my Acai power bowl.

"That was a trip you and him were supposed to go on and because he couldn't go, due to work, I got lucky."

I almost forgot those facts.

"Who knows if he really had to *work*." I rolled my eyes and then immediately took a deep breath in. I was not about to let my mind go there. "But let's not talk about him."

"We definitely should not, but I thought it'd make it easier to segue into talking about our new bestie without you biting my head off."

"Stop calling him that."

"Don't be mad at me because you've made me team Midnight. Let's not forget, because of him I just had the best massage of my life." I shook my head at my best friend. "Anyway, how did that 'thank you' conversation with him go?"

"Not bad except for the fact that he asked to take me out tomorrow night."

Nene leaned away from me dramatically. "And what did you say?"

I finished chewing the food I had in my mouth before I spilled the tea that I already knew Chenethia wouldn't be happy about.

"You left that man on read after he paid for us to be here, Tyme?!"

"This is why I didn't tell you."

"Because you know you're in the wrong?" she asked before taking a bite of her sandwich.

"I'm going to respond eventually, but what do I even say to that?"

"Yes or no. It's not rocket science, babe."

"It's not that simple, Ne."

"What if it *is* that simple, and you're *choosing* to make it hard? I already said my piece. You deserve to be happy. I think you should lean into happiness, especially after the shitty year you had. If you miss him, tell him. If you want to see him, see him. If you want him to take you out, let the man take you out."

I heard her, but that didn't mean I had an answer for Midnight.

"And maybe if you see him, you'll give *Kofi* a break for at least one night."

"You are such a bitch." I playfully frowned.

"A cute bitch, get it right. Either way, the worst that can happen, in my opinion, has already happened and that's Malachi finding out. But do we even care about Mal's feelings? Last time I checked, *we* don't." She looked down at her phone as she finished the rest of her food. "Anyway, I gotta head back in for my mani-pedi. The last thing I'm going to say on this is do what's best for Tyme. See you in a bit."

Who would have thought that I'd miss the days when Midnight Drayton and I hated each other? It was so much easier to despise him than to feel like I'd lost a part of myself without him — a piece I never even knew was missing until we went from enemies to lovers.

I had tried so hard to stay away from him, knowing that it was the *right* thing to do. Our relationship was supposed to be temporary, a mere fling. Falling for my ex fiancé's twin brother was never part of the plan.

The next two hours were spent indulging in a luminous facial followed by a nap in the tranquility room. I wasn't sure if it was the binaural beats or the culmination of the entire spa day, but by the time we were back in the changing room getting dressed to leave, I had a newfound clarity about what I wanted to do.

All I needed was a lot of courage.

As Nene did her makeup, I used the complimentary curler to give my hair some volume. "I know earlier we said we were going out to dinner to celebrate my sister's life, but would you mind if we take a raincheck on that?" I caught Nene's gaze through the mirror. "I want to go see Midnight."

Nene's response was playful. "So, you're ditching me for the D?"

"I'm ditching you for a conversation."

Nene chuckled at my response. "Either way, I'm okay with being dropped like some mediocre peen. I'm happy you hit him back."

"Actually," I pursed my lips, feeling the nerves creeping up on me. "I haven't texted him back yet. I was thinking of just popping up at his house." My words stumbled out, hesitant and uncertain. "I remember how to get there, so it's not a problem."

"Ummm," she hummed, her tone noncommittal. I inwardly smiled, knowing she was trying to figure out the best way to support my irrational actions. "Don't you think you should check if he's home first?"

"Yeah, you're right," I admitted, unplugging the curler. "I'll text him on the way there at least."

"Okay, cool," she replied, her tone soothing.

Unfortunately, that was a lie.

CHAPTER 24

I saw her at my front door before her text came through.

SWEETS

Are you home?

> It'd be weird if I wasn't since you're at my door.

Who you telling? It's cold, hurry up.

As she rang the doorbell (as if I didn't know she was there), I felt a mix of excitement and nerves. I never expected her to show up after leaving me on read for hours, but once again, Tyme never failed to keep me on my toes.

"Pull it together, bruh." I tapped myself on the cheek as I jogged down the stairs just as the doorbell rang again. My mind was racing, and my stomach was doing flips.

It was unnerving to feel so out of control around a woman. Even with my ex, no woman had ever caused this kind of reaction in me.

That's why I knew I had to be honest with Tyme and myself. It wouldn't be fair to either of us otherwise.

"It ain't even that cold out here," I joked, swinging the door open and taking her in.

She was glowing. Her skin was flawless, her hair was styled to perfection, and her eyes shone brighter than I'd ever seen them before. It was clear that the spa had worked its magic on her, and, per usual, I couldn't take my eyes off her.

The icing of course, was her glossy lips.

She was dressed appropriately for our cold weather in one of those all-over long sleeve jumpsuits and knee high boots. The one piece had to be made by the devil himself in the way it hung to her curves and had my dick coming alive by the second. She had on a trench coat that kept her ass hidden, and I lowkey needed it to stay that way.

"Yes, it is," she retorted, wasting no time coming inside.

She stood in the foyer as I closed the door and gave myself — and my dick — one more pep talk because I knew we were about to put our arms around her soft ass body.

"Even after I got you flowers, you still not nice to me."

"Oh please," she waved me off and walked further inside. Falling into our *new normal* banter came easy as if we hadn't gone days without communication. "It's nice and cozy in here," she commented, removing the coat.

Now God, why would you let her do that?

"I know. So you can stop whining about the cold."

As I took Tyme's coat, she asked, "Do I need to take off my shoes?"

"Yes, but I got you," I said, gesturing to the chair next to the console table. I knelt down and unzipped her boot, my hand lingering on her left thigh. Flashbacks of the last time my face was buried between her legs lived rent free in my head. "I didn't think you were the pop-up type," I remarked. "Especially after you left my ass on read."

"That was rude of me," she admitted. "I didn't know what to say or how to take what you said because we shouldn't be missing each other, Midnight." I removed her other shoe. "I shouldn't even be here but—"

"No buts." I gave her a knowing grin.

"Don't start that," she said, smirking.

I returned the smirk with a wink. "Start what?"

"And that devilish wink tells me you know exactly what."

"So why are you here then...if you shouldn't be?" I asked, meeting her hesitant gaze.

"To say thank you in person. Today was great, I needed it. And," she paused, "I did want to see you, too."

I stood and offered my hand to help her up. "You could have just said yes to me taking you out tomorrow."

"How about you show me around," she suggested, changing the subject, "I've only seen the living room and the half bath." She let out an awkward chuckle, and I found it endearing. After all, she had only been to my house with Malachi less than five times, and on two of those occasions, she didn't even step inside. It was a pleasant surprise that she remembered where I lived at all.

"I can do that."

"Yay," she sang, looking around with a mixture of awe and amusement as she ventured deeper into my humble abode.

The open floor plan and large floor-to-ceiling windows allowed natural light to flood in, making the space feel open and inviting. "Feel free to let me know if it's up to your interior designer standards," I joked as she took in the contemporary decor I'd chosen. I liked my home to be sleek and stylish yet still warm and comfortable.

"So far, so good," she said.

I pointed out the oversized fireplace in the living room, knowing that it would be the perfect spot to cozy up on a chilly night like tonight. "I need to be snuggled up in front of that," Tyme teased.

"You're welcome to it whenever you like, Sweets," I said, winking at her before leading her to my spacious kitchen. The gleaming stainless-steel appliances and marble countertops were not only beautiful but also functional, with ample counter space for preparing meals for a large group— or for placing takeout in my case.

"This is where you turn your cup noodles into masterpieces, huh?" Tyme chuckled, running her fingers across the oven handle.

I grinned at her. "You remember that?"

"Of course I do," she replied, circling the kitchen island.

When we first bonded over our shared love for ramen, I boasted about my ability to turn a simple packet of noodles into a gourmet meal.

I laughed. "Yeah, that's me. The noodle master," I confirmed, noticing her subtly scanning my wine rack embedded in the island. I cleared my throat. "You want a glass?"

Her gaze snapped back to me. "Yeah, I do actually. I was trying to peek and see if you had my favorite."

I walked over to the wine cooler and pulled out a bottle of the Double Barrel Cabernet Sauvignon that was already chilling. "Do I get to cop a lil' feel if I do?" I asked, holding it up for her to see.

She looked at me with a mixture of shock and curiosity. "One, I'm starting to think you've been peeking through my windows, because how did you know that was one of my favorites?"

I chuckled. "Apparently, when people become the bane of your existence, they start to haunt you in your dreams. And before you know it, you end up knowing things about them that you never asked for."

She flipped me off. "And two, not you trying to blackmail me with wine."

Neither one of us had initiated a hug, so I was trying to get one by any means necessary. "Aye, what them strippers say? You gotta use what you got..." I started as I grabbed a couple of glasses. Tyme's laugh echoed throughout the kitchen as I poured us each a generous serving.

She took a sip and closed her eyes, savoring the taste. "Mmm, never gets old."

I raised my glass in a toast. "To good wine and even better company."

She clinked it. "You still not getting a feel." She giggled, continuing to torture me, as I guided her towards the door that led to one of my favorite spots.

I had converted the basement area into an entertainment space. It wasn't your typical 'man cave' — it was so much more than that. The sleek bar area, comfortable seating, and state-of-the-art audio and visual equipment made it clear that I had put a lot of thought and care into creating a space that was both stylish and functional.

"I like the vibe in here." Tyme said, leaning against the pool table. "You have a thing for high tech gadgets, don't you?"

"I can't help it," I chuckled, running a hand along my goatee. "They just make things so much easier. I really do have a thing for convenience."

"I see, but I like it," Tyme said with a smile.

"Whew," I feigned worry, "I almost thought you were about to come for my house."

"*You're* the judgmental one. Don't get us confused." She stood in front of me, and it took everything in me not to place my lips on hers.

Having constraint was ghetto as fuck.

"Oh!" Tyme exclaimed as something caught her attention. I watched her as she made her way over to my display case filled with model airplanes. She leaned closer to examine each plane, her eyes lighting up with excitement. "Wow, you have an impressive collection here," she said, tracing her finger over the glass.

I walked over to join her and pointed out my favorites, telling her a little bit about each one. She listened intently, asking questions and expressing genuine interest. It was refreshing to be around someone who appreciated my passion for aviation and didn't dismiss it as a childish hobby.

We continued the tour, and to simmer my Tyme craving, I placed her hand in mine as I led her up to the second floor, where three out of the four bedrooms were located.

As we walked, I pointed out the unique features of each room, like the skylight in one and the built-in bookshelves in another. We ended the tour in my master suite, which was truly fit for the king that I was.

The room was expansive and luxurious, with plush carpeting, a comfortable seating area, and a massive bed that we could do a lot of grown-up things on.

I turned to Tyme and gave her a playful grin. "So, what do you think?"

"I think," she sang, placing her empty wine glass down on my dresser next to mine, "that this mirror is a dream and on that alone, I gotta give it a ten out of ten."

I watched her as she headed towards the oversized mirror in the corner, which was a personal favorite of mine as well.

"Yeah, I love it, too."

As I approached her, my phone dinged, and I pulled it from my pocket to see a reminder about a food delivery I had scheduled for tonight. "Shit."

"What?" Tyme asked.

I ran my hand over my goatee. "Your ass popping up had things completely slipping my mind. It's *fellaship* night."

On the second Wednesday of every month, my boys and I had a standing tradition of getting together to chill, vibe out, and catch up. Tyme was no stranger to this routine because even though Mal and I had our differences, we were still brothers, and our close circle of friends was intertwined.

Recognition slowly dawned on her face. "Oh hell," she cursed, "Is—"

"Nah," I interrupted, knowing what she was about to ask. "I don't think Mal's coming. He hasn't said anything in the group chat, and he only got back yesterday. Besides..." I trailed off, not needing to state the obvious — that Mal probably didn't want to be in my presence.

I knew I had to squash the beef I'd intentionally caused with my brother, for the sake of our parents. Looking back, I didn't fully consider how my plan to get under Mal's skin, by helping Tyme, would have repercussions beyond him. But when this all began, all I cared about was lifting Tyme out of her funk, even if it meant putting myself in the line of fire.

The problem was that our chemistry and underlying feelings for each other got in the way. Now, instead of just letting Mal think we hooked up once, I needed to tell him that I planned on pursuing her and he needed to be okay with that.

I hadn't talked to him yet because Tyme's decision was just as crucial. If she wasn't willing to take a chance on us, there was no point in having a conversation with him. So, I took a leap of faith and decided to surprise her with a sweet gesture on her sister's birthday.

Taking it a step further and asking her on a date, was to give us an opportunity to define our relationship. I needed to know exactly where we stood before I had that conversation with my twin.

"Good," she relaxed. "What about Mr. Jabberjaws?" she asked.

I paused, trying to pinpoint who fit that description, and the first name that came to mind was, "Liam?"

"The fact that you barely hesitated tells me you know he's always running his mouth," she commented.

"He'll be here."

"Well, that means I definitely need to be heading on out. Liam will be too thirsty to let Mal know I was here if he sees me."

I chuckled at her accurate observation. Liam definitely couldn't keep a got damn thing to himself most times.

There were five of us in the circle, and we'd all been cool for the last ten years. Outside of my brother and me, there was Rohany, Keone, and Liam.

Rohany was our jeweler. He had designed a one-of-a kind ring for my mom for my parents' twentieth wedding anniversary twelve years ago, which was how we got introduced to him. His vibe was right on par for our crew, so he fit right in.

Keone and I met in college when we were both bright-eyed and bushy-tailed freshmen, getting our tires slashed by the same girl whom we had messed over. We bonded over the fact that she was mad at us for *allegedly* cheating on her when she was clearly doing the same thing. We'd been great friends ever since.

And Liam's ol' motor mouth ass had been Malachi's partner-in-crime since high school, but we've always been cool too.

They were all used to Mal's and my "frenemy twins" dynamic, so it wasn't a surprise to them when we had beef over something stupid.

But this time, things were a little different.

Although I was sure they were already in the know about the drama, none of them had brought it up in our group chat. Keone had hit me up on the low with the looking eyes emoji after he saw the pictures on social media, but I shut that down quick.

Back then, it was all in good fun. But now, I was hopelessly caught up in the beauty that stood before me.

"Nah, I ain't letting you leave just yet. They won't be here until around eight-thirty." It was only a quarter to seven.

"Mid, if—"

"I'll make sure you're gone before they get here. Don't stress," I assured her.

"Yeah, you better. Besides, the tour is done; I don't even know why you still tryna keep me hostage," she joked, turning her attention back to her reflection.

I stole a glance at her through the mirror. It immediately brought me back to the memory of us standing in the bathroom, right before we had sex for the first time.

Standing behind her, I inhaled her mesmerizing scent before burying my head in her neck and planting a kiss on it. The sides of my lips turned up as I basked in the way she shivered in my arms.

"Midnight," she purred my name as my kisses continued around her throat. "We can—"

"I've missed you so fucking much, Sweets," I cut her off, "That's why I don't want you to go yet. Let me have you, baby," I whispered into her ear, watching as she tilted her head to the left and sucked in a sharp breath. Through her reflection, I watched as her eyes closed and her cheeks flushed with desire. "Please," I added, my lips pecking at her shoulder as I felt my own excitement building.

I let out a playful grunt of annoyance, pulling away slightly. "Why are you so damn irresistible?" I teased, my eyes locked on hers through the mirror." Got a nigga begging. That shit ain't normal."

She let out a light chuckle, holding my gaze, "I kind of like it."

"Because you're evil." I slapped her on the ass. "Can we take this off?" I breathed against her ear, tugging at the one piece as I pressed my hard dick against her backside.

"Do we even have the time?"

I licked my lips. "We'll make the time."

"Mid—"

"You know you could already be riding my face, right?"

Lust flashed across her eyes. "I really hate you," she stated, lifting a hand up to her shoulder.

"Show me how much." I placed my palm around her throat,

forcing her mouth my way. The way her body melted into mine as we kissed was enough for my dick to see if it could explode. "Shit," I hissed, smacking her ass again as I stepped back and watched her undress for me, never once letting my eyes leave from the prize before me.

It didn't take long before I was splayed out on the floor in front of the mirror and she was riding my face, calling out my name, and telling me how she couldn't take one more orgasm.

I ignored that lie because I clearly had more faith in her orgasmic abilities.

And I was selfish and couldn't get enough of her natural honey.

Almost nothing pleased my soul more than being suffocated by Tyme's thighs and her juicy ass pussy while she fucked my face— except for her doing that while watching herself in the mirror. It must have turned her on even more to see herself in action because her sweet essence drenched every part of my nose, mouth, chin, and neck.

We went from me pleasing her, to her pleasing me, and then us sexing the hell out of each other in the middle of my bedroom floor — rug burn be damned. I was positive that sex with Tyme would never get old. I couldn't imagine getting tired of the way her pussy walls sucked me in every-single-time, or the way she moaned and whimpered when I stroked her just the way she liked.

As I showered and got ready for boys' night, I convinced Tyme to take a quick power nap before she headed out, promising her she still had almost an hour before the homies would arrive. When I emerged from the bathroom, I smiled at the sight of her, knocked out and sprawled on my bed with her mouth open. I loved seeing her in my space. It made me feel like she belonged there.

Part of me wanted to be selfish and let her sleep so that I could come back to her at the end of the night. But I knew she'd be pissed if she woke up and my boys were here.

At this point, I no longer cared who knew about us. As soon as I opened the door for her tonight, it became clear to me that I didn't want what we had to be just a fling.

I wanted to explore the possibility of forever with her. In my heart, I knew it was always meant to be us. I could only hope that she felt the same way. The time we'd spent apart had led me to this realization, and I hoped it had done the same for her.

"Bae." I caressed her side, coaxing her awake. She hummed and slowly opened her eyes, stretching her arms out and smiling. "Hey, beautiful." She playfully scrunched up her face before poking out her lips for a kiss.

Of course, I obliged because what wasn't I willing to give her at this point?

What was this life and how did I let this woman get me here?

She lifted herself up on her elbows. "Remember when I had to beg for a lil' funky kiss?"

I shook my head. "Not you waking up being a menace."

She giggled as she tossed the sheet back and climbed out the bed. "Would you have it any other way?"

I snatched her fine naked ass to me and gave her another kiss, while caressing the sides of her stomach. "Nah."

"Exactly what I thought." She tapped me on the nose with her pointer finger and then toyed with my nose ring. "I wasn't supposed to let you talk me out of my panties."

Giving her ass a squeeze, I smirked. "That was never my plan, *and* had you agreed to the date instead of popping up, you may have at least gotten fed before you got—"

She covered my mouth with her hand. "Don't finish that sentence unless you wanna fight."

Taking a step back, I held up both my hands. "Ion want no smoke, big homie."

"For a change."

I was about to ask her if she wanted to shower before she left, but that all went to hell when the doorbell rang.

"Midnight!" she squealed, "I knew I should have left earlier."

"Calm down," I inwardly laughed at the death stare she sent my way before searching the room for her clothes, "I'm sure that's just the food I ordered for tonight." I pulled up my camera app. "Yeah it's the —shit."

"*Shit?*" she repeated.

I didn't make eye contact with her because I wasn't about to let her kill me where I stood. "Rohany just pulled up."

"Fucking hell."

"Look, get dressed and I'll take him downstairs so he won't see you." Ro was honestly the last person she had to worry about. He was the poster child for 'I just mind my business'.

She ran her hand over her face. "I knew this was gonna happen."

"I'll make it up to you tomorrow when I take you out."

"I didn't agree to that."

"Because I'm no longer asking you. I'm letting you know that I'll be at your house at seven-thirty tomorrow night, and you're going to let me take you out."

She crossed her arms over her chest. "Is that right?"

I wrapped an arm around her waist, drawing her to me once again. Reluctantly, she let her arms fall to the side. "It is." She tucked her bottom lip into her mouth, and I could sense her wanting to push back but also wanting to give in. "Don't overthink it, Sweets."

"Now why on earth would I do that?" The sarcasm was evident.

"Have you met *you*?"

"Hush, but fine. You can take me out this *once*."

Once? *Yeah, okay.* She must mean once this week.

"Bet. We need to—" I was cut off by the ringing of my doorbell again. That quick, I had almost forgotten about them motherfuckers outside.

"*We* need to get me out of here sight unseen." She pecked my lips. "Now go."

"I'll text you when all is clear."

CHAPTER 25

Tyme

I released the deep breath I was holding as I stepped out of Midnight's house without being seen. There were parts of me that still wanted to believe it was wrong to continue to see him, but the most important parts of me couldn't help the way *we* felt. From the moment he opened the door, I knew I wouldn't be able to resist him—nor did I want to. I *tried* to play hard to get, but truth be told, I would have dropped my draws in the foyer if he'd asked me.

Because as my bestie said, he deserved to be thanked.

My head was so in the clouds that I didn't notice the additional car in the driveway, but when I heard, "What the hell are you doing here?" I froze in place.

Not out of fear, but as if I'd gotten caught red-handed in the cookie jar.

Malachi Drayton was ten feet in front of me. He hadn't been this close to me in months, and instead of feeling weak in the knees like I once did, all I felt now was a surge of disgust. It was almost surreal to think that I had once been so in love with him, so blinded by his charm and good looks that I had ignored all the red flags.

But now, after experiencing the better twin, I knew that it was just an illusion I had created for myself. As I looked at Malachi, I couldn't help but compare him to Midnight.

Midnight's presence felt like home, like I belonged there. Being with him felt natural, effortless, and comforting. It was like a warm blanket on a cold winter's night, like a cool breeze on a scorching summer day, like the first sip of hot coffee in the morning. In contrast, Malachi felt like an ill-fitting suit that no longer suited me. Being near him made me feel suffocated, like I was trapped in a small room with no windows and no air conditioning.

In just seventy-two hours, Midnight had given me so much more than Malachi ever had in two years. Despite that, seeing him still brought a pang of pain to my chest, like a sharp twinge of regret for all the time I had wasted on him.

Our eyes met, and his were flashing with anger.

"So y'all really are fucking, huh?" he asked, disdain dripping from every word. "You foul as hell, Tyme."

Snapping myself back into reality, I started walking towards my car again. Thankfully, no one had blocked me in, and I could get the hell up out of here because I didn't have a damn thing to say to my ex. My best bet was to pretend he wasn't talking to me.

"So, you ain't got shit to say, now?" he continued as I unlocked my car. "How do you think this makes me feel?"

Against my own volition, my body whipped back around towards him. The disrespectful audacity. "How does it make *you* feel?!" I repeated and I was sure the neighborhood heard me. "You?" I reiterated, pointing at him. "The person who allowed a bitch to be in my face, knowing you were having sex with her?!" Hot tears sprang to my eyes as memories of our past flooded my mind. "And then, because that wasn't enough, you married her and now you want to be in my face like I'm betraying you?!"

"You are! That's my family!

I grabbed my head, wondering if I was in some sort of nightmare because he couldn't be serious. "And you fucked your "family" too! So, I guess we're even!"

I was shaking so hard that I dropped my keys. They rolled down the driveway, giving Malachi more time to spur bullshit.

"So, you admit that you did this to get back at me?" he seethed.

Snatching my keys from the ground, I stood back up and squared my shoulders, wiping my tears away. Just then, Midnight emerged from the house and saw what was brewing between us. I barely blinked before he was by my side, his fists clenched.

"What the fuck did you say to her?" Midnight demanded, his voice low and dangerous.

"You think because you smashed MY ex, you can be in my face, asking me questions with yo' bitch ass?"

"Mal." The veins in Midnight's face made me instinctively wrap a hand around his elbow. "Watch your mouth."

"I ain't gotta watch shit," he spat. "You think you that nigga now because you stole my girl from me?"

"Last I checked, I didn't steal her; you fumbled and now you the one who wanna whine like the bitch made nigga *you* are."

Malachi's jaw twitched.

"You ain't got no right to be coming at her about shit," Midnight continued. "You got a problem, you deal with me."

Malachi laughed bitterly. "Here you go, playing captain save-a-hoe again."

That was the last straw for Midnight. He was out of my grasp in seconds as he lunged at Malachi. The two of them started grappling with each other, and my screams for them to stop were completely ignored. It was as if they were both possessed, and nothing I could say would make them stop fighting.

As soon as I saw Rohany sprinting out of the house, I made a beeline for my car.

I had to get out of there.

Tears streamed down my face, and I could hear their voices growing louder behind me, but I didn't stop until I was safely inside and driving away.

THE STEAMING HOT CUP OF CHAMOMILE TEA DIDN'T HELP TO CALM MY nerves.

Neither did the shower.

And apparently, sipping wine straight out the bottle wasn't the key either.

Nothing seemed to help me process what had happened less than two hours ago.

How did we get here?

How were my ex and his brother fighting over *me*? Two grown ass men literally throwing blows over *me*.

I know Midnight and I had said to hell with everyone else, but it was easier said than done when we were miles away, in our own bubble. It was easier to not care about anyone else or the consequences of our actions; however, it was a completely different ball game when things turned violent.

I never expected they'd end up physically going at it. An argument with some very choice words, yes, but what happened tonight was something I didn't see coming, and I hated how much it made me start to regret my decision.

My phone vibrated against the bedside table, and I glanced at it to see Midnight calling for the third time. I couldn't bring myself to answer it. What was there to say, other than something that would be what neither of us wanted to hear— no matter how much we wanted to, we couldn't do this.

He called right back, and I took a deep breath, reaching for the phone. It stopped ringing right before I accepted the call. The sigh of relief I felt was only temporary because immediately, a text message came through.

> TIN MAN
>
> I'm outside.

Shit.

I might've thought — or hoped — he was lying, but then the doorbell sounded throughout the house.

Without my permission, my legs moved me from the safety of my bed, down the stairs, and to the foyer.

The camera proved what I already knew— Midnight Drayton was at my door.

But I couldn't open it.

He called out my name as he knocked, and my heart skipped a beat.

I froze.

So many questions flooded my mind, but the one that stood out was how had I allowed my heart to open up to the one person I refused to even have a decent conversation with for the last two and a half years? But now... I couldn't keep my composure in his presence. Even with a door positioned between us, I became complete mush.

I pressed my back against the door, in an attempt to pull myself together, but then a text came in that only made my palms sweat.

TIN MAN

Tyme, baby, please open the door.

One word, four letters.

> No, Midnight. We can't do this. Today was proof.

I hated how hard I squeezed the phone as I awaited his reply.

Sweets, let me in.

One word, six letters.

> You just fought your brother over me. We can't do this.

Running into Malachi definitely knocked my ass back into reality. I had to be logical about this and not allow my emotions to lead.

We boys. This ain't the first time I beat that nigga ass.

I wanted to laugh, I did. But I couldn't. This situation wasn't funny.

> This was what I didn't want to happen. This is why we were supposed to stop before we got too far gone.

> The problem with that is, I was already gone before this even began.

One phrase, eight words.

The air going into my lungs ceased, but I somehow still managed to open the door.

"What?" The word escaped the confinements of my inner thoughts.

He didn't say anything; instead, he enclosed his hand with mine as he walked inside and guided us to the couch. We sat down and I couldn't stop my leg from bouncing a thousand times a *minute*.

"What did you mean by you were already gone before this even began?" I reiterated.

"It's always been you, Sweets, and our time together proved that." He placed a hand on my knee, calming me down before putting my hands into his. "I know things ain't ideal, but that's what I planned to tell you at dinner." My heart was beating erratically as I listened to him spill his truth. "I can't pretend like what we shared didn't happen, move on from it and go back to life without you. Tyme, I want every part of you, and I won't deny it again."

His words sounded good— *hell better than good*, "But—"

"No buts—" he cut me off but this time, I couldn't sit back and say nothing because my mind kept screaming, *'how could we ever continue this?'*.

That run in with Mal was just a taste of what could come.

His family would hate me.

There would always be drama.

I would cause a bigger rift between him and his brother.

His dad would probably cut him out of the company, and everything would be a big disaster, all because I had to be the girl who got her lick back *and* fell for her enemy.

Was I worth all of the possible turmoil that would ensue?

"Yes, Midnight," I pulled my hands from his grasp, "this time, there has to be buts. Because who's to say if what we feel is even worth it? What if we're still on a high from our experience together? What if—"

"And what if you're just afraid?" He called me out. "I know you, Tyme. You're afraid of what everyone else is going to think, or about everyone else's feelings, instead of putting yourself first. But we can't live like that." His words hit me like a ton of bricks. "When I asked you to let me show you what you needed, I had no idea how much that would backfire on me, seeing how much I needed you."

"Mid," I mumbled. "I don't want to be the cause of more family drama."

"I get that, and I know things went left earlier between Mal and me, but that's not on you. It's on me. I wish I could have handled that better, but I will never tolerate anyone disrespecting you."

"And I will always appreciate you for protecting me, I just…" I blew air out my mouth as I ran my fingers over my eyebrows.

What was a girl supposed to do when her ex's brother was the epitome of the type of man she not only wanted, but needed and deserved?

"I'm not saying shit will be easy but if you weren't worth it, I wouldn't be here asking for you to take a chance with me." He grabbed my hands, placing them back in his. "I was willing to let you go when you were with Malachi. I respected it at the time, but I always knew you were the one I let get away because of my bullshit. I'm not letting that happen again, not if you're willing to take a chance with me to figure out if there's something worth exploring here." He squeezed my hand before saying, "Because if you're open to it, I would love to date you, fall in love with you, and be the man you deserve to have."

I wanted to hide from his words. I wanted to look away from his beautiful ebony eyes that never stopped staring at me as he laid it all out on the table.

But what I wanted more— was him.

As scared as I was, it was time for me to let go of my fears and enjoy the present. After all, who knew what the future held? All I knew was that I didn't want to look back and regret not taking a chance on something that could have been great.

I couldn't let my ex-fiancé stop me from potentially finding my husband.

"You gon' say something, Sweets?"

Straddling his lap, I planted a sweet kiss on his luscious lips before I took him out of his misery.

"I never belonged to him in the way I want to belong to you. And you're right," I confirmed, "I am scared. I don't wanna jump into this and it end up being another failed relationship, *and* I've ruined things between you and your family for nothing." He opened his mouth to say something, but I stopped him. "That said, I also know as long as you're by my side, I'll be protected and we can face whatever comes our way because this," I motioned between us, "feels more real than anything I've ever felt."

There was so much relief in doing and saying what felt right and trusting that my life hadn't unfolded this way for nothing. I had already started to convince myself that the second half of last year had been so full of turmoil, that there was no way this wasn't the silver lining.

We stared into each other's eyes for a moment before leaning into one another and sharing the sweetest kiss.

"But," I said as we pulled away, playfully causing him to drop his head, "we have to take things slow." I elaborated on what I meant by taking it slow. At the end of the day, what mattered most was us, and if we truly wanted our relationship to thrive, I emphasized the significance of getting to know each other deeply and intentionally taking our time to date and progress.

"I'm more than happy to find a pace that works for us both, as long as you're willing to go into the fire with me, Sweets."

"I mean, I guess," I teasingly sang, "since you are kinda fine." He grinned. "Besides, either we're gonna crash and burn *or* you're gonna be stuck with me aggravating you for the rest of your life."

"Let me start praying for God's favor now. Maybe he won't let you ask me fifty-eleven questions."

"Hush up!" I pretended to push away from him, and he only held me tighter. He buried his face into my neck, trailed kisses up my face, and then blessed me with one on my lips.

"I want a lot more twelve-oh-ones with you," I whispered against his mouth while tracing the hoop of his nose ring.

He let a devilish smirk dance on his lips. "Look at my lil' freak."

I rolled my eyes. "I meant, more new beginnings, new days, new weeks, new years, and new moments by your side."

His eyes gave me a look of adoration as he said, "Tell me anything." I wanted to respond but somewhere between my explanation and his ugly sexy smirk, he'd managed to slip his fingers between the folds of *his* pussy.

I had no more words, only actions.

Within minutes, I transitioned myself from sitting on his lap, to sitting on his dick.

The purest sigh escaped both of our lips as he slid into my home base, and I knew without a doubt, no one else would ever complete me like Midnight Drayton.

And from his next words, he felt the same way. "You're timeless, Sweets, and I want a lot more twelve-oh-ones with you, too."

FIN

12:01: The Aftermath

Wanna know what happened leading up to the epilogue? Dive into **12:01: The Aftermath** on the next page. This is a novelette that was created to give you a glimpse into Midnight and Tyme's first year together *(i.e. between the end of the book and epilogue)*. It's a timelapse of the next chapter of their journey filled with heartwarming (& hilarious) text threads, juicy social media posts, and key scene snippets chronicling their first year together. Please keep in mind that this is not a story where you're going to get every single aspect of their year together as that is not the purpose.

The purpose is to bridge the gap between the end of *12:01* and the epilogue.

I wanted to create this because I felt like their situation was so "unique" *(i.e. messy lol)* that though I could sum it up in the epilogue (which you will find after this), we all know that the likelihood of everything being all peachy during their first year together was going to be slim. So I wanted to create what I originally called an "epic epilogue" that gave my lovely readers a little bit more through a timelapse-style novelette.

If you wish to skip this and jump straight into the future with the epilogue, it's up to you. But if you're as invested in Midnight and Tyme as I am, I think you'll love 12:01: The Aftermath *(and yes I'm biased)*.

12:01
the Aftermath

BELLA JAY

January

ALMOST ONE MONTH AFTER 12:01

JANUARY 29TH

TYME

sliding down the wall crying gif

NENE

??? You okay?

TYME

No :(

NENE

What's wrong? Do I need to put out a hit on Midnight already?

TYME

No…

I ran into the hoe half of the kissing cousins today at Lattes & Bagels.

NENE

Shit.

Did you hit her?

TYME

My claim to fame on SM is finally dying down, so I couldn't risk it.

But why did she have the audacity to approach me on some 'you and Midnight should be ashamed of yourselves.' Bitch, BFFR!

NENE

I woulda slapped her because what TF do you mean WE should be ashamed? Did you not just marry your "cousin"??

Are you not embarrassed gif

TYME

Exactly!

NENE

The delusion is at an all-time high.

TYME

Ain't it! So I told her that's really none of her business, and she told me that she didn't appreciate me trying to ruin her 'big day' and that I need to move on with my life because her and fuckboy are happy and...

EXPECTING. *eye rolling emoji*

NENE

mouth wide open gif

Why would she even tell you that?

TYME

Because she's a fucking bitch.

NENE

I'm sorry, babes. It makes no sense why she keeps rubbing her messed-up relationship in your face.

I'll be home in an hour with hugs and wine.

TYME

Honestly, I don't even care because I have bigger problems...

NENE

looking eyes emoji

TYME

Ne, when she told me she was pregnant, I realized I haven't gotten my period since December.

attached image of a positive pregnancy test

NENE

complete shock gif

TYME

What the fuck am I supposed to do, Ne? I can't be pregnant.

February

FEBRUARY 10TH

TYME

Do you think we're making a mistake or moving too fast?

MIDNIGHT

Hell no and no.

What's wrong?

TYME

Nothing.

MIDNIGHT

Why aren't you picking up my call?

TYME

Because I can't talk right now.

MIDNIGHT

Stop lyin. You know I'll show up to your house, right?

TYME

You're not even in town.

MIDNIGHT

And?

Tell me what's wrong.

TYME

Nothing... I'm just in my head today.

Am I your girlfriend?

MIDNIGHT

Who's asking?

TYME

I'm serious.

MIDNIGHT

You wanna be my girl, Sweets?

TYME

Answer my question or ima take that as a no.

MIDNIGHT

I know we agreed to take things slow but I still thought that was obvious.

TYME

We didn't discuss it, so no.

MIDNIGHT

Say less.

FEBRUARY 14TH @ 9:32PM

Liked by midnightdrayton and 554 others

onceuponatyme Stepped on a helicopter single. Stepped off a girlfriend. 😊😊 #happyvalentinesday

View all 121 comments

nenenene I KNOW THAT'S RIGHT!!

bookswhitme I hope she don't take a bat to this one 😬

mosaidit The upgrade is upgrading. Love that for you sis

nenenene @mosaidit I need a do over babe 👀

takeahlatimore The standard!

mosaidit @nenenene I can't see I'm blinddddd

keepingupwithkay And a helicopter? Or she must got a rich ninja. Is it my turn yet God?

garygotsnolove if that nigga slip up, i'm next

pole_n_pour I love this for you! 🙌

onceuponatyme: Stepped on a helicopter single. Stepped off a girlfriend. #happyvalentinesday

nenenene: I KNOW THAT'S RIGHT!!
bookswhitme: I hope she don't take a bat to this one
mosaidit: The upgrade is upgrading. Love that for you sis.
nenenene: @mosaidit I need a do over babe.
takeahlatimore: The standard!
mosaidit: @nenenene I can't see I'm blinddddd
keepingupwithkay: And a helicopter? Or she must got a rich ninja. Is it my turn yet God?
garygotsnolove: if that nigga slip up, i'm next
pole_n_pour: I love this for you!

FEBRUARY 14TH @ 10:02PM

NENE

Okay GIRLFRIEND.

TYME

Please don't start

NENE

MIDNIGHT'S GIRLFRIEND!

TYME

You're aggy.

NENE

Have you told him yet? *pregnancy related emojis*

TYME

No because we don't know for sure yet.

NENE

3 yeses is pretty sure.

TYME

and 1 no. My appointment is on the 16th.

NENE

Denial is so cute on you. Rub your tummy and
tell my niece I said to hold on because her
daddy finna try to put another baby in HIS
GIRLFRIEND tonight.

TYME

I don't really like you.

FEBRUARY 19TH

Tyme

NENE

On a scale of 1 - 10, how awkward are things?

11.5. We just sat down for dinner. His mom is
working overtime to make things seem normal,
but this shit is weird. I wanna go.

I know, but it's something y'all gotta get
used to.

I know.

Also, something is making me wanna gag
every other minute.

Tell my niece to calm down for you since she's
still a secret.

I knew you'd bring that up.

You need to tell our bestie we finna be parents.

"How was Zanzibar, Mama K?" Tia's voice pulled my attention from my texts. Her calling Kinley 'Mama K' after referring to her as 'auntie' for years must've felt strange. I mean, it sent a queasy ripple through *my* stomach. Though, everything seemed to make my stomach flutter in an unsettling way. How the hell was I going to make it through dinner like this?

"It was two weeks of pure bliss," Kinley replied, "I've already told Marcus we need to plan our next trip to Africa, this time along the coast of South Africa."

"And I've already told you," Marcus chimed in, "I ain't flying that many hours ever again."

A soft chuckle escaped my lips. I always enjoyed the banter between Marcus and Kinley Drayton. Everyone at the table, including Marcus himself, knew he was lying through his teeth because his wife tended to get her way. I loved that for her.

As we started to eat, I let the conversation drift into the background, focusing on keeping my composure and preventing any unwanted surprises — like vomiting — at the dinner table.

"You okay?" Midnight's voice whispered in my ear, bringing a smile to my face.

"Yeah."

"You're barely eating."

My eyes followed his down to my plate. I hadn't piled much on it, and even then, I had only managed to take three bites, mostly of the salad and cornbread.

"The nerves of this dinner have my stomach feeling uneasy," I confessed, "but I'm fine. I promise."

"We'll leave right after dinner, okay?"

I nodded, feeling relieved. I knew how these family gatherings typically went, having been through more than a few. There would be pre-dinner mingling (which we intentionally missed by arriving just before dinner), the meal itself, and then the post-dinner festivities, which could involve a movie, games, or more socializing. So, I was grateful that our escape plan was in place.

Midway during dinner, Tia and Malachi dropped the news that they were expecting. It baffled me because I had assumed, given Tia's *gracious* advance notice to me about the pregnancy, that she'd already shared it with the family. Clearly, I'd been mistaken. Thankfully, I hadn't disclosed that information to anyone outside of Nene, not even Midnight, as I was too absorbed in coming to terms with my own pregnancy. As they shared their announcement, I managed to put on a brave face, forcing a smile as everyone congratulated them, all the while battling waves of nausea. All I wanted was to find some corner of solitude to throw up. I couldn't decide if it was Tia's over-the-top enthusiasm about their impending parenthood or the overpowering smell of the curry that was triggering my discomfort.

As dinner concluded, our plan to leave immediately hit a snag when Midnight's dad pulled him aside for a quick chat. With barely a minute gone by in Midnight's absence, I excused myself to the bathroom. As everyone else prepared for the post-dinner festivities, I was desperate for a moment of relief from the lingering uneasiness brought on by the food I had reluctantly forced myself to eat.

ME

Do not bring anything with curry around me. I am dying. *vomit emoji*

NENE

Ah damn and noted. Y'all still there?

Yeah, I'm hiding out in the bathroom while Mid's with his dad. We're about to leave though.

You might as well face the kissing cousins and the Draytons with your head held high, they stuck with you. *pregnant woman emoji*

I know. I still need more time to adjust. It's so easy when Mid and I are in our bubble, but being around his family makes me feel like I'm the villain.

You are not! That bitch ass son they raised is. Let him and his lil dusty wife feel uncomfortable.

I gotta log onto my IDGAF zoom lol.

Exactly, 'cause I know our bestie would agree with me.

You really think y'all friends now. *eye rolling emoji*

And is. Now go back out there and own being the baddie that bagged both brothers.

I took in a deep breath and swung open the bathroom door, determined to find my strength and stop worrying about Malachi, Tia, and anyone else who might disapprove of Midnight and me.

Easier said than done.

As I stepped out into the hallway, my phone chimed with a text from Midnight, pulling my attention to it. He asked where I was since he had finished his conversation with his dad.

"You okay?" I almost jumped out of my skin at the familiar phrase, causing my phone to slip from my trembling hands and crash onto the tiled floor. Unfortunately, it wasn't tied to the person I'd wished it was. Instead, Midnight's mom stood just two feet away, offering me a bottle of water.

"Yes, I'm fine," I replied, retrieving my phone, "my stomach was just feeling a little uneasy." I echoed the same lie I had told her son. She continued to hold out the water, her eyes locked onto mine. I accepted it, hoping the gesture would put an end to her scrutinizing gaze, but it didn't.

"I didn't know what to expect today," I began, my voice steady, "with me and Mid and..."

But Kinley raised a hand to stop me. "How far along are you?"

I stumbled over my words, my composure cracking. "What? I'm not—"

She took my hand in hers, her expression softening. "Tyme, I've been pregnant a few times, and my friends think I have a sixth sense about these things. I've been watching you all through dinner. The curry is driving you crazy."

Crazy is an understatement.

"There's no reason to lie about it when eventually, you're gonna have to tell us. Unless…"

I let my shoulders drop. "Almost nine weeks."

Her smile widened. "Does Midnight know?"

I shook my head no. "I didn't know how—"

"You're pregnant?" Both of our heads snapped toward the voice that had interrupted. "I know you're kidding me."

Malachi stormed away, headed for the den area, with Kinley and me following closely behind.

"You got her pregnant?" He snapped at Midnight, causing everyone else in the room to go mute.

"What the hell are you t—" Midnight began, stumbling over his words as Malachi's words sunk in. "Pregnant?" His eyes darted to mine. "Wait..." He sprinted toward me. "Are you?"

His hands found my waist before his eyes landed on my stomach.

"Yes," I whispered, my heart racing. This wasn't how I had wanted him to find out, and I wasn't even sure how I planned to tell him, given that I had been avoiding the truth.

"Oh my gosh!" I heard Mickie squeal. "The plot thickens!"

"Give me a fucking break." Tia's voice cut through the silence. "This girl really wants into this family by any means necessary. Disgusting."

"Excuse me?" My head whipped in her direction.

"Tia," Kinley chimed in, her tone firm. "I thought I made it clear that we were going to respect one another in my damn house."

"I'm sorry, Mama K, but her pregnancy seems real convenient. Couldn't keep one brother, so she went after the next."

"Girl, go to hell. I'm not the one who was sleeping with someone else's man for years, waiting to get picked!"

"At the end of the day, I got him though." Her eyes fluttered as if she couldn't be prouder of her dumbest accomplishment.

"By default. Don't forget that." My attention turned back to

Midnight. "Let's go. Unlike some people, I don't want to keep disrespecting your parents' house."

March

MARCH 7TH @ 11:22AM

FELLASHIP GROUP CHAT

LIAM

Don't get married.

MALACHI

Too late

LIAM

I warned your ass.

KEONE

Been there, done that. What sis done did?

LIAM

Let's just say I see why you got divorced.

MIDNIGHT

Don't put Kassy in the same boat as Deztiny crazy ass.

LIAM

You know what... you right. Dez was on one.

KEONE

I ain't know this was come for my BM day.

MALACHI

Nigga you know we speaking facts.

KEONE

Anyway what Kas do?

LIAM

Y'all know I love that girl to death but like why she thought it'd be funny to hide all my boxers and only leave a g-string for me to wear

MIDNIGHT

BRUH Imboooooo

LIAM

Now she talmbout she holding my draws ransom and I gotta Zelle her $200 for lunch. LUNCH NIGGAS.

ROHANY

This why I keep my notifications on mute.

But did you send the money?

LIAM

Only because I ain't feel like free balling it today.

MIDNIGHT

Not because you whipped?

LIAM

Fuck off. Long story short, I need this fellaship night tomorrow 'cause she gonna prank her ass into a divorce.

ROHANY

Yeah right lol

MALACHI

At least y'all a few years in, Tia already working my nerves and we ain't even at 3 months.

KEONE

That best friend to lovers story a lil iffy ain't it?

MALACHI

Fuck you. LOL

But on some real shit, y'all don't be on y'all bullshit tomorrow. This pregnancy got her steadily on my ass.

ROHANY

Shit it ain't us she gotta worry about. You and Mid the ones who can't act civilized. Had to take a break last month after y'all wanted to throw bows and shit back in Jan.

LIAM

Still mad I missed a front row to that.

KEONE

Grow up @Liam

MALACHI

Won't be no problems because that nigga ain't invited to my house

MIDNIGHT

shrugging emoji

MARCH 7TH @ 6:12PM

MIDNIGHT

For the sake of our boys and our fam, we need to have a conversation. 'Cause the side comments and shade is already getting old. If nothing else, we can at least clear the air.

MALACHI

Ain't no fucking air to clear.

I ain't got shit to say to you

You fucked her, you got her pregnant, congratulations.

Don't bring your ass to my house, that's all I got to say. Me and my wife don't want you here.

MIDNIGHT

Bet.

MARCH 25TH

Midnight

"I can tell you gotta girlfriend, look at you getting my angles right," Mickie said, grinning as she swiped through the pictures I'd taken of her outside the restaurant and lounge where we had celebrated her birthday dinner.

I chuckled. "You still have a fat ass head, though," I joked, and she playfully pushed at my shoulder before leaning against me. The atmosphere was relaxed after the dinner, but tensions were still lurking beneath the surface. Malachi's presence was a constant reminder of the complicated web of relationships we were entangled in.

"Tell that girlfriend of yours that she owes me breakfast or something for missing my dinner party."

"I will. Your nephew is giving her a hard time," I replied, going along with the story Tyme had concocted about her pregnancy.

Since the blowout at Sunday dinner last month, Tyme had been avoiding any situation that could bring her face-to-face with Malachi and Tia. I didn't like it, but I understood the need for her to avoid added stress, especially now that she was pregnant.

"Y'all found out it's a boy?!" Mickie looked up at me with excitement, her eyes sparkling.

"Nah," I shook my head. "I'm just putting that wish out into the universe. We've decided to be surprised."

"Aww okay. Well, I hope it's a girl then." She stuck out her tongue playfully, and I playfully mushed her in the face. "See how you treat me? That's why I miss Tyme."

"You'd probably be the only one." Our banter was interrupted by a sudden shift in the conversation. Tia's voice had cut through the air, and from the stilted look on her face, it was clear that she hadn't meant for us to overhear her words.

"What?" she feigned innocence, but it was clear that we had caught her disrespectful comment.

"You know we heard you, right?" Mickie pointed out before I could react.

"It ain't like she lied," Malachi chimed in from beside her. Our strained relationship was palpable, and while I wanted to address the issues between us, I wasn't about to kiss his ass in order to do it.

"Exactly," Tia agreed, seemingly empowered by Malachi's support. "She just makes things weird. Last month's dinner was a mess, and she ruined my baby announcement on purpose."

I scoffed, shoving my hands into my pockets and biting back the retort that threatened to escape. But Mickie wasn't as willing to hold back.

"You don't think it was weird because you slept with her fiancé and then married him?" Mickie's voice was laced with incredulity, and I turned to face Tia and Malachi, fully aware of the tension in the air. I knew that my sister still didn't want to pick sides, but she also wouldn't let bullshit slide.

"And then she slept with his brother," Tia gestured towards me, "so what's the big deal? She's not innocent in this mess."

"Come on, babe, let's just let it go. We ain't even gotta address this shit no more," Malachi surprisingly tried to diffuse the situation, but Tia wasn't having it.

"No, because I thought Micks and I were cool, and now she wants to act like we're in the wrong. Things didn't get awkward until Midnight brought Tyme back around. Everyone was fine with me and Malachi's relationship."

"I never thought it was cute that you were sleeping with my brother while he had a whole fiancée," Mickie's voice was firm, "but that was none of my business—"

"Exactly."

"However, I'm not going to let you act like Tyme is the only one who has made shit in our family messy. It's all of y'all," Mickie pointed around, "so grow up and take some damn accountability."

"Whatever," Tia murmured.

"Ain't no whatever," the words tumbled out of my mouth. "Y'all always knew what you were doing was wrong."

"And you don't think you were fucking wrong for what you did?" Malachi's gaze was fixed on me, challenging me.

"I was, and now what?" I shot back. "I was willing to own up to my mistakes and acknowledge that we went about it the wrong way. You didn't wanna have a conversation."

"Because having a conversation wouldn't have changed anything," Tia interjected, once again adding her two cents that no one needed. "You let her use you, and now you're stuck being her baby daddy, all because she still wants Malachi. That's the real issue here."

"You know what, Tia? I don't understand why you keep inserting yourself into a conversation that should be between me and my brother. I know you think that because you fucked him and he was cheating on Tyme with you, that *that* somehow makes you a part of what's going on between us right now. But it doesn't. What happened between me and Tyme has nothing to do with you. Yet, you seem so pressed about her, when in reality, you're the one who slept with the nigga she was in a relationship with, not the other way around."

Mickie grimaced, Tia's face dropped, and Malachi stood there, clenching his jaw.

I was done with this. Thankfully, my rideshare pulled up. "And on that note, I'm out."

April

APRIL 3RD 12:30PM

withshadeontop

#WSOTMESSYMONDAYS PREGNANT BY YOUR EX'S BROTHER?!

Oh, Baby

Liked by pole_n_pour and 72,125 others

withshadeontop #WSOTMessyMondays Shadies we got some messiness for you TA-DAY! Y'all remember that one #batshitcrazyex who showed up to her ex's wedding with a BAT back in December? Well someone with inside knowledge sent us some updated tea with some receipts (unfortunately they didn't give us permission to share them). Either way turns out #batshitcrazyex (who's name is #TymeHenley) is now PREGNANT by her ex's TWIN brotherrrr ! Somebody write the book!

If you missed that end of the year wedding drama, swipe for the video.

Is this the ultimate lick back or what? Let us know in the comments!

#MalachiDrayton #MidnightDrayton #MDWinery #TheDraysWineBar #Southgate #ClamptonCounty
View all 5952 comments

kamikrishauna Ohhhhh this is messyyyyyy. Definitely a top tier lick back! 🐍

chaletnthecity I mean I heard he cheated on her first so he lucky she didn't go for his daddy 🐍

xoskyemoon Ain't this @pole_n_pour brothers we talking about?

authortialove I love a bad bitch, I'll write the book.

missdazia Fareal?! I love @thedrayswinelounge in Southgate! Talk about family drammmaa

imatroll.abih @onceuponatyme is a low class bitch

missfancyreads Is this true @pole_n_pour?

kris3marie Have y'all seen those twin brothers though? I mean I ain't exactly mad at sis.... 🐍

renaissanceman6721 Hurt hoes be vicious 🐸

shontheauthor Not his brother being a short king. Ew.

crown.me.bookish Wait wait wait... getting knocked up by his TWIN is nasty work

smutmeplease @theemalachidrayton played in that girl face. Karma came back hard AF. I hope @onceuponatyme is happy with @midnightdrayton

joe__justified I check ol' girl page, she thick as fuck. I woulda folded too if I was his brother. 🐍

tanontales I used to date the twin who got married and I never trusted the hoe he married. He told me that was his cousin y'all so if he told ol' girl the same and then married HIS COUSIN... I wish nothing but chaos for him and a pretty baby for our lick back queen.

harlemsheatatl Bro code is dead. You niggas wack.

tiadraytontoyou but if i speak...

tanontales @tiadraytontoyou if you do speak I hope it's about how you were his side chick for years until he finally picked you. But congrats? 🐸🐸

quaywantit BRING BACK SHAME

withshadeontop: #WSOTMessyMondays Shadies we got some messiness for you TA-DAY! Y'all remember that one #batshitcrazyex who showed up to her ex's wedding with a BAT back in December? Well someone with inside knowledge sent us some updated tea with some receipts (unfortunately they didn't give us permission to share them). Either way turns out #batshitcrazyex (who's name is #TymeHenley) is now PREGNANT by her ex's TWIN brotherrrrr! Somebody write the book!

If you missed that end of the year wedding drama, swipe for the video.

Is this the ultimate lick back or what? Let us know in the comments!

#MalachiDrayton #MidnightDrayton #MDWinery #The-DraysWineBar #Southgate #ClamptonCounty

kamikrishauna: Ohhhhh this is messyyyyyy. Definitely a top tier lick back!

chaletnthecity: I mean I heard he cheated on her first so he lucky she didn't go for his daddy

xoskyemoon: Ain't this @pole_n_pour brothers we talking about?

authortialove: I love a bad bitch, I'll write the book.

missdazia: Fareal?! I love @thedrayswinelounge in Southgate! Talk about family drammmaa

imatroll.abih: @onceuponatyme is a low class bitch

missfancyreads: Is this true @pole_n_pour?

kris3marie: Have y'all seen those twin brothers though? I mean I ain't exactly mad at sis….

renaissanceman6721: Hurt hoes be vicious

shontheauthor: Not his brother being a short king. Ew.

crown.me.bookish: Wait wait wait... getting knocked up by his TWIN is nasty work

smutmeplease: @theemalachidrayton played in that girl face. Karma came back hard AF. I hope @onceuponatyme is happy with @midnightdrayton

joe__justified: I check ol' girl page, she thick as fuck. I woulda folded too if I was his brother.

tanontales: I used to date the twin who got married and I never trusted the hoe he married. He told me that was his cousin y'all so if he told ol' girl the same and then married HIS COUSIN... I wish nothing but chaos for him and a pretty baby for our lick back queen.

harlemsheatatl: Bro code is dead. You niggas wack.

tiadraytontoyou: but if i speak...

tanontales: @tiadraytontoyou if you do speak I hope it's about how you were his side chick for years until he finally picked you. Congrats?

quaywantit: BRING BACK SHAME

APRIL 3RD @ 2:03PM

Tyme

"Shit!" I muttered under my breath as my phone flashed with my mom's incoming call. Panic surged through me as I accepted the video chat, knowing that the WSOT post had reached my mother. I had been dreading this conversation since I confirmed my pregnancy. Midnight was even getting a little annoyed that I hadn't told anyone close to me, outside of Nene. But I didn't need anyone's judgment when I was trying to get used to a little gremlin taking over my body.

"So, you're pregnant?" My mom said before I even came into view

good enough. "By Midnight? Tyme, what the hell." There was concern in her voice mixed with a wild amount of confusion—as expected.

I nodded, my throat tight. "Yes, Mom. I'm pregnant with Midnight's baby."

Silence hung in the air as I vividly watched her process me confirming the truth. Her face didn't reveal much for me to go off of, which didn't make this any easier.

"I know it seems crazy, and I should have told you sooner," I began to ramble, "but I didn't know how—"

"You're a grown woman, Tyme," she said, cutting me off. "Am I disappointed that I had to find out through a social media post? Yes. Am I confused that you're pregnant by Malachi's brother? Yes. But you don't owe me an explanation. I'm just trying to process it all."

She ran her fingers through her freshly styled Senegalese braids. Following their European adventures, she and Luke had opted for Africa as their next destination. Currently, they were exploring countries in West Africa.

"Midnight? Wow." She let off a sigh. "I'm not mad, so stop looking like I'm about to ground you."

My shoulders slumped with relief as I let off a chuckle, but I still couldn't shake my anxiety. "I just didn't want you to find out this way, so I feel like I have to explain myself to you."

She offered a reassuring smile, going into mama bear mode. "Let me tell you something I learned in my thirties, Tyme. I don't owe anyone an explanation for the choices I decide to make. No one but myself. And I want you to remember that, especially now that you're on your way into motherhood. At the end of the day, the only thing I care about is if you're happy."

A wave of gratitude washed over me as I was reminded that my mom was always going to support me.

"I am, Mommy. I'm really happy."

Her face lit up. "That's all that matters, my baby."

Tears welled up in my eyes, touched by her unwavering love. "Thank you, Mom. I love you."

She smiled warmly. "I love you too, Tyme. Now, how far along are you?"

I raised the phone slightly to point it at my barely visible baby bump. "I'm about fifteen weeks, a little over three months."

Her eyes sparkled with excitement. "That's wonderful, sweetheart. How are you feeling?"

"The morning sickness is finally starting to give me a break, so I'm feeling better these days. I'm scared, though; I know nothing about being a mother."

"None of us do, and that's the joy of it. You'll learn as you go, and I know you're going to be an amazing mother. Plus, you won't have to do it alone. I'm always here for you."

"I know."

"Now," she raised a brow, "it seems like you've been having a little too much fun, so I need to know all about how this got started…"

APRIL 3RD @ 3:42PM

THE CUZZOS GROUP CHAT

HALANA

attached image of the WSOT post

Not me finding out on social media that I got another cousin coming… um congratulations? @Midnight

& Who spilled the tea. 'Cause I know I'm messy but I'm innocent this time.

RILEY

Shit I ain't know either. Damn Mid! You came for Mal's neckkkk. But congrats big cuzzo.

NEO

This shit cutthroat. Congrats nigga. @Midnight

JORI

I'm about to add Tia & Mal back to the group so we can get some answers lmaoooooooo

HALANA

You bet not Jori!

JORI

I'm not but if not ussss then....

MICKIE

Tia did that shit, let's be fucking fareal

JORI

I wasn't gonna say it but I'd believe it

MICKIE

This is getting so unnecessarily messy with ppl in my comments & DMs asking me about it like I KNOW NOTHING nosies!

HALANA

crying laughing emojis Storytimeeeee

NEO

She know better

MICKIE

And do LMAO

MIDNIGHT

We were gonna share the news soon but Tyme hadn't told her mom yet so we were waiting but I guess that's a dub. Either way, thanks fam. We appreciate it.

APRIL 3RD 6:11PM

Midnight

"Mmmh, it smells good in here," I commented, my lips curling into a smile as I entered the kitchen to find Tyme. She greeted me with that warm smile of hers, her barely noticeable baby bump catching my attention. Every day, the sight of her growing our child filled me with an overwhelming sense of joy. It might not have been in our original plan, but I couldn't have been happier about it. Knowing that Tyme was carrying my first child made each moment more beautiful, and I cherished her presence more than ever.

"Hey, my Tin Man," she said sweetly. "Baby M was in need of some s'mores," she explained.

"What kind?" I asked, genuinely curious.

"Peanut butter cup s'mores," she replied. Tyme really did have a knack for creating unique s'more recipes, and I'd tasted a variety of them since January—cookies and cream s'mores, mint chocolate s'mores, and caramel s'mores. Each one was delicious, and I was in s'more heaven.

"Sign me up for about four of them." I pulled her closer to me, planting a kiss on her lips. Her laughter was music to my ears. Each day, I found myself falling more and more for her, and it scared me, but I continued to lean into it.

"Got you, boo," she replied, giving me another quick peck before returning to making our evening treats.

As I settled on a stool across the counter from her, I couldn't help but express my concern. "You really okay?" I asked, recalling the social media post that had revealed our pregnancy to the world. I'd called her earlier, and she'd reassured me that she was fine, but her texts had hinted at something different.

"Yeah, I mean it sucks that my mom had to find out like that, but like I told you, she took it better than expected," Tyme replied, her tone calm.

"So, she's not gonna come down here and beat my ass?" I joked, hoping to lighten the mood.

"I mean... don't rule it out just yet," she teased, and we shared a laugh.

I snagged one of the mini peanut butter cups that was to be used for a s'more from the baking sheet, earning a playful glare from Tyme. I couldn't resist grinning as I devoured the sweet treat.

"Jerk," she muttered, though her affectionate tone didn't hide her amusement.

"A jerk who's your baby daddy, though," I retorted playfully.

"Disgusting," she replied with a mock scowl.

I laughed heartily as she carefully positioned the baking sheet in the preheated oven, placing it on the middle rack.

When she turned back to face me, I could sense her underlying concerns. "I just hate how I'm seen as the person who's most in the wrong in this whole situation. I had to block so many people today," she confessed, her vulnerability showing through.

"So, how can I fix it?" I asked sincerely, wanting to ease her distress.

"You can't. It's just social media being social media," she replied with resignation.

"Nah, I can do something. Go upstairs and pack a bag. Let's go on a little baecation. You need it," I suggested, my tone firm. I knew there was genuinely nothing I could do about the post itself, but I'd do whatever it took to put her back in her happy space.

"Midnight, we can't just run away from our problems or go on a trip every time there is one," she protested, though I could see her resistance fading.

"Says who?" I countered, a glimmer of determination in my eyes. "Now go pack while I watch the s'mores."

May

MAY 14TH

onceuponatyme

Liked by **whereisaprylnow** and 714 others

onceuponatyme Mom, your love, strength, and endless support has shaped me into the woman I am today. I'm forever grateful for your guidance and the countless memories we've made together.

As I journey into motherhood myself, I can't help but reflect on the incredible example you've set. Your unwavering love and kindness are the qualities I hope to pass on to my little one. 💕

And who knows, maybe I'll be blessed with a little girl who's just like the one I once was. 👧🏽

Here's to all the amazing mamas out there – Happy Mother's Day!

#ThrowbackonaSunday #Motherhood #Mommytobe #MothersDay #ILoveYouMom

View all 91 comments

queenbeemama Yaaas, mama-to-be! Your mom set the bar high, and you're leveling up. Can't wait to meet the little one!

midnightdrayton Happy mother's day to the finest woman on the planet. I can't wait to do parenthood with you.

midnightdrayton And stop trying my son like that.

onceuponatyme @midnightdrayton Don't come on here starting your mess 😑

ght_swx @midnightdrayton You should just want a healthy baby

pole_n_pour some of y'all don't know how to laugh obviously he wanna healthy baby

pole_n_pour Anyway I can't wait to meet my niecy pooh! 😍 @midnightdrayton

gurlyougottareadthisshyt This post hit me right in the feels! 😭 Your journey into mommyhood is gonna be lit! 💕

whereisaprylnow I love you my baby.

nenenene This is the cuteststtt throwback! I can't wait to meet my niece (or nephew)!

halanaxhalana Big congrats on joining the mommy club! Can't wait to meet my new little cousin.

beingmrsdrayton You and your mom were beautiful. Your mom's legacy shines through you and I can't wait to meet my grand baby. Happy Mother's Day, mama!

onceuponatyme: Mom, your love, strength, and endless support has shaped me into the woman I am today. I'm forever grateful for your guidance and the countless memories we've made together.·

As I journey into motherhood myself, I can't help but reflect on the incredible example you've set. Your unwavering love and kindness are the qualities I hope to pass on to my little one.

And who knows, maybe I'll be blessed with a little girl who's just like the one I was.

Here's to all the amazing mamas out there – Happy Mother's Day! #ThrowbackonaSunday #Motherhood #Mommytobe #MothersDay #ILoveYouMom

queenbeemama: Yaaas, mama-to-be! Your mom set the bar high, and you're leveling up. Can't wait to meet the little one!
midnightdrayton: Happy mother's day to the finest woman on the planet. I can't wait to do parenthood with you.
midnightdrayton: And stop trying my son like that.
onceuponatyme: @midnightdrayton Don't come on here starting your mess
ght_swx: @midnightdrayton You should just want a healthy baby
pole_n_pour: some of y'all don't know how to laugh obviously he wanna healthy baby
pole_n_pour: Anyway I can't wait to meet my niecy pooh! @midnightdrayton
gurlyougottareadthisshyt: This post hit me right in the feels! Your journey into mommyhood is gonna be lit!
whereisaprylnow: I love you my baby.
nenenene: This is the cutesttttt throwback! I can't wait to meet my niece (or nephew)!

halanaxhalana: Big congrats on joining the mommy club! Can't wait to meet my new little cousin.

beingmrsdrayton: You and your mom were beautiful. Your mom's legacy shines through you and I can't wait to meet my grand baby. Happy Mother's Day, mama!

MAY 15TH

To the incredible man who's sharing this incredible journey with me, thank you for making my first Mother's Day so special. Here's to many more beautiful moments together.

~ With love, Tyme.

MIDNIGHT

I never got flowers before. Thank you baby.

TYME

You're welcome. Do I win a prize?

MIDNIGHT

If you tryna have me knock you up while you're already knocked up... just say that.

TYME

Come handle this pussy then

MIDNIGHT

I'll be there in fifteen.

midnightdrayton: Get you a woman who sends you flowers.

keonedidit: okay princess treatment
neodray: look at you in your soft boy era
paperbacksandpoundcakes: Oh you must have delivered premium peen
missfancyreads: The way you showing off the things YOUR BROTHER'S EX do for you is NASTY work
pole_n_pour: Awwww how sweet!! Love this for you big bro
readlexread: It's giving pick me but if that's what you like

imatroll.abih: Not you letting your brother play in your face like this @theemalachidrayton

nenenene: not her sending you my flowers... um @once-uponatyme ... where mine?

aninjanamedjeri: that's how the h*es coming nowadays? I need to get me one.

June

JUNE 18TH

Tyme

MIDNIGHT

You okay?

TYME

Yeah, she's fixing me a snack :) How's the brunch?

I settled into Kinley's tastefully decorated living room, my growing belly making itself known as it had expanded significantly over the past month. Our agenda for today was to finalize the details of my upcoming baby shower, scheduled for next month. With Midnight off to a Father's Day brunch, it left me available for a *"Sunday Funday"* with his mom.

"Texting my son?" Kinley's voice broke through the quiet, accompanied by the rhythmic tap of her heels as she emerged from the kitchen, bearing two bowls brimming with summer fruits. The cozy atmosphere of her home helped alleviate some of my initial discomfort.

I mustered a smile. "Yeah, he was just checking in."

Kinley placed the bowls of fruit between us. "Well, tell him you're in good hands and to enjoy his first Father's Day brunch," she suggested.

The Drays Wine Bar had been hosting a Father's Day brunch for Black dads for the past five years, and Midnight was thrilled about attending it as a dad-to-be. Seeing his excitement only deepened my appreciation for the incredible father he'd be.

I let out a forced chuckle. "I'll let him know."

As Kinley sat down and glanced over at me, I couldn't help but notice the intensity in her eyes. Kinley's gaze, while not as dark as Midnight's, was just as penetrating.

"You sound like you don't believe that yourself."

I furrowed my brows. "Believe what?"

"That you're in good hands." Kinley picked up a binder from the table, her focus now seemingly directed at the pages within. Her serious demeanor was nothing new; she'd exhibited the same meticulousness when planning my wedding to Malachi, a wedding that had ultimately fallen apart. Nevertheless, I appreciated her attention to detail.

"Oh." I faltered, feeling caught off guard. This marked the first time I'd been alone with Kinley since everything had transpired with Midnight and me. Even before that, when I was with Malachi, we hadn't spent much one-on-one time together. Kinley had never been unkind, but she hadn't been overly warm either. Her relationship with Tia was markedly closer.

"I know that when you were with Malachi, we didn't really get a chance to bond, and I will admit that was more on my part," Kinley admitted. "But now that you're with Midnight, I do really want to change that."

I nodded. "Okay." My response came almost reflexively. I was curious about why she wanted to forge this new relationship, but at the same time, I was no longer as invested in the past.

"To be clear, it's not only because you're pregnant with my grand-child, but because I truly see how happy you make my son," Kinley continued. "And as a mother, you will see that, at the end of the day, we just want our children to be happy. I see that he loves you, and he's happy—" She paused abruptly. "What's that face for?"

I realized I'd unconsciously displayed a puzzled expression.

"You don't believe me?"

"No," I quickly responded, "it's not that. It's…you think he loves me?" Kinley's words had me spinning.

Kinley chuckled warmly. "You don't?"

I ran my hand through my hair, trying to make sense of my thoughts. "Well, we've never said that. We've— we've never said it."

"Seriously?" she asked, sounding incredulous.

I nodded. Was it crazy that we hadn't said it yet? I mean, I've wanted to say it, but I wanted him to say it first. Was that wrong? "We wanted to take things slow, and obviously, Baby M changed that. But I don't know, we never said the words."

"Do you love him?" Kinley inquired, tilting her head slightly. The question churned my stomach.

"Yeah," I replied softly, placing my hand on my belly as Baby M gave me a gentle kick, almost as if they knew we were talking about their daddy. "But I don't want to say it first because I rushed into so many things with Malachi, and it scarred me. Malachi and I were saying 'I love you' two months in and look where that led us."

"Midnight isn't—"

"Trust me, I know that more than anything. They're complete opposites. Things are so different… I guess I'm just afraid."

"I'm sure you know how things went with his last relationship." Kinley's words held empathy, and I nodded. "Veronica did a number on my baby, and I didn't think I'd see him bounce back from that for at least five years. So, I can only imagine that he's feeling somewhat the same. I do think he will say it, but if you want him to say it first, you're gonna have to be patient. However, know that he does. I'm one hundred percent sure of that."

"Okay." I exhaled deeply. "I'll consider saying it first."

"Good, because sometimes men just need to hear it first. They're annoying."

I couldn't help but laugh along with Kinley. "Facts."

After a moment, she leaned over, placing a hand on my knee. "I truly do want to build a better relationship with you, Tyme. If you're open to it."

The corners of my mouth curled up. "I'd love that."

JUNE 21ST

Tyme

You up? How about some late-night leftover s'mores and bestie time?

NENE

Absolutely. Last one to the kitchen is a rotten egg!

As the clock ticked past midnight, Nene and I met in the kitchen, the soft moonlight casting a gentle glow through the windows. We gathered the remnants of our late-night s'mores, and with our sweet treats in hand, we made our way to the inviting outdoor lounge couch on the adjacent balcony that overlooked the ocean.

Nene beamed at me, her eyes reflecting excitement. "I just realized it's past midnight! Happy birthday, boo!" She embraced me tightly, her warmth radiating through our hug.

I was officially thirty-one.

"Thank you, friend," I replied, a wide grin spreading across my face as we settled onto the comfy couch. The gentle ocean breeze brushed against our skin, and the distant sound of waves crashing against the shore provided a soothing backdrop.

Midnight had surprised me with a trip to an island for a baby moon and birthday celebration, and he'd thoughtfully invited Nene and Mo to join us, ensuring they could share in the festivities.

The beach house we were staying in was spacious, allowing each couple to have their own private quarters. It was a thoughtful touch, especially considering that Midnight and I had been getting it in quite frequently lately, thanks to my heightened sex drive this month. In fact, we had just finished a hot and heavy session before I texted Nene.

Nene reached for one of the s'mores and asked, "Why are you even up? I thought y'all were calling it a night."

"We were, but this baby won't let me sleep," I confessed with a chuckle. "I mean, I did put *him* to sleep, though." I couldn't help but grin mischievously.

Nene chuckled, shaking her head. "Okay, lil' nasty, putting him to sleep!"

"Well, you know I had to because..." I paused dramatically, savoring the moment, "He said I love you!!"

Nene's mouth dropped open, before a joyful squeal escaped her lips. We bounced around on the couch like two excited schoolgirls.

"Oh my god," she sang.

"Yeah," I said, grinning from ear to ear. "I know I told you that I was going to take his mom's advice and say it first after he surprised me with this trip, but... he beat me to it." My heart fluttered as I replayed the memory of him saying those three little words for the first time.

"Awwww, y'all are all in love. Next stop: marriage."

"Fingers crossed," I said, holding up my crossed fingers. "Because I've never been this happy. It's crazy because I was afraid that things were moving so fast because of Baby M," I continued, placing my hand over my pregnant belly, "when we originally agreed to take it slow. But honestly, everything just feels right and different than anything else I've ever experienced. I really do love that man, Ne. He's my person.

Nene smiled warmly, her eyes reflecting genuine happiness as she grabbed the second-to-last s'more. "And you're his. I'm so happy for you, boo. You deserve it."

"I do," I replied, my heart full of gratitude and love, savoring this moment of bliss.

JULY

JULY 15TH

"A lot of people don't know this but Baby MJ is our rainbow baby. At the very beginning of last July, Malachi and I, found out we were expecting our first child together. Unfortunately our baby became an angel instead, but now they get to watch over their brother."

KEONE

Bruh tell me I'm hearing this wrong. She didn't just say last JULY? TF.

MIDNIGHT

Nah your ears good.

KEONE

Mal look like he pissed AF and damn near as shocked as everyone else

MIDNIGHT

Because he didn't want it to get out

KEONE

Not him looking right at Tyme as soon as she
said it though.

MIDNIGHT

He better look the fuck somewhere else before
I ruin their baby shower

———

MICKIE

Why she say that???? She could have left it at
rainbow baby.

At least Tyme doesn't look like it fazed her

MIDNIGHT

She just got her poker face on. You know she
don't even wanna be here.

MICKIE

She definitely a better woman than me. How
you get so lucky?

MIDNIGHT

Shut up fathead.

Midnight

"You okay?" I asked, my voice low and careful as I looked into Tyme's
eyes. As soon as everyone started getting their food, I pulled her to the
side.

"I'm fine, babe," she replied, her smile a touch forced.

"Tyme," I stressed, my fingers lightly brushing her arm. I couldn't
shake the feeling that Tia's timing with the miscarriage reveal was too
deliberate. A calculated move to nudge Tyme into piecing together the
puzzle we'd kept hidden.

Tia seemed hell-bent on causing Tyme more pain than Malachi ever did. Her motives were becoming murkier by the day. The Tia she'd become over the past year was like a distorted version of the girl I once knew. Familiar face, but everything else — her actions, her aura — it was all different, twisted.

I hadn't the faintest clue what kind of dark magic Mal's dick had her under, but I was damn tired of her games. It was about time he got a grip on her and reeled her in before I got tired of being the bigger person and decided I'd had enough of taking the high road.

Her gaze met mine, a hint of defiance in those beautiful eyes. "I can do the math. She was pregnant before we were supposed to get married. But I don't care."

I reached out and cupped her cheek, my thumb grazing her skin as I searched her face for any hint of underlying emotions. "You don't have to be strong for me, Sweets."

"I'm not," she sighed, leaning into my touch. "I'm at the point where nothing they can say or do will shock me anymore. Nor do I care." She paused before saying, "But you knew and didn't tell me."

"I did and—" I started, but her words cut me off.

"It's okay. Really," she said, her voice softening. "I know you well enough now to know your intentions were to protect me, and I'm glad you didn't tell me six months ago when I was still navigating the pain. Now, I'm happy and whatever they did in the past is their business and none of my concern. Fuck them both."

I chuckled, my fingers playing with a strand of her hair. "There's my girl." I grinned.

"You just like me to be violent."

I shrugged, my grin widening. "A lil' bit. Can't be having no punk raising my son."

Tyme rolled her eyes, a playful smirk tugging at her lips. "You are aggy."

"But you love me anyway," I teased, my voice warm.

"Shoulda kept that to myself." She chuckled, her eyes shining with affection.

JULY 16TH @ 7:11PM

onceuponatyme: Got him ready to knock me up again . But seriously, we had a TYME at our shower today! Thank you to everyone who came out to shower us with love for Baby M. We are overwhelmed by all the gifts and truly appreciate each and everyone of you. #ThirdTrimester #AlmostTyme #GirlOrBoy

midnightdrayton: no lies told witcho fine ass.
imatrollabih: since they twins isn't that like your ex's baby too? Ew.
nenenene: you hoes need to go back to school @imatrollabih
nenenene: Look at OUR baby mama.
neodray: I'm voting girl but don't tell Mid
whereisapyrlnow: now get some rest, you're not superwoman.
midnightdrayton: @neodray nigga I can see your comment. Punk.
thelibraryofrae: honestly I need this love story written in a book immediately.
readlexread: it's all fun and games until karma comes back around.

JULY 16TH @ 8:43PM

BESTIES & BOOS GROUP CHAT

NENE

Nobody else will say it, but y'all baby shower was the superior one

TYME

You ain't even go to the other one

NENE

Your point?

MIDNIGHT

Babe, just agree. She right.

MO

The testosterone has spoken.

It was the most lit baby shower I been too.

TYME

I knew creating this group chat was a bad idea. We need to disband it because All of y'all are a mess...

& accurate. *shrugging emoji*

Our meatballs was definitely hitting better than theirs

NENE

PERIOD.

August

AUGUST 22ND @ 11:24AM

MIDNIGHT

Where do you think you're off to?

TYME

Oh, come on *crying laughing emoji*. Are you spying on me now?

MIDNIGHT

Can't trust you not to get into trouble when I'm not around.

TYME

side eye emoji Alright, fine. I might be sneaking out for a bit.

MIDNIGHT

shaking my head gif

You know you're supposed to be taking it easy.

TYME

Dr. Nina said I could do light activities if I'm feeling fine, and I haven't had any problems lately.

MIDNIGHT

I understand that, but I don't want you pushing yourself too hard.

TYME

I promise I won't, my love *fingers crossed emoji*. Just need a breath of fresh air and a change of scenery.

MIDNIGHT

i.e. shopping. But fine, just keep me updated, and don't be gone for too long.

I love you.

TYME

LOL you know your baby mama so well lol. But you got it, boss. I love you too. *blowing a kiss emoji*

AUGUST 22ND @ 2:17PM

Tyme

What began as a simple Target run somehow morphed into a two-hour shopping spree, where I found myself picking up items for Baby M that were more impulse buys than necessities. The nesting instinct had taken over, fueled by the fact that I had spent the majority of the past four weeks confined to strict bed rest.

As if the shopping spree wasn't enough, I found myself at Lattes & Bagels, despite having just told Midnight that I was on my way home. Tomorrow, he was definitely gonna give me an earful about it when he returned from his work trip. But with Midnight out of town and Nene attending a real estate conference, I seized the opportunity to break free from what had started to feel like a personal prison.

My pregnancy had been progressing smoothly until a few weeks ago, when a routine prenatal checkup revealed that I had developed placenta previa. It was unexpected news that hit me like a ton of bricks. This diagnosis meant changes to my daily life, unexpected limitations, and a heightened sense of caution—particularly from Midnight. However, despite the initial worries, I was determined to make the best of the situation for Baby M's sake and my own. It didn't take much for me to convince myself that a quick outing wouldn't hurt. After all, I had been feeling perfectly fine lately—no signs of discomfort or pain. So why not savor a moment of freedom?

Standing in line, my thoughts danced between guilt and excitement. Guilt for possibly overexerting myself during my time out, and excitement for the simple pleasure of enjoying my favorite summer tea and bagel. Little did I know that this seemingly innocent decision would lead to an unexpected turn of events.

After placing my order, I settled into a corner seat by the window, intending to rest before hitting the road. Sipping my Sunshine Limeade tea and taking a bite of the warm, toasted poppyseed bagel felt liberating. The flavors offered me comfort, but I couldn't ignore the faint twinges of pain that had started to surface. This familiar sensation was like a warning bell in my mind, urging me to head back home to rest.

Or was I just in my head and imagining things due to my growing paranoia?

I tried to focus on the familiar surroundings and the quiet buzz of activity around me. However, my attention was drawn to the entrance just as Malachi walked into the café.

First Tia, now him—clearly, I needed to find a new favorite café.

I wondered whether he had noticed me as he went straight to the counter to place his order. I regretted even looking in his direction because, as if he could sense me, our eyes met. I quickly averted my gaze, my grip tightening around my teacup.

His steps brought him closer to my table, and I cursed myself for not choosing a more inconspicuous spot. I kept my focus on my tea as his footsteps grew nearer. A mixture of apprehension and frustration swirled within me because I didn't have the energy to deal with his shenanigans today. Since that day in Midnight's driveway seven months ago, we hadn't spent more than a minute alone together.

As if the universe had decided to have a bit of fun at my expense, Malachi walked right up to my table and pulled out the chair opposite me, seating himself without an invitation.

"Mind if I join you?" he asked, his tone deceptively casual, masking the complicated emotions simmering beneath the surface.

I forced a small smile, trying to keep my composure. "Actually, I was about to leave."

Undeterred, he offered a brief nod before settling in. "I promise not to take up too much of your time. Just a quick chat, if you're willing."

My fingers drummed softly on the tabletop, torn between wanting to dismiss him and a nagging curiosity about what he had to say. Despite my better judgment, I found myself reluctantly agreeing. "Alright, but make it quick."

"You look good. Pregnancy suits you," Malachi commented with a hesitant smile.

"Compliments won't buy you extra time," I retorted, my tone cool and distant.

He chuckled nervously, the tension palpable. "Fair point. I was just... wondering how you're doing."

"Small talk won't buy you much time either. You've got about four minutes left."

He shifted uncomfortably. "Right, right." Clearing his throat, he seemed to gather his thoughts. "I heard from Mom that you've been on bed rest, and I wanted to check in."

I sighed inwardly, already bracing myself for the impending apology. "I'm fine, Malachi. Let's not drag this out. I really should be heading home."

He nodded, seemingly understanding. "Okay, okay. I wanted to take this chance to genuinely apologize for my actions this past year because I know they were immature, selfish, and fucked up. I know I said sorry when things fell apart, but I can see how that might not have meant much, considering how quickly I moved on with Tia."

Suppressing an eye roll, I maintained a neutral expression, letting him continue as I mentally braced for what I anticipated would be more excuses and justifications.

"So, Tyme, I'm sorry. Truly sorry," he said earnestly. "I see the way you and Midnight are together, and while it stung, and I wasn't exactly thrilled at first, I can tell that you both genuinely love each other. You're happy, and that's what matters."

"I am," I replied, my words falling easily from my lips. "I'm very happy." My hand found its way to my stomach, subconsciously cradling the tiny life growing within me. The pinches of pain had been persistent, and I couldn't shake the feeling that something wasn't quite right. The unease settled in my chest as I acknowledged that these twinges were no longer figments of my imagination.

Malachi continued, "I also want to apologize for Tia. Her behavior has been out of line, and I'm well aware of that. It wasn't until she mentioned the miscarriage, knowing you didn't know, that I realized the extent of her malice. Selfishly, I didn't want you to find out about it because I knew how much I'd hurt you already."

Maintaining my silence, I allowed him to keep talking.

"I believe Tia's been struggling with her emotions," he went on, his voice tinged with concern. "Losing the first baby and everything else has taken a toll on her. This isn't the same woman I once knew or who I sacrificed our relationship for. And I can't keep ignoring the change in her."

I gave a noncommittal shrug, feeling no obligation to respond.

"I don't know what you want me to say to that," I finally spoke up, my tone guarded. While I wanted to tell him that maybe he never truly knew her in the first place, I kept my words to myself. None of this was my problem anymore.

He let out a sigh. "I'm not expecting you to say much, Tyme. I just wanted to explain things from my end and own up to how I handled things."

His words hung in the air, and I felt the weight of the past year's complexities lingering between us. Despite his apology and explanations, it didn't change the fact that I had moved on. My focus had shifted, my priorities rearranged, and my heart found solace in a new place. And as the twinges of pain continued, a reminder of the life I was nurturing, I realized that my time was running out — both in this conversation and in the way my body was signaling me.

"Okay. Well, like you said, I'm happy. I've long stopped worrying about you and Tia because I'm too focused on me, Midnight, and our child. I never quite understood Tia's animosity towards me, and I eventually stopped carrying that weight but good luck to you figuring it out. Anyway, I should be getting back home. Have a good evening."

With that, I excused myself, heading towards the bathroom before my departure to make sure I wasn't spotting.

After I checked myself out and convinced myself that it might just be Braxton Hicks contractions I was experiencing, I gave myself a pep talk before exiting the bathroom.

As I made my way back through the café, a sudden, sharp pain gripped my lower abdomen. It was unlike anything I'd felt before, and a jolt of panic coursed through me. Grasping the edge of a nearby table, I attempted to steady myself while my thoughts raced.

Another wave of pain hit me; this time more forceful. A sensation of warmth rushed through me, sending a shiver down my spine. My heart raced as I locked eyes with Malachi, who had clearly noticed my distress. In seconds, he was instantly by my side.

"Are you okay, Tyme?" His voice was laced with worry.

I tried to put on a brave face. "I'm fine," I managed, though my voice betrayed my unease. In his concerned gaze, I saw a flicker of doubt and genuine care that momentarily cracked my armor.

His hand landed gently on my back, offering support as I stood upright.

"Let me at least take you home."

"No, really, I'll be fine. I just need some rest." My reassurances fell flat even to my own ears.

The pain receded enough to allow me to make my way to the car. Yet as I started my journey home, the discomfort returned with a vengeance, escalating by the minute.

Each pang reminded me of my vulnerability, a stark contrast to the strength I had always projected. Nevertheless, I remained determined to downplay it, treating the pain as an inconvenience. Clenching the steering wheel, I took a deep breath to calm myself, only for another wave of agony to crash over me, causing me to pull over.

Tears welled up in my eyes as I struggled to cope with the pain. *I was fine. I had to be fine. We had to be fine.* Blinking away the tears, I fumbled for my purse, searching for my phone, only to curse as I realized I had left it in the café restroom.

Fuck!

I shut my eyes briefly, attempting to quiet my racing heart before rejoining the flow of traffic. Despite the growing dizziness, my mind was set on reaching home. However, the universe had other plans.

A knock on the window startled me, and I turned to find Malachi standing there. Had he followed me? His eyes carried a mix of worry and resolve.

Rolling down my window, I rushed to assure him before he could even ask. "I told you, I'm fine." Yet, my pretense of strength wavered as another sharp pang coursed through me, causing me to wince.

His eyes locked onto mine, his intensity mirroring the anxiety I felt inside. "No, Tyme, you're not. We're going to the hospital."

Shaking my head, I struggled to process the situation. "This can't be happening now," I murmured to myself, my voice strained. "It's too early. I'm only thirty-five weeks."

Malachi leaned in, unlocking the car as he gently assured me that everything would be okay.

"I need Midnight. I can't do this without him."

"I'll call him. But right now, let me get you to the hospital," he insisted.

"No, no, I need him now." I pleaded as he helped me out of the car. Glancing back at my seat, I spotted a small pool of red, sending a fresh wave of panic surging through me. The world spun around me as Malachi guided me into the passenger seat. The sharp pain persisted alongside a growing dizziness that enveloped my senses as he shut the car door and returned to the driver's seat.

"Please, I need Midnight," I kept repeating, desperately clinging to consciousness in the passenger seat.

"Calling him now," he said, pulling away from the curb. "Shit," he cursed under his breath a few times before I heard him instructing someone to pull Midnight out of whatever meeting he was in.

My grasp on reality was slipping, the world becoming a blurry whirlwind of lights and sounds. Malachi's voice was a distant echo, urging me to hang on, to keep fighting, but it was a battle I was rapidly losing.

The hospital loomed in the distance, a flicker of hope amid the chaos. Each jolt of the car intensified the pain, a searing reminder of the life and urgency coursing through me. My strength waned, my body weakened, and the darkness approached.

"Midnight's on his way," Malachi's words were like a lifeline. "Okay, Tyme? He's coming. Everything's going to be okay."

I managed a nod as I clutched my stomach, silently praying that he was right.

"We're almost there," he reassured me. Tears pooled in my eyes as I fought to hold on, to make it to the hospital. I refused to surrender to the darkness tugging at my consciousness.

However, as the car pulled into the hospital parking lot, the pain surged, and I felt myself losing the struggle. The world spun, the sounds of sirens and voices blending into a disorienting symphony. My body felt heavy, every movement a monumental effort.

The car came to a stop, and I heard the distant sound of Malachi's voice, urging me to stay conscious. I wanted to respond, to let him know I was still present, but my voice failed me. Darkness closed in, and I couldn't fight it any longer.

When I regained awareness, I was lying on a stretcher, surrounded by bright lights and unfamiliar faces. I attempted to focus, to understand what was happening, but my thoughts remained foggy.

The stretcher moved, and I was rushed into the hospital. Machines beeped, voices overlapped, and I felt a sense of helplessness wash over me. Yet, amidst it all, I clung to the hope that both my baby and I would be okay. As the medical team worked tirelessly around me, a surge of determination coursed through my veins. I couldn't surrender to the darkness, not when there was so much at stake.

Lying in the post-op recovery room, a blend of relief and exhaustion washed over me. The haze of anesthesia was gradually lifting, and I struggled to piece together my surroundings. The rhythmic beeping of machines and the soft hum of activity filled the room, serving as a reminder that I had just undergone a C-section to bring my baby into the world.

Slowly, my eyes fluttered open, adjusting to the sterile brightness of the room. A figure by my bedside captured my attention, and my heart skipped a beat as Midnight's face registered. Relief flooded through me, and a small smile tugged at the corners of my lips. He was here. He had made it.

"Hey," he whispered, his voice exactly what my soul needed.

I tried to respond, my voice a mere whisper, reflecting my weakened state. "Midnight..."

His hand reached out, fingers tenderly brushing against my cheek. "You did amazing, Tyme. Both of you."

The tears that had been threatening to spill finally escaped, sliding down my cheeks. The weight of the entire journey, from the placenta previa diagnosis to the emergency C-section, had been heavy on my shoulders. But now, with Midnight at my side, the burden seemed to lighten.

"I'm just happy you're here," I managed to say, my words carrying a mix of emotions.

He smiled, his eyes reflecting the depth of his emotions. "Me too, Sweets. I'm just grateful you both are alright."

My gaze shifted towards the bassinet placed near my bed, where our baby lay swaddled. Mira-Serenity Alise Drayton, a tiny and precious miracle, was a living testament to the love shared between Midnight and me. The journey to this moment had been tumultuous, filled with uncertainty and challenges, but now, with her in the world, it all felt worth it.

"Is Malachi still around?" I never thought there'd come another day in this lifetime when I'd be thankful for Malachi Drayton's presence, but today proved me wrong. I was wholeheartedly grateful for how he'd stood by me, even accompanying me into the surgery room when Midnight couldn't.

"He left once I got here, but Dr. Nina let me know he didn't play about you. I guess we gonna have to be nice to him now," he laughed, bringing a lightness to the situation.

"How ghetto," I concurred.

"Very. See what happens when you don't listen to *Daddy* and stay your ass home."

I playfully scrunched up my face, knowing that it was only going to be a matter of time before he brought that up. "Yeah, yeah, yeah."

Midnight's smiled before his eyes returned to our daughter. "She's absolutely beautiful," he breathed, a sense of wonder lacing his words.

More tears welled up in my eyes as I nodded, overcome by a wave of emotions. "She really is."

"Just like her mother. I'm incredibly proud of you, Tyme," he declared. "You're even stronger than I imagined."

His words resonated deep within me, and I managed to smile through my tears. "We did it, Midnight. We have our own little family."

Leaning in, he pressed a tender kiss to my forehead. "I love you, Tyme. And I love our piece of serenity."

"We love you too."

His words enveloped me, filling me with warmth and a profound sense of completeness. We had come through so much to reach this moment, and now, as we faced the journey ahead as parents, I knew that no matter what challenges lay in our path, we would face them together.

September

SEPTEMBER 16TH

MIDNIGHT

Congratulations. MJ is beautiful.

MALACHI

Thanks, bro. How's Tyme and my niece?

MIDNIGHT

They're doing pretty well. It's amazing how much she's already grown in less than a month. Tyme's handling everything like a champ.

MALACHI

Not surprised.

MIDNIGHT

How's Tia holding up?

MALACHI

Yeah, the delivery went surprisingly smooth. Although, I gotta admit, watching the whole head coming out thing was wild AF. No one prepares you for that.

MIDNIGHT

Haha, I can only imagine.

Anyway, I know things are gonna be hectic for both of us in the coming weeks, but I want to remind you of what I said at the hospital. I still want us to sit down and talk, clear the air completely.

MALACHI

Yeah, I'm down for that. Let's plan to do it next month when things settle down a bit. It's time to put the past behind us — after all, we're somebody's dads now *mind blown emoji*.

MIDNIGHT

damn we're getting old gif

SEPTEMBER 22ND

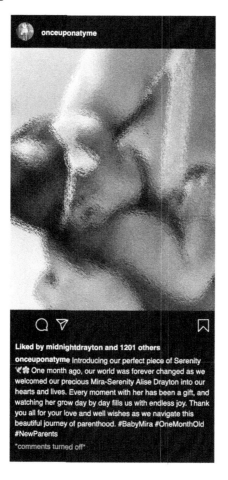

onceuponatyme: Introducing our perfect piece of Serenity. One month ago, our world was forever changed as we welcomed our precious Mira-Serenity Alise Drayton into our hearts and lives. Every moment with her has been a gift, and watching her grow day by day fills us with endless joy. Thank you all for your love and well wishes as we navigate this beautiful journey of parenthood. #BabyMira #OneMonthOld #NewParents

comments turned off

SEPT 25TH

midnightdrayton

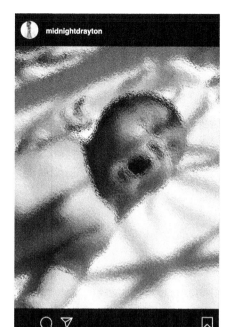

Liked by onceuponatyme and 1212 others

midnightdrayton Today was supposed to be the day we anxiously awaited your arrival, but you had other plans, being dramatic just like your mama and showing up five weeks early. Mira-Serenity, you have completely stolen our hearts. The overwhelming love I feel when I look at you, especially when you're snuggled up with your mama, is beyond words. Loving two people this intensely is a feeling I could have never imagined. You are our greatest blessing. P.S. If your mama ever tells you that I wanted a boy first, she lying!

View all 317 comments

theemalachidrayton 😂😂😂

keonedidit baby girl about to be spoiled AF

rohanythejeweler @keonedidit you speaking facts bc I already made her a little bracelet 😍

paperbacksandpoundcakes awwww she's precious!! I want one!

pole_n_pour look at this cutie pieeeee! Auntie loves you so much Mirabean~

liamferguson your ugly ass made a cute baby, must be @onceuponatyme genes coming thru

questxwine congratulations from Quest & Wine!

beingmrsdrayton your glamma loves you baby girl

onceuponatyme @liamferguson AND IS lmboooo! Look at my baby. I am in LOVE. 😍 ...but my man fine, so not too much on him na 😒

imatrollabih were you screaming my man my man my man when his brother was your man? @onceuponatyme

shontheauthor she gon' be short like her daddy

onceuponatyme are you obsessed with me? LMBO @imatrollabih

pole_n_pour @beingmrsdrayton you spelled grandma wrong lady

midnightdrayton: Today was supposed to be the day we anxiously awaited your arrival, but you had other plans, being dramatic just like your mama and showing up five weeks early. Mira-Serenity, you have completely stolen our hearts. The overwhelming love I feel when I look at you, especially when you're snuggled up with your mama, is beyond words. Loving two people this intensely is a feeling I could have never imagined. You are our greatest blessing. P.S. If your mama ever tells you that I wanted a boy first, she lying!

theemalachidrayton: *heart eye emojis*
keonedidit: baby girl about to be spoiled AF
rohanythejeweler: @keonedidit you speaking facts bc I already made her a little bracelet
paperbacksandpoundcakes: awwww she's precious!! I want one!
pole_n_pour: look at this cutie pieeeee! Auntie loves you so much Mirabean~
liamferguson: your ugly ass made a cute baby, must be @onceuponatyme genes coming thru
questxwine: congratulations from Quest & Wine!
beingmrsdrayton: your glamma loves you baby girl onceuponatyme: @liamferguson AND IS lmboooo! Look at my baby. I am in LOVE.... but my man fine, so not too much on him na
imatrollabih: were you screaming my man my man my man when his brother was your man? @onceuponatyme
shontheauthor: she gon' be short like her daddy
onceuponatyme: are you obsessed with me? LMBO @imatrollabih
pole_n_pour: @beingmrsdrayton you spelled grandma wrong lady

October

OCTOBER 17TH

Midnight

I was busy sifting through paperwork when Malachi walked into my office at The Drays. I looked up and greeted him, knowing that he was here for a conversation we had both finally made time for.

"What's up?" I asked, setting aside the paperwork.

"Shit, nothing but my lack of sleep," Malachi replied, sinking into one of the chairs across from my desk.

"Felt," I said with a knowing smile. "Fatherhood is wearing my ass out, but I love it."

"Same. Every single day, there's something new that MJ does, and I'm just in awe." Malachi's eyes lit up as he spoke about his son.

We spent a few more minutes sharing our experiences of the highs and lows of being new dads before we transitioned into the real reason for his visit.

"I'm glad we're finally able to be in the same room alone and it not be so much animosity," I commented, acknowledging the change in our relationship.

"Same. Earlier in the year, I admit that I was nowhere near wanting to have this conversation, but time and perspective have really changed that for me. No pun intended," Malachi said with a chuckle.

"Speaking of," I said, leaning forward slightly, "Tyme did tell me about the conversation y'all had the day Mira was born."

Malachi nodded, his expression more serious now. "I expected her to. It was a long time coming, and I truly meant what I told her. The way I acted when I found out about you and her was out of pure jealousy because had she moved on with anyone else, I would have never acted that way. But also, I was in a space of still trying to figure out if I had made the right decision with Tia and seeing Tyme with you had me spiraling. I admit that.

"I said and did some foolish and out-of-line things. I accept my role in everything, and now I'm honestly happy for you both. We really didn't even need to have this conversation," he said with a playful air of confidence, "but I also know it's the only way to get yo' mama to stop texting them Bible verses."

"On God!" I sniggered. "Like woman, chill."

We shared a genuine laugh before he said, "But I appreciate that, and I can tell you that Tyme does too. This year has been a lot for us all, and it's clear that we're trying to move past it. And we all played our parts," I fidgeted with my goatee, "Tyme and I never intended for things to turn out the way they did, but it happened. I don't regret it, but I would never intentionally have done it out of malice. So, I apologize for the way in which things happened." My words were sincere and so was the fact that I wouldn't ever apologize for Tyme being right where she belonged.

"Thank you. On some real shit, I've been doing a lot of reflecting, especially since MJ arrived. And one thing I can admit is that I definitely regret how I handled things back then. From the cheating to the aftermath because I'm still seeing how my actions have consequences.

Even after I decided to focus on my relationship with Tia, because I do love her. Shit still can't seem to get on track."

"Trouble in paradise?" I asked, shifting the conversation to the topic that was clearly weighing heavily on Malachi's mind.

His shoulders slumped slightly, and he glanced away for a moment before meeting my eyes again. "I don't know, Mid. It's been a struggle. I want things to work out, but the trust issues and the constant tension are taking a toll on both of us."

I listened attentively, realizing that he needed to vent.

"It's like I can never do nothing right. She's on my ass every time I leave the house, wanting to know where I'm going. She wants to come with me every time I gotta go out of town. The trust isn't there."

I sat back in my chair, digesting his words. It was clear that the wounds from the past still ran deep.

"Plus," he continued, his voice tinged with frustration, "she still has slick things to say about Tyme and our relationship *or* you and Tyme's relationship. It's like she can't let go of the past and is aggravated by the present, and it's causing problems for us."

"Have you considered counseling or therapy? It might help you both address these issues and find a way to rebuild trust."

He ran a hand over his fade and down his face. "I've suggested it, she's against it. She says our focus needs to be on MJ right now, while *I* think we need to make sure he's not in a toxic environment."

I leaned forward, my expression neutral. "You're right. MJ needs a stable and loving environment, and that includes a healthy relationship between his parents. If counseling can help you both communicate better and work through your issues, it might be worth pushing for."

My twin sighed deeply, his eyes reflecting a mix of exhaustion and gratitude. "Yeah, you're right. I just hope she comes around to the idea. I don't want us to keep going down this path."

I got up from my chair and walked around my desk, leaning against it next to Malachi. "Give it some time, man. Sometimes people need a moment to see things differently. Just be patient and keep communicating with her."

He nodded in agreement, and for a moment, the weight seemed to lift from his shoulders. And if not, at least things between us could go back to normal, and Kinley Drayton could get off our asses.

OCTOBER 29TH

TYME

BABE

What that one girl sayyyy

IMA RIDE YOU LIKE A RODSO.

RODEEEEEO.

MIDNIGHT

crying laughing emojis Brunchween wild, huh? How many drinks you done had?

TYME

2 and a p;ossible 4

MIDNIGHT

yeah right gif

TYME

Okay you got me. 5.

Your sister keep bring ing me the spookymosas

they're so good

MIDNIGHT

Clearly so strong.

TYME

I love you so much.

You love me?

MIDNIGHT

To infinity

TYME

& fucking beyond

See that's why I'm knocking you up when I

get home

MIDNIGHT

Nah take your ass to Nene's house, you ain't
about to take advantage of me. Ima lady.

TYME

3 rows of crying laughing emojis

You betta take this cocohie like a G!

MIDNIGHT

No means no young lady.

TYME

I bought a new pack of full rollups

batting eyes gif

fruit*

MIDNIGHT

Oh.

TYME

And you gonna be the one blindfolded.

RODEOOOO

MIDNIGHT

LMBOOOO. Slut me out then.

TYME

And will.

MIDNIGHT

Your ass bet not fall asleep with all this big shit
you talkin

TYME

RODEEEEEOOOOO!

November

NOVEMBER 22ND

onceuponatyme: The Cutest Apple in the Orchard. Mira's first time picking apples was a blast! Our little explorer turned 3 months today. She's growing up so fast and embracing the magic of the changing seasons. I have a feeling that Fall might just become her favorite season. #AppleOfOurEye #Family-Adventures #FallFun

comments turned off

DECEMBER 24TH

BESTIES & BOOS GROUP CHAT

TYME

Sooooo why did Mal show up without Tia???!!!!

MIDNIGHT

Not you already sharing the mess, we barely finished eating

MO

looking eyes emoji

MIDNIGHT

Then we overheard him on the phone with Tia telling her she agreed to drop off MJ but she playing games

NENE

GASP.

TYME

Now who being messy?

MIDNIGHT

You left out details like the fact that he told us they decided they would separate after the new year.

NENE

SHUT THE FRONT DOOR

& I love messy Mid

TYME

rolling eyes emojis

NENE

Won't God do it.

MO

You not shit bae *crying laughing emoji*

TYME

He's always on TYME .

MIDNIGHT

you got a point gif

TYME

Seriously though I feel a little bad that this is happening and MJ is only 3 months.

NENE

Yeah, that's a tough situation, but honestly, with everything that's gone down, can't say I'm too surprised about how it's playing out.

TYME

Me neither but it's the way the cookie has crumbled.

MO

I'm glad you got your happy ending though best fren.

MIDNIGHT

Thanks sis.

TYME

She was talking to ME! *eye rolling emoji*

MIDNIGHT

sure Jan gif

DECEMBER 25TH @ 3:45AM

Tyme

The soft hum of the refrigerator filled the dimly lit kitchen as I sat in front of the stove stirring a pot of my favorite ramen. The house had finally calmed down, which meant Midnight had succeeded at getting Mira back to sleep. We were almost sure she would sleep the night away after being passed around all evening at her grandparents, but the joke was on us because like clockwork, she woke up screaming at three this morning.

I couldn't have been more thankful when Midnight told me that he would handle it and took her to her nursery. However, less than ten minutes of him being gone, my stomach and greed got the best of me, so I came downstairs to make *us* a late night snack.

As I stirred the Udon noodles once more, I heard the creek of the stairs, signaling that my baby daddy had noticed I'd gone missing from our bed.

"Not you down here fixing food at four in the morning."

I let off a chuckle as I turned to see him entering the kitchen. "Just a little late-night snack. I couldn't go back to sleep after YOUR daughter woke me up."

"Aye, not too much on my baby," he teased, slapping me on the behind. He placed a kiss on my cheek, and I couldn't help the goofy grin that spread across my face.

"I figured I'ma be up, I might as well eat. Besides, don't act like you're not about to try and get some of my noodles."

"Definitely will, but I thought you were down here tryna open up some gifts."

That got a hardy laugh out of me because I'd thought about it.

"You know me too well," I said, doing one final stir before turning off the eye.

"That I do." He tapped my hip, before he gingerly moved me out of the way, signaling for me to sit down somewhere. I obliged, hoisting myself up onto the countertop as I watched him grab our favorite over-sized bowl to pour the ramen into.

As I stared at his tattooed covered bare back, I couldn't help but think about how different my life was a year ago. Last year, the holiday season was a constant, painful reminder of loss, loneliness, and heart-break. I was full of anger and couldn't let go of how Malachi had hurt me.

And now, I was completely healed from that and in the most loving and fulfilling relationship with someone I had a whole ass child with. Someone who steadily took care of me in ways I didn't even know I was missing.

"Come on," he said, snapping me out of my thoughts. He used one hand to hold the bowl of ramen and the other to help me down. Midnight led us into the living room, where the twinkling lights of our beautiful, decorated *Elf* inspired Christmas tree flooded the room with a soft, warm glow.

I loved it.

We cozied up beside one another on the couch before digging into the ramen that had been calling my name. The spices tickled my nose and warmed my heart at the same time.

I twirled a forkful and fed it to him, smiling at the way he winked at me.

Moments like *this* had become one of our things. Pregnancy kept me up many a nights, and so we'd find ourselves fixing a late night snack and having conversations about any and everything— our fears about parenthood, how we were feeling about us and our progression, places we wanted to visit, if we thought we were real life Sims — anything.

It was a type of intimacy that only made me fall more in love with him every day.

Midnight cleared his throat after setting the empty bowl of ramen off to the side. "Since we're already down here, I'm thinking we should each open one gift."

I giggled. "That's why you were hoping I was down here opening gifts, because *you* wanna open gifts. You're such a big kid."

He grinned. "It's Christmas."

I was not aware at all how big of a Christmas person Midnight was until November first hit. He had Mira and I out all day shopping for decor. Then, it was the weekly movie days to binge holiday movies. It was the cutest thing ever, but of course, I teased him about it.

"Not you tryna open gifts before my baby."

He kissed his teeth. "Forget that little girl, let's focus on *Daddy*." He winked and of course, my yoni thumped which meant I had no choice but to give in.

"Fine. One gift." We had a myriad of gifts under our tree for ourselves, family and friends, but had planned to wait to open them until the afternoon. My mom was in town and was hosting Christmas brunch, so we thought it'd be fun to unwrap the presents with our family.

"Bet." He clapped his hands as he stood. Rubbing them together, he headed towards the tree with me in suit. Nerves immediately rushed over me as I picked up the perfectly wrapped gift that I wanted him to open.

We settled back on the couch and Midnight handed me a small, rectangular box with a silver ribbon adorned on it.

Not wasting anytime, because clearly, I was just as much of a big kid as he, I unwrapped the gift and opened the box. A light squeal escaped my lips as I saw the Rose gold Diamond Paved 'Mama' necklace that I had been hinting at I wanted. My fingers traced the pendant as I glanced up at Midnight, "Babe, it's perfect! Thank you!"

"You're welcome."

I threw my arms around his neck before handing him the necklace to put on me. "I love it," I reiterated, feeling it pressed against my chest.

"Okay now your turn," I said, leaning over to grab the box off the floor. The nerves had my hand trembling, but I tried my best to hide it as I handed it to him.

"I know this might not be something you wanted for Christmas, but I hope you're happy about it either way."

His eyes locked on mine, a mix of curiosity and anticipation, as he took the gift from me. "I'm sure I'll love whatever it is, Sweets."

"You better," I said, giggling, even though my stomach was doing front and back flips.

He unwrapped the box and opened it. Inside was a specialty bottle of his favorite wine from a small vineyard in Burgundy, France. With the help of his dad, I'd been able to order a bottle of vintage Chardonnay that supposedly embodied the region's rich history and promise of new beginnings.

"Oh snap," he smiled, lifting the bottle of out the box. I eyed the back of it, my heart rate increasing as he turned it around. "Why would you think I wouldn't wan—" He paused mid-sentence and I watched as his eyes scanned the custom back label: Do not open until Baby M2 arrives. Coming next summer.

I was pregnant. *Again.* Nine weeks.

Apparently, things got a little *too* wild after Brunchween, and I will *not* be drinking Spookymosas ever again.

Midnight's deep, dark eyes widened as they met mine. "Are you saying…" His voice was barely above a whisper.

I nodded vigorously, as the tears pooled at the corners of my eyes. "Yes," I stammered, "We're gonna have another baby."

When I found out earlier this month, I was damn near as scared as I was when I found out about Mira. Things were finally settling down on the crazy rollercoaster ride we'd been on, and now I was about to shake things up again with back-to-back babies?

I'd thought about ripping the Band-Aid and telling him on his birthday but decided I'd wait to tell him on his favorite holiday. I wanted him finding out this time to be more sweet, intimate, and thought out since the last time was a shit show. The plan was to have him open it before everyone arrived for brunch and then decide if we'd tell our family today or wait.

But since he wanted to open gifts now, *surprise*.

My palms turned sweaty as I waited for him to say something. *Anything*. But instead, his initial shock transformed into a wide, joyful grin as he stood up. He reached for my hand, pulled me up, and then scooped me into the air, causing a yelp to escape my throat, followed by a slew of giggles.

"Does this mean you're happy?" I asked as my legs settled around his waist.

"Very."

I cupped the sides of his face as we shared a tender kiss. I felt the tears of relief glide down my cheeks.

He sat down with me still straddling him.

"Why are you crying?" he asked, using his thumbs to wipe away my tears.

"I didn't know how you'd take it," I admitted.

"I'm not gon' lie, I'm nervous about having two babies under two. *And*, I'm also excited about you being pregnant with another one of my babies." He leaned me back so that he could kiss my tummy. "This one is definitely my son."

I rolled my eyes. "Do not start that already."

"Too late," he grinned. "I love you, Sweets. You're it for me, so I won't ever be upset about us growing our family."

"I love you too, Tin Man." I leaned in to kiss him. "But let me find out that you just don't want me to have another hot girl summer so you set me up."

His head tilted to the side. "Now we both know this baby probably was a product of you taking advantage of me after Brunchween."

My head flew back as I let out a deep laugh. "No comment," I said between chuckles.

"Yeah, that's what I thought." Another peck. "This is the best

Christmas gift I could have asked for," he said as he transitioned me from his lap to laying on the couch on my back. "Outside of you, of course."

"Of course." I bit down on my lip as he removed my underwear, positioned his face between my legs, and gave me the best Christmas orgasms I'd ever received.

Thank you, God *(and Santa)* for this man, and this life, I now get to call mine.

Epilogue

DECEMBER 31ST | ONE YEAR AFTER 12:01

Tyme

Knocks sounded against the bathroom door. "You ready?" Midnight's voice came flowing in as I finished up my sleeked back bun with face-framing curls. In an instant, a wave of déjà vu rushed through me of this very moment exactly one year ago.

Some things were the same, but there were a lot of things that were *very* different.

We were at the same luxury hotel and getting ready for another fun and wild night at 12:01. I almost couldn't believe I had willingly wanted to come back to Chasington Beach and bring in my new year at a play party.

I had been officially turned out.

But that was where the similarities ended.

This time, I wasn't battling what I considered *ill* feelings brewing inside of me for my arch nemesis; instead, I was completely head over heels with the man who stood on the other side.

The door swung open seconds after he asked the question because what was personal space when you were in love?

"Almost," I responded, giggling to myself before my breath got caught in my throat at my sexy ass man.

He still was aging like fine wine, and I couldn't help but take a moment to bask in him in his wine-colored suit, tailored to perfection. This year's theme for 12:01 was Bosses and Baddies, and I planned to match Midnight's style with a gown in a similar shade that was just the right amount of sexy and softness.

"You look good, baby," I said, turning towards him for a quick peck.

"I would say the same, but…"

"No buts." I stuck my tongue out, proud of myself for using his catch phrase against him.

"Oh, you think you cute?"

"So cute." I batted my eyelashes before pushing him aside. "And I know how to be on time, so shut up." His laugh echoed behind me as I headed into the room to get dressed.

"We gonna miss our reservations, messing around with you."

I rolled my eyes, undoing my robe and tossing it on the bed. Midnight's eyes darkened a smidge at my nakedness. I loved how he still looked at me as if I was his most prized possession, even after I'd gained some weight that wasn't going anywhere anytime soon.

Not with baby number two on the way—yes, number two.

So much for taking things slow liked I'd wanted to.

At the beginning of the year when I found out I was pregnant with our daughter, Mira-Serenity, I was scared out of my mind. Clearly, our last night in Chasington Beach had been the catalyst for the perfect ending to our lick back story—one we didn't ask for.

The three positive pregnancy tests glaring back at me raised so many questions: What would Mid's reaction be? How could I ever tell my mom? What if Midnight wanted me to get an abortion? Would I? Did I want one myself? How messed up was it if I was pregnant by my ex-fiancé's brother?

In the end, the only question that mattered was if I wanted my baby or not—and I did. Prayerfully, so did Midnight, and now we have a beautiful four-month-old and yet another *oops* baby on the way.

This one was entirely my fault.

A Halloween Brunch event, combined with way too many Spooky-mosas, led to me coming home and attempting to knock that man up.

However, because God was still clearly watching my life for his own enjoyment, the joke was on me when I found out earlier this month that I was a fertile heaux.

I waited until Christmas to tell Midnight, and we're both nervous yet excited about having back-to-back bundles of joy.

All I know is, he got until next New Year's Eve to propose because I'm not about to keep popping out babies as someone's girlfriend.

He better wife me up; he saw what happened to the last dude that didn't.

"See, this how you gonna make us late," I said, picking up my dress off the bed. "Looking at me like you trying to quench your thirst."

"*Shid*, when am I not?" He scratched at his goatee, his voice dropping to a husky, seductive tone. "But I'ma chill. We got all night."

He winked, and I shook my head as I slipped into a mesmerizing gown that seemed to embody my every emotion. The dress, a tantalizing blend of lace and tulle, flowed elegantly as I moved. Its sweetheart neckline framed my features delicately, adding a touch of softness to my allure, opposite of the front split that revealed a whole lot of leg, sure enough to turn heads.

"Wine is definitely our color," Midnight commented, standing behind me as we took a mirror picture.

We did look damn good.

"It is," I replied, playing with one of my curls to fix it.

"Come on, let's go. This restaurant is almost forty minutes away." He slapped me on the butt and then gave it a squeeze before grabbing my clutch for me.

Midnight had suggested we have a nice New Year's Eve dinner before going to 12:01 to celebrate. After all, this year had been not only a rollercoaster but a whirlwind; we were deep in the trenches. With so many ups and downs and events unfolding rapidly and unpredictably, I didn't expect us to be where we were now for at least another year, maybe even two. Finding out I was pregnant with Mira, definitely took the drama to a new level, mainly due to Malachi and Tia. Because plot twist. Not only were we expecting at that time, but so were they. Of course, Tia was not happy about that.

At every turn, she tried to hurt me or belittle me. At first, I just didn't get it. Why was she so bothered by me? I wasn't the one who stole her man, and I wasn't the one who pretended to be her friend while I was sexing her man. That was all her—yet, she treated me as if she were the victim.

But then I stopped trying to get it and focused on me, Midnight, and our child. Once I did that, the rollercoaster became a lot more tolerable, and I just had to keep up with how quickly my life was changing — *for the better.*

Now as we got ready to enter a new year, I loved where things were going. Malachi had owned up to his mistakes, and while we weren't exactly friends, I respected his role as an uncle to Mira because he loved his niece down. He and Midnight had also mended their relationship, and it was less volatile than before. Tia, however, was still a ball of negativity, which only led to her and Malachi planning to separate at the start of the year.

Couldn't say I was mad about it because karma always showed up on TYME. The only person I felt bad for was Malachi Junior.

"By the way, I called my mom before we left to check on Mira," Midnight said halfway into our drive.

I shot him a teasing grin. "Of course, you did."

My *baby daddy* was a hands-on dad, and I loved him even more because of it. This was the first time we were hours away from our daughter, and he'd checked in with his mom more than me.

"My baby good, though?"

"Yeah, but she ain't wanna talk to you, though."

I cut my eyes at him, scrunching up my face, even though Mira really was already a daddy's girl. Little did she know, her big-headed daddy was calling her a boy my whole pregnancy. Now look at him, completely wrapped around her teeny tiny finger.

Fingers crossed that I have my own little mama's boy growing within me.

As we continued our drive, I reflected on how my relationship with Midnight's parents had evolved over the past six months. My connection with his dad had always been warm and welcoming, and that hadn't changed. However, my interactions with his mom had been a bit uncertain initially.

At first, things between Kinley and me resembled the dynamics I had with her during my relationship with Malachi. However, something shifted back in June when she opened up to me in a way I hadn't expected. From that point on, we began building a genuine relationship.

Just a few weeks ago, we'd spent two hours on the phone as she spilled grade A tea about the rich wives in her circle. This was a far cry from my time with Malachi when the only phone conversations I had with her were when he had his phone on speaker during their talks. I felt grateful for the positive changes in our relationship, especially because when I first found out I was pregnant, I had no idea how Mama Bear Kinley was going to handle me bringing dishonor to her family.

As we pulled up to the restaurant's valet, I couldn't help but let out an amazed "Whoa." Cascade had quite the reputation in Chasington County, and it wasn't just because of the food. The place was renowned for its breathtaking views.

Perched on a hill, Cascade boasted a truly magnificent panorama that seemed right out of a fairy tale. They clearly didn't name it Cascade for nothing. The restaurant sat directly across from a mesmerizing waterfall, and that's where the enchantment began.

As we stepped inside, the view of the outdoor patio caught my eye. It was a spacious and inviting area, aglow with the warm twinkle of charming string lights. The soothing sounds of the cascading water filled the air, creating a serene ambiance that made me want to unwind.

The atmosphere was lively, and both the indoor and outdoor seating areas were nearly at full capacity, which only added to the restaurant's charm.

My favorite part so far was the large glass windows that offered every table a premium view of the waterfall, as if nature itself was joining them for dinner.

"Hi, welcome to Cascade. Can I have the name on the reservation, please?"

"Midnight Drayton."

The hostess gave Midnight a smile before redirecting her attention to her tablet. She cleared her throat before asking him for his name once more.

"Could it be under another name? I don't have anything here under Drayton or Midnight."

"I'm positive it is," Midnight responded, fidgeting on his phone.

"Maybe you put it under mine," I said, squeezing his bicep. "Can you check Tyme Henley?"

"Sure." She tapped on her screen a few times before telling me she didn't see my name either.

"Here's my confirmation," Midnight said, holding his phone towards the woman.

"Hmm okay, um. I'm going to have to get a manager for you because we don't have any available tables. We're completely booked for the night with a waitlist."

"Well if he has proof, wouldn't we go to the top of the waitlist?"

"Actually, the waitlist consists of people who also made reservations. It's not a walk-up waitlist."

"But—" I started before Midnight stopped me and told her to just get her manager. She scurried off and we sat down on a bench across from the welcome podium.

"I can already see that little annoyed vein of yours popping out." I gingerly tugged on his nose ring.

"You know me too well," he replied with a smirk, reaching for my hand and giving it a gentle squeeze.

"I mean, if this don't work out, at least we can still get food at 12:01."

"True, but I know you were excited about this place. Your ass already know three things you plan to order."

"Oop." I popped his knee. "Not you judging me when I'm carrying another one of your big-headed children."

He chortled and gave me a kiss on the cheek before the restaurant's manager, a tall and sharply dressed gentleman, approached us with a friendly smile. "I apologize for the inconvenience, but it seems there's been a mix-up with your reservation," he began.

Midnight nodded, maintaining his composure. "Yeah, we had a confirmed reservation for tonight."

The manager looked genuinely apologetic. "We take reservations very seriously here at Cascade. It appears there was a glitch in our system, and your reservation was canceled. I'm truly sorry about this."

A glitchhhhh? They better glitch us a table out of thin air.

That's what I wanted to say, but Midnight handled things much more graciously. "Is there anything you'll be able to do for us then?" he asked politely.

"As I understand, you're Neo's cousin?" Midnight nodded, offering a friendly smile. "He was the one who suggested we get your company's wine in stock. It's one of our patrons' favorites."

"Thank you," Midnight replied, his smile growing appreciative.

"Off of that alone, we want to make sure you have a good experience, so I do have one option, if you're open to it," the manager explained. "We have bar seating on our rooftop, which offers a fantastic view of the fireworks and the waterfall. Plus, we've got cozy heaters and a firepit up there to keep you warm. If you don't mind waiting for a few minutes, I can arrange that for you."

I glanced at Midnight, considering the offer. The idea of a rooftop view sounded good to me; either way, I was more interested in securing a seat and enjoying good food than fussing over a reservation mix-up.

Midnight met my gaze, a question lingering in his eyes. I smiled and nodded. "Sure, that sounds great. Rooftop dining with a view? I'm in."

The manager's smile widened. "Excellent choice. We'll get everything ready for you. Just give us about ten minutes to prepare, and then we'll escort you upstairs."

"Not my man getting us royal treatment."

He shook his head at my antics. "Bar seating is not royal treatment."

"But he definitely made it sound good." We shared a laugh as a text came in from my best friend.

NENE

Have a great night being all freaky deaky best fren! Next year I'm convincing Mo to go.

> Girl hush. How's New York?

I'm already over it LOL. We're about to head out to some spot with a great view of the ball drop. I just wanted to check in right quick and tell you how much I love you and I'm so happy you found your person in our enemy turned bestie.

> Don't get mushy on me. I love you more *revolving hearts emoji*.

I glanced up from my phone, forcing back the tears. My friendship with Chenethia only got better and better. She not only was a great friend, but she and Mo were the best aunties. My goal for next year was to try to rebuild some of my other friendships but for right now, I was good. Plus, my friendship with Mickie had also flourished. We'd been cool when I was with Malachi, but Tia's continued shenanigans this year only put a sour taste in Mickie's mouth, and that pushed us closer.

All in all, I was grateful for my small circle but even more grateful for the man beside me. Making sure he knew that became my mission.

"You know," I said, putting my phone away and capturing Midnight's attention, "With all we went through to get to this moment, I can't say I wouldn't do it again because I just love what we've become, and I love you."

"I love you too, Sweets, and I plan to show you how much very soon."

"Promise?" My coochie tingled at what we knew was a challenge that we were up for. I was very curious to see if we could out-do our current standing record of twelve orgasms in one night.

"I absolutely do."

I grinned. "Kiss," I poked out my lips, and he obliged as he always did.

"Thank you for your patience," the manager said, returning. "We truly appreciate it. Your bar seating on the rooftop is ready. If you could kindly follow me, we'll get you seated right away."

Midnight nodded, standing up. He offered me his hand, and I took it, rising gracefully from the bench. With the manager leading the way, we made our way through the bustling restaurant, my eyes greedily scanning people's food as we passed by. I was thankful that, so far, Baby number two wasn't as uncooperative as Mira had been when it came to morning sickness and smells.

We climbed the flight of stairs, and as the manager pushed the door open, a refreshing breeze swept past me, causing me to let go of Midnight's hand as I adjusted my coat.

"Watch your step," I heard him say, causing me to glance down. My eyes caught the glint of something white: rose petals.

"Why are there r—" I began to question, my voice trailing off as my gaze shifted back up, capturing the stunning scene before me, stealing my words and my breath.

The rooftop, bathed in the soft glow of candlelight, had been transformed into a romantic paradise. A path of white rose petals and glowing candles stretched out before us, leading to a heart-shaped arrangement made entirely of white roses.

"I hope this will do," the manager said, smiling at me before he disappeared back the way we had come.

I stood in awe, everything happening in slow motion as the images of our family and friends came into view. They held red tulips and white roses, their smiles radiating love and excitement.

To my surprise, my mom and Luke, who were supposed to be in Jamaica for New Year's Eve, stood ten feet in front of me. My best friend, who had told me five minutes ago she was in New York, was standing a few feet away, grinning right alongside Mo.

Midnight's parents, his sister, and even his close guy friends and their significant others were all there as well.

"Don't worry, Mira's with her uncle," Midnight said, reading my mind. The moment I spotted his parents, I wondered where my baby was, but I also noticed that among our immediate family and close friends, Malachi was the only one missing.

As Midnight guided me towards the heart-shaped arrangement, hot tears streamed down my face. In the center of it, a neon sign illuminated the night with the words 'It Was Always You' in elegant white script.

I knew what was happening the moment I saw our loved ones, but those four words sent my heart into overdrive. I couldn't believe this was happening right now, and Midnight had completely surprised me, even enlisting the restaurant staff in his plan.

My tears fell harder as I accepted the roses and tulips that were being handed to me. When we stood in front of the arrangement, Midnight gently turned me to face him, and I was sure I looked a mess because I was full on ugly crying.

"Before we came up here," he began, his voice filled with emotion, "you said that with all we've been through to get to this moment, you'd do it again because you love what we've become... and Sweets, I can do nothing but agree. Every part of our journey to this moment has been worth it because I knew a long time ago that it was always going to be you.

"Since being with you, my life has been filled with love, happiness, laughter, and growth. You've shown me what it means to truly love and be loved, and all I want to do is continue waking up to you, coming home to you, and doing life with you.

"So, Tyme Falice Henley," he paused, pulling a small box from his pocket and dropping to one knee, "Will you marry me?"

As he opened the box, it revealed the stunning engagement ring, a work of art with a round-cut diamond set in an intricate rose gold band. The diamond sparkled brilliantly, and its design was timeless, classic, and elegantly untamed, mirroring the wild and beautiful journey of our love.

Overwhelmed by emotion, I nodded vigorously, my voice failing me as *more* tears of joy filled my eyes.

"You know I need to hear it," he teased, with that ugly sexy smirk on his face that I couldn't wait to be stuck with forever.

"Yes!" I exclaimed, unable to contain my excitement, and the rooftop erupted in cheers and applause from our loved ones.

With trembling hands, he slid the ring onto my finger before standing and wrapping his arms around me. We fell into a passionate kiss, sealing our love and commitment under the starlit sky and the soothing sounds of the waterfall.

The night transformed into an engagement party. We took pictures, enjoyed a delicious meal, and had a blast with our family and friends. It wasn't until we were preparing to bring in the new year that we finally had a moment to ourselves.

I pulled my *fiancé* closer, his big bold eyes locked onto mine. *How did I ever despise this man?*

"You sure you wanna be stuck with me for forever?" I teased.

"You sure you wanna be stuck with ME? You know I only know how to make ramen and cereal," he replied, a sly glint in his eyes.

"Oh, I'm locked in. Who needs a man who can cook when you can get free wine, luxurious trips, and premium peen for life?" I smirked. "Besides, you ain't about to make me a single mom," I continued, my heart swelling with love as I thought of our growing family.

"I guess we stuck then," he said, his smile warm and full of promise. "All thanks to a bat and a truce."

I let off a hearty laugh, my head falling back. "I will die on the hill that the truce was definitely a set up!"

"You can't prove that," he shrugged. "All I did was give you what you needed—me." He winked and licked his lips, causing my skin to prick.

I really let Midnight Drayton 'trap me' and was now on the way to being his wife and loving it?? What is life? I had gone from reasons why I hated him to reasons why I didn't want to spend life without him.

"And here I thought I was getting that again tonight," I said, hinting at our play party experience. My inner freak was looking forward to releasing our inhibitions once again— this time as an actual couple.

Midnight's smile reached his eyes. "Oh, trust and believe you will still be getting the 12:01 experience when we get back to the hotel. It'll just be a lot more intimate. Don't expect to sleep." My entire soul tingled at his words as everyone around us began to chant.

"Ten! Nine! Eight!", they yelled, their voices rising in unison.

I wrapped my arms around him, resting my chin on his chest. "I'm glad we didn't crash and burn, Tin Man."

"Seven! Six! Five!" the countdown continued around us.

"And I'm glad you trusted me, Sweets."

"Four! Three! Two!"

As the clock struck midnight, we shared one final, lingering kiss.

"One! Happy New Year, Mr. Drayton," I whispered against his lips.

"Happy New Year, Future Mrs. Drayton," he replied, sealing our love with the first kiss of the new year.

Cheers to more new beginnings, new days, new weeks, new years, and new moments by each other's side.

I couldn't wait.

Afterword

I hope you enjoyed Midnight and Tyme's love story.

12:01 was supposed to be a fun little NYE novelette, and clearly, Midnight and Tyme had a lot more to say and I could do nothing but go with it and tell their story.

Writing this was definitely fun because who doesn't love a little mess and drama? This one was for the girlies who deserve to get their *happily ever after* after an ex did them dirty. I knew that I wanted this to be the ultimate lick back, which is why when the idea for me to take it up a notch with an *oops* baby, I had to do it.

As always, this story is theirs and no one else, and I hope that if nothing else, you can appreciate it for that.

Don't forget to let me know what you think inside of my reader's group. Search: Bella Jay's Book Bar on Facebook!

Extras

House Party Inspired Cocktails List

THESE WERE THE COCKTAILS BEING SERVED AT 12:01

1. Bilal's Blueberry Bourbon Smash - a sophisticated and bold drink that combines blueberries, lemon juice, honey, and bourbon. Muddle the blueberries and garnish with a lemon twist.

2. Jamal's Jive Juice - a smooth and groovy vodka-based drink that combines fruity notes with a subtle hint of spice. The perfect companion for those looking to groove the night away.

3. Kid's Kool-Aid Crush - a playful and colorful drink that combines various Kool-Aid flavors with a splash of soda and a shot of vodka.

4. Pee-Wee's Bubblegum Bliss - a sweet and bubbly drink that captures the essence of bubblegum, invoking a sense of nostalgia and joy.

5. Play's Punch - a euphoric drink that blends fresh mangoes, sweet pineapples, and a cannabis tincture to bring this fruity concoction to life. Served over ice and garnished with a fresh pineapple slice, it's the ideal party sip for good vibes.

6. Sharene's Seductive Sip - a sultry drink combining black vodka, blackberry liqueur, and cranberry juice, garnished with a skewer of fresh blackberries.

7. Stinky's Minty Mojito - a refreshing and herbal white rum cocktail with zesty lime and muddled mint leaves, topped with soda water. Perfect for a cool and invigorating sip amidst the party vibes.

8. Sydney's Sensational Spritz - a lively and bubbly drink with a citrusy kick. This spritz combines the lemon juice, champagne, and a touch of sweetness, resulting in a sensational sip that's perfect for celebrating.

9. Zora's Sweet and Spicy Cocktail - a fiery yet sweet drink that combines tequila with a tropical twist and a kick of heat, perfect for those who dare to indulge in sweet and spicy flavors.

12:01: The Rulebook

THE RULES THE ATTENDEES MUST ABIDE BY

1. Consent & Communication is essential: Consent is key, and any sexual activity must be consensual for all parties involved. Clear communication is crucial to ensure that everyone is on the same page and comfortable with what is happening.

2. Respect everyone's boundaries: Everyone's boundaries should be respected, and no one should be pressured into doing something they are uncomfortable with.

3. No means no: If someone says no to something, it means no, and their wishes should be respected.

4. Confidentiality: What happens at 12:01, stays at 12:01, and participants are expected to keep everything confidential.

5. No judgment: Participants should be non-judgmental and respectful of others, regardless of their preferences and desires.

6. Safety first: Participants should prioritize their safety and take necessary precautions, such as using protection during sexual activity and being transparent about their sexual history.

7. Cleanliness: Participants are expected to practice good hygiene and cleanliness to maintain a safe and healthy environment. Participants should also clean up after any sexual activity or messes made in public areas.

8. Recording: Cellphone usage should be limited. No means of recording or photography is allowed in public areas. In privacy, please do not record or take photographs without the explicit consent of all parties involved.

9. Substance Usage: Outside alcohol, drugs, and illegal substances are not permitted. Neither is excessive use of substances that will leave you unable to function. Please be mindful of your liquor and other approved substances intake.

10. Safe Zones: Be mindful and respectful of sex free zones.

11. Respect the space: Participants should respect the property where 12:01 is being held and ensure that it is left in the same condition as it was found.

12. Have fun: Ultimately, the goal of 12:01 is be a fun and pleasurable way to bring in your new year. Everyone should be respectful of each other's desires and boundaries to ensure that everyone has a good time.

12:01
Level of Play Color System

BLUE	Means the attendee is here alone.
ORANGE	Means the attendee enjoys being watched.
BLACK	Means the attendee is not here for sex, but here for the experience. It's also for those who enjoy watching people engage in sexual activities.
YELLOW	Means the attendee is open to discuss sexual actions with other.
GREEN	Means the attendee is down for whatever.
RED	Means the attendee is not interested in engaging in sexual activities with anyone other than the person they came with.
WHITE	Means the attendee is a first-timer / guest of someone.

- Blue - Means the attendee is here alone.
- Orange - Means the attendee enjoys being watched.
- Black - Means the attendee is not here for sex, but here for the experience. It's also for those who enjoy watching people engage in sexual activities.
- Yellow - Means the attendee is open to discuss sexual actions with other.
- Green - Means the attendee is down for whatever.
- Red - Means the attendee is not interested in engaging in sexual activities with anyone other than the person they came with.
- White - Means the attendee is a first-timer / guest of someone.

Thank you!

Hey You!

I want to thank you for reading my book. Each of my book babies mean so much to me and I'm grateful for you reading it and hopefully falling in love with it.

If you enjoy this book, **I would really appreciate if you could leave me a review on Amazon and/or Goodreads (or Storygraph).** I would love to get as much feedback as possible from my readers, and reviews really do make a difference.

I plan to read each and every one of them and would love to hear your thoughts.

Thanks so much!

~ Bella Jay 🤍

Acknowledgments

I'm so happy to release another book! I hope you enjoyed it!

As always, thank you to everyone that continues to encourage and inspire me as a writer.

Thank you to my cover creator. I love it so much and it is perfect for what I wanted!

Thank you to my alpha / beta readers: Alvina G., AreAle, JaNiah K. Richardson, Joie S., Lex S., Meko, Salene Whyte, Shon, Sidni, Tiff H., and Tracey Whitehead! I value your thoughts and feedback more than you may think and your feedback really helped to shape the final version of this project.

Thank you to my ARC Team, Cover Team and Street Team! Each and everyone of you are truly appreciated and I am grateful for you wanting to tell others about this book!

Thank you to my editors, Jasmine Gaines and the ladies of Hopeful Heartbreakers! Y'all came through, per usual!

Thank you to anyone who has helped me and/or supported me in any way, big or small. I truly appreciate you more than you know.

Thank you in advance to every person who purchases, reads, reviews, and/or shares any of my book babies. I am appreciative of everyone!

Peace. Love. Write.

Standalones

Power [Jolee x Amare]

Holidaze [Nola x Bricks]

Here Comes The Sun [Bee x Mari]

Bookmarked [Books x Juice]

12:01 [Tyme x Midnight]

Jacobs Brothers Series

Finding Kristmas [Deuce + X]

Kookie Dough [Nelly + Yadah]

Four Letter Word Series

A Little Bit of Love - A Real Kind of Love Prequel [Ave + Siah]

A Real Kind of Love [Ave + Siah]

A Toxic Kind of Love [Addie + Landon]

A Selfish Kind of Love [Tessah + Kyree]

The Ways of Love [Addie + Waze]

*Each book in the FLW Series is a standalone but the books are meant to be read in order as the first three books take place during the same time. Book four, The Ways of Love takes place a year after the first three. If nothing else, it is **highly** recommended to read book two, A Toxic Kind of Love prior to The Ways of Love.*

Nobody But You Series (Collab with Skye Moon)

Completed Series Books 1 - 3

Holiday Dare Series

Mistletoe Blues [Joie + Blue]

Holiday Reads

Finding Kristmas

Holidaze

Mistletoe Blues

For my most updated catalog in order of release, please visit my website:
www.authorbellajay.com

About the Author

Miami bred, Bella Jay (born Precious Rodgers) has had a love for books since she was a little girl. Getting lost in them was a favorite past time but writing them has become a true love. In 2018, with a little push she stepped out on faith and released her first novel to the world allowing her writer alter ego, Bella Jay, to take flight into the writing industry.

She writes spicy & contemporary Black love and romance books with unapologetically flawed characters who she loves to fix.

When she's not wrapped up in her characters, she can be found traveling the world, building her empire, sipping on tea or wine while reading a book, and wishing healthy eats were pancakes or cupcakes.

Website: www.authorbellajay.com

facebook.com/authorbellajay

tiktok.com/@authorbellajay

x.com/authorbellajay

instagram.com/authorbellajay

pinterest.com/authorbellajay

Printed in Great Britain
by Amazon

43451572R00219